Ribbons
of Scarlet

Ribbons of Scarlet

A Novel of the
French Revolution's Women

**Kate Quinn,
Stephanie Dray,
Laura Kamoie,
Sophie Perinot,
Heather Webb,
E. Knight**

With a foreword
by Allison Pataki

An Imprint of HarperCollins*Publishers*

RIBBONS OF SCARLET. Individual pieces copyright © by their respective author as noted on page 642, which constitutes a continuation of this copyright notice. All rights reserved. Printed in the United States of America. No part of this book may be used or reproduced in any manner whatsoever without written permission except in the case of brief quotations embodied in critical articles and reviews. For information, address HarperCollins Publishers, 195 Broadway, New York, NY 10007.

HarperCollins books may be purchased for educational, business, or sales promotional use. For information, please e-mail the Special Markets Department at SPsales@harpercollins.com.

FIRST HARPERLUXE EDITION

ISBN: 978-0-06-294469-6

HarperLuxe™ is a trademark of HarperCollins Publishers.

Library of Congress Cataloging-in-Publication Data is available upon request.

19 20 21 22 23 LSC 10 9 8 7 6 5 4 3 2 1

This novel is dedicated to the women who fight,
to the women who stand on principle.
It is an homage to the women who refuse to back down
even in the face of repression, slander, and death.
History is replete with you, even if we are not taught
that, and the present moment is full of you—
brave, determined, and laudable.

Contents

Foreword

*L*iberté, égalité, fraternité. That rallying cry, along with the new "Marseillaise" national anthem and the tricolor flag, emerged as one of the French Revolution's most vaunted and inspiring calls to action. And yet, at a time when French reformers, philosophers, and revolutionaries boldly trumpeted the equality of citizens and fought for the expansion of rights both civil and human, they largely, if not surprisingly, meant the rights of men. Liberty, equality, fraternity, after all.

But what of the sisterhood? What of the women who believed, suffered, fought, and died? Now is the time for the novel in your hands. *Ribbons of Scarlet* is an important and invaluable gift for readers because it presents a full half of the story that has heretofore gone largely untold, buried in the history pages that were penned primarily by and for men these past three centuries. The backdrop could not be more of a reader's—and writer's—dream. If history provides the best raw material for compelling fiction (and I believe it does), then the French Revolution provides arguably the most compelling historical moment in modern Western history upon which to base that fiction. Compelling, yes, but even more than that: singularly dramatic in its grandiosity, incredible in the scope of both its events and its players, important in its lessons of the best and worst of human nature, and endlessly intriguing in just how jaw-droppingly juicy its raw material proves.

What is less well known about the French Revolution, however, is the leading role in which women fought to bring about some of its most important triumphs and inspiring changes. From influential salonnières in glittering drawing rooms to the hungry peasant women who marched on Versailles to demand bread, women were waving the tricolor at the forefront of the Revolution. This "best of times . . . worst of times" era marks one of the earliest appearances in the Western world of women demanding expanded rights—including the right to vote. Their thinking was shockingly modern on issues as diverse as gender equality, racial equality, judicial reform, and the distribution of society's wealth. As such, the attitudes of the women in this book may even seem unlikely in how evolved and contemporary they feel to us, but these were truly women ahead of their time, and there is no attitude espoused in *Ribbons of Scarlet* that was not in fact historically espoused. The impact of these female revolutionaries and their struggles still reverberates today.

And yet, wherever these women fell on the socioeconomic spectrum, on whichever side of the struggle these women found themselves, they shared an immutable commonality: they were defined, judged, even condemned based on their gender. These women experienced the age-old sexism encompassed in the French saying "cherchez la femme"—search for the woman—that makes women convenient scapegoats, implying that women are naturally troublemakers and always to blame.

Many stories of the French Revolution are tragic, and many of the stories of the women of the French Revolution—royals, aristocrats, bourgeois, and peasants—are tragic. But even tragedies can inspire, and they can certainly teach. And the authors of *Ribbons of Scarlet*, in bringing to life such a varied, meaningful, and worthy cast of characters, are doing just that: they are not only entertaining us, they are teaching, inspiring, and even transporting us.

The French Revolution was complicated, and so, too, were the living and breathing women who rose and fell through its turbulent years, the women who fill the pages of this novel. These women are not simply virtuous heroines or evil villainesses. The authors of *Ribbons of Scarlet* show that like these women, the Revolution as a whole, and particularly women's experience of it, was marked by cataclysmic change and conflicting beliefs, brutality and community, rapidly shifting alliances and new factions sprouting up by the day.

So, reader, you now have the chance to enter Paris during these years for a front-row seat to all the action and drama. You'll meet an enlightened noblewoman whose privilege provides both opportunity and obstacle. A streetwise revolutionary who hungers not just for bread but for justice. A Bourbon princess who fights for her family even as God, king, and nation are ripped from her royal hands. A patriot with a passion to serve her new republic, only to find that both her pen and her voice are silenced by the self-serving radicals in power. A woman of faith whose commitment to the Revolution sharpens to the tip of a knife. And a belle of Parisian society whose beauty and charm launch her to such heights that these same gifts soon turn to fatal burdens.

Each one of these stories, like the real-life women within them, stands on its own. And yet, when taken in its entirety, the novel provides a whole view of a conflict that was peopled by living, bleeding, inspiring, and complicated individuals who each have an important and unique voice. We are better for reading these tales and knowing these stories. We are enriched by this novel's meaningful quest to "search for the woman," to bring their voices to the fore, and to find a rallying cry all its own: *liberty, equality, sorority.*

Allison Pataki

PART I

The Philosopher

Freedom is the first need of the
human heart.
—SOPHIE DE GROUCHY,
IN HER *LETTERS ON SYMPATHY*

Paris, Spring 1786

Sympathy is our most natural and moral sense. And its origin is pain. From our first wail of infancy, we're creatures who suffer. Perhaps women most of all. From cradle to grave, we gather bruises, scrapes, and cuts. And all of us—from peasant to queen—stumble and fall.

What's more, every injury hurts infinitely. First, when the bone breaks. Then in every remembrance of it, such that when we see another person in pain, we feel the echo in our own body.

That's why, blinded by tears, I shuddered with every crack of the hammer over the scene of torture playing out before me in the majestic place de Grève, where a doomed prisoner screamed for mercy as the executioner shattered his bones.

I didn't know the condemned criminal strapped to the cartwheel. I didn't know his family. I didn't even know if he was guilty. I had no relation to him whatsoever except the most important one—that we were both human beings. But when the executioner raised the steel rod to break the victim's forearm, I quite nearly prayed for him to miss his mark and kill the man. Let the blow end his suffering. Let the victim's senses go quickly, like mine were beginning to as I grasped my uncle's gloved hand to fight off a swoon.

But I *didn't* pray, because this suffering to which I bore witness was in the name of the king's justice, supposedly ordained by a god I didn't believe existed.

Any god who ordained this would be a devil. And I didn't believe in devils, either, unless they be men.

"I shouldn't have brought you, Sophie," Uncle Charles whispered as, in anticipation of death, black crows gathered on the rooftop of the nearby Hôtel de Ville. "Come away now."

His voice was a rasp of emotion with an uncomfortable awareness of the peasantry, for whom this horrific spectacle was meant to be both entertainment . . . and a warning. Those peasants bold enough to peek up from beneath dirtied caps to look at me and my uncle seemed to say, *You don't belong here.* And perhaps we didn't. Though I wore only a plain somber gray Brunswick gown unadorned by ribbon or lace, and my uncle was dressed in black, the people knew aristocrats on sight.

They also knew that even minor aristocracy, like my family, would never be made to suffer the torment of being broken upon the wheel, shrieking and begging for a swift death. We had the money and connections to avoid such a fate. The common people knew it and I knew it too.

So I didn't obey my uncle, but smeared away my tears, forcing myself to watch as the screaming wretch's bones were shattered, brittle ends breaking through skin, spattering crimson blood on the cobbles. His screams were indescribable, but they seared my soul, and I reminded myself that I was here because of my uncle's important work—*our* work, he often flattered me to say . . .

Uncle Charles was a magistrate, not a street vendor hawking his wares. But he knew we might be the only chance to end suffering like this, and for that reason he addressed the crowd. "I represent three peasants of Chaumont who've been sentenced to die this same way," he told the knot of people standing nearest. "I authored a defense of them." I held one of his pamphlets now, crumpled in the tightness of my grip as my uncle raised his voice. "Perhaps you've read it . . ."

His words made no impression upon a burly bricklayer who had climbed atop a crate for a better view and cheered every hammer blow. But we'd captured the attention of a fishwife in brown homespun and a young fruit seller in dirtied skirts, basket in hand and tears in her eyes. Neither were likely to have the education that would allow them to read my uncle's pamphlet, but they'd heard about the three peasants of Chaumont. Oh yes, they'd heard. And word passed.

"It's Charles Dupaty," someone whispered. "He's here."

My uncle had gained renown (or perhaps infamy) by taking on the case, and more heads turned our way when he shouted, "Three innocent men! Forgotten by our barbaric system of criminal justice, left to rot in prison for thirty months, then condemned without evidence or credible witnesses!"

A priest in the crowd hissed at us, "For shame."

I *did* feel shame for using the occasion of one man's death to draw attention to the plight of three others. The dying man deserved, perhaps, the witness of every person for his suffering. But we couldn't save him. We could only, if we were lucky, deprive the executioner of his audience and make the end quicker for the dying man.

"If the three peasants of Chaumont were rich men," Uncle Charles continued, undaunted, "they'd never have been forgotten in jail. Rich men would've been able to appeal . . ."

My part, now, was to say what my uncle couldn't. Ordinarily, it outraged me that the things women said were easily dismissed, but now I wished to take advantage of it. I was just twenty-two. I'd be thought a termagant for speaking about legal matters in public, but not a criminal. So with at least fifty pairs of eyes trained upon us, I found my voice. "But rather than reform a merciless system that celebrates suffering, the Paris Parlement resorts to judicial *murder*."

Several men turned with hostile glares. "Good thing you're a beauty," one snarled. If I were not a noblewoman on a magistrate's arm, he would've beaten me into silence.

As I swallowed my fear, murmurs in the crowd grew louder, nearly drowning out the screams of the shattered man. Sensing the change, the executioner ended the prisoner's suffering with the coup de grâce—a blow to the torso that ruptured every organ.

Then all was silent.

The dead body was left upon the wheel, like carrion to be pecked by crows. Some words were chanted about how the criminal's suffering purged us all of sin. Someone else said a prayer, acknowledging our submission to the king. Then the soldiers commanded us to go . . . but some people sullenly took copies of our pamphlet as they went.

Long after our carriage rolled away, the dead man's screams still echoed in my ears, and I retched out the window, my sour vomit spattering the cobbled streets of Paris.

"Poor Grouchette," Uncle Charles said, using my childhood nickname as I fought another wave of nausea. "However brave you are, you're still a gently bred young lady. Now I fear you may never sleep again."

"Should I?" I asked with a sob as the horses clopped along. "Should any of us sleep while things like this take place? It seems as if the whole world has closed their eyes to injustice."

And I wanted to shake the world awake.

But first, I'd have to get hold of myself. Uncle Charles valued rationality not emotion. I feared that if I couldn't stem my tears, he might trust me less in the great legal matter he'd undertaken at risk to his career and our family reputation. A fear that was confirmed when he pressed into my palm a silver flask of brandy with which to rinse my mouth and said, "I think it's time you bow to the wishes of your parents."

"Not that again, not now," I pleaded, taking a gulp to cleanse my tongue.

I'd just seen a man die. It was obscene to speak of my future when the executed man had none.

My parents wanted me to marry—a fate I dreaded. In helping my uncle with his practice of the law, I'd learned the myriad ways in which husbands abused their power. And even if I were ignorant of that, there remained the regrettable reality that my heart already belonged to a young man I could never marry.

A good and brave soldier who risked his life, fortune, and freedom in the cause of liberty. But because my love was a shameful secret, I only said, "You know I've no wish to take a husband, Uncle. I'm much happier to devote myself to our causes like a nun to Christ."

My uncle managed a small smile, perhaps remembering the family row when I renounced my faith. My kindhearted mother had sobbed against her rosary beads. My father, the Marquis de Grouchy, barked, "I'll have no godless girl under my roof!"

Only Uncle Charles took my part in the matter.

Sophie is special, he'd argued. *She consumes Rousseau and Voltaire like breathing air. She's conversant in every subject. Let her leave off the prayer beads, the embroidery, and other feminine occupations. Sophie is a scholar with a man's mind.*

Of course, I didn't feel as if I were a man in body or mind. And I believed other young ladies would be scholars if only such qualities were prized and encouraged in us. Nevertheless, I didn't protest against my uncle's defense, because he'd persuaded my parents to allow me to study with him. *If she were a man, I'd take her for a legal apprentice. She'll be a great help to me . . .*

I liked to think I *had* been a great help to Uncle Charles during the past year while we fought to save the lives of three condemned peasants. I'd fetched books, researched precedents, taken notes, suggested arguments, and carried his writings to the printer. I'd even suggested that he sell his pamphlet, the funds for which might be used for the benefit of the prisoners. I truly believed we'd save them.

But now in the carriage beside me Uncle Charles said, very gravely, "It's not going to end well, Sophie. My clients will likely die upon the wheel, just as that man did today, and it'll likely be the last case I ever take."

"You can't mean it," I said. "Every day we're overwhelmed by pleas to help other unfortunates condemned by the king's so-called justice."

Even if we didn't save our three prisoners, we might still make a difference. Not just through charity but by opening the public's eyes. That's what my uncle had said at the start, but now he took the wig from his head and rubbed at his thinning gray hair. "I have reason to believe the judges of the Paris Parlement will retaliate against me."

That hardly seemed fair since my uncle's pamphlet hadn't accused any judge of corruption. He'd merely pointed out the unfairness in the system of the ancien régime. "They'll see reason," I argued. "They're learned men. They can learn to see the humanity of peasants and a kinder way of justice."

"My darling niece, were your passion alone to count upon the scales of justice, France would be a better nation. But I can no longer shield you from the expectations of society. I've brought the king's disapproval down on the family name. It will be up to you to redeem it with a brilliant marriage."

I didn't see how my marriage—brilliant or otherwise—would do anything for the Grouchy name, considering that I'd have to give it up. The family hopes more properly rested upon my brother, the heir to my father's title. But the lines of worry on my beloved uncle's face made me wish to give comfort. "I don't believe you *have* brought down the king's disapproval upon us, Uncle Charles. I don't believe the king knows half the crimes committed in his name while he gorges himself on dainties at Versailles without any concern whatsoever for the people over whom he rules."

"Be fair-minded," Uncle Charles chided, as he always did when my passions got ahead of me. I did not like to be strident, but I had, as Maman often told me, an unladylike temper. "King Louis is still relatively young, and those who know him say he's well intentioned. He can learn, if he's well advised. But I'm not enough connected at court to have the king's ear."

Neither was my father.

If we wanted to save the lives of the three peasants and save my uncle's career—not to mention preserve me from an unwelcome marriage—we'd need the support of someone *very* wealthy and sympathetic to our cause. Someone with the bravery of a lion. Someone both respected by the king and beloved by ordinary people. And of course, at that time, there was only one such man in France.

The Marquis de Lafayette.

The very man with whom I fancied myself so helplessly in love.

It's disgraceful enough that you skipped Mass," Maman said, catching me in the parlor with my charcoal and sketchbook, my mending unfinished, the doors of our Paris apartments thrown open to the courtyard where my little cousins ran wild without supervision. "Must you also set such an unladylike example?"

I wasn't sorry for not wasting time in prayer. But I *did* feel guilty for having abandoned my mending, because we couldn't afford as many servants as we used to and holes in hosiery wouldn't mend themselves.

Besides, spinster daughters should at least be counted upon for watching the younger children when their governess was away. "I'm sorry, Maman. It's just that I keep thinking, if only I can capture his pain in a portrait . . ."

In the weeks since the execution, I'd sketched a hundred men being broken on a hundred wheels and had never been able to expunge the sadness from my heart. Perhaps I never would. Perhaps it was important for my own humanity that I didn't. And if I could elicit sympathy from even one important person with my art, shouldn't I try?

Maman sighed. "I'll never forgive your uncle for taking you to an execution. If he keeps agitating for these prisoners, he'll land himself in the Bastille and drag you with him."

I shuddered at the mention of the Bastille, the ancient fortress in Paris, with its eight stone towers. No longer needed as a battlement, it had become a jail. At first for suspected traitors, then religious dissidents. More recently for publishers, playwrights, and pornographers. It was a prison controlled by the king's whim. A royal guard might take you unawares, strike your shoulder with a ceremonial white wand, and then you *disappeared*.

The king's defenders said conditions in the Bastille

were much improved, its few occupants ensconced in sumptuous suites enjoying decadent meals. I found that difficult to believe after having read firsthand accounts of prisoners who'd been forgotten in oubliettes, chained up with rotting skeletons. Voltaire called it a *palace of revenge*. The idea of being imprisoned there made me afraid. Yet not as afraid as seeing three more men tortured to death without having done something to stop it. "I believe we can win powerful people to our side, Maman. Uncle Charles has secured an invitation to dinner from the Marquis de Lafayette next week and I—"

"Sophie, this obsession with your uncle's work cannot go on. I, too, once fancied myself an intellectual. Then I became a wife and mother, taking on the duties one must."

"Must one?" I asked, hotly. Men devoted themselves to science, the study of the law, and the pursuit of justice. Because I was female, this and everything else that mattered to me was to be abandoned?

My mother sighed again. "We all have duties. Your father served the king as a page and his country as a soldier, and now serves his family by managing our estate even as it falls into disrepair. In addition to all these responsibilities, he keeps food in your belly and clothes on your back and—"

"Of course," I said, painfully reminded of my dependence. My books, my comfort, and all my intellectual pursuits came at the expense of someone else's labor. As a daughter, I was a burden. Another mouth to feed. That was the reality, and I didn't wish to give my parents pain. "At least I've not cost Papa a dowry."

My mother stroked my arm, softly. "But neither have you secured relations that might help us rise in status. Worse, you have rejected so many suitors you begin to make enemies."

It didn't seem fair that the same men who enjoyed my company in the social whirl of Paris should think me a coquette merely because I did not wish to marry. But the reality was that most noblewomen my age were long since wed. The queen had been only fourteen at the time of her nuptials. Lafayette's wife too. And if I didn't become a wife, I'd remain a daughter all my life. Or at least until my brother inherited my father's title, in which case I'd be at his mercy, perhaps acting as governess if I wouldn't take the veil.

Still, none of that seemed important. "Maman, you taught me we owe a duty to our fellow man. I took that lesson to heart. Please don't prevent me from helping Uncle Charles with this case and, after it's done, I promise to submit myself to your wishes."

My mother sighed a third time.

It wasn't permission, precisely, but neither was it a refusal. And later that week, Maman contented herself to be vexed merely because I wouldn't permit the *friseur* to style my hair under a towering powdered *pouf.*

Such atrocious creations—festooned with everything from feathers to fat stuffed songbirds—were thankfully going out of fashion. And I hoped that would not be the only thing to change in France. "It's only one of Lafayette's American dinners, Maman. We wouldn't wish to make any of the Americans feel underdressed. Remember, Monsieur Franklin used to walk about Paris in a beaver hat . . ."

She sniffed. "Nevertheless, it's important to make a favorable impression."

At her urging I donned my best *robe à l'anglais*—its bold red satin stripes recalled the flag of the new American nation across the sea—and rouged my lips, pleased by the result in the mirror. The truth was, I *did* wish to make a favorable impression. Not only for my family's sake, but for the Marquis de Lafayette, whose help we needed. And for whom I harbored every secret, fevered emotion a young lady could feel for a married man . . .

We'd met five years before at a celebratory ball in honor of Lafayette's return from America, where he'd fought heroically in their cause. I was just eighteen then, and Lafayette himself was a major general of twenty-four, and also the toast of France, fawned over and feted by even the royals. But when we were introduced, I'd had the temerity to ask Lafayette how it was Americans could declare *all men are created equal* and still keep slaves.

Maman had been appalled at my cheek, but the dashing major general lingered at my side to explain the dreadful compromises Americans had made to unify, and the ongoing work to abolish the slave trade. Lafayette had lingered with *me* while impatient men in satin suits cleared their throats, and jealous noblewomen flapped their fans.

He made me feel as if it were not impertinent at all for a young woman to take an interest in humanity.

I'd loved him each day since, despite my attempts to reason the feeling away like a philosopher. I agreed with Adam Smith's contention in *The Theory of Moral Sentiments* that love was ridiculous. Certainly, it'd been the ruin of many women. Nevertheless, I couldn't shake the feeling. Each time I came into Lafayette's presence, I found myself as tongue-tied and giddy as a girl half my age.

Knowing this, I belatedly wondered if I should let Uncle Charles go without me—better to stay home than to make a fool of myself in front of Lafayette, or perhaps even his wife. For though Lafayette's wife did not seem to mind his alleged dalliances—what self-respecting French wife would stoop to notice a mistress?—I didn't wish to be one of the many bejeweled women who flung themselves at the man.

However, the importance of the dinner to the cause of our prisoners renewed my determination to simply compose myself. That I loved Lafayette ought to be of no consequence—there could never be more to it, for I was no coquette.

So why, then, did my heart kick up its pace that night upon entering his town house on the rue de Bourbon?

In the entryway, a portrait of George Washington—the rebel general under whom Lafayette served in America—was given the place of honor amongst the glittering mirrors, crystal chandeliers, and upholstered neoclassical chairs—none of which were threadbare like ours. Unlike my father, of falling fortunes, Lafayette was one of the wealthiest men in France, and we meant to recruit that wealth and influence to our cause.

The dinner guests were a mixed company. Men and women. American and French. The tall, distinguished new American minister Thomas Jefferson was present, along with his ginger-haired daughter, Patsy, who looked to be about fourteen. Also present was a ward of the Lafayettes'—a colorfully dressed young Iroquois who hailed from the North American forests. But even in such varied company, I spotted someone *quite* unexpected: Madame de Sainte-Amaranthe.

She wasn't precisely a courtesan, but rather a kept woman—a so-called *dame entretenue*. Once, she'd been the mistress of the Vicomte de Pons, more recently the mistress of the Prince de Conti, and it was suspected she took more lovers besides. Of noble blood, the beauty hosted her own salon, welcoming gamblers at her card tables. She was rarely shunned in society, but Americans could be shocked by French norms when it came to marital fidelity. So it surprised me to find Madame de Sainte-Amaranthe here, wearing pink from head to toe—frothy rose bows, pale peony petticoat, and a pink gemstone bracelet on her wrist that dazzled as she offered her hand to my uncle for a kiss.

Then she inclined her head of golden ringlets to me. "Mademoiselle de Grouchy, where have you been hiding yourself? I haven't seen you since the Opera last year where you charmed every young man in my box, then broke their hearts." I started to tell her that I'd been crusading on behalf of condemned peasants, but she interrupted. "Allow me to present my daughter, Émilie."

Madame de Sainte-Amaranthe pulled from behind

her skirts a delicate swan of a girl, already powdered and pinned, her youthful beauty on such display that there could be no question her mother meant either to sell her virtue to the highest bidder or find a wealthy husband before the temptation should arise. "Just thirteen years old, but too pretty to keep under wraps . . ."

Émilie looked younger than thirteen; perhaps not even twelve. Uncle Charles tried, in vain, to hide a frown at Madame de Sainte-Amaranthe's transparent ambitions. Meanwhile, little Émilie greeted us with great poise, showing that her mother had taught her well. "Magistrate. Mademoiselle de Grouchy . . ."

Émilie's adorable curtsy so charmed me that I replied, "Oh, but you must call me Grouchette, like my friends do."

The girl's nose nearly twitched in amusement.

Behind us, a man's voice intoned, "May I also call you Grouchette, mademoiselle, or have we become strangers again after all this time?"

I turned to see our host, the Marquis de Lafayette. And despite my determination to betray nothing, my breath caught at the sight of him. Tall, with auburn hair tied back, he wore a sword at his hip we all knew was more than ornament. He had, at his own expense and in defiance of the king, wielded that sword to help liberate the American colonies so they might govern themselves. Now twenty-eight, the young officer was at the peak of his physical grace, with long, lean, muscular limbs and an easy confidence.

Lafayette took my hand and raised it to his lips.

Which was my complete undoing.

For the moment his warm lips brushed my skin, I was struck with a bolt of base desire. Perhaps he realized it, because his eyes danced with mirth. "Mademoiselle, I'm delighted to see you. I've missed our conversations."

I smiled, thinking of a quick, witty reply. The kind I usually engaged in so easily in social situations. But staring into those gray-blue eyes, I quite forgot what I was going to say. A flush swept over me, and my fingers trembled in Lafayette's hand. *Trembled!* Worse, when I saw Lafayette's wife, I snatched my hand back, as involuntary a motion as if it'd been burned upon a stove.

Startled, Lafayette's brow furrowed. "Have I offended?"

Oh, how great a fool must I make of myself?

"No," I said, swallowing a groan. "Of course you haven't. It's merely that I-I . . ."

Lafayette leaned closer, expectant. For a moment, it seemed as if every guest listened for my excuse. Madame de Sainte-Amaranthe smirked knowingly at my predicament, and I felt young, exposed, and at a complete loss.

Just when I thought I might melt of humiliation, I was rescued by a sweet-faced little savior. "Grouchette is too polite to say that I trod upon the back of her dress and nearly knocked her off balance," Émilie offered, and I cast a grateful look at the young girl for her merciful lie. She beamed in return. "I'm new to satin heels and clumsy in them."

Laughing, Lafayette offered his arm to Émilie. "Well then, my dear girl, kick them off and make yourself comfortable in my home!"

Lafayette ushered us into the dining room where democratic informality reigned, the seating was unassigned, and we were meant to serve ourselves from a stack of plates. This was, Lafayette said, how meals were served in America and not, as someone jested, on tree trunks eaten with bare hands.

I must have been staring too admiringly, still, because Émilie's mother whispered in my ear. "I'm afraid Lafayette is a lost cause for you, my dear. To him, you can be nothing more than a charming child."

I wanted to lie and say, with a flutter of my lace fan, that it made no difference what Lafayette thought of me, or whether he did at all. That was the game to be played in the parlor and it was a game I usually played quite well. But that night I felt too disgusted with myself to dissemble. "We're nearly the same age . . ."

Madame de Sainte-Amaranthe smiled. "It's not the *years* but the experience, mademoiselle. You may be—at least until my Émilie fully blooms—the prettiest girl in Paris, but everyone knows you're still an innocent."

I'm not an innocent, I thought, mildly aggrieved. Not after having watched a man die. I was awakened to the rot in our society and not innocent at all. But what Madame de Sainte-Amaranthe meant was that I was a virgin.

That, as a woman, what remained untouched between my thighs was called *virtue* and comprised the whole of my worth and maturity. To a lady like Madame de Sainte-Amaranthe, who traded in sexual favors, I must've seemed very innocent indeed.

"No Frenchman is above taking a mistress," she continued. "Not even Lafayette. But he would never take an unmarried aristocratic girl to his bed. He may speak like a wild American revolutionary, but his heart is filled with old-fashioned chivalry."

This was nothing I didn't already know, and a familiar ache bloomed in my breast. Both at the impossibility of being with the man I wanted and irritation with my infatuation. As if she understood my dilemma well, Madame de Sainte-Amaranthe patted my hand. "If you're looking for a man to transgress the rules of society, you'd do better with royalty . . ." She tilted her head and laughed. "Or *the Condor*."

I tilted my head too. "The Condor?"

"It's a new world bird," she explained, indicating with a discreet gesture a dour middle-aged nobleman with a beak of a nose. "It's also my pet name for the Marquis de Condorcet . . ."

I knew Condorcet only slightly. He was a prodigy, they said, in philosophy, science, economics, and mathematics. But, to the horror of fellow aristocrats, he'd taken on the habits of the working class, accepting positions as permanent secretary of the Académie des Sciences and inspector general at the Mint. Condorcet rather dressed like a member of the lower classes too. No embroidered waistcoat or lace—just a simple cravat, carelessly tied, and a shabby dark blue coat that had not been brushed of its lint, as if he didn't keep a valet. "He doesn't look like a libertine . . ."

Madame de Sainte-Amaranthe laughed. "Libertines rarely do. Never gamble with the man; you'll lose your petticoats."

I glanced again at Condorcet—a man who looked to be even older than my uncle. As he bumbled at the edges of the table, seemingly unable to find a seat he liked, I wondered if she was making sport with me. "Yet he has a reputation as a cold man of science."

Madame de Sainte-Amaranthe smiled knowingly "Oh, those of us who know him best say he's a volcano covered in snow."

I might've asked what she meant, but I had no interest in Condorcet and didn't wish to engage in malicious gossip. So I politely excused myself in favor of helping Uncle Charles slip mention of his case into polite discussion, which Lafayette conducted in English for his American guests.

Thankfully, I spoke English well. But the talk at the table was all of a mercantile nature. France had paid a high price to help liberate the American colonies but both Lafayette and Jefferson confidently predicted that free trade with the new nation would compensate. Meanwhile, the women shared ugly gossip about our queen, whispering about Marie Antoinette's lovers, diamond necklaces, and foreign ways. Other than myself, the only lady not to indulge in this gossip was Lafayette's wife, a shy woman who gave the impression that she'd have preferred to be in confessional with her rosary beads.

After dinner, Lafayette invited the assembly to his *grand cabinet* and adjoining library to admire his copy of the American Declaration of Independence in a double-paned frame, only half of which was filled with the famous document. Pointing to the empty half, Lafayette said, "I am honored to display this declaration, which spells out the rights of man. But I leave this side of the frame empty . . . do you know why?"

No one hazarded a guess. The urbane Mr. Jefferson, who had been the primary author of this document, merely smiled enigmatically. But earlier in the evening, I'd heard the freckled Virginian say that he hoped the ideals of the American Revolution might spread liberty to the whole earth. My heart filled with hope that might be true, so I dared to guess, "Are you waiting for a French version to match it?"

Lafayette broke into a sunny smile. "*Oui, oui*, Mademoiselle de Grouchy. We must have reform in this country. Until then, we're all left, like this frame, half empty and wanting . . ."

I told myself it was his words about reform that stirred me, and not the playfulness he put behind the word *wanting*. Alas, for me, it was no game. I positively burned with wanting and worried everyone could see it.

Fortunately, Lafayette turned everyone's attention to my uncle. "Dupaty, I've read your pamphlet, you know. I purchased it for a handful of coins, so the proceeds may go to the good cause. And I've guessed you might wish for me to write in support of your prisoners."

We'd only hoped Lafayette might bring our cause to the attention of the royals. That he might *write* in support of it left me breathless. Perhaps our luck was about to change. "Your words carry great weight with the public," said Uncle Charles, eagerly.

With altogether too much adoration in my voice, I added, "My dear Marquis, you may save these men's lives if you write in support of them."

"Mademoiselle, I would attempt it if only for the reward of your dimpled smile," Lafayette replied, taking a gulp from his wineglass. "But you'd be sorry for the result. Give me a battle to win with a sword, and I'll fight. Give me a battle that must be won with a pen . . . and I flop like a fish in mud." I deflated with disappointment until he gestured with his glass. "My esteemed friend Condorcet, though, has great powers of argumentation. I hope you won't think me presumptuous to have asked him to take up his quill in support of your case . . ."

The beak-nosed Marquis de Condorcet, who'd said not a single word to anyone through dinner, made a sound somewhat like a grunt.

I couldn't tell if that meant he'd agreed to help us or not. Or whether or not we should wish him to.

Uncle Charles said we needed the support of a man in the political sphere—not the academic one. But if Lafayette thought Condorcet might be of assistance, then I wished to encourage it. I flashed my most winning smile. "If the Marquis de Condorcet were to acknowledge the merits of our cause, and write in support of the condemned prisoners, he, too, would have my deepest gratitude."

"I wouldn't do it for your gratitude," Condorcet said so sharply his words might have cut. "I'd only take up my pen in this matter to demonstrate the need for a jury-based system of justice."

I startled at his curtness.

And Uncle Charles—who was not so liberal a magistrate as to be entirely easy with the idea that legal decisions should be left up to a jury of uneducated, ordinary persons—looked like he'd bitten a lemon. I could see he was thinking it might actually be worse to be defended by an eccentric like Condorcet than to be left twisting at the mercy of the Paris Parlement. But with the lives of the prisoners in the balance, it was worth the risk.

"Trial by jury I've seen in America," Lafayette was saying. "It better reflects public opinion, but there are those who argue a jury is not wiser or more merciful than a judge . . ."

Madame de Sainte-Amaranthe chuckled.

But Condorcet said, "I can prove otherwise, sir. Mathematically."

"*Mathematically?*" I asked, with a chuckle of my own.

Condorcet's frosty expression told me he was not making a jest. "Yes, mademoiselle. *Mathematically.* I've published an essay on the application of analysis to the probability of majority decisions. A jury theorem, if you will . . ."

Then, with clipped gestures, Condorcet explained what he called the *social arithmetic* by which he could prove that the more reasonably informed people vote on a decision, the more likely they are to reach the correct answer.

It was not, of course, the most stimulating discourse for a dinner party. Or so I gathered from the glazed expression of his listeners. When Condorcet took paper from Lafayette's mahogany *secrétaire* to scratch out equations, people fled the room. But I remained, watching over his shoulder, impressed by his statistical defense for democratic decisions.

"I'm sorry for laughing," I said when he was finished. "I'd no idea mathematics could be applied this way."

Condorcet straightened, stiffly, and tugged his waistcoat. "You're not the first to laugh at me, and I doubt you'll be the last."

I hadn't laughed *at* him, and his prickliness bordered on rude. I would've taken offense but for the fact that he'd explained his work to me rather than assuming, as most men of his stature might, that I couldn't understand. That emboldened me to ask, "Is there not an exception to your formulation? What if the jurors are all uneducated, or unenlightened and ill-informed?"

He lifted an appreciative brow at my question. "In that case, the math would lead to the opposite conclusion, where the ideal jury is one."

"Like a judge," I said, enjoying our intellectual discussion in spite of his curtness.

"Or a king," he replied. "But we're not savages in France. Only give a free secular education to all the people and we can govern ourselves."

Reflexively, I glanced over my shoulder, wary that anyone should overhear talk that sounded seditious if not treasonous. Fortunately, everyone had bolted for the wine trays and no one was paying us the slightest attention. Feeling as if we now shared some manner of confidence, I asked, almost in a whisper, "You favor a free education for *all* people?"

Condorcet nodded. "From serfs to noblemen."

"And women?"

He glanced up in surprise. Perhaps he'd not considered the possibility before. Few men would have.

"Why not? You'd seem to be an excellent example of how education may benefit the female sex."

I tilted my head again, unsure of whether or not I'd just been complimented. *What a very strange man*, I thought as our conversation concluded, never realizing the degree to which Condorcet might change the world, and my life in particular.

My father declared that it was time for our family to leave Paris and return to our estate at Villette for the summer. This would—not coincidentally, I thought—prevent my continued involvement in my uncle's case. So I was thrilled when, before my parents could whisk me away, we received an invitation to call upon Condorcet at the Hôtel des Monnaies, the palace on the Left Bank where he oversaw coin makers and clerks.

Uncle Charles and I arrived precisely at the appointed hour and the liveried servants showed us up the impressive double staircase to Condorcet's office. At his desk, which was cluttered with papers and books, Condorcet came directly to the point. "If I'm to take a public position on this case, I'll need to know everything about your condemned peasants."

I noticed that Condorcet neither questioned my presence as my uncle's secretary nor seemed vexed by it. So I told myself not to be vexed by the fact that he didn't offer refreshments or even a seat. Had the man been raised in a barn?

My uncle and I took seats anyway, and while he reviewed the legal matters, I supplied the information that one of the condemned men had a young son—a youth of perhaps nine years of age—now living on the streets. "He'll be made an orphan if his father is executed," I said. "Then who could it surprise if the poor boy should turn to crime?"

Condorcet didn't look up from whatever he was writing. "A boy with an education wouldn't need to turn to crime. Education is our liberation."

Be that as it may, the boy was too poor to afford an education, so I directed the conversation back to a pattern of recent judicial abuses, which included blameless persons being tortured in front of their children. After this discussion, my uncle rose to fetch some documents he'd left in a satchel with the steward, and I found myself momentarily alone with Condorcet. "Surely you wish to help remedy these crimes against the innocent," I said.

"It isn't the innocence of the condemned that make them crimes," Condorcet replied. "I saw a man burned alive for vandalizing a crucifix. He was assuredly guilty. But it is cruel to subject another person to torture and death. You cannot undo such a punishment if the judgment was in error. More importantly, death is an immoral punishment, unworthy of us."

Condorcet wasn't the first to make this argument, of course. Several reformist lawyers of the time believed the death penalty should be abolished—prominent amongst them, a young associate of my uncle's named Maximilien Robespierre.

But at the time, Condorcet was a far more prominent man. "Have you decided to help us, then?" I asked, hopefully.

Condorcet rubbed his chin. "There's an argument to be made that with the nation's finances in shambles, my time is better spent persuading the royals to rein in expenses and reform our tax system, which burdens the poor for the benefit of the rich."

Maman would've scolded me for arguing with a man of his stature, but I never could stifle my natural predilection for debate. "That *is* an important matter, but less urgent than the impending torture and death of three men."

Condorcet leaned back in his chair. "If I'm asked to weigh the fate of three individuals versus twenty-eight million French subjects . . ."

"That's a cold calculation, sir," I argued. "Moreover, I believe it's a miscalculation. Because our case only requires persuading the courts to show clemency and reason. Whereas in the case of the twenty-eight million French subjects, you must persuade the nobles and the clergy to voluntarily surrender their ancient privileges. It seems to me that the likelihood—"

"The likelihood is that, if I take up your case, I may actually accomplish something for a change?"

I pressed my lips together. "I beg your pardon if I've given offense. My mother says that I have an unfortunate habit of frankness."

I thought I saw him smile, ever so slightly. "Something we have in common."

This emboldened me to say, "Then perhaps you won't mind my frankness in confessing that all this talking has made me quite thirsty."

Condorcet stared. Blinked. Then remembered his manners. "I am terribly absentminded. I should've called for tea . . ."

Grinning, I said, "I imagine you can still do so." And because there'd always been in my breast a desire to provoke, I added, "Maybe even some sweets. Perhaps *puits d'amour* . . ."

Condorcet's cheeks colored at the erotic name of the little treats—slang for a woman's genitalia. And I decided Madame de Sainte-Amaranthe *must* have been making sport of me to imply that he was a libertine. He was red as a schoolboy as he mumbled, "There must be some sort of, um, pastry in the kitchen . . ."

Clearly the man *had* been born in a barn. After calling for a servant, he looked so pained, I decided to rescue him. I noticed a version of Adam Smith's work open on the table. "You're reading *The Theory of Moral Sentiments*. I am an adherent."

He looked vaguely surprised. "I was under the impression all the ladies in France were adherents of Rousseau."

"Only the foolish ones. Rousseau seems to believe a woman's only purpose is to torture men or cater to them."

"And you believe?"

I didn't know how safe it might be to confide my beliefs, so I only said, "I believe this is a bad translation of Smith's work."

He stared with disconcerting directness. "Can you recommend a better one?"

"Mine," I said, recklessly. I'd started translating Smith's work into French—an endeavor I believed might one day be a real achievement. But now I was embarrassed. "It isn't finished. Mostly, I have notes with my own critique."

"I'd like to read your notes."

I flushed, torn between being flattered by his interest and fearful of his mockery. "You don't find it strange that a lady should occupy herself in such a way?"

He shook his head. "I know what it is, mademoiselle, to desire a different vocation than expected. I myself was nearly forced to be a soldier like my father."

I couldn't imagine Condorcet as a soldier. The man of science didn't look as if he'd harm an insect. "Well, you seem to have found a more suitable calling, sir . . ."

"You can too."

My cheeks grew hotter, as I feared he might be mocking me after all. My uncle indulged my scholarship, but Condorcet seemed to be *encouraging* it. It made me curious to see just how far he would continue to do so. "Maman says it's heresy to defy the divine order in which God has ordained women occupy themselves with domestic concerns."

"I believe neither in God nor a divine order," Condorcet replied, leaning to me with what might almost be a smile. "Only a natural order. Thus, if men have natural rights simply because they're capable of reason and morality, then I suppose women should have exactly the same rights."

My breath caught. It's what I believed. But hearing it said aloud was a shocking sensation. Electric. Even Uncle Charles would never have gone so far. Which meant that Condorcet was, quite possibly, the most radical man I'd ever met.

It was for that reason I agreed to send him my notes before I left Paris for the summer. And that is how our correspondence began . . .

Château Villette, Summer 1786

My Dear C, my letter began, *You said you'd like to read my additions to Smith's work, so I've taken the liberty of sending them . . .*

Having been spirited away to our estate in Villette where we awaited my uncle's visit, writing letters was a pleasant enough diversion from the boredom of country life. And when Condorcet's surprising reply arrived, it was not only with praise for my intellectual efforts, but also an enclosure of a pamphlet of his own.

One that lit a fire inside me like a spark to tinder.

"Can you believe the boldness?" I cried.

Having run from the house onto the wide drive in front of our manor to greet my uncle as he stepped out of the carriage, I read aloud one of my favorite lines from Condorcet's pamphlet on behalf of our three prisoners.

The people groan to be obliged to ask once more, not

for a system of laws worthy of an enlightened people,
but just for basic human rights . . .

Condorcet championed a right for all accused to have
the assistance of legal counsel and an ability to confront accusers. He called for an end to interrogations
by torture. And he made an utter mockery out of any
trial, such as the one in which our three prisoners were
condemned, where the prejudices of witnesses were not
questioned and unreliable testimony was given unde-
served weight.

No one was spared from the heat of his fiery
words—not the Paris Parlement, not the king, and not
even those who simply wished to look the other way.
Condorcet's pamphlet was stirring and brave and the
news from Paris was that it had resulted in at least a
temporary reprieve for the prisoners whilst the court
reconsidered their case. Victory!

So why did my uncle look so weary? "The Paris
Parlement might spare the prisoners," he said. "But
they've vented their rage upon me."

My uncle's work was to be publicly burned. He
was also stripped of his magistracy. After dedicating
his entire life to the law, my uncle was discarded in
disgrace. "To save men's lives, I'd do it again," Uncle
Charles said bravely. But he took the retaliation hard.

We all did. Even Maman, who confined her remarks

to this single utterance: "Let's count ourselves fortunate it hasn't come to worse."

"I object to the idea we should think ourselves *fortunate* not to be imprisoned for seeking justice," I said.

I wasn't the only one, as I learned when Condorcet called upon us late that summer. He came without an entourage, having made the day's travel from Paris driving his own little chariot, and because he wasn't expected, I was the only adult member of the family at home to receive him.

"You came alone?" I asked, after explaining that my mother was delivering bread made from potato flour to the poor and that my father, brother, and uncle were hunting. "You're lucky you weren't set upon by highwaymen. We'd have sent a servant to escort you if you'd sent word ahead."

"I was uncertain I'd be received if I sent word ahead," Condorcet admitted as we sat together outside in view of our fountain with its statue of an ancient sea god amidst the spray. With my nephews playing nearby under the supervision of their governess, it was the only place I might entertain a gentleman without suspicion or censure. He'd caught me out wearing only a white muslin gown with blue satin ribbon, and I smoothed the dress over my knees as we settled together upon a marble bench.

"I've come to convey my apologies to your uncle," he explained. "As I've been the cause of his ruin."

"My family doesn't blame you." After all, Condorcet had only done what we asked. And he'd done it brilliantly. I looked at this shabby absentminded man and wondered how he could write prose that made my heart thump. Condorcet's pamphlet had been, perhaps, impolitic. But he'd been *right*.

"Nevertheless . . ." Condorcet took from his coat a letter on very fine paper, and when he handed it to me, my silly heart thumped again in recognition of Lafayette's seal. "An invitation from my young friend for your family to join him at Versailles. It will be quite impossible, of course, to obtain a direct personal audience with the king. Still, there may be powerful people at court who will intervene on your uncle's behalf."

I broke the wax seal and, inside the invitation, found an enclosure. Pressed between the folded page of a brief note, a trio of blue forget-me-nots.

My compliments to the unforgettable Mademoiselle de Grouchy.

It annoys me now to remember how, like a schoolgirl in the convent again, I traced the lines of my name where Lafayette had written it, smiling like an idiot. The soldier-hero was, once again, trying to help. But what did he mean by sending me dried flowers? It could be a mere token of friendship and respect. In spite of all good sense, I still wanted it to be more . . .

"Thank you for delivering this invitation," I said. "There's cause for optimism, then, is there not? After all, Maman feared we'd all be thrown into the Bastille with the Marquis de Sade, and yet, we're still free."

"As free as one can be in France," Condorcet remarked, "where anyone can be jailed on a mere lettre de cachet."

"But in the Marquis de Sade's case, they say he's a deviant lunatic. The list of rapes and crimes he's alleged to have committed is long . . ."

"Perhaps he's guilty and must be jailed, but how can we know without a trial? He might've been released but for the suspicion he's committed sodomy with his manservant."

I gulped in surprise at Condorcet's frank use of the word *sodomy.* "You think that's an unjust reason to imprison a man?"

"I don't believe in crimes without victims. Whether suicide or consensual sodomy, it is no one else's affair. But rape is a violation of the right every woman has to do with her own body as she pleases."

I'd never known anyone to defend sodomites before. Nor to claim a woman's body was her own, though I'd always had an innate sense that I belonged to myself.

Still, again, there was something exhilarating in hearing him say it, and I gave him a radiant smile.

To which he bit his lip and looked away.

A servant came with tea, and Condorcet eyed an easel upon which my latest sketch of the executed man remained unfinished. "That's very vivid. Is it yours?"

"Yes," I admitted. "But despite all my attempts, it doesn't capture the human suffering . . ."

"Because torture consists of more than what we can see. There are smells and sounds and—"

"Pain," I said, swallowing, feeling it anew beneath my breastbone. "Just to witness it."

He nodded. "I feel that when I hear about the slave markets too."

"I'd like to end torture *and* slavery," I said, realizing how grandiose such a statement sounded. Perhaps I should bring an end to smallpox while I was at it, or give men wings and women the right to become jurists. "I might as well wish for the moon, I know—"

"Why not reach for the moon, however out of reach it seems? Torture and slavery have no place in a civilized world."

I felt the familiar pleasure of intellectual camaraderie— the delight of my opinions being echoed. Of an impulse, I touched his arm. "I think, sir, we shall be good friends."

"Because we agree?"

"Surely that helps."

Condorcet blew upon his cup. "I suspect true respect is formed when you find something upon which you *disagree* and yet remain on good terms."

"Unfortunately, I agree with that too. So how will we test the theory?"

"We'll have to find something upon which to disagree."

We made a game of it, discussing, rapid-fire, social and religious subjects, searching for something upon which our opinions differed, and finding nothing. Finally, he asked, "And how do your thoughts run on the matter of marriage?"

I set down my teacup, hoping to vex him. "I believe marriage ought to be abolished."

"*Abolished?*" Condorcet cleared his throat in apparent shock.

I nearly laughed at having turned the tables. "The church holds marriage is a sacred covenant between a man, a woman, and a god who doesn't exist, for the purpose of children being brought forth advantageously. And yet the church permits—nay, *encourages*—fathers to sell their daughters into marriage whilst they are still children, delivering them unto the tyranny of their husbands in an arrangement that can never be undone."

"Regrettably true," Condorcet said.

Since he didn't look ruffled enough, I continued. "Fidelity is openly laughed at—and why shouldn't it be? Husbands and wives, betrothed before adolescence, scarcely compatible, should naturally prefer the beds of others."

Condorcet cleared his throat again.

Perhaps he was succumbing to an illness, so I poured him more tea as I continued, "It's bad enough a woman has no legal standing; before marriage, she's controlled by her father. After marriage, by her husband. Which is why I prefer to remain unmarried. If I must choose between a father or a husband to rule me, it seems wiser to remain with the devil I know."

Not that Papa was a devil, of course. I regretted phrasing it that way. But passion was carrying me away. "So, in summary, my thoughts on the matter of marriage is that it is, at worst, church-sanctioned despotism and, at best, an empty, meaningless farce."

I punctuated my argument by taking up my teacup for a long, satisfying gulp. Meanwhile, Condorcet's eyes were inscrutable. "I see."

Was that all he was going to say? "Sir, I'm not too fragile to endure an attack on my arguments, if you should wish to make one."

"I do not," he said, his finger tapping against the edge of his seat. "It's only that . . ." He trailed off, wry.

"It's only that when I asked how your thoughts ran on the matter of marriage, I didn't mean as an institution . . . but rather, with regard to how you might consider the prospect of marrying *me*."

I laughed, delighted by what I took for a jest.

Then he winced, and my laugh strangled in my throat. He pinched at the bridge of his nose, and I covered my lips with my fingertips, wishing I could call back the laughter.

How had I misunderstood the direction of our conversation? Condorcet hadn't behaved like a suitor. He'd not flattered or fawned or even sent me dried forget-me-nots. I couldn't imagine what would possess him to think . . .

. . . to think what? That I found him interesting? That I enjoyed his company? I did. Perhaps for a cool-tempered scientist, that was enough to justify marriage. It was better justification than most could claim. But I mumbled into my teacup, "We scarcely know each other . . ."

"That's true," he admitted. "Unfortunately, even as a scientist, I cannot explain the mechanics of love."

At the word *love*, I quite nearly choked on my tea. "Please forgive me. I did not realize—"

"I worried it could scarcely be more obvious that I've been struck by the arrows of Eros."

He flushed, which somehow made me flush too.

Had I been expecting a declaration of love, I'd have known how to gently reject his suit as I'd gently rejected many others. But taken entirely off guard, I retreated to flippancy. "How strange that a rational philosopher who has no faith in a Christian god should believe in Eros . . ."

He returned his gaze to his cup. "Well, I have *evidence* of Eros by way of the pain in my heart."

I felt his pained embarrassment. It was a very familiar feeling, as I experienced it every time I thought about Lafayette. *Love really is ridiculous*, I thought. Humiliating, distracting, nonsensical, and undignified. And it could apparently manifest, like a disease, out of thin air. Like a sneeze, it simply must be excused.

I was trying to think of a tender way to excuse Condorcet when he hurried forth to add, "I know you don't share my feelings. Which is why I've been trying to talk myself out of them. Fortunately, your argument against marriage is so persuasive that no fair-minded man could possibly take personally the rejection of his suit."

It was gallantly done and I had no wish to bruise his feelings. "I wouldn't have argued so vehemently if I wasn't trying to make you disagree with me."

He nodded. "Alas, there's no point you made without merit. I've reached the age of forty-two without having taken a bride because marriage, as the church would define it, *is* immoral. But between mature, consenting individuals, I believe marriage can be a useful social arrangement . . ."

"For a man, perhaps."

"For a woman too. A married woman, for example, is freer to mingle unchaperoned," he said, gesturing lightly at the governess, watching us like a hawk. "A married woman is capable of hosting literary salons without censure. And the right husband might leave you free to enjoy intellectual pursuits. In short, given the right sort of husband, marriage could secure your liberty."

It was a notion I'd never entertained because I had never met a man who might allow a wife complete freedom. Because it was an appealing notion, I humored him. "And you'd be the right sort of husband?"

He met my eyes. "I'd attempt to be. If I should fall short, I'd attempt it anew. I'm not a very wealthy man, but I'm industrious. You aren't likely to find yourself impoverished. I'd neither require nor accept a dowry. Nor would I demand to know your whereabouts or circumscribe your social sphere. And I'd not trouble you for children. The world has enough."

I tilted my head. "And on the other side of the equation?"

"The other side?"

"What would you expect in exchange for these benefits . . . other than . . ." I hesitated, trying to think of a delicate way to phrase it. Fortunately, the most appealing thing about Condorcet was that one could be perfectly frank with him. "Other than the conjugal benefits of the marital bed that I assume you'd demand."

His complexion went, almost in an instant, to ash. "Only a monster would *demand* that."

His proposal was becoming a greater curiosity all the time. "What benefit, then, would you receive? I hope you won't say that you wish only for my happiness, because I'm uneasy to be the object of unselfish charity."

"I'm not unselfish." He looked chagrined. Excruciatingly so. "I seek to explore the possibility that you may, in time, grow to care for me, if not precisely the same way I care for you, then in some approximation thereof. I think it quite a high probability actually, as I've done some calculations."

I didn't think he could startle me a third time in one conversation, and yet, he did. Retrieving from within his coat a tattered scrap of paper upon which he'd scribbled indecipherable equations, he began to ramble. "Assuming esteem and trust to be the necessary ingredients of affection, and further assuming that trust and esteem may increase with both proximity and time . . ."

The man who had applied mathematics to juries and democratic decision making had now turned his statistician's mind to the problem of love.

And in spite of myself, I was *inexplicably* charmed.

So charmed I regretted I could not give him serious consideration. Remembering the dried forget-me-nots, I said, "My dear sir, I'm afraid your formula fails to account for the possibility of a prior claim on the lady's heart . . ."

"To the contrary," he said, pointing at his equation. "I've made allowances for the Lafayette variable here . . ."

"Oh," I breathed with instant and intense dismay. "You knew . . ."

Did everyone? How painfully obvious had I been?

At my distress, Condorcet's expression fell. "Oh, no. I knew nothing until this moment. I merely thought to give my variable a clever name and since so many women in France admire him . . ."

"I am just one more," I murmured, wishing the ground would swallow me up. A man of Condorcet's age and stature must have seen gaggles of infatuated girls in his time, and there was no explanation I could give that distinguished myself from them.

"My dear lady, the fact that so many others share your tenderness for Lafayette is merely a testament to your good judgment. As I've said, the more reasonable jurors added to a pool, the more likely they are to reach a correct result . . ."

It was a kind thing to say. And because he was kind, I would not mock his mathematical formulations. "You don't think that love for one man is likely to foreclose all possibility of loving another?"

"I'm willing to test the proposition."

"You're a gambler," I accused.

He folded his arms, but he didn't deny it. "I have flaws, of course. But unless there is some immutable quality about me that repels you, I believe there's a possibility—nay, a probability—that marriage would contribute to our mutual happiness."

I stared at him then. Really looked at him, as if for the first time, seeking his soul in his face. As I would later write, one can hardly doubt that beauty, or at least something interesting in the person's appearance, is necessary for love. Exceptions to this are fairly rare among males. If there are more exceptions among women, that is because we've been taught from the cradle to be wary of first impressions and to value more important qualities.

I noted again his bent beak of a nose.

The Condor, indeed.

There was the shadow of a beard, which he ought to have shaved. His upper lip was too thin and his hairline receding. He slouched, his nails were ragged, and his aging face wasn't handsome. But neither was it disagreeable. He was not ill-made. Beneath his white stockings, I could see his calves were strong. Moreover, I confess, there was something arresting about his dark eyes.

Unfortunately, I felt not the slightest stirring of amorous attraction, but I could find no immutable quality that repulsed me.

And I supposed that was something.

"But what if marriage did *not* add to our mutual happiness? Then we'd be unhappily bound together unless divorce becomes legal in this country."

"If it does not, we'd be precisely as free to take lovers as any other married couple in France and without censure. As I said, I won't demand to know your whereabouts or circumscribe your social sphere. Moreover, I've always had a premonition of an early death, and given that I'm twice your age, I'll likely make you a young widow, whereupon you'll have the means to live independently or marry again, more to your liking."

It guts me to remember how dispassionately he said this. But even *then* I flinched at the thought of his untimely demise. Meanwhile, he concluded, like the scientist he was, "Given your worries, I'd like to test the proposition that equality in marriage can flourish."

"You don't propose a marriage, sir, so much as a social experiment."

"Isn't every marriage a social experiment?"

I remained dubious. "Even the most amiable spouses sometimes come to an impasse. Then the husband is the final arbiter . . . and thus the ruler."

"It's true someone must have the final say. But it needn't be the same person. Look to the ancient Romans, who had a solution between co-rulers. They simply took turns."

He had an answer for everything. On the whole, it was the most unique offer of marriage I'd received. Certainly the most agreeable. Which is why I regretted so very much having to dismiss it. But before I could, he asked, "Would you at least consent to think about it for a little while? Perhaps on your long carriage ride to Versailles . . ."

And I nodded because that was, I thought, too reasonable a request to refuse.

❋

Versailles, August 1786

Versailles had been the seat of French power since the time of the Sun King, and though my father—who had once been a courtier—told me what to expect, I positively gaped to see gardens unfurl like a green leafy brocade on earth-colored satin, each shrub clipped by an army of gardeners into fantastical shapes.

I told myself not to be overawed by the splendor. In the American Declaration of Independence, Jefferson wrote *all men are created equal.* But I couldn't help feeling humbled by such grandeur and staggered by the magnificence of the palace as it rose grandly from its verdant park, surrounded by spraying fountains that crowned the whole with a glittering mist.

We lodged at the Hôtel de Noailles, a stately residence belonging to Lafayette's powerful noble family by marriage, a short walk to the palace gate. "You must attend every function here at court as my guest," Lafayette explained, in receiving us. "That includes the king's *lever* when he awakens, and his *coucher* when he retires, to say nothing of the royal dinners . . . If we're to win allies in the reinstatement of your uncle's magistracy, you must be *noticed.*"

And yet, I'd never felt more invisible.

For Lafayette's manner was strangely changed—polite and chivalrous in every instance, but utterly void of flirtation. He made no reference to the flowers he'd sent and made certain we were never alone together. Not even for a moment.

"There are a thousand petty rules here at Versailles," he warned. "Fortunately, my wife's kinswoman, the late queen's lady of honor, and so-called *Madame Etiquette*, can advise you."

I wondered, at first, if that was the cause of the distance he'd put between us. In Paris he was free to do as he liked. Here in Versailles at the Hôtel de Noailles, he was surrounded by his wife's powerful family and their strict expectations of propriety. But I began to think my mother had something to do with Lafayette's changed manner when she mentioned to him, for the third time, that I had received a marriage offer from the Marquis de Condorcet.

I regretted telling her—for she and my father now pestered me night and day to marry the man. And the pressure of their wishes made it nearly impossible to make up my mind. "Are you trying to make it impossible for me to refuse Condorcet's offer without humiliating him in front of his friends?" I asked Maman when we were alone, our trunks unpacked. "Or are you trying to embarrass me in front of Lafayette?"

"I'm trying to save you from him," Maman replied. "Or at least from rumors that you're his lover. Which will ruin you, Sophie. A woman without virtue is worthless."

I wilted, horrified. "I had no notion of these rumors . . ."

"Neither did Lafayette," Maman said. "But he's assured me that he'll be mindful of your reputation."

How outraged I was by all this. By the rumors—who had started them? By my mother's meddling—why could she not leave matters alone? I was even outraged by Lafayette, who apparently meekly submitted to my mother's warnings to stay away from me without any explanation or consideration of my feelings on the matter.

He may speak like one of those wild American revolutionaries, but his heart is filled with old-fashioned chivalry.

Perhaps Lafayette did think of me as a child. Perhaps he always would. And I simply couldn't allow myself to care. *Enough*, I commanded myself. I must center my attention upon things that mattered, like restoring my uncle's magistracy.

So in the days that followed, I dedicated myself to learning court etiquette—which, in my case, felt like the rules of war. Rituals of who must remain standing and who was permitted to sit upon which sort of chair, depending upon rank. Important courtiers kept one fingernail long because no one must *knock* upon the king's door, but only scratch it. That was to say nothing of the rules about napkins and who had the right to offer the queen a drink . . .

I learned to wear the mask of a courtier as we were introduced to noblemen, courtesans, and ministers at the dazzling palace, where a thousand tall windows cast light over a hundred sumptuous rooms. My own image, a girl in ivory brocade with lace, was reflected back to me again and again in the Hall of Mirrors. And I seemed entirely suited to this arena of sunlit parquet floors, glittering crystal chandeliers, and priceless murals painted on the ornate arched ceiling. But I didn't belong here. For I couldn't ignore that there was a stink to the grandeur. The musk of sweat arose from the crowd and I covered my nose with a kerchief to stifle the whiff of urine, as some visitors had apparently relieved themselves in the potted plants.

A man wearing a luxurious red coat embroidered with black and metallic threads noticed my gesture and said, in passing, "You smell the king's condescension to democracy, mademoiselle."

I'd only ever before seen the royal family in procession, from afar, so I would only later learn that this was the king's youngest brother, the Comte d'Artois. I would see him again, that evening, in the presence of Swiss Guards, amongst elaborate tapestries, while I waited with the crowd in the galleries to watch the king and queen eat their dinner—first a creamy soup, then a sizzling pheasant on a bed of tender greens, followed by beautifully frosted pastries and peaches—all served in dishes of crystal, silver, and gold.

Though King Louis was magnificently dressed, I was surprised to find that he was portly and otherwise dull. At his side, the powdered queen may have been a wax figure, so formal was every motion as she picked at an extravagant meal, the rich scent of it carrying to us where we stood watching them eat—our mouths watering.

What was the point of this? I couldn't entertain the idea that the royals enjoyed this performative farce. Certainly, I'd imagined the role of king and queen to be more magisterial, whereas, in reality, they seemed puppets on a stage.

Cut your strings, I thought. *Look up and see us.*

But they never did.

Which did not mean that I went entirely unnoticed. The Comte d'Artois, with eyelids heavy and lustful, stared at me until Lafayette whispered, "I regret you should come to *his* attention. Artois will be of no help to your uncle or your reputation."

It was a warning I kept in mind the next day on a stroll through the gardens when I found my way barred. The Comte's sudden appearance amongst the rosebushes startled me, especially as he was without the usual knot of attendants who surrounded the royals. "Mademoiselle de Grouchy, I've been asking after you."

Not knowing what else to do, I lowered into a respectful curtsy. "Your Royal Highness, I am—"

"Beautiful," said the king's youngest brother, hemming me in. "An unmarried beauty at that . . ." He didn't wait for a reply. Instead, Artois gestured to the showy red roses. "Exquisite, aren't they? And yet, I am sorry it is late summer, with so many flowers in full bloom, because I have always preferred the *bud*."

Another flower metaphor. First Lafayette's forget-me-nots. Now this.

"How interesting," I said, trying to slip my gaze past his broad shoulders to see who might be watching. And I didn't know whether to be relieved or worried that nearly every eye in the garden was directed our way.

Our growing audience didn't stop the king's brother

from reaching out to snap a rosebud from its bush, trailing its soft petals along my jaw. "Oh, yes. Being the first to *pluck* an untouched bud and watch it bloom in the privacy of my chambers has always given me the greatest pleasure."

I bit my lip to stave off a roll of my eyes and the tart observation that once men start using flower metaphors, the word *pluck* was never far behind. But because it was the king's brother, I couldn't use my sharp tongue to cut him to ribbons. And my stomach knotted because if the king's brother set his sights on a woman to make a mistress or a whore, he'd have his way.

Was there any way to refuse his attentions without giving offense to a man with the power to ruin me and my family if he pleased? Perhaps Madame de Sainte-Amaranthe would've known how to manage him, but I merely pretended not to understand, hoping he'd be too ashamed to make a bolder move.

Alas, he was not ashamed. In fact, he moved closer— a motion I arrested by turning so the hoops beneath my voluminous skirts kept him at bay.

Pretend to be stupid, I thought. *Or he'll realize your contempt!*

"If plants give you such pleasure, you must be very fond of your gardener," I tittered, as I imagined beating him off with my little handbag.

Fortunately, I did not have to. Because at that very moment, a lovely young woman with deep blue eyes rushed over to us to interrupt and embrace him. "Artois! What do you think of my new shoes?" She raised the hem of her petticoats only slightly to reveal ornate silk heels with blue bows and seed pearls—entirely incongruent with her modest gown.

"My dear sister," the comte replied, with a smile halfway between impatience and delight. "They are exquisite."

I curtsied again, this time more deeply as he presented me to his sister, Madame Élisabeth, a princess of France almost my very same age. She had a reputation for kindness and extreme piety and her brother seemed as surprised to see her as I was. "What has lured you from your hermitage at Montreuil, Élisabeth? Surely not a desire to show off your shoes."

"I wished to cheer the king by showing him the new type of apple I've bred in my conservatory," she answered, indicating her lone attendant, who carried a basket of fruit instead of the jeweled fans so ubiquitous amongst the ladies at court. "I would be happy to tell *you* about my studies in botany, too, dear brother, but I believe it's about to rain and that you are missed at the card tables . . ."

Whether it was dread of a scientific discussion, the

lure of the card tables, or fear of rain ruining his perfect coiffure, the Comte d'Artois made haste to leave our presence.

And Madame Élisabeth laughed heartily, watching him flee. "Mademoiselle de Grouchy," she said with a warm smile. "Why don't you walk with me?" When I fell into procession, she added, "You must be flattered by my brother's attention. But be careful. I love my brothers, all three. But that does not make me blind to the fact that the Comte d'Artois is as pleasure-seeking as a man can be."

His pleasure, I thought. That's what he sought. Not mine or any woman's, I'd wager. Yet I feared Madame Élisabeth would believe I called his royal attention to myself—perhaps I'd given some signal of which I was not aware. To pardon myself I said, "I fear I'm new to court, madame, and ill-suited for it."

She laughed again. "We are kindred spirits, then. I am far more at home at my little farm of Montreuil, where I can serve God and the good people of the village. I would never come to Versailles did my brother the king not desire it."

It was a comment, perhaps, only to put me at ease. Still, it struck me that she, too, even at her exalted rank, was expected to be a servant of men and their pleasures, not her own.

As if fearing she'd given the wrong impression, she added, "But you mustn't think ill of Versailles or believe all the wickedness that is said about this place or my family . . ."

I wanted to say that I'd never heard criticism of the royal family, but I'd been a critic myself and heard ugly gossip besides, so did not wish to insult her with a lie.

She nodded, appreciatively, at my silence. "So, mademoiselle, you know I have a passion for farming—what are your interests? Every woman should have some."

It was safe to say that I sketched and painted. If I were braver, I might confide that I read and translated philosophy books. But remembering our purpose here, I willed myself to say, "I've a passion for justice, madame."

"God's justice is a worthy cause." She did not tease—her voice and expression were serious. "How do you pursue it?"

"I assist my uncle, Charles Dupaty. He defended three wrongfully condemned men—peasants of Chaumont. He was stripped of his magistracy for his pains. We've come to Versailles in the hopes someone here might care about these injustices."

"Everyone ought to have a care for those wrongly condemned. Crime must be punished, of course, both by man and, eventually, by God. But we must judge more carefully than God for we do not have His perfect understanding. I hope that if, as you say, your uncle and the men he defended have been judged wrongly, they may find relief. I assure you that if they do not find it in this world, they will be weighed more truly in the next."

I was not at all comforted by her hope or her assurance of justice in another world, but seized upon what she'd said like a lawyer. "Yes, we *must* judge more carefully. Since we cannot know, with perfect understanding, whether any man deserves death, should such a punishment not be abolished?"

She stopped walking. "I have never thought on the question."

I knew that I was being imprudent; *impudent*, even. But I couldn't count on such an opportunity to come again. So I took from the pocket in my skirts my uncle's pamphlet—the one that was condemned to be torn and burned. "Perhaps this might be worthy of your consideration, madame?"

She took it and tucked it into the basket of fruit. Then she offered me an apple. "In exchange for the pamphlet. I will read it. My friends will tell you"—she cast a glance at her companion—"that I buy even more books than shoes."

I wanted to shout with joyous triumph that I'd put the pamphlet into her royal hand. And I believed her when she said she'd read it. After a week of roaming Versailles trying to catch the attention of a notable man, it was a notable *woman* who deigned to take an interest. "Thank you, Madame Élisabeth."

"I must warn you," she said, lowering her voice. "I've not much influence here. I am not a creature of the court—in truth, I would have taken the veil if my brother would have permitted it. It was my fondest desire. But obedience to the king is a duty and sacrifice that God commands."

I didn't tell her that I believed only superstition and tradition gave her such a duty, or demanded such a sacrifice. I didn't wish to be unkind. Especially since I felt that she, too, was trapped by the rules of society in France. Just as I was. Just like the king and queen seemed trapped upon their stage, spooning soup into their mouths like puppets.

And all of us were still freer than the falsely imprisoned, the impoverished peasants, and the enslaved in our distant colonies.

These thoughts troubled me long after Madame Élisabeth took her leave. And I started out on foot for the Hôtel de Noailles, hoping to reach it before the cloudy sky opened up.

I didn't get far before it poured rain.

Taking up my skirts, I splashed down the rue du Vieux Versailles past an alley cat and an abandoned wagon until I was forced to duck into the doorway of the nearest building for shelter—the royal tennis courts, as it so happened.

I did not expect to find anyone else inside, but as the drum of rain beat against the roof, a lone slouching figure stamped water from his buckled shoes and when he turned, I saw it was Condorcet.

"We'd no idea you were here in Versailles," I said when he offered me a seat on the bench beneath the indoor awning. "Why didn't you send word?"

He frowned, water dripping from his neck cloth as he fiddled with an umbrella the wind had all but destroyed. "I'm only here for an evening to discuss finances with the new minister. Besides, I wanted to give you time to consider your decision. I couldn't imagine you wished to be subjected to my painful anxiety while you made your choice as to whether or not you might agree to wed."

He *was* anxious and it pained me to see it.

"Also," he began, seemingly unable to meet my eyes, "I've been trying to find the courage to confess something I've done. Something quite unforgivable."

That sounded serious. He looked so mournful that

I tried to comfort him by saying, "Surely you haven't killed someone."

"No. But I've forfeited your esteem. You see, when I last spoke to the Marquis de Lafayette, your name became the subject of our discussion. In a complimentary way, of course . . ."

None of this sounded terribly unforgivable. "And?"

"I told him I'd proposed marriage."

"I'm afraid that's no secret, thanks to my mother . . ."

"Yes, but I also told him that I am in love with you."

Ah. Another reason for Lafayette to keep his distance. Not just because of my mother's warning, but also in deference to his friend Condorcet. Who had all but lifted his leg on my metaphorical skirts like a territorial dog. *Men, really!* What was wrong with them?

"You staked a claim to me," I accused.

Condorcet rubbed at the back of his neck. "It wasn't my intent, but it was the result, and for that I'm humbly sorry. My behavior wasn't in keeping with the spirit of equality of the sexes I promised you."

"No, it wasn't," I said, vexed and feeling hemmed in on every side that afternoon. Condorcet pinched the bridge of his nose in genuine regret, and my anger began to dissipate. "But you might be the only man in France who would realize that. You're certainly the only one who would confess it, so I forgive you . . ."

"You do?" he asked, as if he didn't dare to hope.

I nodded. "That doesn't make it right," I said, trying to wring the rain from my skirts, hoping that I'd not irretrievably ruined my best gown. Maman said that in a masquerade, I might wear it with an ivory mask and look like an angel. But I was exhausted by court masks and when I looked up at Condorcet, I felt anything but an angel. "It's grotesque the way you men pass us from the father who guards our chastity as a family asset, to the lover who threatens its value, to the husband who expects to claim it for his prize."

Undone by my parents and rumors about my virtue and my brief encounter with the royals and by rain—stripped of my powder and cosmetics and every artifice and illusion—I knew only one thing. That I didn't want to be *plucked* like an unripened bud.

I wanted to blossom on my own.

Condorcet made me an unorthodox offer. Now I intended to make one in return, if I could find the courage. I remembered what Madame de Sainte-Amaranthe had said about him.

If you are looking for a man to transgress the rules of society . . .

Well, I would find out.

I began, "You've said that a woman's body is her own . . ." Condorcet's eyes narrowed as he tried to

follow the direction of my thoughts, but he didn't interrupt. "What I do with my chastity, I wish to do without
anyone else's sanction. Without promises, obligations,
or entanglements of any kind. And if you consent to it,
I would like you to help me be rid of it." I swallowed
hard. "Here and now."

At my words, Condorcet went purple and a vein
pulsed at his temple. Fearing what he might say, my
heart thumped painfully beneath my rib cage. I knew
the words he might be thinking. *Slattern. Wanton.
Whore.* Those words were weapons. Even if Condorcet was too mannerly to utter them, he might erupt
in anger, accusing me of impugning his honor with an
immoral request. At best, he might tell me that though
I had a right to ruin myself, he wouldn't be the instrument of my ruin.

That's what Lafayette would've said.

What Condorcet said was, "Mademoiselle, to be
taken here in haste will likely be painful for you and
without any compensatory pleasure."

I could see the lust in his eyes and knew that he
wanted me. But he didn't press it upon me in the way
of the Comte d'Artois. Nor did he deny me my wish,
though I sensed it was not his own. He wanted me, but
not here, not like this. Nevertheless, he simply stood
there, exposed. Doing his best to leave me with an in-

formed and genuine choice. One of the only choices I'd have the opportunity to make.

That was a potent elixir.

So I said, "It can only be done in haste, because if we're caught, my father might kill you."

"Might?" Condorcet replied, sarcastically.

My father would *certainly* kill him. If not my father, my brother or uncle would attempt it. But Condorcet was either a fool in love, or braver than anyone guessed, because he situated his umbrella in a hopeless attempt to bar the doors. Then he came closer, saying, "Well, then . . ."

My mouth went instantly dry. I couldn't have made this request without expecting he might agree. And yet, as I lifted my sodden petticoats out of his way, I felt aquiver. Hot and cold, all at once. He paused at the sight of my thighs where crimson garters held up my sodden stockings. For a moment, it seemed as if those garters reminded him of the bonds of social propriety that held everything together, and I thought he'd come to his senses and talk us both out of it. Instead, he unfastened the scarlet ribbons, letting each fall to the floor.

I didn't know where to put my hands. And to my surprise, once he'd undone his breeches, he didn't seem to know where to put his hands either.

"You've done this before?" I asked, suddenly frightened.

"Yes. But never like this . . ."

Still, his hands were steady. So I said, "Hurry."

He eased me down onto the bench, then our eyes locked and he pressed his damp forehead to mine. Our lips seemed to inch together but did not meet in a kiss because I pulled him closer to get on with it. As our bodies came together in awkward congress, I buried my face in the wet fabric of his coat to stifle a cry at the invasion.

It went swiftly after that, in the way of nature. And in the crucial moment he spent himself outside me so we wouldn't make a child.

Then it was over. I'd been relieved of my virginity as gently and surgically as such a thing could be done. But as I caught my breath beneath him, it was Condorcet who trembled. I'd taken something from him. I hadn't known, until that moment, that the sexual act could render a man so vulnerable. And of an instinct I could not then name, I stroked his cheek.

"I will agree to marry you," I said. "If you still wish it."

"I do," he answered, holding me tighter.

"But I wonder, how, in the end, can we be equals

in a marriage when the law gives a husband authority over me?"

"I wouldn't exercise that authority," he whispered into my hair.

"But I'd always know that you *could*."

"I suppose then, my dear lady, there must be an element of faith even in a godless marriage."

Château Villette, December 1786

My family was overjoyed, insisting we marry by Catholic rite in the little chapel at Villette. Condorcet told me, "I shall not mind. The religious ceremony will be nothing but farce and mummery but will prevent anyone from interfering in our affairs."

That made good sense. Unfortunately, when it came time to take our vows, it was *worse* than farce and mummery because of all the men in the world that Condorcet might've asked to stand as witness to our nuptials, he chose Lafayette.

I knew my groom meant well by this. A gesture of good faith, to demonstrate that he would never again try to warn a man away from me. But how indignant it made me to see Lafayette in the chapel, dressed in winter finery, beaming benevolently as if he were releasing me from a love affair we'd never consummated.

All while I said my vows to another man.

"I, Marie-Louise Sophie de Grouchy, take thee, Marie-Jean-Antoine-Nicolas de Caritat, the Marquis de Condorcet . . ."

I paid little attention to the promises we made beneath pine boughs and holly berries. I believed they meant nothing. Our first kiss was a peck; I'm ashamed to say I scarcely remember it. More ashamed that I remember vividly how Lafayette kissed my cheeks. "Congratulations to the rosy bride, Marquise de Condorcet!"

Yet there was some grace in that the first kisses I received from Lafayette were given while he called me by another man's name and title. It was a reminder that while I had no choice whatsoever in the ridiculous humiliations of love, I'd had a choice in marriage. And I knew I had made the right choice.

Especially that night when, alone in our bridal chamber—for I would not allow servants to undress us—Condorcet frowned. "I fear I misstepped in inviting Lafayette to the wedding and made you unhappy."

"No, of course not, I—"

"Let us always be honest."

Swallowing, I tried. "It's a pang that will pass. In fact, I think it has already passed." Something eased in me. "Please forgive me."

"There's nothing to forgive," Condorcet said, removing his coat and throwing it over the end of the divan, making as if ready to sleep there. This seemed faintly silly as we'd already shared physical congress, but he didn't presume it was his right. Even on this night.

"Sophie—may I call you Sophie?" When I nodded, he continued, "And I would like it if you called me Nicolas."

"Yes, of course."

"Sophie, it will only work between us if you have freedom to love what you admire. If that is Lafayette, then go to him. I won't stop you. You're not bound. And regardless of whether you wish to go to him tonight, if you regret this marriage, you may press for an annulment. I won't contest it."

He said this with the utmost sincerity, and a truth stole over me that lightened my spirit even more. I had married an *extraordinary* man. "Even I am not so irreverent a creature as to attempt adultery on my wedding night, and I've no regret, other than causing you unease."

He smiled. "To the contrary, madame, you've made me happier than I've ever been."

I slanted him an amused glance. "I fear you've a low threshold for happiness."

"Perhaps. But now we're done with rituals, the worst outcome can only be that we live separately and give each other no trouble for the rest of our days."

I blinked. "I assumed you wished for me to live with you."

"I do," he replied. "Very much so. But what do you wish?"

Was he suggesting I might continue here in Villette with my family? Or live at his ancestral estate? Or even take a separate residence in Paris? The options— options I never expected—were dizzying. And his willingness to give me options warmed my heart and lodged a little lump of gratitude in my throat. "I see no reason to complicate things. I should like to live with you in Paris."

"Thus making me even happier," Condorcet replied, snuffing out the candle so we were plunged into darkness.

Me in my bed, he upon the divan.

I was so tired that I ought to have faded to sleep. But instead, I asked across the dark divide, "How did you come to be different from other men?"

"I'm no different," he said.

He was wrong. Men might be born with the same

natural rights, but not the same natural endowments. Or the same personalities. "I feel as if you somehow know just what a woman might need to hear to make her happy."

He laughed. "I assure you, madame, you are the first person to ever accuse me of that." Then he laughed again.

He had a wonderful laugh. Rich and sonorous. I realized I'd never heard it before. And I hoped the fact I desired to hear it more frequently meant we'd get on well together.

❧

Paris, January 1787

On the day we arrived at Condorcet's residence, I admired a portrait in the hall, my fingers itching to reproduce it in a sketch. "Who is this darling little girl? A relation of yours?"

Unexpectedly, the question made my new husband cringe. "In a way."

His reaction made my stomach knot. Was this a bastard daughter? Given our arrangement, it wasn't my right to know, but my voice was sharp. "In *what* way?"

He glanced at me warily. "My mother was a good

woman. A loving mother . . . but she kept me in dresses almost until the age of eight. *Years* after other boys were breeched and began to attend school. That portrait is not a girl. It's me. You can, perhaps, easily imagine the cruel laughter and mockery of other boys that I endured."

Sensing a lingering pain, I took the liberty of reaching for his hand. "We should be rid of this portrait if it humiliates you."

"No, it *educates* me," he said, squeezing my fingers. "That's a good thing. The experience taught me the indignities to which girls are subjected. It taught me to sympathize."

Sympathy.

We had that between us, at least.

And that was the start of everything good in this world.

I soon found it easy to be married to Condorcet, who left me to be entirely my own mistress. No one scolded me if I stayed abed all day or read legal books into the wee hours trying to find something useful for my uncle's case. No one told me which wig I must wear to social outings. Nor did anyone stop me from strolling the nearby Pont Neuf where I chatted pleasantly with a tart-tongued fruit seller named Louise who was convinced that nobles were hoarding all the grain and driving up the price of bread.

I had no mending to tend to, no children to look after, and no duties whatsoever. Which I found unexpectedly intolerable.

Freedom, I liked. Purposelessness, I couldn't bear.

So while we awaited the appeal of my uncle's case, I helped Condorcet translate pamphlets that interested him from English into French. That's how I learned that my new husband's work ranged from science to mathematics to economics to politics, philosophy, and the law. Such an astonishing intellect might have shut himself up amongst the safety of his books.

But I greatly admired the way Condorcet committed himself to public service. He was hard at work designing new schools, roads, hospitals, and canals—inventing a new kind of hydrodynamic science in the process. Such industry made it even more surprising how little he imposed upon his household staff, the latter of whom took advantage of his bachelor habits.

"It should go without saying," he said, one morning in passing by my door, "that you have my support if you might like to bring about some changes here."

"I would, actually," I replied. "Starting with breakfast."

"Breakfast?"

By unspoken agreement, we didn't share the intimacy of a husband and wife, but I enjoyed his company and wished to take better care of him if he would not take better care of himself. "I should like for us to take breakfast together, if you don't find that prospect disagreeable."

"Not at all," he replied. "It's only that I never formed the habit . . . and neither has my cook . . ."

His cook, like all his servants, was woefully underemployed and if I was to host a salon—which I was keen to do—I'd have to find a way of changing that. Breakfast seemed like a good start. "A hearty omelet invigorates me and gives me hope for the new day. Perhaps it will have the same effect upon you."

"Perhaps it will," he said.

So began our morning ritual.

The cook's first attempt, with too little butter and a sprinkling of bitter herbs, was unpleasant, though Condorcet ate without complaint as we discussed the news: that an Assembly of Notables was to meet to address the country's debt.

Lafayette had been chosen as one of the notables. My new husband was less notable. And since we didn't have to go to Versailles, we talked instead of plans to create a new public school for adults across from the

Palais-Royal. "I'll teach mathematics," he said. "Perhaps you might consider educating persons in literacy, philosophy, and what you know of the law."

I quite nearly dropped my napkin. "You'd want me to teach?"

"Only if you wish. You're among the most learned women I know, which is, of course, one of your most appealing qualities." His flattering confidence was only slightly less breathtaking than his vision for the school itself. "And we'll invite anyone who would like to learn."

"Even Louise, the saucy fruit seller on the Pont Neuf? Her skirts are filthy but her eyes are bright."

"Why not? She sounds as if she'd get on well with my new valet . . ."

"You've taken a valet?" This surprised me because I'd never met a nobleman less concerned with proper dress.

Condorcet nodded. "He's being fitted for livery as we speak—if any can be made for a boy his size."

"A boy?" I asked, even more confused.

Condorcet sat back with the utmost satisfaction. "The son of one of our three prisoners. I sent for him, with enough money to keep the family from starvation whilst the case works its way through appeals. He says to call him Pierre Simare . . ."

Tears pricked at my eyes, this gesture touching me deeply. "You rescued that boy, Nicolas. And if his father is pardoned, it will be your doing."

"Your uncle is his true savior. And *you*."

The way Condorcet looked at me in that moment made me wish I'd done more to be worthy of his esteem, because he was certainly worthy of mine. "Did you do this only to please me?"

"No," he said. "But everything I do now carries with it that hope. For the chance of a day, or even an hour, that you might return my feelings in passionate harmony, I'd give years of my life."

And here I'd thought him a scientist and not a poet . . .

He was so good and decent—I could see already many admirable traits in him that justified an answering in my heart beyond friendship. So why wouldn't it come? Perhaps because love *was* ridiculous, it wasn't possible with Condorcet. But I remembered a feverish moment in the tennis courts when I felt an intimacy with him. Now I wished to feel it again. "As we're on the subject of education, sir, I'd like to take instruction from you . . ."

His eyes brightened. "I'd be happy to teach you hydrodynamics . . ."

"I'm more curious about biology." When he showed

no comprehension, I decided I must be more frank. "I want to learn the science of physical satisfaction and wonder if you'd consider visiting my chambers this evening for a less hurried lesson than we enjoyed in the tennis courts."

Condorcet put down his fork. Picked his fork up again. Put his fork down. Then, at last, he lifted his gaze, crimson spreading up his neck as if he were a virgin maid. He started to say something. Then changed his mind. For a moment I thought he might actually refuse. Had I misunderstood his intentions for our arrangement?

Finally, a slow grin worked itself onto his face. "Why wait for this evening?"

Such unexpected waggishness made me laugh. But I didn't like to be outdone in boldness, so when my laughter subsided, I asked, "For that matter, why bother with my chambers?"

That made *him* laugh. And as I've said, I loved to hear him laugh.

More than an hour later, we lay panting upon the Turkey carpet, one of the dishes broken, egg on the floor—neither of us could remember how that happened—and I felt as if I knew a great deal more about what satisfied appetites of the flesh. Condorcet had made an experiment of my body, and nearly everything he did with hot hands and fevered breath delighted me.

A volcano covered in snow, indeed . . .

But in the end, he again pulled away so as not to make a child, and that did *not* delight me. Still, the whole experience was pleasurable enough that I wished to repeat it. I hoped he would too. So I was gratified that though he groaned—the floor did nothing good for his aging back—he said, "I'm beginning to see the value in breakfast."

The students at our new school near the Palais-Royal called me Vénus Lycéenne. Or so Louise told me when I invited her to leave off her fruit-selling for an hour each day so that I might teach her to read.

Despite my marriage, or perhaps because of it, I'd received in Paris several offers from would-be paramours for illicit trysts. "Might as well let a man seduce you if you fancy him," Louise said as we sipped cups of chocolate at La Maison du Chocolat Léon in Saint-Germain—a special treat for her that I wished to give so as to bolster her confidence. "Because I hear things in the market, and everyone is already saying that you've made your husband a cuckold with his friend Lafayette."

"That's malicious gossip," I said, wondering for

the thousandth time what I'd done to give rise to it and if such gossip was merely something women must endure. Still, I worried that Condorcet might overhear such whispers, and that—whatever our agreement—they might give him embarrassment.

I was resentful, too, that everyone seemed to have an opinion about our marriage, including my new student. "Seems an odd match, if you don't mind my saying so. You're young and vibrant, and the marquis is a terse old fellow."

Most common fruit sellers wouldn't dare to express something like that about their supposed social betters, but I'd encouraged Louise to speak her mind. Unfortunately, now I felt outraged on Condorcet's behalf. It was true he was no good in public; with strangers he fidgeted and his fuse was short. But in a small circle of friends, he could weave a tapestry of predictions for the future that beguiled his listeners—rhapsodizing about how, through science and reason and harnessing the sun, the world could be made a utopia.

"He's different in private," I protested. "Extraordinarily charming, actually."

"If you say so." Louise raised a dubious brow as the chocolatier, Mademoiselle Léon, refilled our cups. "But if that nose of his ever makes you cringe, I s'pose you can console yourself with his money."

"There's nothing about Condorcet that makes me cringe," I said, a little heatedly. "And I didn't marry him for money. I married him for equality."

At that, Mademoiselle Léon gave a little snort, nearly spilling her pot of chocolate. Meanwhile, Louise shrugged, smoothing her skirts, which, for once, and in honor of this outing, were *clean*, even if stained and in need of mending. "I'm just a fruit seller. But seems to me, you're only as equal as he lets you be. Like the king, he could shut you up in a dungeon or a nunnery or abandon you to a brothel if he pleased."

"He'd never do such a thing," I replied. Really, where did she get these ideas?

Louise, who had lived a hard life fending for herself on the streets of Paris, broke into a toothy grin, as if she thought *me* a simpleton.

I might've forgotten this exchange, if, the next morning, our little valet hadn't said to me, "When I get big, I'll steal a kiss from you, madame. The Marquis de Condorcet is a kindly grandfather, but too old and ugly to make you happy for long."

"When you get big, Pierre," I said, ruffling the little wretch's hair. "I hope you'll know better than to steal anything. Even kisses."

I liked Pierre—and I liked having the boy in our

home, since we were unlikely to ever have children. A happenstance I should've considered more carefully from the outset. Still, Condorcet wasn't old enough to be my *grandfather*. He could be addlebrained, losing pens and ink and mislaying his tobacco. But I counted that as a product of his brain at work with more important matters, not age.

Besides, he was in no way *ugly*, inside or out.

So I abandoned my sketches of men dying on wheels in favor of painting my husband's portrait, determined to capture those moments when he smiled wryly from the side, his mouth caught between scholarly severity and good-natured amusement. Or the even rarer moments when he laughed. For I wished for the world to see him as I was beginning to see him, with very kindly eyes indeed.

Versailles, August 1788

At long last, our three peasants of Chaumont were declared innocent and set free.

What's more, the vengeful verdict against my uncle had been reversed too. I didn't know if Madame Élisabeth had anything to do with it, but I flattered myself to think so. Certainly, Condorcet deserved much of the credit.

Victory was sweet and ought to have satisfied us, some said.

But before we could celebrate, we'd learned of another young man who was to be broken upon the wheel in Versailles, where no one believed him guilty of the crime for which he'd been accused. I hadn't wanted my uncle to make this trip; he was feeling in poor health. I myself did not wish to witness another execution ever again. But we both believed that our presence there might somehow help matters, and Condorcet understood that it was something I felt I must do.

"It's not even sunrise yet," I murmured to my uncle when the prisoner's cart rattled into the square. Yet if the executioner had hoped to be done with this deed before an angry crowd could gather, he was mistaken. For a multitude of men, ranging from burly blacksmiths to satin-clad courtiers waited near the scaffold.

One glance at their faces, and I knew that our work had changed minds—and that *this* time the people would not meekly submit. Instead of quieting during the prayers, they began shouting for the prisoner, encouraged when the soldiers fell back and the executioner looked wary.

I felt infected by the righteous enthusiasm of the crowd, adding my voice to theirs.

At least until, all at once, the people stormed the scaffold. It all happened so quickly, I had not even the time or the presence of mind to cry out against it. My uncle feared a violent clash, but somehow, that didn't happen . . .

Instead, while the rest of us moved to block the soldiers, the burly men in the crowd freed the prisoner and carried him off. I felt nearly faint with exhilaration at what we were doing—what we'd done!

When the executioner tried to run, fearing for his own life, he was promised safe passage. How humbled I was by this power of the people to do good together.

Not a drop of blood was spilled, but we broke the scaffold, broke the wheel, broke every cruel vestige of torture to pieces and set it on fire. We then held hands and formed a circle around the beautiful bonfire that must have awakened the king with its glow. For the word soon came from the palace that the prisoner was pardoned and that never again would any human being be broken upon the wheel in France.

We were all awake now!

On our way back to Paris that afternoon, we gave way to a royal carriage. And when the royal carriage's window passed mine, I recognized Madame Élisabeth. To my surprise, I think she recognized me, too. She smiled, making a sign of blessing upon me as if she knew what I'd done to end torture on the wheel, what I'd been a part of, and approved. And though I did not believe in divine blessings, somehow my heart lightened to think we were all now, royals and common people alike, working together for a better world.

That evening, Thomas Jefferson raised a glass in my honor. "Let us drink to the Marquise de Condorcet, the loveliest and most influential salonnière in Paris . . ."

Though I felt that day I had been more than that, I couldn't help but be flattered by a toast from the elegant and urbane American minister who opined so often in my parlor on the glories of liberty—and how we ought to emulate the model of his country.

My salon was political rather than literary or musical, with frank but polite discussion that I encouraged with a carefully cultivated guest list. Other salonnières, like Madame de Sainte-Amaranthe, centered their entertainments around men. But mine included distinguished women, too, like my friend, the playwright and advocate for women's rights, Olympe de Gouges. Also, the Chevalier de Saint-Georges, a mixed-race fencing champion, maestro of the opera, and music instructor to the queen.

That night was a celebration that included even the three prisoners we'd set free.

Our only sadness was that we'd lose Pierre from our home, just as we'd begun to love him like our own child. "Your papa may be changed from his ordeal in prison," Uncle Charles warned the boy. "So you must be kind to him, and be the solace of his days. As Sophie has been mine."

Beaming, I kissed the top of my uncle's beloved head. How many more persons would now go free because of our work? Reform, at long last, was happening. I couldn't help but burst out, "It's a glorious time to be alive!"

"So it is," my uncle said, kissing my hand. "Now go, Grouchette. Go instigate matters as you do best . . ."

What I did best was organize under the guise of entertainment. I invited people to partake of wine and dainty delicacies with a purpose. Now that our prisoners were free and my uncle's reputation restored, I was free to take on new causes. We'd abolished the wheel; now I meant to abolish slavery too. Which is why I'd invited Jefferson and sought out his daughter, Patsy, who had been educated at a convent school and spoke French perfectly.

I tried to impress her with my English. "We have

hopes that your father will join the Society of the Friends of the Blacks."

Given Jefferson's enlightened reputation, I was surprised to see her wince. My husband had joined the abolitionist society founded by Jacques Brissot, a prominent reformer and critic of the queen. But of course, it was argued that because we didn't own slaves, we couldn't possibly understand the pragmatic concerns of ending the institution of slavery. Jefferson, on the other hand, was a slaveholder in his home state of Virginia. Might not his authority as a revolutionary and his skill with a pen lend greater authority?

"I think"—the young Mademoiselle Jefferson fiddled with her fan—"my father must be careful that his private opinions aren't mistaken for *American* opinion. Still, Mr. Short has joined your society, and he's my father's representative in sentiment as well as mine . . ."

With that, she stole an altogether revealing glance at her father's handsome young secretary, William Short. She was plainly smitten, and I envied her the uncomplicated nature of her affections, for nothing about my own were uncomplicated now.

For a year, Condorcet and I had enjoyed an amicable arrangement of increasing physical and intellectual intimacy. My breath didn't catch when Condorcet entered a room, but I felt the lack of his presence when he left.

The brush of his kiss on my hand didn't send me into a swoon, but I liked the lingering scent of him on my pillows. And sometimes, on nights like this one, seeing my quiet husband, the social scientist, standing beside Lafayette, the dashing war hero, I couldn't help but compare.

Lafayette was still handsome and charming, but I could no longer even imagine tracing my name upon a paper simply because he'd written it. Perhaps the crippling emotion I'd felt for him wasn't *love*, but merely the fly-wisp imaginings that we shared an intimacy, when we did not.

After all, I'd known of Lafayette's glories, but he'd never confessed his insecurities. I knew Lafayette's principles, but never watched him struggle to prove an idea, scratching out formulas. Everyone knew of his battlefield bravery, but I'd never heard him share detailed dreams for the future. Condorcet did that, and I was sometimes struck by the absurd thought that I'd married the more courageous man.

Not that anyone else would've thought so.

"Will the king call the Estates General?" a guest demanded of Lafayette, hanging on his every word. "What did he say when you were brave enough to propose it?"

"Nothing else will fix our finances," someone else

added. "When the Assembly of Notables couldn't provide relief, you were right to ask for a representation of the whole nation."

The Estates General, composed of the nobility of the First Estate, the clergy of the Second, and the common people of the Third—hadn't been called together in nearly two hundred years. Yet we all hoped the king, at Lafayette's suggestion, would revive the old tradition.

France was, after all, the richest and most enlightened nation in Europe. There was no need for our government to be bankrupt or corrupt and unrepresentative. We could, together, remake our country into a glorious beacon of freedom throughout the world, just as our American friends like Mr. Jefferson encouraged us to do.

Yet my husband was unusually apprehensive. "What principles should govern such an election?"

It'd been so long since the Estates General had last been summoned that no one had the faintest idea. "Can it not simply be left to *common sense*?" I asked, with a bit of mischief since I'd started to translate a pamphlet by Thomas Paine with that title.

Jefferson chuckled at my wit.

Meanwhile, Condorcet rubbed at his chin. "But Americans had experience governing themselves. Time to form the common sense of which my lovely wife speaks. Tyranny is any violation of the rights of mankind. It can emanate from a king or from a majority vote. What guide does the average Frenchman have in respecting the rights of his fellow human beings? Especially when slavery continues in French colonies and he does not protest it."

My husband glanced rather too pointedly at the slave-holding Jefferson, who only sipped at his wine, for the American minister was a man who knew the value of silence. Keenly aware of the presence of the Chevalier de Saint-Georges, himself born of a French father and an enslaved mother in Guadeloupe, Lafayette was not so silent. "This is why we must have a declaration of the rights of man to serve as a guide."

"What about the rights of women?" Olympe de Gouge asked.

"Man is a universal term," my husband replied.

"Oh, is it?" Olympe smirked, looking to me as if disappointed I wasn't offering my support. She was an opponent of marriage, calling it "the tomb of trust and love." Which is why she believed I held my tongue in wifely deference. In truth, I held my tongue because I didn't know which one of them was correct, and somehow the respect my husband always gave *my* opinions made me more considered.

————

Perhaps I should've been more considered that glorious summer when the king did, in fact, summon the Estates General to convene the next May.

"Everything is going to change now, Nicolas," I said, grasping his hands. "That beautiful future you're always talking about—it's in our grasp!"

"Maybe it is," he said, and together, we threw ourselves into the excitement. I hosted salons night after night, until I was weary. My purpose was to nudge important persons to form a consensus about the Declaration of Rights we so badly needed and to sway the deputies to abolish slavery in the French colonies. I couldn't vote in the upcoming elections, but at least I could do this.

Meanwhile, Condorcet created a scientific method by which to determine the winner of an election that most represented the will of the people. And he worked so feverishly that I discovered his strange habit of falling asleep under his desk so as not to waste the steps it might take to come to and from his bed.

He was adamant that slaveholders should be banned from standing for election altogether, but Lafayette pointed out such a stance would've prevented Jefferson from drafting the American Declaration of Independence. "Compromises must be made," Lafayette said, and perhaps he was right.

But at breakfast one day, I asked my husband, "Why don't *you* stand for election?"

Poking at his omelet, and distracted by the fact that he'd mislaid his wig somewhere now that little Pierre wasn't here to find it for him, Nicolas seemed flummoxed. "Me?"

"You're eminently qualified," I replied. "More than qualified. And if you worry about your discomfort in crowds, well, you've been perfectly amiable in our salon for months now. I heard you laugh the other night, surrounded by strangers. Twice. Everyone has noticed the change in you."

"That's your doing," he replied. "As you truly *are* the most gracious and lovely salonnière in Paris . . ."

I smiled at his compliment, which I liked even better coming from him than from Jefferson. "And *you* are the most enlightened man in France. The country needs you, Nicolas."

"I'm no orator," he replied. "My voice doesn't carry."

"Yet your *words* resound like thunder," I said, remembering the way I felt the first time I read his pamphlet.

There are those now who say it was all my doing.

That if Condorcet hadn't married me, he would've sailed above the political whirlwind. That the national treasure of his giant intellect would have remained untouched by the revolutionary convulsions of my heart and our age. His politics are attributed to me, as if he had no will of his own, but in matters of intellect and philosophy, they say he was always my master.

Of course, the people who say that never understood the man or our marriage.

And I was only beginning to.

"Sophie," Condorcet said, knocking lightly upon my door. "Please answer or I must assume you're in need of a physician . . ."

Prostrate with grief, I'd been unable to rise from my bed in the three days since my uncle's funeral. I was worrying my husband, which now added shame to my grief. "Come in," I said, wiping tears from my cheeks. "I merely feel wretched, and for that there is no tonic. I cannot even bring myself to comb my hair . . ."

Condorcet furrowed his brow. "I'll comb it for you, if you like."

I could imagine no other man offering to do the job of a lady's maid. And though I appreciated it, I did not wish to affect the air of an invalid, even if I felt like one. "I know death is natural. I keep telling myself that

Uncle Charles lived to see that his work wasn't in vain. That he died content." So why couldn't I be? "I told him it was a wonderful time to be alive. I believe that. So why do I feel now as if I can hardly bear life?"

"Perhaps because you've shut yourself up alone," Nicolas said, drawing my hands into his own. "Doesn't your favorite philosopher say that the sympathy of others comforts?"

"Adam Smith says that," I said softly. "But my favorite philosopher is Nicolas de Caritat, the Marquis de Condorcet . . ."

He smiled and kissed the top of my head. "Well, Condorcet believes the proverb that grief is halved when shared. Your uncle is gone, but our lives will always include him, Sophie, because he's shaped all you are. All that you accomplish will be his legacy."

Condorcet's words consoled me, and he stroked my back to soothe the pain away. I welcomed his touch, realizing that he'd become so infinitely dear to me. And so I wrapped my arms around my husband's neck and kissed him with a much more fervent emotion.

We'd kissed before, in experiment and fondness. This was different, and he knew it. "What does this mean?"

"It means I should have told you before now that I return your love," I said, drawing him down upon my tearstained pillow. *This* was love; not some frivolous emotion, but, like him, a necessary part of my existence. And it was in no way ridiculous. It was salvation itself. "I love you, Nicolas."

I expected to see the self-satisfied smile of a scientist whose experiment had come to successful conclusion. Instead, he whispered in the hollow by my ear, "You can break me, Sophie."

"I won't," I promised. For his fears, and his joys, were all my own, in perfect sympathy.

"But I'll always know that you could."

I twined my fingers with his. "I suppose then, in the words of a philosopher who is even more wise than famous, there must be an element of faith even in a godless marriage . . ."

It was lovemaking that night. We remained entangled during the crucial moment, for I couldn't bear to let him go and he didn't pull away. After, I enjoyed stroking his hair, his face, and even that beloved beak of a nose.

Yet he was rueful. "I should've been more careful just then."

"You needn't be. I think I'd like to make a child together." I'd felt the desire to be a mother for some time—even before little Pierre left our household. I thought the desire would pass. But now, at the age of nearly twenty-five, the yearnings of nature were too strong to ignore.

I believed my words would please my husband, a nobleman in need of an heir. But Condorcet's dark eyes narrowed in consternation. "I don't think it wise."

I could make no sense of this. He'd been wonderful with Pierre. Nearly all my husband's thoughts were consumed with how to feed, educate, and liberate the children of France. "Why shouldn't you want children of your own?"

He brought my palm to his lips for a kiss. "Do I *want* a child? Of course. If I close my eyes, I delight to imagine a precious little girl in my arms, calling me *Papa*. But I'm forty-five years old, Sophie, and your dearly departed uncle was three years younger than I am now. Do not forget that my father died when I was an infant, leaving me at the world's mercies. I would not wish to do the same to another child." I didn't wish to imagine Condorcet's death—couldn't bear to imagine it, actually. Especially when he said, "I couldn't leave you, a young mother, to fend alone with a child in this world."

"But we're making a better world," I argued, emotion lodging in my throat. "Don't you say the evils of the world are the product of ignorance, and that through education, we will eradicate them?"

He nodded. "I believe that better world will come,

but not soon enough for our child." He said this soberly and I realized that in the matter of our childlessness, we'd finally stumbled upon a matter of disagreement.

One we couldn't solve. That's how I knew it was truly love, I suppose. Because I disagreed with him but respected him just as much.

Perhaps our legacy could be our work together. Because from that day forward, we wrote together against slavery and tyranny, and in favor of women, education, and human rights—speeches, pamphlets, letters, and more. His words seeping into mine, my words seeping into his as we scratched out ideas at the breakfast table in our bedclothes, feeding each other bits of omelet.

I told myself that my happiness did not depend upon a child. There were so many other things I wanted to accomplish. Portraits to paint. Treatises to translate. Philosophies to formulate—including my own theories on moral sentiment.

It could be enough.

Even if it wasn't.

That winter was so frigid that wine casks burst open. There wasn't enough firewood to keep anyone warm. Rivers froze solid, which meant mills couldn't grind grain into flour. That meant no bread, and all Paris seemed to be rioting. In desperation, French business-men loaned the nation millions to import food for the king's hungry subjects, and Ambassador Jefferson arranged shipments from America to stave off starvation. But would help arrive in time?

Meanwhile, we were buried in snow while howling winds destroyed orchards and hailstorms killed everything that the winds did not. Then all at once came a thaw and the flood washed away whatever grain was left in the silos.

During this catastrophe, Nicolas never said to me, *You see how many children are going hungry? How could you wish to expose a little one to this?*

But I knew he was thinking it.

What he did say was that the price controls implemented by Jacques Necker—who had been recalled from exile to advise the king on financial matters again—were bad policy.

"It's hard to support free trade when bread is already more than fourteen sous a loaf," I argued. That was almost all of an average worker's daily wage, a thing I learned from Louise on the morning I braved the frigid weather for a moment's sunshine on the Pont Neuf. I bought two desiccated pears from her, and she recited a pamphlet that I was teaching her to read, which said,

What is the Third Estate? Everything.
What has it been hitherto in the political order? Nothing.
What does it desire to be? To become something . . .

When I told Nicolas this, it brightened his mood. He'd lost his election to the Estates General as a deputy—the nobles thought he was too radical, and the people thought him too much an aristocrat. But that didn't stop him from advising Lafayette, who had been chosen by the nobles of his home district.

"After the opening ceremonies, all three estates should become one national assembly," Condorcet argued. "As soon as this comes to pass, we can draw up a new constitution and change a whole nation."

"I argue this *every day*," Lafayette said, with a sigh. "You know that my heart is with the people. But my constituents—"

"Are wrong," I interrupted, willing to give up every dubious honor nobility had ever conferred upon me. "Your constituents are nobles who wish to hold on to their privileges and those days are over. They must be over if we're to bring liberty and equality to France. You were elected to *represent* your constituents, not bow to them."

"What does it mean to represent them?" Lafayette asked. "To violate the instructions of the people who sent you to be their voice—how can that be honorable? A thousand times in America I saw General Washington obey Congress despite how often they were wrong."

This was a fair point, but George Washington was a slave owner whose deference to Congress, or at least his own interests, resulted in the continuation of slavery. I didn't say this. Lafayette, too, was an abolitionist. But our friend worshipped Washington as a father and would hear nothing against him. I was frustrated. Lafayette was still the most influential man in France. More than the king, I believed. Certainly more popular. I wanted him to be bolder.

"I hope you won't judge him too harshly for his caution," Condorcet said as we snuffed out candles before bed. "I know you admire courage, but don't mistake heat of the head for heat of the soul. Because what you want is not heat but force. Not violence but steadfastness."

He'd described his own virtues, and he was right about what I wanted. I wanted him. I still wanted his child too. He must have sensed it when we made love, because afterward he said, "Sophie, I won't be a tyrant of a husband who says *this is how it must be, and that is the end of it.* I'll never tell you what you must do with your body. And you don't need me to make a child with it."

This remark was, of course, the natural product of his honorable heart and the promises he'd made me. I know that now, and I knew it even then. Nevertheless, I took powerful offense. "Are you suggesting I take a lover?" We'd agreed that if we couldn't be happy together we might seek happiness with others, but everything had changed. Or so I thought. For him to suggest this *now* infected me with rage. "Or do you think I've already taken one?"

"I don't permit myself to think anything of the sort—"

"If you think I'm bedding Lafayette, you're a perfect idiot."

I would regret stooping to insult. But the more rational Nicolas remained, sitting there quietly in thought, the more I burned. I wanted to tell him how foolish it would be to think that any child of mine would not also be his, if only by law. Instead, I snapped, "Have *you* taken a mistress, then? Is it Madame de Sainte-Amaranthe? She once suggested you were a libertine and that if I gambled with you I'd lose my petticoats. Which is true—in a fashion, I did. Still, she spoke of you with the intimacy of a lover, of which she has several. Are you one?"

His mouth twisted as if he couldn't decide to be angry or absolutely *delighted* by my jealousy. Thankfully, his hesitation gave me the necessary pause to recover my senses.

My hands went to my cheeks. "I'm sorry. That was beneath my dignity and yours."

"Nevertheless, I'll answer you, quite happily. First, it's Madame de Sainte-Amaranthe's vocation to pretend at intimacy. Second, my connection to her is a long friendship formed after having won a fortune at her gambling tables by employing mathematics to guess which cards my opponent might play. Third, I don't have a mistress or desire one. And, finally, it confounds me that you don't realize there's no one else for me but you, nor could there ever be."

Relief, love, and wretchedness all warred in my breast. "As it confounds me that when I say I want a child, you don't realize I want *your* child. No matter what you hear whispered outside the Palais-Royal, I'm not a harlot."

That made him offer his arms. "I've never believed that." Once I was soothed, both of us embracing and murmuring apologies, he said, "It seems that in the matter of children, one of us needs to decide. You should have the first turn. Like a Roman, I'll abide by your decision."

This concession was irrefutable proof that I'd always been right to trust in him. Still, the thrill of his sur-

render was temporary as I considered that he was sur-
rendering to me the use of his body for a purpose he
didn't approve—and not for the first time. Having re-
sented, all my life, the power men had over my person,
I simply couldn't exercise it over him. Not when he'd
told me I could break him, and I'd promised I never
would.

"We'll simply leave it an open question," I said.
"Reasonable people can change their minds . . ."

Versailles, Spring 1789

My husband was chosen as one of the six who would
prepare the complaints of the nobles to the king, an
elector for the Luxembourg district, and a *commissaire*
in the Paris General Assembly.

He was, overnight, a politician. And I was a politician's wife. Which meant we must go to Versailles.

Everyone was excited. Joyous, even. Even those who
would later oppose the changes in France would later
admit it was the most joyous time in our lives. The
roads were clogged with the traffic of horses, wagons,
carriages, and litters. So crowded was the king's capital that none of our friends could host us and we were

forced to take rooms at La Boule d'Or Inn to witness the festivities that opened the Estates General.

I woke early, bright-eyed, filled with nervous excitement, chattering away with my lady's maid as she fastened my mother's pearls at my throat. Condorcet, too, donned his best. Silk stockings I'd chosen for him to wear beneath his *culottes* because they showed off his calves. A black coat embroidered with gray, worn in sympathy with common people—for the deputies of the Third Estate were ordered to dress in the traditional black of the lower class.

"It's getting off on the wrong foot," I fretted. "The people's deputies and the nobles should all dress the same. Instead, the Third Estate has to march in black sackcloth like beggars with leprosy."

"Surely that's to exaggerate a little," Condorcet said, taking his place beside me at the balcony rail. But I knew he agreed such distinctions were harmful.

Along the route onlookers pressed together at every window and beneath every awning, craning their necks to see the parade. From bejeweled aristocrats to plain-faced scullery maids and sooty chimney sweeps, it seemed as if every person held their breath in anticipation of the march of the deputies. The trumpets announced them.

The king was at the head of the procession with the

Swiss Guard in his wake, their gold-hilted swords glinting beneath red coats with braiding. And the people shouted *Vive le roi!*

In later years, when I took up my pen to call for the end of the monarchy in favor of a republic, I'd be accused of harboring hatred for the king and perverting my husband's formidable mind with that same hatred. The truth is, I never hated the king. Especially not that day when he'd called together the people to remake the laws under which we all lived. That act was the king's greatest and most noble.

So I, too, shouted, "*Vive le roi!*"

Fewer people shouted for the queen. For my part, I waved to the king's sister, Madame Élisabeth, though I doubted she could see me through the crowd. Nor did she look up, as her gaze remained always on her brother the king, her expression pinched with submission to the public role he expected her to play.

The royal court was followed by diamond-bedecked nobles in plumed hats, then bishops in violet robes, and then, at last, the Third Estate in black. Lawyers and clerks, but also merchants and farmers, too—men who had come to take up the glorious mantle of governing their nation.

But not a woman amongst them, I thought.

Condorcet didn't laugh when I mentioned this.

"You're right. In all my writings about election procedures and expanding suffrage, I've overlooked half the earth."

"So has everyone else. I think it's because women have so long been denied our natural rights that even we aren't conscious of it."

But I was conscious of it *now*. So was Olympe de Gouges and many of the women who held forth in my salons. Now my husband, the most brilliant mind in France, was conscious of it too. One day he'd call for the enfranchisement of women, echoing my words. But that day, we were still awakening.

The Estates were greeted in the Salle des Menus, and we witnessed the pomp and circumstance from the galleries with American friends. Together we watched one deputy of the Third Estate applauded for refusing to wear black. The representatives of the common people were all seated far from the king when he took his place upon a throne of gold and purple—and many took insult.

As the king gave his speech, he still seemed, to me, more marionette than man. Trapped upon this national stage. Perhaps it would've been better to replace him with one of the automatas that Nicolas sometimes spoke of, a mechanical king that could be wheeled out for public occasions. Then maybe everyone—even the king—would be happier. And Madame Élisabeth could lead whatever life she chose.

After all, despite my enjoyment of this pageantry at Versailles—what was the cost of it all? In teaching in our school, I'd learned how difficult it was for people struggling to survive; with hungry bellies, they had little time to reflect upon finer sentiments like sympathy. I wondered if we might not all be better served with less pomp. Whether the sharing of our wealth, instead of the display of it, would result in a kinder society . . .

When it was announced that each estate should get a single vote, instead of each deputy having an equal vote, the Third Estate erupted in protest. It meant that the nobles and the clergy could always outvote the people's representatives, and so it all came to a messy impasse during which several deputies came to prominence.

Maximilien Robespierre, for one.

Arguments raged for weeks. Debate spilled into the taverns and coffeehouses where, one afternoon when Nicolas was closeted away with colleagues, I stopped for refreshments with Madame de Sainte-Amaranthe and her daughter, the latter of whom cried in greeting, "Grouchette!"

Once an adorable child, Émilie had since grown to

be the prettiest girl in Paris, just as her mother had predicted.

In truth, she was much more than pretty. With flaxen hair, angelic blue eyes, and luminescent skin, Émilie was a moon-kissed beauty who enchanted everyone whose gaze fell upon her. Having learned the practiced art of charm, she was now collecting expensive gifts from various suitors, to her mother's delight. But at a recent outing at the opera, Émilie confided in me a tenderness for a penniless young singer she kept secret from her mother—delighting *me* with the knowledge that she was a less biddable girl than she pretended to be.

As we entered the café together, we saw Robespierre, drawing notice to himself in tinted green spectacles, striped coat, and a fastidiously tied cravat. Except for some pockmark scars and a sallow complexion, Robespierre cut a fine and self-possessed figure amongst the gaggle debating the day's events.

And yet, at the sight of Émilie, he fell silent.

"It's the queen's fault," someone else was saying. "She doesn't want to give up her diamond necklaces."

Madame de Sainte-Amaranthe scowled at this as we took our seats. Émilie sighed, then whispered, "It's always the queen's fault somehow . . ."

The Sainte-Amaranthes were staunch royalists who

held polite disdain for the reforms we were trying to bring about. Still, Émilie had a point. From market women to princes of the blood, everyone blamed the queen for everything. They called her *Madame Deficit*, and I won't say that Marie-Antoinette was blameless. But that day, we couldn't bear to hear it, for the little dauphin, heir to the throne, had only recently perished at the age of seven, stricken by tuberculosis. How cruel it seemed to speak ill of the queen while she grieved for her child, so I couldn't help but turn to the crowd to interject, "Can we not spare just a few days' pity for the queen, who has a mother's broken heart?"

"Madame la Marquise." It was Robespierre himself who addressed me, while methodically peeling an orange. "Whatever the private sorrows of the royal family, the business of the nation must go on. And insofar as pity interferes with the nation's business, then *pity is treason.*"

His words were chilling, but in those days he wasn't anyone to fear, so I argued, "What is the business of the nation if it is not easing the suffering of every French person, man, woman, and child?"

"The queen's not French!" someone cried. "She's Austrian."

Robespierre simply took a bite of orange and smiled at Émilie, as if he hoped to impress.

"You mustn't let him trouble you," Condorcet said when I recounted this later. "I've listened to him speak these past weeks. His sole mission is to preach his religion of reform, and this he does almost constantly. But it is only talk. Robespierre aspires to be a priest and will never be anything else."

One rainy day in June, not long after, Condorcet rushed into our rented rooms, damp and disheveled. I assumed he'd returned for his umbrella, which he'd forgotten in the morning.

I was half right.

"The Third Estate has been locked out of their chambers," he said, breathlessly, his eyes on the windows overlooking the avenue.

"By the king?" I asked. "To keep them from meeting?"

"Perhaps an accident." He moved the curtain aside, no doubt looking for the royal cavalry, for we had no idea if this meant some kind of war. "The guards said it was only to make repairs to the hall. Yet it looks ill-intended, given that the king has been demanding that they meet separately and remember their place as inferiors. Either way, the Assembly has made its way through the rain to the tennis courts."

"To do what?" I asked.

Condorcet turned and met my eyes. "To write a constitution. They're going to do it. With or without the king."

Reassured the king's dragoons weren't galloping toward the tennis courts to put a stop to it all, he crossed the room and kissed me full on the mouth. Then he reached for his umbrella and started for the door.

Abandoning everything—paper, quill pen, and book—I grabbed my shawl and followed.

"Where are you going?" he asked.

"To witness a revolution," I said, feeling the impact of my own words in my bones.

He nearly smiled, but then his brow furrowed. "Sophie, it might be dangerous. There's no telling how the king will react, whether he'll surrender to the will of the people or have his Swiss Guards blast the tennis court to smithereens with cannon."

"All the more reason to go," I said. "To be with you. Whatever may come. Now, more than ever."

It was, after all, my revolution too.

A different sort of man would have flatly refused. Condorcet held out his hand to me. My heart pounding with thrill, I put my hand into his and together we splashed through the streets of Versailles, joining the gathering crowd to watch as the nearly six hundred brave, rain-drenched deputies swore a solemn oath "never to separate"—not even if the king should send an army against them—until they'd drawn up for France a true *constitution* and a Declaration of Rights for every citizen.

I was terrified. I was terrified for the deputies. I was terrified for *myself* in bearing witness. I was exhilarated too. Because I knew—we all knew—it was a defining moment. The moment that would change everything. And I believed, like a kind of faith, that we would prevail. That after all the pamphlets and debates and societies and all the years of calling for reform, we could, as a people, simply claim our natural right to self-determination through reason, courage, and legislation, without war . . .

Not even the Americans had done that!

It wasn't seemly for a husband and wife to hold hands in public. I didn't care. I clutched my husband's hand, marveling at his steadiness. Remembering, too, how steady his hands had been a different summer in a different rainstorm in this very place, during a moment that had liberated me as much as this one . . .

Tears misted my eyes. I wasn't alone in the emotion. My husband's voice was thick when he murmured, "I've been wrong."

"About?"

"*You.*" He stared with those arresting dark eyes and

I felt his joy. "I've worried to bring a child into this world, imagining that she'd be left without guidance or protection or strength without me. Now I know she'll have her courageous mother. I've given power to my fears instead of my hopes, but no more after today." He gestured at the oath-taking deputies, every one of them glowing with hope, courage, and determination. "Here is proof that we're remaking the whole world for her. Right here and now."

"Do you mean it?" I asked, almost afraid to believe.

He took my face in his hands and nodded. "Sometimes minds, governments, and marriages do change."

Ours *was* a marriage, I realized. No mummery or farce. Not defined by religious tradition or constrained by social rules or tainted by the tyranny of his sex over mine. It was a beautiful creation of our own self-determination, just as the nation would soon be.

And it was, indeed, a glorious time to be alive.

PART II

The Revolutionary

Men took the royal Bastille,
women took royalty itself.
—JULES MICHELET

Paris, June 27, 1789

A westerly wind swept across the rooftops, turning the weather vanes in a new direction.

The sun had long since set, yet the streets were alive with errand boys, blacksmiths, and fishmongers heading to their favorite tavern, and women scampering home after a long day at the shops. The heavy air hung about my shoulders like a damp blanket. Hot as a circle of hell, it was, and after a long day of selling fruit, I wanted nothing more than to collapse by the river's edge—after this last mission. I pushed the hair out of my eyes as the steady flow of gilded carriages carted their powdered and bejeweled cargo to the evening salons. I muttered foul words under my breath. Not a single carriage paused so I might cross the street. Neither did their passengers look at pedestrians with anything but disdain. And we were to believe they felt differently about us, we commoners.

It was a glorious time to be alive. Or so said the Marquise de Condorcet yesterday when I'd finished my lessons at her school. A sharp retort had sprung to my lips, but I'd clamped them shut, knowing she meant well in spite of her rank. But what did nobles know?

It was always a glorious time to be alive for *them*.

Change, many said, was on the wind. This was the reason for the Marquise de Condorcet's optimism. But I had my own opinion. Nothing had changed in hundreds of years, and this country was no America. It was a waste of breath to pretend otherwise.

"The nobility," I grumbled, wiping my nose on my sleeve. To say I had conflicted feelings about them would be like saying the queen bought an occasional trinket.

I had followed Maman's advice all my life: do as the nobility asks and your belly will always be full. But she had lied, God rest her soul. Sometimes, doing all that was asked of me wasn't enough. Sometimes, I was knocked about, or went home empty-handed at their whim. Those days reminded me where I ranked in this world: among the lowly selling fruit to survive, or playing courier for noblemen and salonnières day after day. All for a little coin that disappeared into the landlord's purse. On a good day, someone like the Marquise de Condorcet paid me well, even smiled and offered a kind word or two. Those days kept me coming back for more, like a rat to a crumb of bread.

My stomach growled in accordance with my

thoughts. *Bread*, fresh hot bread. Manna from heaven, if any could be found in the city. I groaned, a hand pressing at my midsection, hollow after a long day of eating only a potato. Thankfully, tonight's errand would pay well so I might afford something more.

For I was on an errand for Monsieur Maillard, a notary clerk and brother of the master bailiff in Paris known to support the Revolution, who had hired me to find the chocolatier Pauline Léon. More and more, he'd taken to speaking on behalf of the people. He spoke with passion, and the people listened to him, so I'd agreed to undertake the task instantly. I'd also undertaken the task of reading the note—now that I'd learned to read. Something about a meeting with the Duc d'Orleans, a meddling nobleman who liked to pretend he was one of us. I didn't trust the oily duc and his weak chin.

I stepped from the shadows and took a chance, dashing between a carriage and a cart bumping over the cobbles.

Luckily, I knew Pauline slightly, as the Marquise de Condorcet once took me to her shop, La Maison du Chocolat Léon, to sip cups of warmed chocolate. I'd also seen Pauline buzz about the grounds of the Palais-Royal like a worker bee, where the wealthy and wicked spent their livres shopping and gambling, or on whores and fortune-tellers; and more recently, where the dissatisfied went to bark at the crowd and whip everyone into a frenzy. These days that made it the best location to sell fruit—and the perfect place to keep abreast of the news from Versailles.

I slipped inside the bustling chocolatier and noticed the usual mix of patrons: merchants, barristers, soldiers, a handful from high society, and even a few women. More and more often, members of all classes mixed in the taverns and cafés of Paris. They liked to play friends with one another while they spouted their nonsense about the king. I couldn't help but roll my eyes at their stupidity. It was nothing but a fantasy to pretend we were all equals, to pretend something might change.

Pauline rushed to and fro, delivering cups and whisking away dirty saucers, all the while slipping coins into the pocket of her apron and smiling at patrons. I headed in her direction.

"Mademoiselle, I have a note for you." I held out the creamy envelope.

She snatched it from my hand without a word and tucked it inside her apron.

"You're welcome," I said, sliding a chair out and plopping into it. "Ah, that's nice. My poor feet ache. Can you bring me a *chocolat chaud*?"

"*Pas ce soir,*" Pauline said through tense lips. When I stared back at her in surprise, she bent closer to the table and said, "You need to leave. Your . . ."—she winced—"odor is offending my guests."

I glanced at the tables nearest me. One man scooted his chair as far away as possible. Another regarded me through narrowed eyes, his mouth pinched. It took a lot to embarrass me and my thick skull, but heat flared in my cheeks. Did I smell *that* horribly? It had been a searing hot day, the kind where exposed skin burned quickly and moisture clung to your dress. I'd spent most of it running messages all over Paris. Apparently, I needed to wash tonight.

To salvage what little pride I still had, I stood to go. But before I could stop my dagger-tipped tongue, I said, "You don't look like an aristocrat, Pauline, but you sure do put on the airs of one. Maybe a little powder for your complexion and a rod up your backside will complete the charade."

Pauline's face darkened. "I'll thank you to leave my café—now. Before I toss you out on your hind end."

I bit down on my bottom lip to suppress a laugh. That was another thing Maman had lied about: my wit did *not* always serve me well. At least half the time my mouth got me into more trouble than a good teasing was worth, especially with my five brothers, who loved nothing more than to give me a good knock on the arm. I shrugged and headed toward the door.

At that moment, a man barged into the café, his breath ragged. He leapt onto a chair and shouted above the patrons, "The king has joined the First and Second Estates with our National Assembly. We have a voice in our government, at last!"

Cheers erupted, drowning out the remainder of the man's speech. Not even my typical cynicism dampened the excitement suddenly churning in my belly. If what the man said was true, we now had a merging of royalty, clergy, and the common man into one. We were no longer a country divided.

When all had quieted once more, he tried again. "The king promises to change our taxation laws, and abolish the letters de cachet. We'll have no more directives from the king without consensus! *Vive le roi!*"

The cheering arose again, and for the very first time, my heart swelled with the urge to believe things really could be different. Chairs scraped over tile and the clatter of spoons tossed on a forgotten dish filled the room as customers stood to beat each other on their backs in happy gratitude.

"Friends, come, celebrate at the Palais-Royal tonight! *Vive le roi!*" the man said and jumped to the ground.

Laughing and cheering, and some even crying, everyone poured into the lamp-lit street. Like a legend of old, we all knew how the deputies from the Third Estate, the representatives of the common people, had gathered inside the tennis court, prepared to face bayonets of the Swiss Guard if necessary in the name of forming a new government. When the news of their courageous stand arrived in Paris, joy had seized the city. And now this—the National Assembly represented a united France. As was my nature, I couldn't help but wonder if the Assembly would hold, or if its power and influence would shift with the king's mood.

Still, the streets were alive with celebration, and seeing the jubilation of my countrymen, I had to admit that perhaps my cynicism had been misplaced. Perhaps all the Marquise de Condorcet believed would come to pass. My mind reeled with how those changes might affect me; no more hunger, a safer home, perhaps even different work.

The sound of explosions echoed off the buildings, and a sudden burst of light in the night sky elicited cheers from citizens rushing to see the display. My breath caught as I tilted my face upward. Fireworks flowered over the Palais-Royal. On my right, I caught sight of Pauline.

When she noticed me, her eyes narrowed. "Don't

ever use that filthy word around me again, or you'll regret it."

"Aristocrat?" I asked innocently, unable to resist goading her.

She eyed me coolly. "I lost friends in the bread riots, executed by the king's men. You can be certain I don't consider our monarch, or the nobility, my ally."

And I had lost a mother under the boot of a vicomte who'd had one too many glasses of brandy in the household where she worked as cook, and after, my dearest friend, Marion, to an overeager baron at the brothel where she once lived. Wretched memories that I would never forget—or forgive. Yet I knew better than to fight those who paid my wages. I needed to eat, after all.

Still, I felt a stirring in my breast as the fireworks glittered like jewels against the black night. In truth, I needed something to believe in. I might laugh at life's difficulties in public, but privately I sank into more darkness than I dared admit, even to myself. It was dangerous there, in that place.

"Mademoiselle Léon." I held up my hands in surrender. "Am I forgiven? Let us be friends."

Her dark eyebrows arched in surprise. "Was that an apology?"

"Something like that." I grinned. "Call me Louise."

After a moment of studying my face, she nodded.

"All right, Louise." She paused a beat and motioned overhead. "Look at these stupid men, celebrating as if anything has changed."

"We'll see, won't we?" I noticed the twist of her lips as if she'd eaten something sour. Her cynicism put a damper on the hope I'd just begun to feel, and maybe she had the right of it. I quickly added, "They sit around and talk, those deputies, and we're supposed to act as if it's the second coming of Christ."

Pauline snorted in laughter, and then her face grew serious. "Well, we should see what's happening at the Palais-Royal at least, shouldn't we?" I nodded. "And Louise?"

"Mmm?"

"I meant what I said—you really stink."

I howled with laughter and followed Pauline Léon to the Palais-Royal.

Paris, July 12, 1789

A fortnight later, nothing had changed, in spite of our National Assembly. My doubt redoubled, and for a moment, I pitied the fools who believed this new government could bring anything meaningful to our lives.

I peered from behind my fruit cart across the gardens of the Palais-Royal. Sunlight filtered through the chestnut trees, marbling the ground beneath them with dappled gold. A hot breeze rustled my skirts and lifted the hair off the back of my neck. Patrons roamed in and out of the boutiques, arm in arm with smiles on their faces, or perched on a bench in the courtyard of one of the most famous marketplaces in Paris. Just another summer day, and all seemed glorious. All but the odor of the damned chrysanthemums. Why the *fleuriste* felt it necessary to park his cart next to our fruit and vegetable stand each day confounded me. We weren't nice to him, my friend Jeanne or I; well, I wasn't nice to him, and I didn't like the way his flowers reminded me of death.

We needed no reminders of death, as so many continued to starve. The tension I'd felt off and on all morning reasserted itself.

A laughing couple started toward me, and I adjusted my scowl into a faux smile.

The young woman was another of *those* customers—a proper lady in sky blue silk and pearls, ruffled skirts with immense petticoats, and an elegant gentleman at her side. His tricorn hat looked as if it had never been worn. They sorted through apples and pears and stroked the fuzz of a plump peach before deciding on the two largest apples in the barrel.

"Thank you for your patronage," I said, closing my fist around the coins the man dropped into my palm, making an effort not to touch me as he did. I pretended not to notice and bumped his hand with my own.

He jerked away and examined his glove, lips pinched in disgust.

Through a wide smile I said, "Good day, monsieur."

They turned abruptly, swept across the gardens to a waiting coach, and climbed inside. The woman looked past me as the carriage trundled away.

If I had my choice, I'd avoid her type like a case of the pox; she in her feathered hat as fat as a hen on her head, clucking and tutting her disapproval, all the while flaunting her pretty manners. They never looked you in the eye. I sighed. But a customer was a customer, and I needed the sous in a desperate way.

I shuffled pieces of fruit around to make it look like I had more in my cart. Of course the couple had reached for the biggest apples they could find. Bigger and more meant better in their eyes. A dim-witted choice, to be sure. The smaller fruits packed the sweetest punch, didn't they know? But it was just as well. I'd save the best fruit for those who deserved it: the hardworking carpenters, peddlers, laundresses, fishmongers, and poor mothers who struggled to feed their families at all. We all worked like the devil to survive.

I groaned. My stomach felt like it would eat itself, the pangs had grown so bad. I plucked a Mirabelle plum from the pile and bit into its golden flesh. That would come out of my meager sales today, but it was worth it. Three days without bread, a week without meat, and what little cheese I'd come across I'd given to the street rags. I couldn't watch a child go hungry. But with only soured wine and fruit for days, my head felt light as a feather, especially in this suffocating heat. Tonight I'd have to eat something of substance, even if I had to beg for it.

Jeanne, the vendor with whom I shared a cart, snapped the roots off her lingering potato stock. She was having trouble selling too. Perhaps our customers were standing in the growing breadlines, waiting for their share. We'd all believed, come summer, the wheat stores would be stocked and the price of bread would fall to normal and be plentiful again.

We hadn't dreamed the nobility would be cruel enough to hoard their crop. We were wrong.

Across the garden, I spotted a familiar figure. Madame de Sainte-Amaranthe, famed salonnière and courtesan, was so graceful she appeared to float over the path. She wore gold brocade and carried a dainty handbag over her left arm, and on her right, an acquaintance joined her in a promenade. I'd delivered many messages for Madame, running my derrière ragged to please her. She had recommended my services to others, always had a kind word for me, and paid me better than most. I was grateful for her trust. I wondered, briefly, what scrap of gossip held her attention as she appeared deep in conversation.

Just then, a garçon strolled in front of my cart, his trousers tattered at the bottom, his face black with grime. I knew that face all too well. "Don't you—"

In a flash, the little thief snatched an apple, turned on his heel, and ran.

"You'd better pay for that!" I shouted. To Jeanne, I said, "Watch the cart, will you? I'll be back."

I raced after the boy, winding around manicured hedges and pushing through a group of men in heated discussion.

"*Attention*, mademoiselle!" a man called after me.

I skidded on a patch of slick cobbles bathed in liquids I dared not examine too closely. Stumbling slightly, I pitched forward but managed to regain my footing. "*Christ!*"

A puppeteer chuckled and pointed after the boy. "Better move. He's a fast one!"

"He's mine this time!" I picked up my pace, ducking beneath a bolt of fabric outside the tailor's shop that billowed in the breeze.

The boy threw a look over his shoulder—and nearly slammed into a woman browsing an array of pungent cheeses.

I lunged for him, grasping at threads unraveling on the edges of his coat. "That's one too many times, you rat!"

"Sorry, ma'moiselle, got to eat." He leapt over a puddle, ducked under the boughs of a tree, and sprinted toward the shops.

Apparently, the little rodent didn't know I'd have no qualms about whacking him on the skull the minute I caught him, inside a fancy boutique or not.

He barreled toward the gleaming window of one of the city's finest chocolatiers. Surely the shopkeeper would turn him away. They weren't the type to offer handouts. If so, I wanted my own bonbons. Seemed only fair.

The boy reached for the latch, and the doorbell tinkled as he slipped inside. I dashed inside after him—and inhaled a sharp breath.

The store gleamed. Boxes in blue, lemon yellow, and powder pink sat on the shelves, ready to be filled with confections and tied with gold ribbon. Black and white tiles fanned across the floor in a dizzying maze, and a wide brass chandelier hung from the ceiling. A case of glistening confections stretched one whole wall, gold-dusted, glazed, dipped, and swirled, and some that had been painted prettily with tiny brushes. My head dizzied at the sight, or maybe it was the smell. Sugared cherries and vanilla, and the earthy aroma of *chocolat chaud* wafted on the air. For an instant, I contrasted Pauline's simple café with the luxury of this one, clearly designed to attract a certain kind of patron, and saw in the comparison just how vast the gulf was between our classes. I wondered, though, was the warmed chocolate really that much better when served in fancy cups? My stomach growled, eager to make the comparison.

"Mademoiselle Audu, *bonjour.*" The Marquise de Condorcet stood at the counter tucking a box of treats into her basket. "What good fortune, I did not have to seek you out. We will not be having class this afternoon."

The Marquise de Condorcet was a true lady, kind and generous through and through. I'd spent many a day learning to read in the free school she and her husband ran in a building just across from the Palais-Royal. She wasn't like other nobles—at least not much like them—and I owed her more than I could ever repay whether I wanted to admit it or not.

"All right," I said distractedly and leaned over the counter to look behind it. My breath still came in hot bursts. "Where did the boy get off to?"

"You wouldn't mean this young man?" The marquise stepped forward to show the filthy boy, eleven or twelve in age, hiding behind her. In his hand, he clutched my fruit, already half-eaten. The marquise wrapped an arm around his shoulders. "This is Pierre Simare. He was one of my fledglings but we were forced to let him go." Fleetingly, as if even she was not aware of it, the noblewoman smoothed a palm over her abdomen in the way of expectant mothers, then gave the boy the basket. "Here you are, *mon cheri*. Come to me next time, if you are hungry."

He clutched the gift as if it were bricks of gold. "Thank you, Marquise."

I sucked in another ragged breath, faintly noticing I couldn't seem to slow the blood pounding in my ears. "He stole another of my apples. If that little . . ." My words trailed off as stars filled my vision. Clasping my chest, I leaned against the countertop. The spells had worsened over the last weeks, as I barely managed to keep flesh on my bones.

Both the marquise and the chocolatier moved to steady me.

"Mademoiselle Audu, are you ill?" the marquise asked, concern shining in her blue eyes.

"I haven't eaten much in a few days," I confessed.

"Madame"—the marquise motioned to the shop-keeper—"a saucer of your best chocolate."

The shopkeeper disappeared into the back room and emerged moments later with a porcelain cup. "Here we are."

"Fancy dishes," I said, accepting the cup gratefully.

"Nothing but the best for the Queen of the Market Women," the woman said, her voice dripping with scorn.

Queen of the Market Women. It had a ring to it.

I gulped the warm chocolate without tasting the thick liquid as it slipped down my throat. When I'd finished, I gave the marquise a rueful smile. "I suppose I should thank you for saving me from starvation."

She flashed her sweet smile set in a round face. The smile of someone who had never been hungry. "We must all look after one another in these times."

"You're a saint among women, Marquise," I said with a touch of my characteristic sarcasm. Then I grew serious. "Thank you, truly. I am indebted to you, as ever."

She nodded. "Pierre has had a difficult life. You must forgive the boy."

"He's a thief." I shook my finger at him, and he tucked himself farther into her skirts. "I can't afford more lost sales. Do you hear me, boy? Steal from someone else."

A pair of bright blue eyes peeked out from behind the marquise once more. "Sorry, ma'moiselle. I was hungry."

"Me too," I growled. But I felt myself soften. He was just a child, and had I seen him on the street instead of stealing from me, I would have given him a trifle or two.

"Well, now, who is watching your cart, Mademoiselle Audu?"

"My friend Jeanne. She sells vegetables. We set up together every day and help each other. It takes some doing, getting the cart wheeled from the Cordelier to the Palais-Royal, but it's worth it. I make twice the livres as I did on the Pont Neuf."

A rumbling came from outside the shop.

I knew that sound all too well by now—the sound of many voices mixing and mounting in fury. I followed the Marquise de Condorcet outside, and Pierre sped past us, disappearing into the crowd. A *staggering* crowd. The hundreds of people usually milling about the shops had grown to thousands.

I whistled. "Sweet Jesus on the cross. What's going on here?"

A man stood atop a table outside the Café de Foy and was speaking.

"It is Monsieur Desmoulins, the journalist," the marquise said.

As we waded toward Monsieur Desmoulins, we were jostled by prostitutes and butchers, pamphleteers and soldiers, and actors from the Théâtre Favart, including François Elleviou, and the Italian opera singer Marie Grandmaison with her lover, Charles de Sartine. All wanted to hear what the writer of *La France Libre* had to say. I had his pamphlets, which I could now read thanks to the marquise, tucked away in a cupboard at home along with other writings.

Despite the short walk, I struggled for breath. I leaned into the marquise and she turned to me, her eyes deep blue pools of concern. "Are you unwell, Louise?"

I must have looked a fright for the marquise to call me by my Christian name, so perfect were her manners. I inhaled a calming breath to clear away the stars crowding my vision once again. "I drank the chocolate too fast is all," I lied, eager to dismiss her concern—and to hear what Desmoulins had to say.

"*Citizens!*" he began, his dark eyes flashing. "I am just back from Versailles. The king has sacked Necker as finance minister! He was our only ally in the king's service. Next, the king will put down our National Assembly and all we've worked to achieve."

A hush fell over the crowd.

Desmoulins continued, "There is no time to waste! The king has called upon the Swiss and German battalions this very night to murder us all; our only choice is to take arms! To defend ourselves!"

Fear rippled through the crowd in waves of shock, tears, and the terrified cries of children as their mothers gripped their hands too tightly.

"*Non*," Madame de Condorcet gasped, her pallor suddenly ashen.

My heart tumbled to my stomach. Would the king call upon a foreign army to slaughter us, his own people?

"We must take up arms and adopt a symbol by which we patriots may know each other. A cockade." Desmoulins pointed to a green ribbon tied to his hat. "Our symbol of liberty!"

"A symbol of hope," someone shouted.

Desmoulins waved his pistol in the air, his black eyes all afire. "To arms!"

The crowd dispersed in every direction, ripping leaves off the trees to make their own symbols of liberty. I reached for the branches of a nearby chestnut tree, snapping off several twigs festooned with brilliant green leaves. "To wear, Marquise."

She hesitated, and I wondered if I'd been wrong to offer. If it came to a fight, would she side with the king, or with the people? There must be no wavering between sympathies. If the king was sending his soldiers to slaughter us, we needed to know who our friends and enemies were. Could we trust the nobles, even the good ones?

To my relief, the marquise accepted the offering and, removing a pin from her hair, fastened the leaves on her bonnet. "We're all in this together."

Once the crowd stripped the trees of the Palais-Royal, they raided the wax museum to demand the sculpted heads of Necker and the Duc d'Orleans, champions of liberty that we could carry as talismans of good luck. I followed, heart thundering in my ears, though I secretly wondered: What use was a wax head against an army? Were we going to throw them at the cannoneers?

We needed weapons. But most commoners couldn't afford a pike, much less a pistol.

All around me, people grabbed stones, sticks, bricks—anything we could lay hands on. I loaded my apron with stones. Yet I didn't believe for a minute a handful of pebbles would save me.

"To the Hôtel des Invalides!" someone shouted.

An order that was repeated in a great wave. The Invalides was more than a hospital and home for our aging army veterans; it was a place where we might find cannons and muskets. The mass surged in that direction, sweeping us along with it. I lost hold of the Marquise de Condorcet, and she disappeared in the crowd. I couldn't fight the crush of bodies if I'd wanted to; there was nowhere to go but forward. In truth, I wanted to see how this would end. If the marquise was brave enough not to flee, I must be too.

As we reached the place Vendôme, our number had grown into a mass larger than I'd ever seen. And that's when we saw them.

A troop of the king's Swiss Guards posted about the square, weapons drawn, demanding we disperse. Tension crackled in the air. I wrapped my hand around a stone, waiting to see what would happen next. In that instant, a rallying cry arose from the crowd—*To arms!* A hailstorm of stones flew through the air. The soldiers descended upon us.

My pulse pounded in my ears. My breath grew shallow. We were no match for the king's army with our makeshift weapons. Chaos ensued, and people fled in every direction.

In the confusion, I ducked into a doorway. An old man fell at my feet, clutching his bloody gut, cut open by a saber.

We were going to die. In that moment I knew, the king was going to kill us all.

"Run," the old man croaked. "You're just a girl. This isn't your fight. Run!"

I fled across the square, looking for a shrub to cower under and hating myself for it.

I'm just a girl. What could I do? For a moment, I wondered if my brothers were in the melee, if they had left their places of work and now tangled with the Swiss Guard. Would they be ashamed I cowered here in the bushes?

The clatter of horses' hooves, the crack of muskets, and the cries of the fallen sounded from the square, but I didn't dare move. What had we done to deserve this treatment? We had asked our sovereign to look after us, as he was ordained to do by God.

In spite of the prickly bush against my skin, I crouched for hours, my muscles aching, my ears straining for some sign it was all at an end. When the bells finally rang to celebrate that we had held the king's troops at bay—at least for now—I went home, mind racing with dark thoughts, thoughts that threatened to disorder my mind.

Through the night, I became accustomed to cries in the street and the sound of smashing glass as people took advantage of the chaos to loot the shops. And yet, I was consumed with memories of dear Maman, and of how much she'd longed for freedom from the lives we'd led.

How I'd lost her at the hands of those who oppressed us.

At dawn, I finally felt brave enough to go in search of my abandoned fruit cart.

Once at the Palais, I found good patriot men gathered to form a citizens' army they were calling a National Guard. "We'll protect you, mademoiselle," some of the swaggering boys in hastily assembled uniforms of patched-together cloth promised. They had traded their green leaves for cockades of blue, white, and red and carried pistols and knives stripped from the cutlery stalls and gun shops throughout the city. Yet in spite of having seized all these weapons, and some cannons and muskets from the Hôtel des Invalides, we didn't have enough to truly arm a citizens' National Guard.

Monsieur Maillard pushed his way to the front of the new army. I wasn't surprised to see him there. As a former soldier and emerging orator, he struck me as prepared to lead. "Something more must be done," he said, pulling the hat from his head to run a hand over his sweat-dampened hair.

Whatever it was would be done without me. I would stay out of this mess, at least until I had my own weapon. My hands shook as I dragged the empty fruit cart slowly from the gardens of the Palais, but I didn't get far. Drums had summoned every able-bodied man out of his house to enlist. Including, apparently, the Marquis de Condorcet, the old philosopher who always appeared haggard with fatigue but was now garbed in the new uniform and carried an umbrella. Somehow, the sight of him made me fearful of what was to come.

"How are you going to kill the king's dragoons with that, Marquis?" I asked.

"I could never bring myself to kill a man," he said. "Violence isn't the answer to any of this. But I must stand by my convictions as a patriot and join our citizens' militia. Since that is my truth, I've decided my weapon of choice is an umbrella."

My mouth fell open, I closed it, and it fell open again. An umbrella to defend himself? Fat chance that would protect him. Or any of us. He'd be slaughtered like a lamb, like the old man who'd been cut down by a saber. Nobles really were mad, I decided, even the good ones. I admired Condorcet, but if he were the kind of soldier that had joined the citizens' militia to defend our city, we were doomed.

"Is it true what they say about the king's soldiers, Marquis?" I asked. "I've heard they will attack again tonight."

He nodded grimly. "This is what I have been told. And the governor of the Bastille is pointing his cannons at the city."

I gasped. So we were to be attacked by foreign armies from the outside and by our own government from within? If the governor was willing to threaten us, then the Bastille, that ancient prison and depository for the king's large store of weapons, might be our only answer.

Nay, our only hope.

The idea of storming the Bastille sparked like fire on dry tinder and raged across the city in mere hours. And it was as if hundreds of years of hatred, fear, and rage at that fortress, and all it represented, bubbled over at once. The ragtag army of National Guardsmen began to cry out, "*À la Bastille!*"

Go home, I told myself as the fervor grew, and I pushed my cart once more. *I am just a girl.* Pauline Léon appeared in the crowd at that moment, wearing her chocolate-stained apron over a skirt she'd tied like trousers, and carrying a pike like an avenging goddess.

Again, my mouth fell open, but this time in awe. "What are you doing?"

"I'm going with the men to the Bastille to demand the governor give up his weapons. He says he won't without the king's permission. He thinks we're stupid. That we don't know he's holding those weapons for the king's troops. He's going to help them murder everyone in Paris unless we stop him."

We? Pauline wore a blue, white, and red cockade on her mobcap as if she considered herself part of the citizens' militia. A woman's battalion of one. And now she was looking at me, expectantly, like she meant for me to join.

And so I did.

We marched with the men to the Bastille. The entire way Pauline chanted, "Open the Bastille! Surrender the Bastille!" She wanted to fight, I realized—really fight—but the men thought she was some oddity and kept pushing ahead of her, pushing ahead of us both.

As we rounded the corner of another street, a man shoved past me and lunged for Pauline's pike.

"What the hell do you think you're doing?" Pauline kicked the man—hard—in the shin and then his groin.

He dropped like a stone.

I stepped over him and gave Pauline a bright smile. "I guess he won't try to take a weapon from us again."

Resuming her chanting, she nodded and held her pike up in triumph. Yet, as we continued forward, the men slowly edged us out until Pauline and I were at the back of the crowd.

I wouldn't find out until later that some of our citizen soldiers cut the ropes of the drawbridge of the Bastille and sent it crashing down. That the king's soldiers invited us to take weapons at first—then they opened fire.

And a desperate fight began.

For a second time, I started to run, but Pauline caught me by the collar. "We can at least throw up barricades," she said, "bring water, or tend wounded . . ."

But I was no soldier or nurse. I squirmed away, racing all the way home as fast as my legs would carry me. A lifetime of servility had taught me to survive, above all else. That was all I knew.

The next day, I learned that we'd taken the Bastille. More than that, the people had dismantled it. Carried pieces of it away, stone by stone, destroying the symbol of our oppression. I felt both pride and regret; pride that for a second time the men of France had stood against the king, and regret that I hadn't been a part of it. Not like Pauline had been.

It was a regret I never wanted to feel again.

Paris, Late August 1789

Soon, it came to be said on the streets of Paris and beyond that this was no revolt. This was a revolution.

We flew as high as the king's hot-air balloon on our chance at a new life, at freedom, as stated in our brand-new Declaration of the Rights of Man and the Citizen drafted by our National Assembly. Rights for the common man, and for all. We were one and the same, whether clergy, nobleman, or commoner, each of us pulling on our shoes each day, filling our stomachs to survive. Free people of color and others in Les Amis des Noirs argued before the Assembly that they and their enslaved brethren on Saint-Domingue, too, deserved those rights. So it didn't seem a stretch to believe that even women might benefit from the Assembly's edicts. Or so they said. Especially now that the Marquis de Lafayette had taken command of the National Guard; the war hero would defend us from the king. Again, so they said.

But six weeks after the fall of the Bastille I still found myself asking, what had all this come to? I was still a fruit seller and I was still hungry. The only difference was that my mood had worsened along with the bread shortages. I snapped at Jeanne all day, so we pushed the cart over the bridge and parted ways in complete silence.

As I walked toward home at a brisk pace, a thick fog rolled in like a great puff of smoke from a pipe, shrouding the sky with early nightfall. A man in a cloak scurried from one lantern post to another, igniting the oil with a flame on the end of his pole. He whistled to himself as he walked along. In just a few more steps, his form disappeared into the fog. I could scarcely see the road in front of me.

In spite of our new world of declarations and the National Assembly, the streets had grown increasingly unsafe. I supposed that was something that had changed. When it grew too late, beggars and thieves and all manner of scoundrels emerged from the shadows, ready to pounce on an unfortunate mademoiselle. I'd beaten off a weasel or two when I couldn't avoid being out after dark. Carrying a switch usually put the fear of the devil in them.

Shivering, I picked up my pace and, at last, ducked beneath a tattered cloth awning into Le Sanglier. Though my home was just next door, I didn't need to look in the cupboard to know it was bare. My only hope for a decent meal was at my favorite tavern. I pushed open the door and was met with raucous laughter and a warmth that glowed from the first roaring fire of the season in the hearth on the back wall.

"Mademoiselle Audu!" The barkeep motioned to the last space at the end of the bar top. To the lumps of red-faced men who looked as if they never left the bar, he said, "Move over, you cretins."

They grumbled but did as the barkeep demanded.

"Thanks, Charlie." I slid onto the last stool. "Have you got a spare crust of bread or some stew? I've two sous is all, but I'd take the end of the pot."

He grinned. "Not this time. Unless you make it worth my while."

"You swine." I slapped his shoulder playfully. "You know I'm not a painted lady."

His round cheeks dimpled and a blush stole over his face. "That's not what I meant."

"What then?"

He brandished a bare cheek and pointed to it. "Give us a kiss."

I rolled my eyes and leaned forward. Just as my lips brushed his skin, Charlie turned his face. His lips met mine in a firm but soft kiss.

"Get off." I shoved him in false outrage, but secretly warmed to his touch. Sorry for him—and perhaps sorry for me—I wasn't interested in a sweetheart, and

I certainly wasn't foolish enough to get myself with child. Maybe it would be different when we saw what the future entailed. For now, a man at my side would only create a lot of nonsense.

He roared with laughter as he disappeared into the kitchen, returning with a steaming bowl of stew. "Here you are."

I inhaled the stew's hearty aroma before hunching over it and tucking in. Within seconds, I devoured the greasy meat, softened potatoes, and few stray carrots floating in the broth.

Charlie poured a glass of claret and pushed it toward me. "You *were* hungry."

"I'm always hungry. Got a hole in my stomach." I sipped the wine gratefully.

The noise in the room escalated as more patrons poured in from the street, and the wine flowed freely. I chased the last carrot that seemed intent on avoiding my spoon and finally scooped it into my mouth. Behind me, a pair of passionate voices drifted from the common table. I threw a glance over my shoulder, making eye contact with a large man who spilled over the edges of his trousers.

He removed his tricorn hat and winked at me. I turned quickly, not wanting to encourage him, but bent an ear to their conversation in a not-so-subtle way.

"The king is no fool," the man continued. "He must see what's at stake."

"But he has yet to support the Declaration," said another.

I perked up at the mention of the Declaration. It was all anyone had talked about for weeks at the Palais-Royal.

"We've just upended the king's world. Asked him to change the way he's been taught since birth, and to disrupt centuries of tradition. Give him time."

I sneaked another look over my shoulder.

"I don't think time will make a difference," a third man added, his eyes darkening beneath a shock of unruly wavy hair. "We're demanding he surrender much of his power. What man would do so willingly?"

Several shouted their agreement and another round of ale was poured.

"I hope the king might still see reason." The fat man who first winked at me swirled the contents of his glass and tipped it back.

"Not if that Austrian bitch has her say." A fourth joined them, pulling out a chair. He was a monster of a man with a towering frame and a face that looked like chewed leather. "She'll talk him out of it." He pulled the woman who had followed him onto his lap. She giggled and the capped sleeves of her dress slipped far lower than was modest. Rouge smeared her cheeks and lips. The man planted a kiss on her breast that bulged above her bodice. She giggled again and put her hand on his massive chest.

"Don't ruin the mood, Danton," the fat man said to the newcomer. "We've lots to hope for."

"As long as we continue to pressure the Assembly, we might make a new nation," the man called Danton said, and kissed the whore squarely on the mouth. After, she held his beer glass to his lips and he drank greedily.

"Christ, Danton, can you do that in private?" the dark-eyed man complained.

I turned around to mind my own business. Little did I know how well I would come to know Danton, how often I would see him in the Cordeliers Club and, later, in every newspaper in Paris.

Charlie appeared at my side to collect my saucer. He leaned close enough to my ear to brush it with his lips. "Another claret for a kiss?"

I swatted him again. "Refill my glass and we'll see."

He beamed.

"But don't count on it," I called after him.

He laughed and filled the glass until it brimmed with burgundy liquid.

I took a deep drink and looked up, catching sight

of a familiar face entering the tavern with a bevy of women. Pauline Léon. Frowning, I hopped off my stool and made my way toward her, my mind filled with all the men had said. I wondered what Pauline would say about our Declaration, if she found it as hopeful as the others.

Pauline and her friends snaked through the room to a large table near the back wall. I followed, deciding to make my peace with her once and for all. I had abandoned her at the Bastille and I knew she hadn't looked kindly on my cowardice. But we were on the same side, the same kind of woman, after all. At least I liked to think so . . . I was in awe of Pauline, truth be told. Though young, she had no doubts as to where her loyalties lay, or which path to follow. She had been so brave, and I found that I wanted to be more like her.

"Mademoiselle Léon, *bonsoir*," I said.

"Louise," she said curtly. "You haven't come to insult me again, I hope."

"How can I insult a heroine of the Bastille? You are to be commended."

She scowled. "I would have been a heroine of the Bastille if anyone had let me. A laundress managed to fight her way in, but I was left at the barricades. Still, the Bastille was a victory, as is our National Guard and our Declaration."

"Yet the king has done nothing and we're still hungry." I shrugged. "What should we expect? This is what happens when we leave the men to handle everything."

Several of the women laughed.

Pauline's expression softened into a smile. "Too true."

"Who are your friends?" I asked.

Pauline introduced each of the women at the table; a group of washerwomen, a seamstress, an actress named Claire Lacombe, and a tutor of the pianoforte. "We're going to meet here each week in the Cordeliers. Decide how we women might make something of this revolution."

Instinctively, I felt drawn to Pauline; something about her reminded me of my departed friend, Marion. And somehow, I knew her fight was my own. If I were to become a part of this . . . It now seemed inescapable.

"Are you in need of new members?" I asked.

"We welcome those who are committed to our liberty."

"Liberty is my favorite word." I pointed to the new symbol of liberty at my breast; the red and blue of Paris joined in harmony with the white of the Bourbons on a cockade. "How about I keep my mouth closed for a change and just listen."

"Do you promise?"

I grinned, and Pauline motioned to an empty place at the table, making me feel more welcomed than I'd ever felt anywhere before.

Paris, September 1789

After a second and third gathering with Pauline's group at the tavern, I was left with one burning question on my mind: What could we women do in this revolution?

Many feared the Declaration of the Rights of Man and the Citizen focused on men alone, and that women would once again be left out. Several in the group became disorderly as tempers flared at the meetings. But I knew shouting never changed much—action did. And I planned to learn what that action should be.

Until then, I would try to put food on the table. At the close of another long day, I left the Palais-Royal and found my way home. As I approached my door, I spied a man in front, peering down the street as if looking for someone. Though he was dressed in a shabby brocade jacket and *culottes*, he had the kind of beauty that made you forget your own name. And I knew there could be only one reason this sort of gentleman stood on my doorstep: he needed something.

As I neared him, I felt a vague sense of recognition. Something about his perfectly sculpted face and heart-shaped mouth, his hair . . . Yes, he was a singer or actor that I'd seen at the Palais-Royal. Not a dangerous kind of man. "Monsieur, *bonsoir*. Are you looking for someone?"

"I am Monsieur Elleviou. A gentleman in search of a Mademoiselle Audu. I have been told she is a courier and understands what it means to be discreet."

I recognized the name instantly. My gaze traveled to the tips of his thick, brown hair that he had chosen not to stuff beneath a wig. I guessed I wasn't the only woman who appreciated his choice.

"I'm Mademoiselle Audu."

"I have a favor to ask. I will pay you, of course." He presented a small envelope. "It is a letter for Mademoiselle Émilie de Sainte-Amaranthe. She is with her mother entertaining patrons at their salon this evening."

I knew plenty about Madame de Sainte-Amaranthe and her . . . variety of entertainments, shall we say, as well as the legendary beauty of her daughter. In fact, not only had I delivered many messages for her, but I had seen the mother-daughter pair perusing the shops at the Palais-Royal again just yesterday with a clutch of admirers trailing behind them like a brood of chicks to their mother hen. Madame hosted one of the most renowned salons in Paris with its gambling tables and wealthy patrons, many of whom graced the courts of the queen. Though gambling was illegal, the law was not enforced and those dumb enough to gamble their wages away were left to their own devices.

The gentleman shifted from one foot to the other and looked over his shoulder twice. He was afraid of being discovered, I realized, and in that, I saw an opportunity. "Why should I help you?"

He stared at me a moment, his expression intense as if he were debating whether or not to spill his secret. At last, he said, "I am in love, mademoiselle, and I must know if she feels the same. I have written her a message to meet me. My name is not on the card, as I fear her mother will try to intervene."

Without doubt. A social climber like Madame de Sainte-Amaranthe wouldn't settle for less than a fat old duc for her baby girl. And it amused me to think of how undone she might be to have a mere musician without a pot to piss in for a son-in-law.

Aloud, I said, "So you're not a duc."

He laughed. "I am an opera singer. And as you might imagine, since I am neither a man with a title nor a banker or landowner, Madame de Sainte-Amaranthe finds me unsuitable and is steering Émilie toward better prospects. Mademoiselle has many admirers."

I studied his face. There was something sweet about his demeanor and his perfect diction. He seemed to be a true gentleman. Hell, why not help the lovesick fool? I nodded. "Very well. I'll help you—for a price."

"Of course." He pulled out a change purse. "Would two livres suffice?"

"Is that what your lady love is worth to you?" Haggling was my specialty. At the Palais-Royal they'd say, *Guard your britches or mademoiselle will bargain them right off your hind end.* That may be true, but I would never admit to this fop that a livre was more money than I had seen in a long time.

He smiled and I felt my resolve melt a little. Émilie was a lucky woman.

"Three livres and I'll cover the cost of a coach," he replied.

"Done."

Along with the money, he gave me a small envelope reeking of *parfum*.

I didn't bother to hide my smile. "How will she resist you and that mop of curls? I hope she is swooning in your arms in no time."

He laughed and tipped his hat. "*Merci beaucoup.* Now, shall we find a coach for you?"

Under an hour later, I stood before Émilie de Sainte-Amaranthe's door. Suddenly I was aware of my gauche dress and hat, the way my manners had faded in the years since my mother died. In spite of our revolution, I was still a lowly fruit seller, a woman of meager circumstance and position. But that would change, one day, if I had anything to say about it, and Lord knew, I always had something to say.

I shook off my doubt and clutched the knocker, rapping it hard and with assurance.

A towering servant greeted me, gave me one look, and started to close the door. I slipped my foot between door and doorjamb, and it bounced open.

"*Excusez-moi!*" I huffed, foot throbbing.

The man looked down at me and sniffed. "You, mademoiselle, are not invited."

The cretin thought he was better than me, and he was nothing but a servant himself, albeit in a luxurious home. I stuck out my chin. "Madame de Sainte-Amaranthe hires me weekly as her courier. I've a message for her daughter, and if you don't let me inside, I know a gendarme or two who will help me." A lie of the worst kind, but I wasn't about to return the livres Monsieur Elleviou had given me.

"I will take the message for you," he said firmly.

I shook my head. "Not a chance. I've been paid to deliver it in person and I'm not one to shirk my responsibilities. Now, step aside."

He crossed his arms over his massive chest and spread his legs wide to block the doorway.

I inhaled a quick breath, winked at the buffoon, and dove between his legs.

He gasped in surprise.

In an instant, I scrambled to my feet and rushed through a gleaming marble foyer. As I reached the salon, I slowed, darting expertly around the crowd, vaguely noting the furniture dressed in pastel brocade and walls lavished in floral silk, the plush of fine Turkish rugs. Everything in the room was positioned just so, even the paintings of terribly important men, who—if I were honest—each looked like a mule's ass. There was even a print of the king himself.

Two dozen tables were organized around the room, and an elegant bar spanned the back wall. A smoky haze drifted from the pipes of various patrons. Elegant ladies tossed dice as daintily as they could manage while huddled with a male partner or practicing the fine art of conversation. The gentlemen matched the ladies' elegance in *culottes* and brass-buttoned coats. A few of the guests stared or gave me a disgusted look, but most didn't see me at all, as if I were too far beneath them to warrant notice. It seemed they didn't realize the fall of the Bastille had changed everything, made their lofty ambitions obsolete. They were like fossils in a forgotten world, or children with their fingers in their ears.

A vision of Maman's bloodied forehead and her resigned expression flashed behind my eyes. Of Marion's lifeless body while her lover, the baron, looked at her in contempt. Nightmares with which I'd tortured myself since I'd learned of their deaths. A ribbon of danger and something poisonous snaked through my veins and settled upon my chest. I bit my lip hard, eliciting physical pain to make the images fade.

Focusing my gaze ahead, I stalked through the room, glancing from table to table in search of Mademoiselle. Dealers shuffled cards and counted them quickly, patrons sulked or laughed as they gathered the pile of winnings in the center of the table, pulling it toward themselves in glee. Coins, larger bills, and the odd piece of jewelry or the occasional pocket watch gleamed amidst the spoils. Just beyond the next set of tables, I spotted her, Madame de Sainte-Amaranthe, and several paces away stood her daughter, Émilie, locked in a tête-à-tête with another young lady.

I started in her direction when a strong hand clamped on my arm.

"For the last time, you need to leave," the doorman hissed.

"Unhand me, you *con*." I attempted to pry his fingers from my arm.

"Have it your way." With a frosty glare, he gripped both arms tightly, turned me around, and shoved me toward the door.

I stumbled forward. Acting quickly, I cupped my hands at my mouth and shouted, "Madame de Sainte-Amaranthe!"

The room grew quiet as all paused to see who had the gall to shout and interrupt the festivities. A titter of laughter rippled through the room.

"What in God's name . . . ?" The lady of the house moved toward me, the violet feather in her hair bobbing with each step. Émilie followed closely at her heels.

When Madame stood before me, I lowered my eyes as Maman had taught me, much as it pained me to do so. "Pardon me for being so vulgar, madame, but your doorman would not let me enter. I have a letter for your daughter."

Émilie joined us and I stared at her, shocked again by her beauty. Though I'd seen her many times, she always rendered me speechless. Her skin appeared ethereal in its pearlescence, her eyes flashed with humor, and jewels glittered against her creamy décolletage. Her hair sat high on her head in neat piles of curls, adorned with a nest and a tiny red bird, the perfect accent to her rose taffeta gown fitted with lace. Yet in spite of her beauty and the attention she must command, she seemed as serene and graceful as a swan. Émilie wasn't quite a mirror image of Madame de Sainte-Amaranthe, but there was no question they were mother and daughter. No wonder my eager gentleman thought he must have this creature as his own. I was practically in love with her.

I held out the envelope. "Pardon me, mademoiselle, but I was asked to deliver this to you."

"Louise, what a pleasant surprise," Madame de Sainte-Amaranthe said. "Who has sent the note?"

"A Monsieur Elleviou, madame," I said, more faithful to my longtime patron than to the young man I had met only once.

Madame's eyes grew cold. So she knew of the opera singer. I was suddenly glad I had chosen my loyalty to her over Elleviou.

"You know he is just another admirer, Maman," Émilie said. "*C'est tout.* I will be tossing this on the fire along with those from the others," she added lightly, all the while sweeping the envelope into the pocket of her *robe à la française.* To me, she said, "Mademoiselle, thank you for your service. Would you care for something to eat before you go?"

Madame gave her daughter a stern look before direct-ing her attention at me once more. "I am certain Made-moiselle Audu has things to attend to this evening."

Émilie frowned. "Mother, she is as thin as a rake, and we have a feast tonight."

Madame glanced at me again and I lowered my eyes in respect. "Very well. Enjoy a plate before you go, Louise."

I nodded, gratitude flooding through me. Hunger gnawed at my bones like a rabid dog. It had been days since I'd enjoyed the stew, and all I'd managed were sparse servings of vegetables or fruits to fill the void. "You are very kind."

Madame de Sainte-Amaranthe's mouth softened. "We wouldn't want to send you away hungry."

I glanced at the doorman again and winked. He glared his disapproval.

"If you will excuse me, my guests await," Madame said in a breathy voice, and she turned on her heel, leaving a cloud of orange blossom perfume in her wake. As she returned to the salon, the sound of dice crack-ing over tabletops and conversation drifted through the room.

Émilie touched my hand lightly. "Thank you. It was very kind of you to go to such trouble. You have made my evening a happy one."

"I am glad of that." I smiled. Not only was the young woman beautiful, she seemed genuinely amicable and kind as well. Some women had all the luck.

"Let's visit the refreshments table and then I'm afraid I must return to my guests as well. Please stay as long as you like."

"Thank you." My stomach rumbled as we approached a table loaded with trays. "Just one more thing," I said. "Your gentleman loves you. He told me so himself. He hopes you share his feelings."

Her cheeks flushed and her eyes shone with joy. "You cannot know how happy this makes me. Thank you, mademoiselle. Now I must go." But rather than join the fete, she darted through a door and closed it swiftly behind her. No doubt, to read her letter.

I glanced at the rather stiff but well-dressed servant who stood guard at the refreshments table. He eyed me, disdain rumpling his brow.

I grinned and said, "Don't worry. I won't bite you."

His face reddened, and he cleared his throat. "*Pardonnez-moi.* I did not mean to—"

"Never mind." I waved my hand to shoo him.

His face tightened. "Very good, mademoiselle."

My mouth watered at the sight of row after row of dainty foods: disks of vegetables topped with mousse sprinkled with herbs, wedges of bread featuring flowers of golden butter, and a layered pastry stuffed with creamed spinach and chèvre. I couldn't believe they'd managed to find flour in the city.

I reached for a pastry.

"We use tongs to pick up the canapés." The servant sniffed.

"Is that what these are called?" I forced an innocent expression, picked up the tongs, and scooped five pieces onto a plate, then proceeded to the next tray, selecting the canapé with orange-colored mousse first, and three more of the yellow.

"You don't have to hoard them." His tone dripped with disgust. "You can fill your plate as many times as you like."

"Why don't you make yourself useful and fetch me a brandy," I said through a mouthful.

He winced at the prospect of following my directive but headed to the bar.

I popped two canapés in my mouth at once and groaned at their exquisite taste before helping myself to another. I reached for a serviette, scooped another heap of canapés into it, and stuffed the package swiftly into my handbag for later. Colorful pastries I would later learn were called macarons joined the canapés, for who knew when I'd next see so much food.

The servant returned holding a large glass brimming with amber liquid. "Given your appetite, I trust this will suffice."

I peered at the full glass. "Are you trying to have your way with me, monsieur?"

"I never! Good evening to you!" He huffed and darted away to commence his rounds at the tables.

I threw my head back and laughed deeply. When tears streamed from the corners of my eyes, I wiped them with my sleeve. Before setting down the ridiculous tumbler of brandy, I took two big gulps. It burned going down and within seconds, I felt its blessed warming presence in my blood. I would take a turn about the room before leaving—*Why not?* I thought. The night had been full of surprises.

I walked around the tables, catching another round of ugly stares until a conversation floated toward me and I stopped.

A gentleman laid a stack of pamphlets in the center of the table. "Madame Roland is the woman I was telling you about. She writes articles with her husband for the *Patriote Français* in Lyon. My sister has been sending these to me. What nonsense, this talk of patriots." Several of the gamblers plucked them from the table. "But it is better to know what we are up against, I say."

"I think it's a waste of time," said a man in a fancy uniform. "The king will never publish the Declaration because he isn't going to sign away his powers. The whole idea is absurd. Imagine a life without nobility." The man shuddered, eliciting a laugh from those at the table with him. "A ludicrous notion."

I stared at him in surprise, recognizing him as Lieutenant Colonel François de Sainte-Amaranthe of the king's guard. He was also Émilie's papa—or at least the man forced by law to claim her. He hadn't shown me the kindness his wife and daughter had, and now this . . . this show of superiority and mocking, turned my stomach. So despite his common birth, he'd remain a loyal dog, barking and biting the people for his noble masters. Heat rose to my cheeks.

"A life without nobility, indeed," I interrupted. "Imagine what it would be like to not have servants— actual people, same as you and me—waiting on your every whim." I turned to the officer's aristocratic friends. "Why, you'd have to clean your own clothes, work for pitiful wages, and go hungry most days like the rest of us. Struggle to pay your landlord. How dreadful. I can't imagine it."

The table fell silent.

My eyes roved from one rouged face to the next, settling on one of the aristocratic guests. He wore so much powder his skin looked ghostly and his lips were like two bloody slashes. I'd like to give him a bloodied lip for real. I waved my arm in passion. "Imagine having more to do than gambling away your boredom and swilling spirits until you're senseless. Imagine having passion for a cause greater than yourself. I'm certain you cannot."

"We want what is best for la belle France, mademoiselle. That is all," one of the men said.

Another man smirked.

Fury clouded my vision and I gripped my free hand into a fist. "You want what is best for you alone. And perhaps your whores."

The ladies at the table gasped.

Saint-Amaranthe pushed up from his chair. "I think your visit here is finished."

So it was. I dashed from the room, choking on my anger, and more furious still that I felt foolish beneath their scornful gazes.

Paris, October 2, 1789

Nearly three months after the Bastille fell, still our lot as commoners had not improved, and we struggled to survive. I'd had a row with a gentleman in the tavern the night before to make him see—really see—what must be done for our liberty. *But I was just a girl,* and I'd lost. I had the bruised cheek to show for it. I was beginning to think the men who led our cause did so through strength of might but lacked strength of mind.

Sighing, I dropped a coin in the paperboy's hand and tucked a copy of *L'Ami du Peuple* under my arm. I'd searched for the latest edition of Jean-Paul Marat's newspaper all morning; everyone at the Palais-Royal could speak of nothing else. Every patriot I knew read his columns, if not for news, to fuel their ire.

Eager to read, I didn't bother to sit and delved in immediately. All the rumors about a foreign conspiracy against our revolution were true, it seemed. The king had summoned the Royal Flanders to Versailles to reinforce his royal guard—against us, his own people. And in celebration, the queen had thrown a lavish party. Drunken revelry, music, cards, and even an orgy, some said, had entertained the court.

Several of the soldiers at the fete had pitched their cockades to the floor and trampled them, refuting the nation and swearing their allegiance to the House of Bourbon.

I gasped and reread the text. Didn't those fools know what they'd done? They had declared war on the patriots!

Marat called for a move. He argued the royal household and the National Assembly should move to the Tuileries Palace in Paris, where they could no longer turn a blind eye to the needs of their people. He demanded the foreign armies be expelled and replaced by Lafayette's National Guard.

But even as progressive as Marat was, newspaper columns weren't going to make that happen.

Only we, the people, could.

I stormed back to my cart, journal in hand.

"There you are." Jeanne snatched the paper from me before I could get out a word. As she read, her already-large eyes bugged from her head until she resembled a dead fish. "What are we going to do?"

"We have to march. There's no other way to get the king's attention." My mind raced with the dangers of such a move. If we marched to the palace, would the king send the royal guard to slaughter us like lambs? Versailles was a royal city, after all. It was very likely. There was also the question of who should march. Should we leave such a bold move to the men again? I knew the answer to that already. They would see to their own rights, perhaps, but not ours, not those of the women, and we'd not taste the liberty we now held so dear.

I clenched my teeth, stalking to and fro, unsettled and nervous like a tiger in a cage.

Jeanne squeezed my forearm and pointed to an entryway of the arcade. "Look!"

Citizens poured into the garden from every direction, rushing toward the center of the courtyard, waving their own copies of Marat's paper.

"It's another speech," I said, spotting the familiar dark head of Maillard. He'd been instrumental to the fall of the Bastille and was now captain of the new Volunteers of the Bastille that he'd founded.

Jeanne chewed her lip nervously. "If things get unruly, I'm leaving."

If things became unruly, what would I do?

I looked for Maillard again, but he appeared to be moving through the crowd toward the arcade of shops. I frowned as a short, round woman climbed the bench where he usually spoke. I knew this woman; she was the baker's wife whose shop had been looted and burned after the bread riots at the docks. The crowd fell silent and she began what looked to be an impassioned speech. Every few minutes, she thrust her arm into the air and her audience responded with a mixture of shouts and heckling. Something sinister tinged the air.

I swore aloud, followed by a string of obscenities foul enough to curdle milk. "If we don't want a riot, someone had better get that wench down. Jeanne, can you watch—"

My friend dismissed me with a wave.

I threaded through the audience, a sharp eye on the center of the courtyard.

"My shop was burned to the ground because of people like you!" The woman's words became clearer as I approached. "You don't attack the one who gives you bread, you dolts!" The crowd shouted obscenities, but she went on. "You've made the king angry, brought on the royal guard. Now he doesn't trust his people. Know your place, you idiots, or you'll get us all killed."

I rolled my eyes. They came to listen to this?

"To hell with the aristocracy!" a man shouted, displaying a row of black teeth.

"To hell with you!" she shouted back. "You don't burn down the shop that feeds you!"

The crowd descended into a mass of chaotic jeering. Someone tossed a dummy made of straw dressed in Bourbon blue-and-white livery, and the crowd jostled it overhead. Many began to shove each other.

Breath hitching, I elbowed my way through to the bench and reached for the woman's hand. "Madame, if I could say a word or two?"

"Who in hell are you?" The woman jerked her arm away. "I'm speaking now, and they're listening for once."

Listening? Right before they beat her senseless for her drivel.

I blew out an exasperated breath. "I'd give my left arm for a fresh loaf of your delicious bread, madame. I'm sorry the boulangerie burned, but you might be hurt if you don't step down. This crowd is angry."

The woman's shrewd eyes took in my clothing, the brown waves that flowed from beneath my mobcap and down my back.

"Let me talk to them," I persisted.

Rocks began to sail through the air. A large stone hit a man only four paces away. He took it in the back, gasped at the unexpected impact, and ducked for cover. Another smashed against a firewood cart. A third sliced the air, soaring toward the baker's wife.

I threw my arm around her waist and pulled her to the ground. The stone flew past into a tree and shattered into several pieces.

The woman sat up, a bewildered expression on her face, and adjusted her cap. "They're all yours." She staggered to her feet and darted off.

I sprang onto the bench and stood, waving my hands over my head. I was probably the only person dumb enough to wave my hands like a flag, asking to be stoned. I put my fingers to my lips and blew, and a loud whistle pierced the air.

Most of the crowd stilled, but some continued to shout. I let loose another whistle so shrill those closest to me covered their ears.

"*Écoute, patriotes!*" I shouted.

This time, they grew quiet, and all eyes focused on me. I noticed a few familiar faces; some vendors who were usuals at the Palais and some customers. Captain Maillard reappeared at the edge of the crowd, a thoughtful expression on his face, waiting to hear what I had to say. And what did I have to say exactly? I blew out a calming breath.

"It's true, we're hungry," I began. "And we're tired of looking as if we've been dragged behind a cart at day's end." Raucous laughter mingled with a few cheers. Now, I truly had their attention. "We want change. We want bread. We want no more unfair taxation!"

Cheering erupted. "No taxation! No taxation!" they cried.

A new sensation rushed through me like a river swollen with spring rain. Pride and purpose and passion. I could feel the crowd's expectation and their anger, but most of all their hope. They felt the same pull I did—the pull toward irrevocable change. We would no longer accept our lot as the low, as the inconsequential, as the mud on the heel of society's boot, and the significance of this realization held us in its grip.

"If we're to have change," I called out, "we must band together, not fight amongst ourselves. Together, we are a force. Separate, we are but peasants." Energy shimmered around me and coursed through my limbs. "Together, we are a force who can fight for our *liberté!*" I thrust my fist into the air. "À *liberté!*"

The crowd roared.

"*Liberté!*"

The noise grew to deafening.

Somewhere in the mass, a chant began and quickly gained momentum.

In that moment, I spotted Pauline, who made her way toward me. She joined me on the bench, giving me a quick smile. I returned her smile with genuine gladness and made more room for us both to stand.

Pauline punched the air and joined in with the chant.

I stared out over the crowd, bustling with wives and vendors, bakers and chimney sweeps, and a smattering of aristocrats, fists jabbing the sky. I didn't know what would happen, or how it would end. But we had all changed for good, and I would tuck away my fear and become a part of this great movement. Of that, I was certain.

❧

Paris, October 5, 1789

In the days that followed, citizens emerged from every home, alleyway, and hidden nook in the city, filling the streets to bursting. They voiced their starvation and disillusionment, desperate to be heard. Yet our king still did nothing.

Anticipation knotted my stomach. I knew we must march. *Today*. It would be a show of unity the king could not ignore. And if it should be led by women, how deep his surprise. How eternal and poignant our message would be.

I met Pauline at the already-bustling Faubourg Saint-Antoine. Wives, sisters, and mothers of all ages streamed toward the knot of people in the middle of the street, and soon, it was difficult to hear without shouting. We wanted to feed our families, live without fear of being massacred by foreign armies, make our voices heard. Storm clouds gathered overhead and a stiff breeze rumpled our aprons and tossed our red bonnets. Vendors scurried away, and many ducked indoors to shutter their shops and homes, for we could all taste danger in the air.

I gazed at the masses, their jaws set, their eyes alight.

My sisters-in-arms had something to say, something to fight for. It was a new day for the women of France, maybe even for the women of the world.

Pauline's head inclined toward mine so I could hear her over the din. "This is incredible. There must be thousands of us." Her eyes gleamed, and her cheeks blushed with high color.

"*Incroyable!*" I shouted, exhilaration spreading through me. I fingered the scarlet ribbon I'd fastened to my breast that morning. A gift from Maman on my birthday many years ago. I wore it when I needed to feel her beside me, hear her words of encouragement in my ear. This day, I would make her proud.

A drum resounded near the edge of the market-place, and a hush fell over the crowd. One beat came, then another. A continuous thumping like the sound of boots on pavement.

Like a march.

Bodies flowed toward the sound of the drum until we crushed against one another.

Pauline squeezed my shoulder. "I'm committed until this is over. Are you?"

"I am, friend." And it was true. I felt none of my earlier hesitation.

She smiled and raised her fist in the air. In time with the drum, she shouted, "Bread! Bread! Bread!"

We chanted until our voices became deafening.

The next instant, the mass of bodies shifted and we moved as one down the boulevard.

I gripped Pauline's hand. "Let's move to the front. We're going to need weapons if we march all the way to Versailles."

We forced our way forward, and as we came to the end of the street, Pauline and I directed the crowd toward the Hôtel de Ville, home of the city's administration and a storage facility for weapons.

"First weapons, and then we march!" Pauline cried.

Everyone roared.

"March! March! March! March!" Citizens on all sides of me squabbled over our goals. Should we demand grain and return to Paris satisfied when our good king tended to his people's needs, or should we rally until we seized the Austrian wench who spent our taxes on diamond necklaces while we starved? I clambered on top of a barrel to get the attention of the crowd and made a little joke. "If the queen won't let us have bread, I'll bring back her head!"

Of course, some really wanted the queen dead. Some just wanted the right to be heard and the right to defend themselves. Others wanted no king at all.

Pauline threw me a smile, but I didn't miss the tinge of fear in her eyes. I suppose I felt it too; the fear of failure, of losing the only thing I truly owned: my life. But what good was a life that brought so much suffering? What good was a life without rights, and the hope of a better future?

We clogged the grand boulevards with our masses, halting the flow of carriages and horses and frightening many Parisians, who retreated, scrambling to hide inside. And they might as well hide. If they didn't join us, they were against our cause.

Pride surged through me once more until I felt I might burst. I was a leader, a great part of this incredible movement that raced ahead like a runaway steed. "Bread!" I shouted. "Bread! Bread! Bread!"

The tocsin bells rang incessantly to warn the citizens of Paris of potential danger in the streets. I grinned. We were the danger for a change—imagine, that a woman could be a threat to the men that held us at their mercy.

As the Hôtel de Ville came into view, we roared. We charged the building as if its intimidating structure and guards posed no threat. At the vanguard of the melee, my pulse thundered in my ears. Within minutes, the sound of splitting wood rent the air, and the doors gave way. I glided forward, riding the surge from the swarm of bodies streaming inside. Women raced past me, around me, tearing at everything in sight. A clerk screamed as he was trampled, but no one fought the wave of women.

Moving together as one, we were too strong.

Our collective spirit had become a force of destruction, one that tore away not only the trappings of the Hôtel de Ville but centuries of rules and restrictions and oppression. A flurry of color and voices wrapped around me, and I felt as if I floated through a strange haze, as if I hovered outside of my body. Nothing seemed real, the looting, the intensity of the crowd, the sheer noise of our rally cry.

A woman wrenched a spear from the wall and my instinct took over. I raced ahead, turning down a series of corridors. At last, I found a door with a plaque that read: *Gunpowder Storage*. Before it, a priest stood guard.

"God will punish you," he said, making the sign of the cross in self-protection. "Submit to your king and become a beacon of peace and love as the gentler sex ought."

"Out of the way, old man!" a large fishwife called from behind me.

"String him up," another said. "He's one of the Second Estate!"

Several women jeered—all the encouragement the fishwife needed. She scooped up the petit priest easily and tossed him over her shoulder. I snatched the father's ring of keys and opened the door of the munitions room. We took every musket, every pike. I reached for a sword and measured its weight in my hand before tying Maman's scarlet ribbon to the hilt for luck. Lining the back wall, I noticed a series of small cannons.

"Fetch the cannons," I shouted to a group who was empty-handed.

"What are we to do with them?" a laundress asked.

I grinned. "What the men always do with their little cannons. Point and shoot without care or consequence."

The women howled with laughter.

When the room had been emptied, we flowed out of the building into the streets.

I looked out at the chaos, pulse racing. I knew the crowd needed to be redirected, but I couldn't see how. And then I spotted him, one of the very few men who had joined us—Captain Maillard. He darted furiously from one doorway to another, shepherding people forward. He wore a drum at his waist, and once he'd rescued the priest from harm, he began beating his instrument while shouting and waving his free arm wildly. The crowd's attention pivoted to him, just as it had in the marketplace. I knew with certainty in that instant, if we had any chance of marching to Versailles, he would need to help lead us.

I swallowed my irritation that a man must lead, as always, but started toward him. "Maillard!"

"Mademoiselle, we march, at last!" he said, a look of triumph lighting his eyes.

I peered up at the moody sky and said a quick prayer under my breath. We needed to move before the weather broke.

"*À Versailles!*" I shouted, thrusting my sword into the air as I began a new chant.

Yet General Lafayette, the commander of our National Guard, tried to stop us. From atop his horse, he shouted at us to wait for his men. I wondered if the blue-blooded Lafayette was a traitor to the cause. And I wondered about the other aristocrats I knew. Would I find Sophie Condorcet in this crowd of women? It no longer mattered, because I wasn't her student anymore. And I was ready to teach my betters a lesson.

I shouted louder than Lafayette, "*À Versailles!*"

Within seconds, the chant became a roar and we drowned him out. We women weren't going to wait for the men of the National Guard to take us to the king. We were going with or without them. Like an omen, the sky opened, and rain sheeted down upon us.

Maybe God was against us. It had rained, too, the day the deputies of our Third Estate took refuge in the tennis courts at Versailles. But it hadn't stopped those patriots from taking their oath and fighting for our liberties. And it wasn't going to stop us this day. Let the Almighty thunder. He'd never seemed to like women much, anyway.

We headed southwest through the city gates and along the thickly forested roads that led to Versailles, nearly eleven miles away. Rivulets of water streamed down my arms and legs, and my muddy boots rubbed sore spots on my toes. Despite my defiance of God, I said a semblance of a prayer that our cause wouldn't end before it began. Not after all this, all we'd done.

As we neared the crown of a hill, I turned to look behind me. A great mass of bodies undulated over the road like a giant caterpillar. Citizens carried every variety of weapon and farm tool. Bonnets rouges dotted the crowd, and song broke out among them. In spite of the terrible weather, our fury—and our hope—drove us forward, ever forward. The immensity of our strength took my breath away.

"*Liberté! Liberté!*" I shouted until my voice was hoarse.

Pauline smiled through her sopping hair, waving her spear in the air.

If the king didn't help us, so many citizens in need, he had a heart of stone. And he deserved to be thrown down like the Americans had done with their king.

The miles wore on. Hours passed. Blinded by rain, soaked through, exhausted and cold, I felt my courage slip. I didn't know if I could keep marching, or if I could ask anyone to march with me. *Just one more step, then another*, I told myself, and somehow another mile had gone. At last, Versailles loomed on the horizon. Soon, we would be upon the king. We'd be no match for his guards, I knew, but I had forfeited my chance for safety hours ago.

And, I had, in these rainy miles, breathed more freely than ever before in my life. I would never go back to how it was before, a woman who did as she was told.

As we marched onto the long, royal drive, my heart began to pound furiously. The rain stopped and the clouds parted to give way to a glorious sunset. We cheered, our spirits fanned by the sight and by the excitement of our arrival. The enthusiasm that had followed us out of Paris reignited.

"Bread! Bread! Bread! Bread!"

I gaped at the manicured lawn and the perfect rows of trees lining the drive. When the palace came into view, my heart lurched.

Lord, but it was a sight in all its golden glory. It shimmered in the dying sunlight, as if God Himself smiled down upon our king. A fiery benediction. Silence pressed down upon the crowd, too, as if my fellow marchers felt the same reverence, and many crossed themselves. Perhaps the women doubted what they were doing here. I felt a sliver of doubt lodge itself in my mind.

I shook my head. Christ, if we stormed up to the palace with this attitude, we'd never get what we came for—the king's word that things would change. Surely a *real* God would want His people fed and freed from tyranny. We were created in His likeness, after all, with two sets of hands and feet, same as the king and his opulent, silly queen. Heat built in the pit of my stomach. Why should they sit in such splendor and hoard grain while we starved?

"*Égalité!*" I shouted, raising my sword above my head. Others picked up the chant until it echoed across the gardens.

As we neared the palace, the sun ducked behind a cloud and the fickle sky tore open once more.

Maillard swore as rain washed over us. I laughed at his expression.

He grumbled and then said, "We'll go to the National Assembly. They are our best hope, and I assure you, they are men of reason."

As we approached the door, a deputy with a poorly powdered wig stepped outside. They'd heard us coming and had been waiting. "Captain Maillard, please, join us. We are eager to hear what a conqueror of the Bastille has to say. Ladies." He tipped his head, a show of respect, and swung the door wide.

Upon entering the hall, my breath caught in my throat. The enormous room boasted vaulted ceilings covered in decorative panels and an oval skylight. Rows of benches and chairs faced one another, leaving a center aisle open for passage as well as for a short table hosting the most important of men. A raised platform sat at the far wall with another series of benches, a podium, and a magnificent throne beneath a decorative canopy. We were really here. And the members of the National Assembly looked on in amusement and surprise.

Many of the marchers flooded indoors, and the gentleman at the podium paused, his mouth falling open at the sight of us. Boldly, I slipped onto a bench next to a clergyman and laid my sword across my lap. His eyes registered surprise and then fear, as his gaze rested on my weapon.

I gripped it tighter and grinned. "Share the bench, will you?"

He slid to his left, never taking his eyes from my sword. Other protesters slid in beside me until the bench filled to overflowing. Hundreds of women filed inside, occupying every inch of space.

Maillard stepped to the podium and faced the Assembly. "Esteemed gentlemen," he called out to the crowd, "and ladies."

We cheered.

Maillard continued as we quieted once more, "You may have noticed a bit of a commotion outside."

Several in the audience laughed.

"We have come on behalf of all Paris, nay, the people of all France. We are starving—starving for justice, starving for true leadership from our king." He paused to allow his words to sink in. "We have come to Versailles to demand bread, and to request the punishment of the royal bodyguards who have insulted the patriotic cockade. These soldiers defiled our symbol of progress and liberty under the king's very roof!"

Nearly every member of the Assembly began to murmur, and the man in charge near the podium thundered, "Silence!"

"It is said," Maillard boomed, "the nobility and the king are withholding grain in order to starve us into submission, to put down this revolution. Where is this grain? We believe it is here. Will our king share it? Will he provide for and protect his people? We are rioting at the docks, in the streets, and now we protest even here, on his doorstep. When will he see to the needs of his people? When"—he paused for effect—"will he publish the Declaration of the Rights of Man and the Citizen? We are, one and all, men and women of equal value, and deserve to be recognized by our sovereign."

Cheering broke out in the back of the hall.

Another gentleman approached the podium and Maillard stepped down. The new speaker, dressed prettily in expensive coat and breeches, introduced himself as Robespierre, and the crowd listened politely for only seconds before he was ushered back to his seat. A few other deputies attempted to speak, but no one could hear above the din. Maillard met my eye and waved me toward the back of the hall. I nodded before making my way in that direction. As I reached the doors, a minister touched my shoulder.

"Citizeness, I am Assembly president, Jean-Joseph Mounier. I think it best if we organize a small party to approach the king. You can put forward your concerns and then lead the marchers back to Paris. You will be more successful if you do so without violence." He eyed my weapon. "And you will need to leave that outside of His Majesty's chambers. You understand."

Leaving my weapon behind left me vulnerable— but I would have an audience with the king! A sweat broke out over my already-clammy skin. I'd never have this opportunity again, and nervous as it made me, this was it. This was my chance. I stood on my tiptoes and scanned the room for Pauline but didn't see her. She would have to miss such an event, and perhaps that was best. She despised the king, and I couldn't imagine she would hold her tongue in his company. Suddenly, I was grateful for the years of being a courier and interacting with the nobility.

"I understand." I retrieved my precious scarlet ribbon, fastened it at my breast once more, and surrendered the sword to Maillard upon the condition that he give it back after my audience with the king.

Monsieur Mounier selected several others, six of us in all, and with a flourish, he led us from the hall. "Mesdames, follow me."

Decked in our mud-splattered shoes and sodden frocks, we followed the president of the Assembly across the lawn and around to a palace entrance. As we wound through gilded halls, I tried to contain my astonishment at such splendor and the nerves that twisted my stomach. I was going to speak to the king! As much as I wanted to hate the man, I couldn't deny my awe. He was ordained by God to rule a nation. Who were we to question him? Who was I, a fruit seller, to denounce the actions of a king?

"Right this way." Mounier nodded at a guardsman, whose eyes bulged in surprise at the sight of us. "It's all right. Let them pass."

The guard stepped aside and we trailed down another long corridor with marbled floors, decorative cornices, and royal portraits. I gaped at the decadence of every surface, the gilded flowers on the ceiling panels and carved along the doorframes. My mouth grew drier with each step.

When we reached a heavily guarded antechamber, Mounier said, "Remain here. I will confer with His Majesty."

We watched him disappear through the magnificent doors. My gaze flickered over the faces of the five other women. I didn't know them, and I couldn't be certain of their intentions.

"We need to remain calm and sound like we have a brain in our heads," I said softly. I remembered Maman's teachings, and all the fancy people in the Palais-Royal and the Lycée Condorcet and how they conducted themselves. I had those lessons to guide me and the women with me did not. "If we don't, they will dismiss us easily. Perhaps one of us should do the talking, at least to start. If the king wants to hear from each of us, we can speak in turns. Better prepare what you want to say now."

One of the women nodded, and several raindrops dribbled down her face. "Why don't you lead."

"Is that all right with the rest of you?" I asked.

They nodded silently, as awestruck as I.

The door creaked open, and a woman's voice floated into the corridor. "Louis, it is not to Paris you should go. You still have devoted battalions and faithful guards who will protect your retreat, but I implore you, my brother, do not go to Paris."

A male voice, deeper in tenor but soft, replied, "Élisabeth, I must do something to assuage the protests and the violence."

I frowned. Élisabeth? That must be the king's sister, Madame Élisabeth. And she, counseling the king to do what? To ignore our plight? She had a reputation for godliness and charity. As a good woman, shouldn't she be in our ranks?

"Please, consider more forceful action first," she insisted. "It would be better than retreat. Promise me."

"I will consider everything, sister, but I cannot promise to decide as you would."

A heavy sigh came next, followed by the sound of heels clacking over marble floors. A young woman appeared in the doorway. She had a round face with large eyes and full lips that pursed as she paused, studying us with a mix of curiosity and disdain. Perhaps she knew I was the leader from where I stood, or the way I carried myself, because she asked, "And you are?"

Who was I, after all, to address royalty? That's what

she really meant. She was a princess and I was a nobody in tattered clothing. But suddenly I knew just who I was, and I met her eye boldly. "I am Louise Reine Audu, Queen of the Market Women."

At this last pronouncement, indignant shock flashed across the princess's features, and, without another word, she left, her silk skirts swishing behind her like a dismissal.

Monsieur Mounier joined us in the corridor. "Mesdames, the king will see you now."

I willed myself to appear nonchalant as we entered.

His Majesty stood near a magnificent golden clock such as I had never seen. I recognized his aquiline nose and dimpled cheeks from the caricatures of him found in pamphlets all over Paris, but I wasn't prepared for kind blue eyes. Royal guards stood on either side of him, as did other men dressed in finery and appearing important.

"Your Majesty, I give you the citizens of Paris." The president of the Assembly bowed his head.

The king eyed the six of us warily, but he waved us closer. "Come, I've heard the clamor outside for hours now, and I am anxious to hear my subjects speak."

We curtsied and stood before him. The king and his men trained their eyes on us. No one spoke a word, and tension strained the silence.

"Your Majesty," I said at last, forcing my hands to remain calmly at my sides. "Thank you for seeing us."

He nodded. "I am always willing to hear my subjects."

"We're here . . . you see . . . we are hungry. The queue for bread is monstrous at every boulangerie in the city, and after waiting, we still go home empty-handed. There's talk of a plot organized by the nobility to keep the grain for themselves so we might starve and abandon our cause. We have nothing to eat, and no way to ask for it. Not in a way that we may be heard. We've had to resort to rioting. This is why we came to you, our king and protector."

He stared at me, his blue eyes pensive.

When he said nothing, I continued. "We won't abandon our cause. We are left with nothing to lose. Thus, we are not afraid. You refuse our Declaration and you refuse change. It's not the right thing to do, Your Majesty, to ignore the needs of your people."

He folded his hands. "And what, in your estimation, is the right thing to do?"

"Feed your people," the woman to my right blurted and promptly turned red as a beet.

I glared at her. "First, the nobility should be fined or imprisoned if they hoard grain." I waited for his reply, but he said nothing. Monsieur Mounier nodded, and I took it as a signal to continue. "Also, I would ask you to agree to the reforms proposed by your National Assembly. You'll lose the support of your subjects, Your Majesty, if you do not. I don't say this as a threat but as a certainty. I've seen the beginnings of it already." Realizing I shouldn't be quite as blunt, heat spread across my cheeks.

To my surprise, he briefly touched my shoulder, a gentle smile on his face. "I will consider your advice."

One of the market women promptly fainted. The others tended to her while the amused guards looked on. Apparently the king's presence still had the power to awe his subjects, and I had to admit I, too, was pleased by the simple gesture. Perhaps he meant what he'd said.

"The change will come what may, Your Majesty, but we, your subjects, hope you will lead it, not resist it." I knew that speaking to the king this way broke etiquette. I looked to the Assembly president, and he wouldn't meet my gaze, confirming my thoughts. Inwardly, I cringed. Yet I didn't regret my words.

King Louis began to pace. I watched him as he moved, taking in his elegant breeches and coat, his perfectly coiffed wig, and the way he hunched slightly.

"Please, Your Majesty"—I curtsied again hastily—
"there will be violence if I do not return with some
news to tell the women who have marched all the way
here from Paris."

"She's right," Mounier said quietly.

The king nodded. "Tell those who are with you,
mademoiselle, that I will ensure all have a ration of
grain from the royal reserves. I will let no one in the
kingdom go hungry. You have my word."

A rush of relief washed over me and the other
women smiled. "Thank you, Your Majesty." I hesitated
a moment, wanting to push the issue of our Declaration,
but I sensed this was the limit to his goodwill for now.
At least I could deliver a hopeful message to the crowd,
one they would be grateful to hear.

We curtsied and were then ushered out of the room
and shoved unceremoniously into the courtyard. The
crowd cheered when they saw us reappear.

"The king has promised rations of grain," I shouted.

Cheers arose and tears streaked the faces of many.
We hadn't come for nothing.

"He promises his citizens will not go hungry! He listened carefully. I can attest that he cares for his people."
When I finished speaking, many shouted questions at a
furious pace.

"And what of our rights?" someone called.

"Did you see the queen, or was she too busy eating cakes?"

Laughter rippled through the crowd.

"Did he agree to our Declaration? Do you have his promises in writing?"

"The king is a liar! He's plotting against us."

"*L'Autrichienne* wants us dead."

"I want *her* dead!"

The crowd devolved into a shoving match, and many were jostled or knocked to the ground. The king's guards pressed closer, roughly handling those who would not calm themselves. A soldier fired his pistol into the air, but his attempt at quieting the crowd backfired. A skirmish broke out between several royal guards, citizens, and militiamen.

The people didn't stop until we had the king's promises in writing, for anyone to read. Only then did some of the marchers retreat out of the courtyard and away from the palace, some heading back to Paris, content that we'd won the day.

But I wasn't leaving.

There was still too much at stake. They were right to question the king's commitment to our rights and the Declaration. Grain rations addressed only the simplest of our needs. We wanted liberty! I could not allow our march to amount to nothing. No, we could not leave, I urged those around me. Not until the king came with us to Paris to live amongst his people and share our sufferings.

The rain continued to pour from the night sky on those who chose to remain, but it didn't dampen our fervor. For hours, we chanted, shouted, and sang to push away the exhaustion that beat at us.

Around midnight, Lafayette finally arrived with the National Guard, and I wondered whose side he would take now. Had the king merely been waiting for his general to come and crush us? Perhaps the royal family had simply climbed into warm beds while we stood here shivering and soaked to the bone.

If I couldn't sleep, neither could they.

"Come, *mes amis*, let's remind them we're here," I said as I eyed Lafayette's guard. Pikes, broomsticks, and spears in hand, a group of women followed me toward the gates.

My hand tightened on the hilt of my sword, and I felt something snap inside me. All at once I advanced on a royal guardsman at the palace entrance, only to see that it was Lieutenant Colonel de Sainte-Amaranthe. If he recognized me, too, he was not so smug now, and I wasn't helpless anymore. I decided to show him a thing or two about a woman's strength.

"Now that Lafayette is here, he can escort the king. The king must come to Paris!" I insisted and when he and his men tried to push us back, I swung my sword.

A fight erupted all around me. I fought, like a soldier—no, like a warrior *queen*—and drew blood.

But they drew blood too. First on my right arm, then my left. And the last thing I felt was the stinging slash of a saber across my breast. *Like a warrior queen,* was my last proud thought before I fell to my knees.

While the royal guards retreated under the surge I'd inspired at the gates, someone dragged me to safety, draping me over a cannon so other women could bandage my wounds with strips of cloth they tore from their own skirts. I lay there bleeding, exhausted, hungry, and furious. But still alive. Maybe more alive than I had ever been.

Dawn approached at last, and the king had still not appeared. Would he address his people, or did he hope we would tire and give up?

When the first rays of sunlight brightened the sky, our cries gained momentum once again.

"Bread! Bread! Bread!" we shouted, hearts in our throats, rage filling our empty bellies.

Your Majesty, I pleaded inwardly, *when will you do something?*

Though I was weak both from hunger and loss of

blood, I staggered upright to lead the chants. But as I would later learn, while the crowd parted for the Queen of the Markets, the Queen of France had narrowly escaped with her life. A group of commoners found an unguarded entrance to the palace and broke into the queen's rooms. Finding it empty, they stabbed her mattress with pikes and swords. But all I saw was the aftermath. Several women with clubs and pikes bolted away from the crowd, and it was then I spotted Pauline among the pack who had called for the queen's murder during the march from Paris. Eyes wide, I watched as three armed soldiers on horseback raced after them. More gunfire rang out and screams echoed against the golden walls of the palace. I said a quick prayer that Pauline was safe.

A new chant began, one of endearment for His Majesty. We beseeched him to speak to us. To be the leader he was meant to be.

"Papa! Papa! Papa!"

"Come on, Louis," I muttered under my breath, hoping he would not make those of us who had put our faith in his word look like fools.

Just then, General Lafayette stepped onto the balcony overlooking the courtyard.

He raised his hand in the air and shouted, "Citizens! Silence!" None obeyed, and he attempted it several times until, at last, we quieted. "Your king," he began in a commanding voice, "wishes to speak with his people, and to confer glad news for all."

A shadow filled the doorway on the balcony for an instant. Lafayette retreated, and the king stepped outside.

My heart leapt into my throat. He wore the tricolor cockade. Many bent to their knees, others bowed their heads.

"Citizens of Paris." He paused a long moment. "I accept your Declaration of the Rights of Man and the Citizen. I shall go with you to Paris to rule from our beloved capital. It is to my good and faithful subjects that I confide all that is most precious to me."

The throng roared.

Tears pricked my eyes and I shot my wounded arm into the air in triumph. We had done it! "*Vive le roi! Vive le roi!*" I screamed along with my fellow patriots. Our king would not betray us—he had seen reason— and he would curb the excesses of his wicked nobles. "*Vive le roi!*"

"Papa! Papa! Papa!"

The king stood proudly, soaking up the love his people professed for him. After a long moment, he left the balcony. Yet the chanting continued, this time for the queen's submission, lest she try to change the king's mind. Lafayette motioned to have the queen and her children step out together, which was when the chants became darker.

"No children! Only the queen! Make her come out alone!"

I held my breath in spite of the pain of my wounded breast. Would the queen do it? Would she dare, even knowing that some in the crowd had muskets aimed and ready? I didn't think she had the courage.

But she did.

The door opened a second time. An elegant and gleaming figure emerged, pale in her beauty and immediately recognizable from the hundreds of pamphlets that had littered the streets like fallen leaves. Queen Marie-Antoinette stood before us.

Silence fell.

We stood frozen in disbelief and awe as she looked out over her subjects, who clamored at her feet with muskets and pikes; who had published every foul thing imaginable about her; who had abused her name on the long road from Paris to Versailles. Yet despite all this, her presence exuded a calm self-assuredness. As though she believed she was in her rightful place, as our queen.

Riveted by the sight of this infamous woman, I

stared at her, swells of emotion crashing over me. From hatred to reverence and back again.

She touched the tricolor cockade on her gown as she stared down upon us. At that moment, General Lafayette appeared and knelt at her side, theatrically pressing a kiss to her hand in homage. Was it a show for her or for us?

"*Vive la reine!*" someone called. Some followed suit. But the respect shown in deference to King Louis did not hold, and within seconds, the good-natured cheering shifted to a furious chant.

"*À Paris! À Paris! À Paris!*" To Paris, the royal family must go!

The queen ducked inside to safety.

I stared after her, wondering what it must be like to be born into such privilege and responsibility. I could scarcely fathom it.

Hours later, the royal carriage pulled down the drive, with the National Guard acting as escort. We marched with the procession, heads high, and song on our lips. As the royal carriage passed me, it stalled for an instant on the uneven path. I caught sight of a woman's face inside, her features forlorn. I recognized Princess Élisabeth. For a fleeting instant, her haunted face and obvious suffering struck me, and I doubted what we had begun.

Yet I knew her birth and status had trapped her in this moment. Despite her wealth and her brother and her fancy shoes, her status as *princess* forced her to bend to our will. The same way my poverty had forced me to bend to other wills.

But the carriage continued forward, and her face disappeared from view in a blur of my countrymen. And all I saw was *their* faces—victorious, unified, *free.* My doubt faded.

Maman would have been proud to see her daughter fight for what she deserved, what we all deserved. Prideful tears stung my eyes. I would see this through, come what may, for her and for my friend Marion. For Pauline and my sisters-in-arms. Squinting into the sunlight that poured over thousands of heads and shoulders, glinted off sabers and pikes and cannons, I smiled. The women of Paris guided their king home.

PART III

The Princess

We should not say *I will*
until we are sure of being right.
But once said, there should be no yielding
of what has been ordained.
—MADAME ÉLISABETH DE FRANCE

Palace of the Tuileries, Paris, May 1791

An escape is being planned.

After nearly a year and a half of captivity in his own palace, my brother, King Louis XVI, sees reason. He is not truly king in Paris. He is not safe here, nor is his family.

The truculent crowd that blocked us from traveling to Saint-Cloud last month finally tipped the scales in favor of our departure. The mob charged that Louis sought to flee the city. They were wrong—he only wanted to hear Mass with a priest loyal to Rome. But their shouts were prescient, because after hours trapped in our carriage with the National Guard unable to disperse those blocking our way, Louis returned to the palace finally convinced that he must indeed leave Paris.

And so, we will withdraw to a part of France where the air is clear of virulent revolutionary rhetoric. When Louis is among loyal subjects, supported by loyalist troops, he will be king again and make France sane.

Louis came to Paris in good faith. The queen and I both thought it the wrong decision, and when we arrived at this ruin of a château—a palace of dust, disuse, and disrepair uninhabited by kings for many years—we despaired. Not so Louis. My brother took a hopeful view and did all in his power to cheer us. He helped move furniture to barricade doors that would not lock. He urged us to ignore the insults hurled by crowds beneath our windows. And when one of those dreadful market women, the same sort that drove us from Versailles, climbed up the balcony into my room as I slept, Louis ordered new lodgings made ready for me so that I would feel safe.

Again and again, Louis urged us to be as sanguine as he generally appeared, to believe in the inherent goodness of his children, the people of France.

Louis still believes the majority of his subjects are good. He blames not the mobs but the men who he insists mislead and direct them—the deputies of a Constituent Assembly so diseased with revolutionary philosophies that they cannot come to any practical understanding with their king; the leaders of Paris's political clubs each with a different name but all with the same mission: the destruction of France and the holy church.

But I am not fooled. A true and heedless wickedness runs like an illness through the veins of the French people, infecting those at every level of society from street urchins to certain damnable members of the aristocracy.

We have proof of this in the thousand little cruelties inflicted on the king and queen by our officious jailers. And perhaps such disrespect might be forgivable. But the broader proofs are damning. The new government of France casts aside the greatness of her centuries-old heritage. They have abolished the hereditary titles and privileges of the nobles; replaced the fleur-de-lys flag with the republican tricolor; and redrawn the map of my brother's kingdom as if this were their right, dividing it into "departments" in place of the former great provinces.

And all this—all of it, comes from a rejection of God's divine order.

Sitting at my desk, I riffle through the day's pile of political flyers collected for me by my *dame d'atour*. It is a terrible chore and quickly makes me oblivious to the sunny spring sky and the songs of the birds outside my open window. Like their predecessors, these flyers are filled with horrible attacks on Louis and Antoinette. They also savage God's holy servants, alleging unspeakable acts by priests and nuns. Thanks to such scraps of paper, holy sisters are now regularly pulled from their convents and whipped in the streets. Why, only this morning I penned a letter of encouragement to a sweet young woman named Charlotte Corday who is secretary at the Abbey of Sainte-Trinité in Caen. She was formerly a pupil there and wrote to me first in that guise, sharing her dreams of being a holy sister in due course. But now poor Charlotte worries that the time for such vows is over in France. And she fears for the safety of the sisters there who have already consecrated themselves to our Lord.

Those who turn on their divinely appointed king and the servants of God are not good. I cannot see them as such, even to please my brother.

Casting the ugly pages onto the desk, I rise and walk to my bookcase: the one concealing a secret door completed only last night. I run my hand over the face of it, remembering the thrill and the apprehension I experienced these last few evenings, ear pressed to the outer door of my apartment, ready to signal the workmen to be silent at the sound of any approaching footfall.

Before they departed, one of the men showed me how to make the door open. I have only done so once— with his eyes upon me. The urge to touch the hidden lever is very great . . . and surely I ought to practice . . .

The door to my apartment swings open without warning. I pull my hand back from the gilded carvings of the case as if it were made of fire not wood. How glad

I am that I did not give in to the temptation to trigger the door merely for the thrill of doing so! I spin round, expecting the captain of the National Guard who constantly shadows me. I hope that the color in my cheeks will not make him suspicious.

Instead, the Princess de Lamballe enters at an unladylike pace, her own face flushed. "They burn the Holy Father in effigy!" she says, quite oblivious in her distress to the great sigh of relief that escapes me. "If the mob was any closer, we would smell the smoke!"

"Then it is a mercy they are not. Have you told the queen?"

The princess lowers her voice. "She is with the count."

She means Swedish Count Axel von Fersen. I know what infamy those who defame the queen would infer from such a tête-à-tête. Only theirs is not a romantic meeting, but a logistical one. The count is one of those most intimately involved with planning our exit from Paris.

I cannot say this to Lamballe, who is dear to Antoinette but also related by marriage to the Duc d'Orleans, who makes shameful common cause with the revolutionaries. This is a time for extreme reticence, so the princess will not know we are going until we are discovered gone.

Lamballe stands looking forlorn, and I wish to cheer her. So I say, "Come see the shoes that have arrived! I will put a pair on and we can walk in the garden."

"More shoes! How many pairs is that this month? It must be at least one for every day."

Shoes, books, my farm—after my family, these are my earthly loves. Fortunately, none of them are included in the seven deadly sins. And at a court where so many pursue more morally compromising ambitions and desires, I hope to be forgiven my desire for divine and decorative footwear.

"I do not apologize." I say to Lamballe. "In these grim times we must take our pleasure where we can." I open the box with the two pairs of taffeta shoes that arrived this morning from the rue Neuve des Augustins.

"*C'est joli celui là!*" Lamballe picks up the puce pair, embroidered at the toes with pink roses and festooned with mossy green bows. "You have excellent taste. But I think you meant these to be a gift." She smiles saucily, hiding my shoes behind her back. "Give me one reason I should not take them?"

"I shall give you two: my very big feet. Those shoes would not stay on your tiny feet for an instant. You would walk or dance out of them at once."

"When was the last time anyone danced?" Lamballe's voice is serious again.

"Well, we shall hope for better things in the future," I reply, holding out the box so she can replace the shoes.

But I have more than just hope. I have faith in the God who has always sustained me and who will surely not fail me now. My family will escape, and my brother will find the strength to restore the world as it should be.

"**Élisabeth, your** priest comes." Lamballe sweeps into the sitting room where we ladies have secluded ourselves, by the queen's command, for a morning of all-too-rare frivolity.

"I know we have much that is serious yet to do and consider," Antoinette said to me last evening as she pressed me to join her this morning. "But if we are not careful, our minds will become too exhausted to go on, like horses driven too hard. And Élisabeth, we *must* be prepared to go the distance with so much at stake."

The queen works relentlessly to find foreign aid for my brother in his difficulties, employing her sharp mind and her abundant ability to charm people—at least people of a certain set. But even the most determined and tireless worker must eventually become fatigued. Now, looking at Antoinette radiant where she relaxes into a silk armchair, cheeks flushed, I believe she was very wise in decreeing there must be no mention of politics, rioters, or any other unpleasant thing at this gathering. She needs, indeed all of us need, refreshing. So this morning only romantic gossip and discussions of fashion are being entertained. These are topics not particularly suited to me. No one has swooned over me in years, and when they did, it was all pretense. Foreign princes wooed me as a king's sister, not a woman. And when it comes to fashion, I am rather too "cherubic," as my sister-in-law kindly puts it, to wear most of what is *à la mode* well.

When I was younger, I wished I could be more fashionable. But for some years now it has not bothered me that the rest of those in the queen's sphere are far more glamorous than I. Today, some of these same beauties are not so sanguine. Madame de Sainte-Amaranthe and her seventeen-year-old daughter, Émilie, are among our visitors. The latter, who is the most exquisite creature I have ever seen, is the subject of many jealous glances. With her exquisitely proportioned figure, perfect curls, arched brows, and a smile that hints at intriguing hidden thoughts, she is a perfect *mignon*. A good number of my companions are feeling very plain indeed. Madame de Sainte-Amaranthe's self-satisfied look suggests she knows this. I suspect that Émilie will be wooed for her own sake, but married off for advantage. Such is the way of things.

"You are not going to leave us for a priest, are you?" Émilie asks, laughing.

"Of course she is. The real question, mademoiselle"— Lamballe offers me a playful, challenging smile—"is whether Madame Élisabeth is going to confess the number of shoes she has purchased this week?"

"Only if you confess how you covet them," I reply, laughing.

I excuse myself and search out Abbé de Firmont. To see him striding through the Tuileries in his cassock and rabat seems miraculous, as if I am witnessing our Savior walking on water.

The Assembly began its attack on religion more than a year ago. First by placing the church's property at the disposition of the government. Then by banning monastic vows and sentencing to death monks who failed to marry. And finally, by requiring all clergy to take an oath of loyalty to France. Most priests refused, as the oath conflicted with their duty to Rome by demanding they put nation before obedience to the pope. Such priests are labeled nonjuring, though I would call them the only true ecclesiastics in France. The clergy attached to our family—including my confessor— refused the oath and were banished from the Tuileries. My new confessor also refused, yet somehow he enters the palace daily, without any attempt at disguise.

The abbé takes my hands. "Madame Élisabeth, how are you?"

I wish to say nervous—to divulge that even as I kept company with the queen and her gay companions, part of me wondered if this is the day our false passports will arrive, the day I will learn the role I am to play during the upcoming escape. But, though I might appropriately confess my most grievous sins to the abbé, to mention our flight would be an act of disloyalty to my brother. So I merely reply, "Better for seeing you, Father."

I go to my table, eager to see what passage from the Bible Abbé de Firmont will raise for discussion. Hoping, in a sign from God, it might be from the story of the Israelites' flight from Egypt. But when he is seated, he only looks at me.

"Madame Élisabeth," he says at last, "in our short acquaintance, I have come to wonder why you are not a holy sister. The calling shines from you like light from a summer sun."

I feel heat in my cheeks. "I do not deny, Father, as a younger woman that was my devout wish." I pause, considering how to explain the most difficult decision of my life, a decision that sometimes leads me to a place of self-indulgent regret.

"I was orphaned young. I have no memories of my

father, and those of my mother may merely be stories I was told by my *gouvernantes*. But my memories of my brothers"—I smile and shake my head—"are the best of my girlhood. Their love surrounded me. And Louis—I mean His Majesty—the bond between us is the strongest bond of affection I have ever known. So I set aside my desire to be a nun because Louis asked me to."

I remember the day as if it was yesterday. I returned to Versailles from visiting the convent at Saint-Denis, and Louis came to the courtyard to greet me. He tucked my hand over his arm and listened to what I had to say, but his eyes told me his thoughts were not on the improvements under way at the convent. At the bottom of the steps, before we were surrounded by courtiers, he stopped. "Dear sister," he said, looking into both my eyes and my soul, "I am willing that you should visit our sisters in Christ, but on the condition that you will not imitate them. Let God have other pious young women, Élisabeth. I need you." At that moment I took a different vow—I chose to devote myself to my brother in his labors as king, to advise him and to put him always before myself.

"I worry sometimes, Father, that God is disappointed," I say now. "Sacrifice is surely something He would approve, but if He thought to have my service . . ."

"He has it," the abbé responds. "Can you believe that I could move among the members of the court without coming to know of your good deeds?"

I look down at my hands. My *gouvernantes* spent years teaching me that good deeds were to be done, not spoken of. And stubborn girl that I was, I resisted the lesson longer than I should have.

"I heard a story from the Princess de Lamballe," he says softly. "A jeweler visited Versailles. He spread things on a velvet cloth for the ladies of the court to admire. There was a pin. You picked it up again and again."

I can see it in my hand, the lovely corsage ornament, with flowers so natural, despite being of enamel and diamonds, they reminded me of a bouquet I might have gathered at my farm, Montreuil.

"The princess pinned it on you, urging you to buy it," the abbé continues. "But you took it off, saying that for such a price you could set up two little homes for families living in want."

"I buy many things for myself," I say, "shoes, books."

Every day when I rise I experience both the pleasure of being filled with God's love and the disappointment of knowing I could be worthier of it.

"You have not taken a vow of poverty." My priest

lays his hand momentarily on my own where it rests on the table. "Countless courtiers with incomes many times your own do less, or nothing at all. I suspect most of your royal pension goes not to things worn upon your feet but to your farm. This autumn, village children all around Montreuil will go to bed with stomachs full because of you."

While I hope the harvest this year is as good as my steward predicts, and I pray that there will be no more hunger, no more bread riots, I can hardly bear to think of my farm. Sometimes, as the date for our escape approaches, I find myself selfishly anticipating not only Louis's restoration to power, but my return to Montreuil. Imagining myself in my gardens, my *orangerie*, my library. And always the same resolution forms in my heart, as tears prick my eyes: I will never willingly quit Montreuil again. Better to die there.

"Please, can we speak of something else?"

"Yes, of course. But first, I must embarrass you for a moment longer. Élisabeth Philippine Marie Hélène de France, you are a woman of true faith, good heart, and perseverance. Remember that always, and have confidence that wherever you walk you will do so in righteousness"—the abbé gives a mischievous smile—"whichever pair of pretty shoes you wear."

Sunday, June 17, 1791

We spend the evening as a family: Louis and Antoinette; my niece, Marie-Thérèse, madame royale; my nephew, the dauphin, Louis-Charles; myself; and the children's *gouvernante*, Madame Tourzel. My second-eldest brother, the Count of Provence, and his wife are not with us. Such is our mania for secrecy in these last days before our escape that Provence—who will depart in a small carriage disguised as an Englishman—has refrained from telling his own wife they are leaving. She is a terrible gossip and will not be told anything until the evening of the escape, just before she is trundled off to her carriage.

Antoinette sits calmly embroidering, but I know her mind—as sharp as her needle—is not thinking of the silk flowers she creates. She has been instrumental in organizing our escape plan, developing it in great detail before presenting it to the king. And tonight that plan takes another step forward. She looks at Louis with a soft smile while changing needles as he resets the backgammon board between us after my victory. Six-year-old Louis-Charles plays with toy soldiers at his father's feet, blond curls framing his face.

It is a wonder none of our minders have made a fuss over my nephew's little figures, for they wear the uniforms not of the National Guard, but of the king's disbanded Garde du Corps. But our captors have no interest in things that are royal—unless it is to despoil and disrespect them. *Well, when Louis is safely installed away from Paris, we will soon put a stop to that.*

Madame Royale is reciting from Plutarch's essay on affection between siblings when the softest of raps sounds at the door from my brother's antechamber. Louis's breath quickens where he sits across from me, and I drop the dice I was about to roll, my flesh prickling in anticipation. For while the children do not know it, we await a collaborator. One we have never met.

Only Antoinette manages to appear entirely tranquil, nodding at Madame Tourzel.

"Say good night to your papa and maman," the *gouvernante* instructs.

"Am I not to finish?" Marie-Thérèse looks surprised. It is early. Even the dauphin would not ordinarily retire at such an hour.

"Another time, my *Mousseline Serieuse*," the queen replies, giving her daughter the same gentle, encouraging smile she so often offers the king.

Madame Tourzel leads the children behind an elaborately painted screen where they slip through another of the concealed doors installed to assist in our escape. As soon as they are gone, Antoinette opens the outer door. A gentleman enters, bowing immediately and deeply.

"Majesties, I am François-Melchior de Moustier, for many years a member of Your Majesty's Garde du Corps. My former commander tells me that you have need of my service. I am honored to think so."

My brother rises and embraces Moustier. "The honor is ours, for in a time when few can be depended upon, those I trust tell me you are a true subject, willing to pledge yourself to your king."

If only Louis could meet each of his subjects in such a manner.

In close quarters, he has a way with people. I am convinced Louis's genuine interest and caring would be visible even to the most radical of men—men like Jean-Paul Marat, whose newspaper *L'Ami du Peuple* becomes increasingly influential. For some months I read *L'Ami*, knowing I could be useful to my brother if I keep abreast of the most extreme ideas. At first Marat contented himself with attacking those revolutionaries not rabid enough for his tastes—men like Lafayette. And I did not mind reading his insults against the marquis.

But soon Marat's words went beyond offensive to

terrifying. When he called for the severing of "five or six hundred heads"—royalist heads—as a way of assuring the "repose, freedom and happiness" of his revolutionary followers, I could not sleep for three full days. And I could no longer bring myself to look at his paper. But I still force myself to endure the writings of other radicals, including the so-called philosopher Marquis de Condorcet. Though I merely skimmed his essay denouncing God. Such vile writings do not deserve serious attention.

"Your Majesty," Moustier says, "my honor and my life shall always be yours to command."

"That is good, monsieur, for I will place in your hands not only my safety but the safety of my family, whose lives I hold dearer than my own."

"What would Your Majesty have me do?" Moustier asks.

"For now, acquire three matching suits of clothing. The sort of short coats, suede knee britches, and broad-brimmed hats appropriate to those accompanying the coach of a family of wealth, but not royalty. One is for yourself."

"I will do it straightaway, Majesty." Moustier bows.

He is nearly to the door when Louis speaks. "And, monsieur, though you may tell no one, you will be leaving Paris before week's end. So get your affairs in order." There is strength and certitude in my brother's voice.

It is really happening! In three nights—after months of heated discussions and agonizing planning, after dates chosen and moved, we will ride out of Paris and into our futures!

The young woman is clad in dark, plain, unremarkable clothing, befitting a nurse-companion. "Mademoiselle Rosalie," I ask her solemnly, "are you ready to depart?" The figure does not respond. She is not sure. I am not sure. Now that the moment has come, my heart beats in my throat. I look in the mirror again. I am not Élisabeth of France. I cannot be once I leave my apartment; not until we are safely in Montmédy where we will establish Louis's new court.

That is more than two hundred miles of being someone else.

No, *pretending to be someone else*, I remind myself as I put on the large-brimmed hat that casts my face in shadow. I recall Abbé de Firmont's admonition. *You are Élisabeth Philippine Marie Hélène de France . . . remember that.* That is particularly critical in this moment, for I do not know this Rosalie, but I know myself well, and I will need all the better parts of my nature—my faith in God, my devotion to Louis, and yes, I suspect, my stubbornness—in the next hours.

Glancing at my clock, I hesitate, then snatch up the puce shoes Lamballe so admires. I exchange them for the plain, black leather shoes I wear. Again before the mirror, I make certain they cannot be seen beneath my skirts. Then, to remind myself who I really am, I lift my petticoats and let their pink roses peek out.

Time to go.

I do not regret leaving the Tuileries. I have always hated this palace and the captivity it represents. My wardrobe for life at Montmédy is already on its way in a carriage with Her Majesty's ladies. So I do not need a backward glance at things left behind—I only wish memories of my time here were as easy to discard.

As I trigger the secret door in the bookcase, I carry only my rosary, my prayer book, and Mr. Burke's *Reflections on the Revolution in France*. Of all the books I have acquired to try to comprehend the events that sweep us up, I take Burke because, while he indulges the faulty idea that kings are not divinely ordained, he seems to understand that if the tail of society is allowed to eat the head, comprised of men of property and education with the knowledge and experience to lead the body politic, the tail will not be satiated. Philosophers like Lafayette and Condorcet who hope only to shift the government, but who tolerate or encourage the mobs to that end, will one day be surrounded by the same screaming, distorted faces I saw from my carriage window when I was forced to leave my farm.

Those who stir up these great mobs will be eaten too.

In the dark of the hidden passage, fear surges through me. *O vere adorator et unice amator dei, miserere nobis.* The prayer soothes. I put a hand against the wall, feeling my way along until I find the door into a set of deserted apartments. The dust in the room tickles my nose. Pieces of covered furniture crouch like ghostly beasts in the moonlight, heightening my feeling of peril.

I ease the door to the hallway open, praying under my breath. Empty. When the Tuileries go dark nightly, many of those attendant upon us—both courtiers and menial folk—depart. It is in this nightly exodus that the king and I hope to lose ourselves.

A throng of people crosses the courtyard as I exit by a door befitting my newly assumed station. I brush elbows with a servant, and my mouth goes dry. What if she recognizes me? But she does not pause or give me a glance. Without my fine clothing, and in a setting where no one would expect to see me, it seems that I have become invisible. What a marvelous and, under the circumstances, reassuring thing.

A handful of guards loiter in the torchlight, talking. I look past them to the place ou Carousel, where private carriages mix with coaches for hire. Count von Fersen sits atop one of these unremarkable vehicles. Having cleared the gate, it is my task to find him.

Driver after driver looks unfamiliar. I double back to be sure I have not missed the carriage, then quicken my pace. My niece and nephew are already on board with their *gouvernante*—no, the baronne, I remind myself. Madame Tourzel plays the role of a Russian baronne, traveling with her two daughters. I am eager to be with them.

Finally, near the end of the line of carriages, with panic rising in my throat at the thought that I will never find our party, a footman on one of the vehicles looks familiar. He resembles one of the men who came with Monsieur Moustier for the king's final instructions. But I cannot be sure, so I circle the carriage slowly. I am halfway around when the driver, who had been sitting on the carriage box, hat pulled low and smoking a clay pipe, jumps down into my path.

I spring backward, mumbling excuses, prepared to run.

"Allow me to open the door, mademoiselle."

That voice! I raise my eyes and find myself face-to-face with Count von Fersen. God be thanked!

In my haste, I misplace a foot on the carriage step and pitch forward, treading on Madame Tourzel's gown. A small cry comes from beneath the silk. As I fall onto the seat beside her, Madame raises her skirt to reveal a sleepy Louis-Charles, dressed as a girl, curled on the carriage floor.

"I thought it best, until we are under way," she says simply.

I nod. The curtains are almost fully closed, but the light is enough to perceive the worry on her face, and on my niece's.

"*Ma chere.*" I reach for Marie-Thérèse's hand. "The court was quiet as I left, the halls deserted. Your papa will be with us soon."

"But what if the guards . . ." Her voice trails off.

"Any guards who see him will think, there is that man in the brown-and-green suit we see nightly. Does he never change his clothing? And why does his valet or his wife not tell him that his wig is crooked?"

Marie-Thérèse giggles. And I say a prayer of thanksgiving for the chevalier who has come to the palace each evening for a fortnight dressed in a manner that mimics Louis's disguise. I am grateful not only for his crooked wig that offers us this moment of levity, but because tonight the chevalier's prior visits will help make my brother invisible.

Where is *Louis?*

As if in answer, the door swings wide and the king is with us, settling in beside my niece.

"God and all his saints be praised!" Hearing my voice quaver, I realize I was as worried as Marie-Thérèse despite my bravado.

Louis looks bemused by my show of emotion. "Nothing could have been easier. I stopped to buckle my shoe in the courtyard and not a single guard looked askance."

"You didn't!"

"I did." He laughs at his own prank then gives me a broad smile. "But that is not the most interesting bit. Who do you think appeared unexpectedly at my *coucher*?" He slaps his thigh. "Our jailer-in-chief, La-fayette!"

Madame and I gasp.

"Think how it will sting him when we are safely in Montmédy and he realizes he was one of the last living souls to speak with me before I departed Paris! He will be mortified."

Good. Perhaps they will punish the marquis for neglect of his duty in imprisoning us—a duty that ought to have been beneath him as a nobleman. And things will get worse still for him when we are at Montmédy, and it is widely known his cousin, General Bouillé, commands the troops defending us.

I remember the faith my brother once had in the marquis. How pleased Louis was when Lafayette was elected to head the new National Guard. How relieved the king was to see the marquis when we were surrounded by a mob of shrieking fruit sellers and ragpickers at Versailles, and a handful of them, led by a woman named Louise who dared meet my eyes with a chilling boldness as she gave her name, were given an audience with the king.

But I was wary of Lafayette from the beginning. After all, what sort of marquis would take a position at the head of troops comprised of commoners from the Third Estate? Men of Lafayette's birth serve in the king's own army. It is their birthright, their duty, and their honor.

"Only Madame Bonnet now, and then we are away." Louis winks at Marie-Thérèse as he uses the queen's false name.

We sit in silence waiting for Antoinette. The walls of the carriage seem to contract with each passing moment, and I find myself short of breath. *Has something happened? If so, will Louis go on, or go back?*

He has been adamant that we all leave Paris together, rejecting a plan that divided us into two parties pursuing different routes in lightweight carriages—a plan both Count von Fersen and General Bouillé preferred.

I suspect if we hear an alarm raised, Louis will surrender so Antoinette is not abandoned. This impulse comes from all that is good, but it is still mistaken. Louis is more than husband—he is king, and preserving the monarchy ought to be the priority, however grim that sounds. I pray I will not have to press that argument upon him.

If Antoinette fails to appear, or worse still, we hear an alarm raised, will Louis consent to flee if I offer to climb down and return in his stead? Antoinette and I are very different women, and for years we were cordial but not more. In the early months of the Revolution, when I would have preferred direct, firm repression of its adherents by the king, Antoinette supported political maneuverings, encouraging Louis to broker deals with various Assembly factions. In those months, I could hardly stand the sight of the queen.

But seeing the agony in her eyes as we rode from Versailles, I realized we each in our way wanted only one thing—the preservation of Louis and his crown. And in the long months of imprisonment and misfortune since, we have bonded as if we were sisters in blood and not just by marriage. So I would surrender my own hopes of liberty to give my brother peace of mind and to be at Antoinette's side.

Without warning the carriage lurches. I grip the

edge of the seat, readying myself for whatever comes. In a few feet we stop, the curtain twitches and I wish my brother had not flatly refused to carry a pistol. But it is only one of our guards.

"I am sorry, Baronne," he says, "but the Marquis de Lafayette was passing and startled the horses."

I shiver uncontrollably despite the warm summer air at the thought of the commander of the National Guard so close.

"And here is Madame Bonnet." The door opens to reveal the queen, so unornamented in her plain black garments that I myself might mistake her for a *gouvernante*. As Antoinette is handed in, my brother rises. Without waiting for the privacy of a closed door, he takes his wife into his arms and kisses her on the lips.

I feel a blush rise. And as the king and queen sit down, hands clasped, I have my answer. The king has no intention of being separated from Antoinette; it is not a point he can think rationally upon.

Finally, we are under way.

As we roll toward rue de l'Échelle, I push back the curtain for a last look at the Palace des Tuileries. How different from the moment I leaned out of our carriage from Versailles for one last glimpse of my beloved Montreuil. That moment was agony—this one is ecstasy.

With the help of God and by our own hard work and fortitude, when we next return to Paris, Louis will be secure in his crown and the old order will be firmly restored.

"I do not understand," Fersen says, his face grave. "The carriage ought to be here."

"We must get out and look," Louis replies.

We are at the Barrier Saint-Martin; it is half past one in the morning, and the larger vehicle in which we are to ride for hundreds of miles to safety is missing.

"Your Maj—Monsieur," the count catches himself. Even in this dark, deserted spot it is best not to use the honorific, best not to forget for a moment that the king will be hunted. "Monsieur, it would be better if you let me look—"

"I wish it had not taken me so long to be free of the palace." The queen's hands twist in her lap.

"No, my dear." Louis lays a hand on hers. "You did well to pause when you saw Lafayette. He was preoccupied this evening, but not so much so that he could overlook the most beautiful face in France had he run upon you."

I finger my rosary. Instead of hearing the comforting litany in my head, a little voice whispers a thousand doubts. What a feeble soul I am. I focus my will, and this time the familiar words come. I am halfway through my second set of Hail Marys when I hear the clinking of horse harnesses and turning wheels.

Please let it be our berline, not merely some travelers offering assistance. That would be a disaster.

This time, when Fersen's face appears at the carriage window he smiles. "The berline is found."

Bathed in the light of the gibbous moon, our carriage is a thing of beauty. Not because of its green and black paint, or the flashes of yellow on its wheels, but by its very presence. The others climb inside, but I stand transfixed, watching Fersen and two guards unharness the horses from the carriage we just exited. They send the beasts off with slaps on their rumps, then push the empty vehicle into the ditch.

Moustier, straightening from the effort, spots me. "Mademoiselle Rosalie," he says with a little bow. "We must go."

The berline is spacious. Even with its white velvet upholstery it is not to the standards of a vehicle from the king's collection, but it is comfortable, and more importantly, entirely appropriate for a baronne making a long journey. Its construction was funded by a wealthy financier and adviser to the king, the Baron de Batz. The baron saw to it that the berline is outfitted so we may travel for miles without depending on the hospitality of anyone. When one wishes to go unobserved, the less stops the better. So we will eat on board and relieve ourselves in the berline's leather *pots de chamber.*

As I close my eyes, exhausted and ready to rest, I hear the count yell, "Take them full speed! Be bold, be quick!"

"*Réveille-toi,* sleepyhead." Antoinette's voice is as warm as the sun I feel on my face. "You do not want to miss breakfast."

My eyes flutter open to reveal the queen with a hamper in her lap, putting cheese, cold beef, and peas in aspic onto plates. Out the window, fields stretch as far as I can see.

"Where are we?"

"Close to Charmentray." My brother looks up from a map spread on his knees. Louis-Charles, every bit as keen on maps as his papa, sits beside the king looking earnestly down at our route. "You have slept through two relays."

So Count von Fersen has left us. I glance at the queen to see if I can detect any unease. But she is a master of composure, so she appears completely content. I am sure she does not feel so.

Nor, for that matter, do I.

Throughout May, as the plan we now pursue took

firm form, everyone who had a voice in the matter understood the division of responsibilities. Funded by our friend Baron de Batz, General Bouillé, the loyal royalist commander at Metz, would take charge of troop movements to ensure that the king was properly received at Montmédy, with adequate forces to rule from a position of strength. Count von Fersen would deliver us to that place of safety. But on the evening Fersen brought our faux passports, my brother announced the count must leave our party at Bondy.

Fersen bowed to the king's decision. The queen and I did not. As soon as we had Louis alone, we pressed him as to why he made this change. Louis replied that Fersen was a foreigner, and should our escape be discovered his presence might lead some to doubt their king—to believe that he intended to cross the border and take up arms against them in what so many already believed was an existing foreign conspiracy.

And perhaps you should take up arms and join forces with our allies, brother, I'd thought.

I look outside again. The carriage moves smoothly over the paving stones, shaded by tall, slender trees. Antoinette hands me my plate, and I use my fingers to devour my portion. I begin to feel better, lighter. It is silly to dwell on Fersen's absence.

As dishes are put away, Louis says, "We ought to

have gone into the countryside, among our people, earlier. Do you remember our trip to Cherbourg, Antoinette, when the harbor was under construction? That was five years ago, and yet it was the last time I traveled this far from Paris. Remember the scarlet coat I had embroidered for the trip? It would not button now. But never mind, my dear." He smiles. "Soon I will be in the saddle again, hunting and inspecting troops, and I shall regain my vigor and my figure."

Louis sighs and looks out the window.

"How the crowds cheered us," he says after a pause. "How beautiful you were standing under the great arch of flowers they built. I long to hear '*Vive le roi*' shouted by a crowd so large that my ears are left ringing."

"And you *will*, Louis," the queen says, her voice brimming with conviction. "Once we're away from the nest of vipers in Paris, you will." The look she gives my brother is so fiercely fond that it makes my heart ache.

"And, brother," I add, "you can shout '*vive mon peuple*,' in return. I remember you telling me how your people loved that."

The morning passes with a sweet, simple pleasantness. There are no spies within the four walls of the berline. No need to guard words or looks. The children are gayer than I have seen them in months. When we make a stop by the roadside, Louis-Charles chases butterflies, and Marie-Thérèse, forgetting the gravitas she often adopts as a young lady of twelve, spins in circles watching her cotton skirt billow. I lift my own skirt, exposing the pink roses on my shoes to the summer sunlight, and run after Louis-Charles.

When we pull into Montmirail, the guard who rides ahead is waiting with eleven new horses and our next driver. I reach to shut the curtain as it was agreed we would as a safeguard when stopping. But before I can, my brother opens the door and descends.

What is he thinking?

I am assuredly less recognizable than the queen, so I clamber down after Louis.

"Monsieur Durand," I say, catching up to him. "Is it wise, given your *condition*, to be in the open air?"

"A little air will do me good," Louis replies. "I wish to use the necessary shed and stretch my legs."

"Exercise is a fine idea"—I lay a hand on his arm—"but we must not delay the baronne. Perhaps a walk when she next draws off the road?"

This is not what I want to ask. I want to ask *why*. Why take any chance of being recognized? I give my brother a piercing look, hoping to convey these unspoken sentiments.

"Nonsense," he replies blithely. "I will be back before the new horses are harnessed."

And then, as if he were indeed the unknown Monsieur Durand, instead of Louis XVI of France, whose image is on the fifty-livre *assignat*, my brother wanders away. He does not get far. Noticing a wagon driver, examining the ties securing his load, the king speaks to the man.

I cannot hear what either says from this distance. But the driver cocks his head first one way then the other, after which he suddenly snatches off his hat. He is clearly not certain that my brother is the king, for he offers no bow, but the skin on my arms prickles with unease. I am relieved when our driver climbs atop the carriage and calls that we are ready to depart.

As Louis takes his seat I bite my tongue to keep from chastising him. My *belle-soeur* has spots of color in her cheeks. Perhaps she will remind Louis of the need for caution.

"How well things go!" she declares. "If we were going to be stopped, surely we would have been before now. Knowing we are gone—and our captors must know it by now—is very different from determining our destination and route. There are a hundred possibilities."

"They will assume Austria," I say. Given that Antoinette is sneeringly called *the Austrian whore*, the southern roads will probably be explored first. Perhaps

Louis's indiscretion was not so important as my dread would make it.

Sometime later the queen asks, "How far have we come?"

Louis consults his map then hands it to the dauphin. "More than sixty miles. There is little to fear now, and once we have passed Châlons there will be nothing at all."

He has barely finished speaking when a terrible thump jolts the berline, setting it swaying with such force that Louis-Charles is thrown, still clutching the map, from his seat. I slide into my niece, who crushes Madame Tourzel against the sidewall. Outside, the air is full of the distressed whinnying of horses and shouted curses.

"What has happened?" the king demands as if we know something he does not.

"I will find out," I say decisively. The last thing we need is for Louis to expose himself again.

I wrench the door open. Our driver is off the box shouting at our guide: "What is the point of you riding the lead horse if you are going to take us into a road marker!"

I look back. Sure enough, the nearest marker is streaked with black and yellow from our wheel.

The guide grumbles and begins inspecting the animals. As the guard sitting on the box climbs down to join him, the smaller carriage carrying the queen's ladies pulls up, followed by Monsieur Moustier. The guard beside the horses calls to him, "Are you any good with harnesses?"

"What does that mean?" All eyes turn to me. "What," I stammer slightly, "shall I tell the baronne?"

"Four of six animals broke harnesses in the stumble. We must repair them before we can be on our way."

"Nothing to worry about," Louis opines when I relate our situation. He stretches out his legs, clasps his hands behind his head, and closes his eyes. But, like me, the queen glances at her watch.

Fifteen minutes later, Madame opens the carriage door and takes the children to stretch their legs. The sun is hot, they return thirsty, and still we show no sign of moving. Is Louis really sleeping? Antoinette fans herself with her hand and looks at me. "Surely it cannot be much longer."

But it is. When the berline at last rolls onward, we have lost more than three-quarters of an hour.

"What time are we expected at Pont de Somme-Vesle?" I ask.

"Between half past two and half past four," the king replies, proving he is indeed awake. He opens his eyes, sits up, and retrieves his map from the floor where it has lain since the dauphin dropped it. "Here," he says to Louis-Charles. "This is where we are now, and this is Somme-Vesle."

So far. We must stop at Chaintrix and Châlons before that! There is no chance our rendezvous will be on schedule. Am I the only one concerned? It appears so. For Louis and the dauphin play a game with the map, and the queen and Madame Tourzel chat animatedly. Surely then my unease comes from my own nature—I am fiercely punctual, a point in my character that has provided fodder for good-natured jests.

I force a calming breath and take solace in knowing the royal dragoons will wait for their king at Somme-Vesle—and once we are surrounded by regiments, the last reasons to fear will fly off like a flock of birds we scare up from a roadside field.

"They are not here." The queen's voice conveys a quiet agony.

It is after half past six in the evening, and we stand near a tiny relay on the outskirts of Somme-Vesle. Great fields, lush with crops, stretch in every direction. There is not a single uniformed dragoon in sight. Not one.

"I could not ask directly," one of our guards says, drawing us off to where we cannot be overheard by the strangers changing our horses. "But in making conversation, I mentioned soldiers on the road, and the post-master told me they *were* here.

"The post-master said they made him nervous. Since the start of June, there have been many soldiers in these parts, some speaking German." The guard pauses, licking his lips. "He said for all anyone knows they could be Austrians, and Austrians are a vile people who cannot be trusted." He glances at the queen. "Begging your pardon."

"Do not apologize," Antoinette replies. "I have heard many worse insults, and we must have your candid speech, monsieur, because it is vital that we know what goes on."

"Apparently, all here know that General Bouillé has troops on the march. The mayor, a cousin of the post-master, was told they guard strongboxes carrying money to pay armies at the frontier. But the post-master puffed himself up and assured me that he does not believe that, nor do his fellow members of the Friends of the Constitution Club."

The name of the club puts me on my guard. In Paris, a club by the same name is also called the Jacobins. They are radical revolutionaries of the worst sort.

"The fellow had the temerity to ask why good Frenchmen should wish to see troops at the frontier paid. When I pointed out that they defend him and all France, he laughed and said it is clear I am employed by an *aristo*, because the troops at the border are not made of good and respectable citizens, but a collection of noblemen and foreigners who answer to the king."

And this is the part of France in which we are to be safe? Never for a minute did it occur to me that the poison spewed in Paris had spread so many miles from the capital.

"So what happened to my troops?" the king asks.

"Local farmers drove them off." Our guard looks stricken.

"Impossible," Louis replies as my own stomach drops. If the troops were driven off, how shall we make our way? But the king will not hear such talk. "I am sure that is not the explanation we will have from the Duc de Choiseul when we see him."

If we see him.

All the debate over Choiseul's appointment comes rushing back to me. Fersen and Bouillé sought to dissuade the king from including him in the plan. The general argued, "He is only thirty-one. Let us choose someone older, and more experienced."

But my brother was unmoved. "My dear Bouillé, we cannot all be your august age. I am not yet forty and I rule a nation. The duc can be trusted to secure horses, and he can *afford* to do so, which, given our situation, is very useful."

Are we to ride without soldiers because we could not pay for our own horses and Antoinette's Austrian relations demurred when asked for money?

"Let us get back in our carriages and go on," Louis says. "I am sure Choiseul merely moved his men where they will attract less attention. No one enjoys having insults and perhaps worse flung at them—we can affirm that from personal experience."

As we ride on, my eyes desperately scan the roadside and the horizon. There is a silence in the berline as heavy as the summer heat. The children feel it, for Louis-Charles asks, "What is the matter, Papa?" Louis does not seem to notice, nor does he answer. Marie-Thérèse lets out a stifled sob. I want to say something to comfort her, but do not trust my voice. So instead, I take her hand.

At last, Sainte-Menehould appears on the horizon. It is still daylight, but it feels as if the darkness of the Argonne forest, looming behind the town, rolls like a fog over the carriage. I am very glad that, instead of pressing ahead, our advance guard rides just in front of us. I fear we may have need of brave men with swords and pistols.

The relay in Sainte-Menehould is off the main square.

As we pull to a stop, I speak up. "Please, Louis, do not leave the carriage."

My brother nods.

I am about to suggest we shut the curtains, when my attention is distracted by the most marvelous sight. "A dragoon!" I exclaim.

Louis leans out, summoning the man by gesture. The officer's hand rises slightly as if to salute, then noticing the post-master unharnessing a pair of horses, he lets it drop and says, "Monsieur, can I be of some assistance? Are you lost?"

Louis waits until the post-master leads the horses away. "*I* am most assuredly not lost, Captain, but it seems that some dragoons *are* for there were none at Somme-Vesle."

"Choiseul believed that the treasure we expected was not coming," the captain replies. "He told the troops to stand down."

"*Fou inutile*," the queen exclaims.

Useless fool indeed.

The captain's cheeks color. "I command forty men, but they are dispersed about town, and our mounts are unsaddled."

The post-master returns with fresh horses. As he puts them into harness, he narrows his eyes, staring fixedly at my brother. The captain climbs onto the berline's step to shield Louis from view.

"It might be best if you rode on," he whispers urgently. "I will reassemble my men and follow. You are but an hour from Clermont. One hundred and forty soldiers should be waiting there. They will make you safe."

As he climbs down, seeing that the post-master still has his attention on the carriage, the captain says, "I hope, Baronne, you will soon feel better." Then, turning to the post-master, he barks, "Is that all the faster you can work? There is an elderly lady in this carriage who is indisposed, and the members of her household are eager to get her to her night's rest."

Clever man! I'd wager had he been the commander at Somme-Vesle, the dragoons would have found a way to wait.

As soon as we are clear of the town, a whip cracks and the berline flies. The way is rough. We are jarred horribly. I hope we do not break a wheel, for that would certainly make things much worse.

Looking out into the thick forest, Louis says, "Our luck *must* change." Gone is the optimism that marked his voice for many miles, replaced by desperation.

We reach the heart of Clermont. It is not much more than a pretty church and a handful of buildings at the crossroads where we will, at last, turn north. In such a place, one hundred forty soldiers should be quite noticeable—and we spot a pair of dragoons, but not as we hoped to find them. They sit outside of an inn, glasses in hand, coats off, with a bottle of wine on the ground between them. We quickly learn that these soldiers, like those in Sainte-Menehould, were told our plan of escape had been abandoned. And again those who were to escort us have dispersed and must be collected, or at least those who are still sober enough to ride must be. We cannot wait for such an event. Every moment we delay increases our chances of discovery and apprehension.

As we ride on again, still unaccompanied, a terrible anger rises in me at the coward Choiseul. Was he so shaken by the attention of some peasants that he was willing to declare the whole escape abandoned without receiving word that we were captured or had failed to leave Paris?

The long light at this time of year was considered a blessing as our escape was planned. Roads are more dangerous in the dark. But now, as twilight finally begins to transform the sky, I wish fervently for darkness. I feel exposed. We ought to have been on this stretch of road more than three hours ago accompanied by nearly two hundred mounted men.

Who shall keep us safe now? Who but God, and, though it pains me to think it, He may have abandoned us too. I suppress a sob and, as the cloak of darkness at last slips into place, I pray as I have never prayed before.

Then, the thunder of hooves approaches—horses riding at a gallop.

I stiffen, and the queen does likewise. She carefully parts the curtains. I hold my breath, hoping with all my might that some of the dragoons who should by now be catching up with us have arrived. Two riders streak by in the darkness, gone so fast that I do not get any sense of who they are—only of who they are not. They lack the brightly colored coats and swords of military men.

Ahead, the tiny village of Varennes, lit by moonlight, clings to two different sides of a river. We have barely entered the upper end of the steep central street when our carriage stops. I expect to see a post-master, lantern in hand. But I see nothing.

"Where is the relay?"

"There is none," Louis replies, "but Choiseul arranged for horses to wait in the upper town. I am sure they are here."

You are sure of something Choiseul arranged? I wish I had such faith in God at this moment as my brother exhibits in a man who has already failed us spectacularly.

"Where are they then?" The queen's tone is less generous.

Moustier comes to the carriage window. "Our horses are not where we expected. We will search in some of the little streets."

"I'll help," I say, restless with the need to *do* something before all is lost. Before Louis can object, I am out of the carriage.

The guard on the box argues with the postilion. "We must go on," he says. "We cannot sit here stupidly in the dark, in a village too small to even have an inn sufficient for the baronne's comfort!"

"You *would* say that," the postilion retorts. "The baronne pays you, but the owner of these poor beasts pays me. They are due back by morning. If I let you drive them farther, they will be too tired to return. As it is"—he points an accusing finger—"you've used them hard; look at them!"

Our guard throws up his hands. Moustier stands beside me. I touch his arm. "Monsieur, I will look to the right, you take the alleyways to the left."

There are not so many little lanes as I would like. The first reveals nothing more than a few scuttling rats. As I continue my frantic search, I hope to hear shouts calling me back—to hear the horses are found. Instead, my own ragged breathing and the clatter of my puce shoes on the cobblestones are my only company. Stumbling, I put out my hand and skin my palm on a rough stone wall. The sting of this is nothing compared to the sharp ache of my fear. Increasingly desperate, I consider knocking on a door. But what would the inhabitants think seeing a young woman in the dark asking after horses? Turning back, I glance uphill toward the carriage, glowing slightly thanks to its lamps. There are now multiple figures beside it.

Some of our dragoons at last! I snatch up my skirts and run, only to find, when I arrive panting, that the king and queen have joined the guards in the road. They make a ring around the postilion.

"Just to the lower end of the village, it may be that my mistress's next horses are on the other side of the river," Louis says, holding out several gold coins.

The postilion eyes him, then pockets the money. "To Le Bras d'Or and not a yard farther. If your horses are not there, then perhaps your baronne can take a bed for the night"—he gives the guard with whom he argued earlier a defiant look—"if that is not beneath her." And as he turns to remount the lead horse, I hear the distinct and ugly mutter, *"Aristo."*

We climb into the carriage and set off down the steep hill.

A bell rings. I glance reflexively my watch. "It is not the hour," I exclaim, dismayed.

The clanging continues, punctuated by the crack of a whip. The speed of our carriage increases. I hear shouting and wonder if it is the surly postilion. I dare not open the curtains. Marie-Thérèse clutches her mother's arm. My brother says, "Come on, we are not thirty miles from Montmédy, we have come more than five times that far already."

A second bell joins the first, and through the curtains there are flashes of light, and shouts. *It is over,* I think. Then stubbornly, *No, it cannot be over! God would not allow that.*

A horrific jolt throws me from my seat, leaving me half atop my terrified niece.

A great many voices speak indistinctly. Then one rises above them. Our guard atop the carriage shouts, "Release those horses! What sort of place is this where innocent travelers are set upon! You behave like high-waymen!"

"We behave," comes a drawling reply, "like citizens of France and, as such, we demand to see who rides in your carriage."

"Why should that concern you?"

"Because," the same insolent voice responds, "I know who sits behind those curtains." The low and angry voices muddled together resemble the growls of an animal.

"You are acquainted with the Baronne de Korff?" Our guard's voice drips with incredulity.

"No, but I am Jean-Baptiste Drouet, post-master of Sainte-Menehould. I served seven years in the army of France, so I can recognize the king when he sticks his head out of a carriage window."

My heart pounds so hard that I fear it will burst from my chest. So close to freedom, is all to be lost upon the word of a man who handles horse teams along the road?

"The *king*?" Our guard tries disbelief again.

"Yes, Louis XVI of France."

Without warning, the doors on both sides of the carriage are wrenched open, and the doorways fill with torch-lit faces. A man leans in, his face a twisted mix of eagerness and contempt. I recognize him as the too-attentive post-master who stared at Louis while he conversed with the captain in Sainte-Menehould. His impertinent gaze sweeps over my brother. "Your Majesty," he says. From his lips it sounds like an insult.

To his credit Louis does not respond—merely looking at the man blandly.

"Young man," Madame Tourzel says sternly, "you mistake yourself. This gentleman is my man of business. I must ask you to close the doors before my daughters—whom you have terrified—are sickened by the night air, and let us proceed."

"We will close the doors, but the only place you are going is to see the mayor." The doors slam and a moment later the berline is being turned. Oh, to have even twenty dragoons at such a moment, let alone two hundred!

Madame transfers Louis-Charles, who, with that special gift of the very young is still half asleep despite all that has happened, to the queen's lap. "We must paint a picture," she says softly.

I know what she means: there is still a chance our story can save us. Which means there is no time for panic or despair.

I pull out the passports and hand them to Louis. "The officials in this little *ville* will surely wish to see them," I whisper.

This time when the carriage stops, only one door opens. Some number of National Guards, their uniforms askew, keep the crowd from pressing too close, allowing only Drouet and another better dressed individual to draw near. This second man clears his throat. "Messieur et dames, I am Monsieur Sauce, mayor of

Varennes, I regret this inconvenience, but I must ask you to descend so that I can see if your papers are in order."

"Nonsense!" Madame Tourzel sits ramrod straight, giving him the glance she used for decades to silence children in her charge. "My man has our papers"—she gestures to Louis who holds out the leather pouch— "You may look at them here, and then we will be on our way."

"Alas, Madame—"

"Baronne," Madame corrects him.

"Baronne, it is too dark for me to read properly here, but if you will only take a few short steps you will be in my home where I can examine your papers better."

The crowd presses closer. They lay hands on the vehicle and it begins to rock.

"Fine," Madame says. "Madame Bonnet, your hat, the children."

Antoinette retrieves the black-veiled hat she stowed so many miles ago in a more optimistic moment and places it on her head, obscuring her face.

Moustier helps me down, squeezing my hand by way of encouragement. The small cabriolet has been pulled up behind us—the queen's ladies, still inside it, clutch one another in apprehension. I am led toward the lighted doorway of what appears to be a shop. Entering,

I am surrounded by candles—piled, boxed, hanging by wicks not yet trimmed. So the mayor of this place is a candlemaker. He is bold indeed then to ask a person of birth and title, even if he thinks her only a baronne, to interrupt her journey.

Monsieur Sauce makes a great show of looking at our papers: bending over, moving his light along. But I have the distinct impression he is not reading—for his eyes do not move as one would expect them to.

Straightening, he says, "I regret to say there are some irregularities here. I must call for some of my fellows on the Municipal Council to have a look."

Moustier takes a step toward the shop door. I see what he is thinking: the moment to overrule this candlemaker has come. I put a hand on Louis's arm as the queen, with little Louis on her hip, takes Marie-Thérèse's hand. Moustier reaches for the door handle.

"I would not, monsieur," the mayor says. "The crowd is agitated. We have a company of guard, but I cannot vouchsafe that it will be sufficient to keep the crowd from rushing you."

I take a step to follow Moustier, ready to brave the crowd despite the mayor's bluster. I tug on Louis's arm and my eyes meet his, willing him to take a step. *Now, Louis! It must be now!* But his gaze breaks from mine and his shoulders slump.

None of us are going anywhere.

Madame tells her well-rehearsed story—a trip to Germany with her daughters—while we are ushered up narrow stairs. As we enter a tiny sitting room, I cease to hear her. On the wall opposite the door is a framed etching of my brother.

Sauce hovers as the queen transfers a sleeping Louis-Charles to the settee, and he plumps a cushion on a small chair for the exhausted Marie-Thérèse.

The mayor's wife ushers in three men. Two wear ribbon decorations; the third is an ancient fellow, dressed in the fashions of my grandfather's court. He is no sooner across the threshold than he sweeps off his hat and goes down on one knee.

"Your Gracious Majesty!" he exclaims.

We are undone. Not by an act of cruelty or bad intentions, but by a man showing a deep love and respect for his king. There is a wicked irony in this so strong that my eyes prick with tears.

Louis holds out his hand to raise the man up. "And you are?"

"Jacques Destez, Your Majesty. My wife is from Versailles where, when we were both younger men, it was my honor to see you there—but never so close as this."

Louis turns to the others. "Messieurs et madame, it is true," he says, smiling gently. "I am your king. I have come to live among you, my faithful children. I hope that you will welcome me."

My cheeks flush with pride at my brother's calm, heartfelt words. Without a moment's hesitation he embraces each villager in turn. Then stepping back, he nods.

"You have heard much about me lately that does me no credit. And perhaps, seeing me here, so far from Paris, you will believe the worst—believe that I make plans with France's enemies and would cross the border to wage war on her. Not true.

"What is the truth?" His hand sweeps out. "This is my beloved family. A handful of radicals have stirred Paris into a stew of violence, mistrust, and hatred, so that the city is no longer safe for us."

Madame Sauce gives a small sob, clearly moved by my brother's candor, and lays a hand on her husband's arm.

"Having been forced to live in the midst of daggers and bayonets, I have come to this beautiful part of France to seek the same freedom and tranquility you yourselves enjoy. I am headed to the citadel of Montmédy from which I will strive to restore the public calm and the rightful institutions of this nation."

"Your Majesty," the tallest of the men asks, "how can we aid you?"

"Let me go."

The men look at each other. Monsieur Sauce opens and shuts his mouth several times, but cannot seem to make a sound. And I hold my breath. Will these people be with us, or against us?

It is the tall man who manages, at last, to speak. "Your Majesty, we shall do better. The Municipal Council, which I am honored to head, will escort you to Montmédy at dawn. I will awaken the others immediately that we may organize matters."

Whereas tears only threatened me before, now they stream down my cheeks. These are tears of pure joy. My faith in mankind, and the divine order, is restored. The poison of the revolutionary thinkers has not, as I earlier feared, corrupted my brother's entire kingdom.

"I am grateful for your loyalty," Louis says. "Your honorable behavior and aid to me in this time of distress will never be forgotten."

Three of the men beam. But the face of the last— the member of the Municipal Council who has never spoken—is very different. His eyes are wary, considering. I do not like their look. I push that unworthy thought away. We have a fair promise from the council's head. Oh, how I wish dawn were minutes, not hours, away!

Madame Sauce brings cold meats and serves us

with a self-effacing kindness. She is smitten with little Louis-Charles, watching with a dreamy smile as the queen covers him with a blanket.

"Do you have children?" Antoinette asks.

"Alas, Your Majesty, I have not been blessed."

"Well, after today you must think of my children as also yours. For you have made all of us comfortable here, and in caring for the dauphin, you care for the future of France." The lady is so clearly moved that for a moment she cannot speak, and I know in her we have a true friend.

At last we are alone. I should sleep, but there are disturbing noises from below—voices shout the sorts of slurs and threats that we grew all too accustomed to hearing through the windows of the Tuileries. I try to tamp down my anxiety by remembering the promise of the council members, and the proud devotion of our hostess. They are all good, true subjects of my brother, and in the morning, they will come and see us on our way. As I begin to drift off there is a knock at the door.

The king springs to his feet, calling, "Enter."

The Duc de Choiseul strides in with another officer behind him. Both men are flustered, and both have hands on swords.

"Your Majesty," the disgraced duc says as he bows. "I am mortified by my own failure. I ought never to have left Somme-Vesle. I was a fool and a knave, and when we reach Montmédy you may dispose of me as you will. But for now, I am here, as is the commander of your hussars. We have between us a fraction of your loyal troops, as speed seemed more essential than numbers. But there are enough, I assure you on my life, to take you from this place. On route to Montmédy more will join us. You *will* be safe."

"We are safe now," the king responds. "Men of consequence in this village, including the mayor in whose house you now stand, have assured me so, and say I may depart at dawn."

"Majesty," Choiseul stammers, "are you . . . certain? There is a gathering crowd. They are armed and snarling."

Louis moves to the window, and the queen and I follow. Below, five or six score people, some with pikes and axes, mill about. They are nothing compared to the crowds that have filled the streets of Paris, but they must represent a significant proportion of the village populace.

"There he is, traitorous king!" a man shouts. "Following his Austrian whore into the arms of the Swedes and the Germans! Leaving us to die on their sword points!"

The king raises a hand for quiet and tries to speak,

but those below have no interest in hearing him. They are nothing like the good mayor and his tall friend. And suddenly in my mind's eye I see the cold eyes of the third councilor. Eyes I would not willingly trust.

"Remark, brother, many of them wear those horrible bonnets rouges," I say.

Choiseul adds, "Your Majesty, I do not know whether you should trust the assurances of those you spoke with here, but you may trust mine."

Can he? Can any of us have faith when you left us defenseless?

"Look beyond the rabble," Choiseul continues. "There are my men, *your* men."

Sure enough, a mix of dragoons and hussars are neatly assembled in rows, swords gleaming in the light of the rioters' torches.

"Give the order and we will harness your horses and part the crowd so that you can reach your carriage."

"And if they should rush you?" Louis asks.

"What are axes and pikes in the face of trained soldiers? If they are the sort to attack their king, we will answer them with force."

"And I will give Your Majesty my own sword"— Choiseul's companion pulls his weapon from its scabbard—"so that you may defend yourself if necessary."

"Strike down my own people?" Louis's dismay is palpable. "But they are my children."

I want to shake my brother. I want to point to Marie-Thérèse and Louis-Charles and shout: *These* are your children! But I cannot—to behave in such a manner before the duc, to show disrespect for my brother as king, would only demean us both.

So instead, I say quietly, "Your Majesty, surely being a king, as being a parent, sometimes means punishing. Sometimes a child cries because it is truly hurt, and if someone has hurt your subjects then, yes, you must right that wrong. But sometimes a child cries simply because it does not get its own way. This is true even when what it clamors for would be harmful to it. Your people do not know their own interests."

Both Choiseul and Antoinette nod vigorously.

And you do them no favor by coddling them.

"Majesty," Choiseul urges, "give the order, and we will be on the road north."

Louis puts his hand on the hilt of the proffered sword. I will him to grasp it. Indeed, were I king I would surely take it. But instead, Louis pushes it away. "No, gentlemen. I am moved by your devotion, but I cannot allow my poor subjects, however misled, to be injured—perhaps slaughtered—merely to be on a road that I have been assured I shall be allowed to take once daylight comes."

The dismay and disappointment that I feel are mirrored in Choiseul's eyes, and because of this I forgive his earlier failure. As the duc stands, at an obvious loss for what to say or do next, Louis arranges himself in a chair and closes his eyes. In only a short time he is snoring.

But I cannot sleep, nor can the rest. Choiseul and his companion sit on the floor at either side of the door, their backs against the wall. Glances pass between them, especially as the noise outside swells, but they do not speak.

Antoinette and I likewise exchange looks. I sense we are in accord: were the decision ours, the party would go on immediately. Frustration rolls over me in waves, leaving me equally nauseated and angry. I consider rising, shaking my brother awake and trying to reason with him—suggesting that since the majority of us believe we ought to proceed at once to Montmédy, perhaps that is the better course of action. Then my cheeks grow hot with shame. The divine order is the divine order; if I forget that, I become no better than the pompous Assembly members and misguided mobs we left behind in Paris who boast about how they are wise enough to rule themselves.

As man, as husband, as brother, as king, Louis's will governs our various fates.

That is God's law, and therefore it is as it should be.

As dawn arrives, so does Madame Sauce with water for washing. She says little. And when the king thanks her, she bursts into tears and runs from the room.

"Overwrought by my attention," Louis says confidently. "It won't be long before the good mayor returns with the members of the council and we are on our way. Perhaps the National Guard is assembled to escort us already."

I'm not so sure. For the rumble of the mob has grown louder outside. When the king goes to look and I join him at the window, I see my worst fears manifested. There *are* men wearing the uniform of the National Guard below, but they stand *facing* the royal troops! And the crowd is no longer to be counted in scores but in hundreds!

"Look who's awake!" a familiar voice calls. The post-master who so proudly denounced his king stands below the window with . . . Monsieur Sauce!

A little tremor moves my brother's hand where it rests on the windowsill. "I do not understand," he murmurs.

But I do. I have never been as good-natured or

good-hearted as Louis, so I understand immediately, the mayor and the council are not coming to see us on our way. *Why? What has diverted them from their honorable intentions?*

Shouts and the sound of horses moving at speed send a frenzied wave through the crowd. People turn this way and that, some run into side alleys or flatten themselves against buildings.

Please, God, let it be our royal troops; then despite my brother's miscalculation we will be saved.

Antoinette joins us at the casement, and our soldiers press in behind, discarding formality in their eagerness to have a view.

Half a dozen riders clatter down the steep street, dressed in the uniform of the National Guard. What a terrible sight, made the more so when Antoinette proclaims, "Monsieur Romeuf rides at the front."

Sure enough, there is Lafayette's aide-de-camp, a man we saw nearly every day of our captivity at the Tuileries. Like Lafayette, Romeuf—all earnest, youthful foolishness and democratic fancy—is a traitor to his noble family's history. As they draw close, I recognize the man beside him as another of Lafayette's minions, and in my stomach, more so even than in my heart, I know that the brief period when we might have gone onward—might have reached Montmédy and freedom—has closed.

Dismounting, Romeuf speaks with Sauce. The mayor points to where we stand, and surely Louis must notice how studiously he keeps his eyes from following the direction of his finger.

"Let us receive them with dignity," the king commands.

The queen sits, pulling the dauphin into her lap. The king stands behind her with his hand on her shoulder. The rest of us fall in about them. It is a marvelous tableau of family, royalty, and power. But a pretty picture is not much in the way of a defense.

Romeuf speaks the moment he crosses the threshold, "Your Majesty, we come with an official decree from the Constituent Assembly ordering your return to Paris."

Ordering! This puppy, this boy younger than I, presumes to give his king orders!

My brother takes the piece of paper Romeuf holds and glances over it. "There is no longer a king in France," Louis says solemnly.

Antoinette is less collected. Snatching the order from Louis, she jumps to her feet, leaving little Louis-Charles scrambling to find his. "Insolence!" she cries, casting the order to the floor and pointedly putting a foot on it. "What audacity, what cruelty! How dare the Assembly write such a thing, and how dare you present it without blushing in shame?"

Romeuf's cheeks do color, but he does not respond to the queen. Instead, looking pointedly past her, he says to Louis, "General Lafayette asked me to tell Your Majesty that Paris is in uproar over your departure. Rioters are everywhere, and accusations as to who may have helped you run wild. Property is being destroyed, but he fears greater violence—fears that women and even children might be killed."

"But not by royal troops!" Marie-Antoinette is not done with Romeuf. "Monsieur Lafayette worries about women who have taken to the streets armed. But who fears for *your* mother's children, *Baron*?"

Romeuf winces at his title as if it is an insult.

"Who fears for me and for my children? Am I not a mother also? And the king is a father, yet you ask him to carry his children back into the jaws of the mad dog that Paris has become."

"I ask only that the king acknowledge the authority of the Assembly and understand that his place is with them in calming Paris."

"We will need time to make ready," Louis says.

My stomach lurches, and tears course down the cheeks of the queen's ladies.

"Perhaps you could wait downstairs," Louis continues. "Surely neither your authority, nor the authority you insist the Assembly has, requires you to watch my family perform its morning toilet."

The moment the pair has withdrawn, Antoinette says, "Louis, I beg you, do not go with them! It will be the end of everything."

My brother gathers his shaking wife into his arms. "*Calme-toi,*" he says softly. "Calm yourself, my love."

"We must delay as long as we can," I say, collecting my thoughts, looking for the one chance that may yet save us. "With luck our dragoons will arrive, and the balance will shift in our favor."

Then the streets of Varennes will run with blood— blood of a quantity that might have been avoided had you ordered us on the road last night when Choiseul urged it. I am not fool enough to say it aloud. Not that I personally will regret such deaths—the members of the crowd have shown themselves implacable enemies of their king—but because Louis may well reject my plan if I say it. As it is, I worry he will not agree to delay.

But at last he nods.

"Perhaps I can play the invalid," I suggest. Louis does not dissuade me, so when the impatient Romeuf returns to press our departure, I put on a performance: swooning, shaking, and collapsing. The queen calls for wine and cool cloths for my head, then sits beside me on the settee, murmuring soothing words. And all the while Choiseul stands at the window.

When we are momentarily alone, he reports grimly, "There is no end to the crowd now, Majesty."

The door swings open without warning. Startled, I sit bolt upright.

Romeuf strides in. "I am glad to see Madame Élisabeth is recovered." His tone suggests he suspects the truth. "Because, Your Majesty, there must be no more delay. The crowds outnumber my men, your dragoons, and your hussars combined. Soon you will not be safe. It is time to go to the carriages."

He does not ask, he commands.

Louis nods. "Gentleman," he says to Choiseul and the commander, "stay close to Her Majesty and my children. I shall take my chances, but do not let them be harmed."

"We will die if that is necessary to protect them," Choiseul replies.

"I am afraid, Duc, that I must have one of you with

me," the puppy says. "The hussars and dragoons will not take orders from me."

"Why should they?" Choiseul gives the aide-de-camp a withering look.

"The salient fact," Romeuf replies coldly, "is royal troops are needed to provide a path for Their Majesties to safely reach their carriage. On the point of the king's safety I do not believe we are enemies."

"Sir," Choiseul replies with conviction, "from this day forward we are enemies on every point until one of us is lowered to the grave."

At seven thirty in the morning on June the 22nd, we emerge from the home of the duplicitous mayor of Varennes, making our way along a narrow path, bounded on each side by hussars holding back the angry mob. I make a point of looking at my watch, knowing this moment marks the turning point between bold action and retreat.

The crowd shouts, shoves, and spits, but I pay them no mind. To do so would be to dignify these ugly, ungrateful, and treasonous people, to give them power. *No*, I concede as I mount the carriage step, *they have power already—and having snatched it, they will not give it back.*

What will become of us?

Palace of the Tuileries, Paris, July 15, 1791

I sweep into the queen's bedchamber. "Dear sister, I must burden you with a delicate matter of my health." Antoinette offers a convincing look of concern, though she knows I lie. We simply need to be rid of the guard standing inside her doorway.

The number of guards placed upon us has more than doubled since our forced return. They stand beneath our windows as if we would fly down into the gardens, despite the fact those gardens themselves are so carefully watched that I do not believe a kitchen cat could escape them. The king and queen are required to sleep with their doors open, their beds visible to guards stationed just beyond their thresholds. These soldiers cannot be ordered out, and even the fiercest of Antoinette's glares does nothing to intimidate them. But we have discovered nothing frightens them away faster than allusions to women's private matters. Sure enough, the present spy steps gingerly into the antechamber, pulling the door shut behind him.

"Two women together, what could be dangerous in that?" Antoinette gives a wicked smile. "Do you have it?"

"Yes." I draw the decree from one of my pockets and hold it out. "The Assembly officially declares that the king was abducted, and that is how he came to be on the road to Montmédy."

"Delightful fiction! We must have wine," Antoinette replies, eyes glittering.

It may seem an odd thing to celebrate—this story that must stretch the credulity of even the most simple-minded, but it is the first decree of the Assembly that I have ever applauded. For this is a most expedient lie: it may save my brother's crown.

Shortly after our return to a palace full of broken furniture, slashed paintings, and a stench that made it clear members of the mob—come in a rage on word the king was gone—had used the corners of our home as a necessary, Deputy Condorcet rose in the Assembly declaring that since the king had tried to free himself from France, France could, without compunction, be freed of the king. This maddest of ideas came from one of the mousiest of men, for Condorcet called for a republic not in grand ringing tones, but so softly that the other deputies had to sit perfectly still to be certain of hearing him. As Condorcet finished, the Assembly exploded with delegates leaping to their feet, and soon half of Paris was in the streets shouting for Louis's overthrow.

When word arrived at the Tuileries, I was terrified. But my fear woke me from the self-pity I had allowed to swallow me. "Let us not lose heart in doing good; for in due time, if we do not faint, we shall reap." The passage from Galatians sprang to my mind and sent me running to offer Antoinette help in cultivating a young Assembly deputy named Monsieur Barnave. We met Barnave—if you can call it that, given he was a travel companion forced upon us by the Assembly—during our torturous ride back to Paris. And over those ghastly hours sweltering in the berline, Antoinette and I discovered the deputy was intelligent and far more pragmatic than many of his ilk. Certainly he has a better head on his shoulders than Condorcet.

I suspect it would horrify Condorcet to hear he helped us greatly in wooing Barnave, and in our scramble to preserve my brother's throne. Condorcet's radical rhetoric reminded men like Barnave—with property or prosperous businesses—that a complete overthrow of everything that has gone before would assure many months, perhaps years, of uncertainty, marches, and violence, all of which disrupt commerce. Such gentlemen might soon find themselves reduced to the poverty of the sans-culottes. An unappealing thought. So Barnave led the more moderate members of the Jacobin Club in breaking from it. These more reasonable men are in the process of forming a new political faction, a club that he tells us will be called the Feuillants. And this new brotherhood of more moderate delegates is the reason that the declaration Antoinette now peruses declares the monarchy inviolable.

Finished, Antoinette lays the pages on the settee beside her. "I can guess one of your favorite details—our guards were not named among our abductors."

"Yes!" Monsieur Barnave gave me his word that he would protect those faithful men who aided us in fleeing Paris. And it seems he has kept that word, although true-hearted Moustier and the other former members of Louis's Garde du Corps might easily have been made scapegoats.

What a blessed relief. I've worried about our guards since we descended the step of the berline in the courtyard of the Tuileries and I saw them dragged off. I sent Abbé de Firmont to inquire after them and bid him to say masses for them. The masses were said, but information on the men was not as easy to find. At last the abbé discovered where they were imprisoned, and I sent monies to make certain they had clean linens and food in case their families could not afford such niceties.

"How I wish I could hear Barnave's speech on the floor of the Assembly today in support of the Declaration." Antoinette sighs. "He read me a portion of it arguing for Louis's restoration under a conservative constitutional monarchy, and declaring republicanism contrary to France's true interests."

"I am in perfect agreement with his views on republicanism," I reply. "But I fervently wish no restoration was necessary." I am thinking of a supplemental decree, enacted today alongside the one I brought the queen, suspending Louis's political duties until a new constitution is adopted.

"Élisabeth, we could not move forward without compromise," Antoinette chides.

"Perhaps," I concede, "but no one has yet been able to satisfactorily explain how a king can be suspended from the duties placed upon him by divine right." I know Antoinette will not take up the point, for it is philosophical and she is, to her core, focused on the practical in a way that I alternately finding admirable and infuriating.

"You have not heard the boldest thing our Monsieur Barnave has planned." The queen lowers her voice. "He will conclude his speech with an appeal to *end* the Revolution."

The flesh on my arms tingles. "May God open the ears of the deputies to that wisdom. Will Barnave come to tell you how things went?"

"Yes," the queen says, "but in the meantime what else do you have in those pockets of yours?"

Antoinette has correctly concluded that the same servant who ran for the Declaration collected the latest slanderous flyers for me. How I wish I had told her to deliver the odious stack to my desk.

"Just the usual slurs."

"Nothing on the rights of women?" Antoinette laughs lightly. She refers to a document we received yesterday—not among the flyers collected on the streets, but from a boy who came over the garden wall while we were walking and pulled a packet from inside his dirty shirt. A note on the first page, from an actress named Olympe de Gouges, declared it to be a draft of her soon-to-be published Declaration on the Rights of Woman, which she was dedicating to the queen as "the most detested of women."

"It is quite something," the queen had said, more bemused than offended, "to be designated in pen and ink as the *most* detested of my sex, as if that were a badge of honor."

With a sigh I grudgingly pull the day's flyers from my pocket, laying them in a pile on the settee beside the queen. "Nothing so well written as Mademoiselle de Gouges's work," I say.

With a sweep of her hand Antoinette spreads the

papers like a fan. A great many are primarily comprised of pictures not words. Variations on the common caricature of the queen, skirt lifted to reveal her sex, with some politician—the perceived enemy of whatever faction printed the particular handbill—pushing eagerly between her legs, abound.

No matter how many times I see such depictions, I am mortified. Yet Antoinette merely says, "Apparently these *artists* have not heard how my appearance has changed; they still show my younger self."

The four nightmarish days we spent traveling back to our cage at the Tuileries aged the queen overnight. Antoinette's once luxurious hair turned white, as if she were a woman of six and sixty, not six and thirty. She is noticeably shrunken, reminding me of a flower that, falling from a vase, becomes desiccated before some servant discards it.

Antoinette slides one sheet from the jumble. "Poor Monsieur Barnave, this is the first time I've seen him depicted with me *in flagrante delicto*. His support of Louis is the reason behind his defamation." She shakes her head.

I quickly select another flyer and place it over the offending one. "Here is a novelty. What are you and my brother supposed to be?"

Louis and Antoinette are shown as animals joined

at the middle: my brother with hooves of a goat and white fur, the queen with spotted fur and cat feet. Snakes writhe on her head, among fashionable decorative plumes.

"'The two make but one,'" Antoinette reads the caption. "Who would consider this an insult? Is not every wife joined to her husband by the church so that the two are one?"

"You have forgotten, these revolutionaries have no use for the church, and even as they idealize domesticity in every other family, they revile it in ours."

It enrages me how pious praters like Robespierre, who insist politics is public morality, consistently overlook the happy domesticity of our royal family. Two nights ago I watched the queen sitting beside little Louis-Charles, holding his hand until he fell asleep because he suffers from nightmares. As I gazed upon mother and child wreathed in the light of bedside candles, I wished the villains in the Assembly could see what I saw. Then my stomach fell as I realized that even should there be deputies standing in the shadows with me, their eyes, clouded by misunderstanding and hate, would be blind to the touching scene.

"Let me take these away," I say, eyes pricking.

As I hurriedly gather the papers, one catches my eye. I ignore the figure's bawdy pose and one bare breast, in favor of the pleasant, round face with lively eyes under arched brows. I am transported to a better time: a warm day in the gardens of Versailles when I met a bright young woman who gave me a pamphlet on the need for judicial reforms. There is no mistaking her. But that girl's name was Sophie Grouchy, and here, beneath the slanderous depiction of her as a common street whore, alongside the proclamation "*res publica*," is the name Madame de Condorcet.

Good heavens, could the girl I met be married to the republican who calls for the dethronement of the king? I knew Condorcet had a wife, and I've heard of their salon—a meeting place for every sort of dangerous upstart. She and I, then, are on opposite sides, but even so, this ugly bit of paper saddens me. It seems that royalist or revolutionary, if you are a woman, those who consider you their enemy will make free to call you a whore.

Never mind, Sophie, you are no more "public property" than the queen. And like those slandering her, this piece of paper shall go on the kitchen fires.

The queen reaches out to touch my arm. "Courage, Élisabeth, there are surely more in France who, like Monsieur Barnave, can be turned to reason. Stability is needed, and your brother and the long line of kings before him represent that. Why even the Marquis de

Lafayette seems, in the light of recent events, to have become fonder of the idea of the monarchy."

"Has he?" I ask mildly.

Taking my leave, I head toward the kitchens. As I walk, my mind wanders to General Lafayette, who came upon me in the gardens shortly after our return.

I was burying the puce shoes ruined in our failed escape.

Discarding a pair of shoes is common enough. I give the women who dress me two or three pairs each week. Burying a pair of shoes, however, was a unique act. But our return to Paris felt like a death. So I buried the shoes to have a grave to mourn beside.

I was on my knees mounding dirt over them when Lafayette found me.

"Madame Élisabeth, have you fallen? Let me help you." He held out a gloved hand.

"Monsieur," I replied, "I do not need your help. In fact, I would never seek it."

"I am sorry to think that."

"Sorry, perhaps." I rose so that I could look him in the eye. "But you cannot be surprised, for you dragged my family back to a city that would destroy us."

"Madame Élisabeth, would you believe me if I said I wish I had let you go?"

His belated regret did no good, and only stirred my

anger. "Why? Because men like Danton and Robespierre, who have long slandered and threatened my brother, now call you traitor?"

He stood straight beneath my withering gaze, unflinching. "No, because I too easily dismissed such men as outliers, but they are able to command multitudes. I fear where they will lead. I want a constitutional rule of law, not anarchy and violence."

"And I want nothing but my peaceful life at Montreuil. I long to wake and find this time at the Tuileries a dream, and my family not in danger thanks to an angry populace you helped foment. I would suggest, Marquis, that we both resign ourselves to disappointment."

I shook the dirt from my skirt and prepared to go, but Lafayette stepped in front of me. "I will not ask for your trust or forgiveness, but I will tell you truly: I have never wished His Majesty harm and will do what I can to prevent his injury or abuse."

"If you do, Marquis, you will be blessed. Not by me, for I am an imperfect woman who holds many grudges, but by your far more forgiving Creator."

Leaning in, he lowered his voice. "Let me help you, Madame Élisabeth. You, I *can* help because you are not a crowned king or queen. I cannot return you to your farm, but quiet arrangements can be made for you to join friends in the countryside. Or if you prefer, is not your closest friend abroad?"

I hesitated. To escape and be with my dearest friend . . . I swayed where I stood, tempted.

"You can go tomorrow," the marquis said.

Tomorrow. The word echoed in my head, first in his voice, then in my own. But another voice interrupted—the voice of my abbé saying: *You are Élisabeth Philippine Marie Hélène de France.*

"Marquis, your offer is well meant, but sacred duty keeps me with Their Majesties."

I shake the memory from my mind as I push the slanderous flyers into the kitchen fires. The heat on my face feels purifying. I turn toward my apartments with a firm step. Despair is not in my nature, and not in our interests.

Let us see what the new constitution will say; what powers it will give the king, and which it will take away.

Salle du Manège, Paris, September 14, 1791

We are now to be a constitutional monarchy.

Antoinette and I take our seats to bear witness to its formal enactment. Autumn sun streams through high windows, playing upon the tricolored bunting decorating the side balconies. There is laughter among the members of the crowd, pressed shoulder to shoulder, and nearly all wear tricolored baubles.

I liked the Salle du Manége so much better when it was a royal riding school filled with prancing horses instead of the wicked, prating men who make up the National Constituent Assembly.

Below, deputies mill about. There is Condorcet. No matter how many times I see him, his mild appearance astounds me. This man who presses the most radical viewpoints looks more like the bookish tutor to some duc's son. His expression is entirely pleasant, as if he merely discusses the weather with Robespierre.

The latter's hand can be seen plainly in all the worst parts of the new constitution. His Jacobin Club is much smaller since the Feuillant defection, but that does not lessen his confidence. No man likes to stand on the Assembly floor and hear himself speak more than Robespierre.

Lately he has been ranting about Gouges's Declaration on the Rights of Women. It seems that the greater number of even the most radical men find the so-called natural rights of citizens that they demand for themselves unpalatable as applied to the fairer sex. So Robespierre and his Jacobin rabble vilify Gouges. But in a twist to their ugly attacks, they fixate upon the work's dedication to the queen, calling Gouges "Royalist" in a tone suggesting this is the worst of all infamies. Robespierre employs the same word against the Girondins, politicians he once considered allies, but whose recent desire for moderation has caused him to turn upon them. So the Royalist ranks swell in the agitated minds of the Jacobins, without those of us who are true Royalists gaining any genuine allies at a time when we could sorely use them.

Thinking of allies, I turn my eyes from the avowed enemies of my brother to find Barnave. He meets my gaze and smiles.

"He believes the Revolution is complete," Antoinette told me last evening when I lingered after her *coucher*. "Once the constitution is sworn, we shall stop *becoming* a new France, whatever that term means, and simply *be* one."

I'd found myself wondering how Monsieur Barnave could be so optimistic when every day there continued to be violence in the streets of France. *And violence begets violence*, I'd thought. For word had recently arrived that while revolutionary and royalist landholders argued and clashed in the colony of Saint-Domingue, those enslaved there had risen up in their own sort of rebellion.

"But will those who have found their life's work in marching, shouting, and destroying accept that?" I'd asked. "The worst habits are often hardest to break, and I suspect venting your anger through violence is one."

"I asked Barnave much the same," Antoinette had replied, arranging her bedcovers. "I told him the constitution is but paper, and a disappointing, fragile bit of paper at that. He agreed it is imperfect and says that other laws will be needed. Political clubs must be taught their place. They are private organizations, not a part of the government, and will be ordered to confine themselves to helping citizens understand the new constitutional monarchy. Attacking that government will be treated as sedition."

I stare at Barnave again, wondering how he intends to effectively rein in the clubs. Or rather how his successors will. In a handful of days, the entire National Constituent Assembly arranged below will be disbanded in favor of a new body called the Legislative Assembly. Barnave will not sit in it. *No* current deputies are permitted to. They have done this to themselves, and I cannot make sense of it, though I suppose it fits with their general lack of appreciation for the value of continuity. Will the next Assembly's deputies have the stomach to use prison and troops to suppress violence?

I already know Louis will have no such means at his disposal. No, the time when my brother might have ordered royal troops to fire in his defense is gone. I will always consider it one of his greatest failures that he did not use that power while he had it.

The constitution lay on Louis's desk for ten days before he signified his assent. I made it my business to read the thing in its entirety. Our so-called constitutional monarchy leaves my brother a mere puppet. He is commander of the French army but cannot order troops without the Assembly's consent. His ministers may argue for royal policies on the floor of the Assembly, as if their being heard was a privilege and not a king's right. Perhaps the only true thing of value my brother has been given is the power of veto, although the Jacobins fought hard against it. There is every reason to believe this power will be needed.

This constitution is not the document I prayed for. How I wish my loyalty and duty to the king did not require me to witness his formal acceptance of it.

Someone raps for attention on the Assembly floor. It must be time. As we wait for Louis and the president of the Assembly to enter, I gaze at the small, circular dais below and realize for the first time that two simple armchairs are placed there. Where will the king sit? I look for a throne suitable for my brother. Finding none, my eyes return to the chairs and notice one is painted with fleur-de-lys.

Dear God, they will seat Louis beside the president of the Assembly, with his head at the same level!

If the king is bothered by this insult, his face does not show it. He speaks well and briefly. But even as he swears to maintain their demeaning constitution, to defend it against foreign attack, the deputies cannot show the simple courtesy of taking off their hats.

Behind my fixed smile, I clench my teeth until my jaw hurts. At last the thing is over. As deputies file out, Louis sits unmoving.

"I must go to the king," Antoinette declares. I ought to follow. But I cannot bear to. Instead, I twist and turn through the crowd until I am free of the Salle du Manège. A guard at the westerly entrance to the palace gardens opens it for me. Inside, I pick up my skirts and run so hard that I am winded. I lose a shoe, but, rather than stopping, I kick off the other. The pain of the gravel on the soles of my feet distracts me from the more pressing pain in my heart. It also forces me to slow then stop. In the distance something catches my eye—a great balloon floats in the direction of the Champs-Élysées, streaming with an endless number of tricolored ribbons.

I sit on the nearest bench, put my face in my hands, and cry.

"Madame Élisabeth." The voice is gentle. I look up to find Monsieur Moustier standing before me, hands clasped behind his back, thinner than when last I saw him.

"Monsieur, you are released!"

"All of us, Madame Élisabeth," he replies. "The others are inside awaiting His Majesty, but I came away to thank you, on behalf of us all, for your kind care. The food and wine fed more than our bellies—they let us know we were not forgotten."

I take the handkerchief from my sleeve and wipe my cheeks. "Monsieur, you could never be forgotten, not after the care you took of us on the road to Varennes and the ignominy you suffered on the road back. The members of our royal party decided, eyes open and risks weighed, to ride out of Paris hoping to improve our situation. You followed out of loyalty and duty, expecting nothing for yourself, and risking much."

"That is what true Frenchmen ought to do for their king, and for his family." He smiles broadly. "And I did expect something—I expected to feel as I did during my years in the *gardes*: vital, useful, alive."

"I am so glad, monsieur, that you *are* alive. But how did you know it was I who paid the prison warden?"

"I only know one Mademoiselle Rosalie." Again the smile.

When the abbé took my money to the prison, I knew he might be required to say on whose behalf he acted. I also knew my real identity might harm our guards. So, on the spur of the moment, I decided to adopt the identity used on our journey.

"Shall I escort you inside?" Moustier asks with a slight bow. "Unless I am mistaken, these are yours." The hands that were behind him come forward, holding my lost shoes.

"Thank you." I laugh. Not in the contrived manner of the court, but heartily as I have not in a long time. My mood changed, thanks to this good man, who looks conscientiously away to preserve my modesty as I reveal my feet to put on my shoes.

Palace of the Tuileries, Paris, November 1791

"Have you new shoes to show me?"

That voice! Casting my book aside, I spring up and close my arms around the Princess de Lamballe, still in her traveling cloak. "I would give every pair of shoes I own to have you in England again," I tell her.

On the day we were discovered missing, Lamballe began her own journey out of France. She has been in fashionable Bath, soliciting help for the king and queen—alas without success. Then last month Antoinette wrote, begging the princess to come home. The queen and I quarreled bitterly about that.

"We must have a high-profile émigré return," Antoinette argued. "Since we were dragged back to Paris, the number of aristocrats fleeing France has increased to a frenetic pace."

"Can you blame those who go?" I had retorted. "France roils, so they go despite being deprived by law of three-fifths of their income by departing. And now the moderates think to persuade them back? Are the émigrés supposed to believe what they have lost will be restored if they return? I would not believe it."

"They would be fools to trust the deputies, but they must put trust in their king," Antoinette had flashed back. "If Louis regains his powers, they will be made whole. But he cannot do so with so many titled French men and women gathered outside our borders where they are perceived as a threat. Some portion of the scores who have fled must return."

And our loyal, darling Lamballe has.

"That's a fine welcome." Lamballe answers my somber face with a light laugh, but when I hold her at arm's length the red rims on her eyes are strikingly obvious. "I'd forgotten what it was to be caged until the gates of the city closed behind me," she confesses. "Still it is a blessing to see you, and I will be glad to be with the queen."

"She has missed you greatly." It is the truth, and as it must be Lamballe's consolation, I infuse my voice with as much warmth as I can. But I cannot help feeling that if Lamballe and others like her are encouraged to return and things go badly, their fates will be on *our* heads.

As though reading my mind the princess says, "I have made my last will and testament, and my peace with God. I cannot say this to the queen; it would feel like a betrayal, as if I do not believe in her. And it is not that."

"Of course not," I reply gently. "You do not lack faith in Their Majesties, but in France—in the thousands who ought to be my brother's subjects but now imagine themselves his equals or even his masters. I feel the same."

It is not only Louis's subjects who disappoint. My brothers, the Counts of Provence and Artois, also give me much cause for vexation. Provence, having successfully escaped even as we were captured, has set up his own court in Coblenz, a city of the Rhineland, where Artois, abroad for months, joined him. Their behavior in Coblenz is being compared to the worst excesses of Versailles by those in the Assembly who oppose the constitutional monarchy. Do Provence and Artois never think of His Majesty? Never think how their behavior might deepen his danger?

"If only the queen could make Emperor Leopold understand how dire our situation becomes," I continue, offering Lamballe a second embrace. "Could persuade him that if the French monarchy falls others will follow. But he seems willfully blind." I cannot keep moroseness from creeping into my voice.

The queen is bitterly disappointed in her brother's tepid response to her endless appeals. She is equally frustrated with the Bourbon king and queen of Spain. Even the king of Sweden equivocates, and he has the Count von Fersen at his elbow arguing for help for Louis. It seems we are completely abandoned by Louis's fellow sovereigns, who stand to lose just as much as he should the contagion of republicanism spread beyond France's borders. Yet Antoinette does not give up. Only yesterday she showed me her hands, ruined with calluses from the many letters she writes daily.

"Or perhaps Leopold has other political interests," Lamballe replies. "But our interests, yours and mine, will always lie with Their Majesties. That is why I came back. Antoinette wrote that she hopes my return will set a fashion. I would prefer to set a fashion for a new hairstyle." She places both hands on her coiffure and strikes a playful pose. "But I will not say that to the queen. No, from this moment I shall be light of heart and witty of conversation. If we are all in a cage, I will act the brightly colored bird."

Lamballe is a better woman than I. Only this morning I told Abbé de Firmont I find it hard not to meet whatever optimism is left in Antoinette and Louis with a myriad of facts that would undermine their hopes. For we had clung to desperate hope once before, and I feared this moment was Varennes all over again. By way of penance, the abbé instructed me to rise each day determined to live without bitterness and be useful to those around me.

I try to be useful to Louis, truly I do.

But my brother's largest fault is his goodness; or rather his inability to perceive what is not good in others. Intrigue is foreign to his soul. So even as Antoinette and I point it out all around him—the disloyalty of his ministers, the constant shifting of factions in the Assembly, and the duplicitous nature of the deputies who make a show of compromise with Louis to his face but mock him in other quarters—he often cannot, or will not, see it.

But to say any of this to Lamballe would be to fail in my penance, and a cruel repayment to a woman who sacrifices so much. So instead, I embrace her again and say, "That is all we can do, dear one: make the best of our captivity . . . and pray for freedom."

"I cannot understand why the Assembly is so angry!" My brother stamps into the queen's apartment. "*They* wrote the constitution, not I, and it clearly promises religious freedom."

"Ah, but *they* did not write it, Louis," Antoinette reminds him, looking up from the tapestry we are working on. "Their predecessors in the Constituent Assembly did."

"But they can read."

"Presumably"—I stick my needle into the work—"some of them."

"So they know freedom of conscience is enshrined in that document, which also gives me the veto. They should not be surprised then that I veto a decree stating that any priest still not willing to swear an oath to the constitution will lose his pension and be driven from his parish. Do priests, like every other Frenchman, not fall under the constitution's protection? Have not holy fathers consciences?"

"They most certainly do, but many deputies do not," I reply.

Louis's veto of the latest law punishing priests is the king's second in as many weeks. The first involved a dreadful decree sentencing émigrés who fail to return to death in absentia, and providing that lands belonging to other members of their families, even those who themselves remained steadfastly in France, would be confiscated. The king could not permit that, for it punishes the innocent for the actions of their relations.

Yet despite the sound logic and moral footing of my brother's vetoes, the more radical members of the Assembly use them to defame the monarchy.

"This is the work of the Brissotins," Antoinette says.

The latest of France's political factions is made up of men expelled from the Jacobins immediately after the constitution was adopted. They are trying to make a name for themselves, and the quickest way to do that is by bringing decrees to the assembly floor.

"They create laws to bait you, Louis," Antoinette continues. "Then publish broadsheets attacking you for exercising the royal veto."

"I cannot do otherwise but veto, no matter how they portray me," the king responds. "Surely you see that.

Barnave does. He told me he himself would veto this measure."

Antoinette looks studiously at her needle and I wonder, *Will she tell the king that Barnave begins to suspect her support of the constitution is a ruse?*

"Monsieur Barnave is leaving Paris." The queen says it matter-of-factly as if it did not have larger implications.

Louis stops walking and his mouth falls open. His eyes take on a pained look. Barnave ought to have confessed this when encouraging Louis's vetoes—ought to have admitted that he would not be here to share the consequences. I've thought Barnave intelligent, and naive, but now see him for a coward.

"So the Feuillants cede the field of battle to these new upstart Brissotins," I say, weary from trying to keep up with the ever-changing realignments among the political clubs.

"Yes," Antoinette replies. "But we will not. There is increasing talk of war, and the Brissotins beat the drum most loudly. Let it come."

Louis looks stricken. "Let it come? But my dear, given the way the constitution is written, I would be required to declare it! To declare war against your brother, whose help we have so ardently sought."

"I will write to Leopold and explain that it is an expedient." The queen's tone is entirely matter of fact. "You will lead France's patriotic defense. If France wins, all will celebrate you and your influence will be greatly restored."

"And if France loses?" My brother begins to pace again.

"I suspect it will." Antoinette shrugs. "And that may be better for us, because the radicals who invited the war will be destroyed, and the monarchy will be reborn of the ashes."

"Élisabeth," Antoinette says, suddenly noticing me, "why do you smile? What could possibly be funny?"

"I am sorry, not the thought of war I assure you. It is just so strange to hear you agreeing with Robespierre."

Among the papers gathered for me by my *dame d'atour* these last weeks there have been dozens trumpeting war as a "school of virtue" for the citizens of France. But one voice has been absent from those braying for battle.

Robespierre opposes war.

Since the dissolution of the Constituent Assembly he has been working as the public prosecutor for Paris. But no matter his position, his word carries great weight with all the worst sorts of people. Radicals and revolutionaries called him "incorruptible" for his alleged purity of principles, modest way of living, and refusal of bribes. As if any man who suborned radical revolution could be said to have pure principles.

"Robespierre says that war will play into our hands," I say.

"How fortunate then that, for once, no one listens to him." This time it is Antoinette who smiles.

The Streets of Paris, April 25, 1792

The streets are crowded. "I should never have agreed to bring you," Moustier says, looking around in the manner of a man accustomed to assuring the safety of others.

"How could you say no to Mademoiselle Rosalie?" I glance into his worried face and smile. That is who I am today, dressed in the clothing I wore to flee Paris—clothing I never thought to don again. But when I heard about the guillotine, I had to see it.

And these clothes were the only way.

"Mademoiselle Rosalie was very persuasive," Moustier concedes. "But if you are harmed, I do not believe His M— Monsieur Durand will absolve me of guilt."

"Monsieur Durand will not miss me, and we have both been in more dangerous crowds." I momentarily recall the twisted, horrible faces lining the route on our ride back from Varennes. How members of the mob murdered an elderly count—shot, trampled, and cut him to ribbons—merely for taking his hat off to his king as our carriage passed.

There is none of that today—no anger in this mob. Instead, there is a jovial mood and a tremendous amount of patriotism.

The Brissotins have had their way. We have declared war on the House of Austria.

But, in a twist of fate, that house is no longer headed by Emperor Leopold. *Odd,* I think, as we make our way through the throng, *while I thought Leopold useless, his death overwhelmed me.* Perhaps it was only the suddenness. But it felt like something more—a presage of further ills. I suspect the king felt a similar portent, because when he stood before the Assembly reading out the declaration of war, his voice faltered, and when the queen and I went down to him afterward, he kept murmuring "sentenced to death" in an odd, absent way. As for Antoinette, as unnerved as she was by the loss of Leopold, she still hopes this war will save us. Given the report of fifty thousand Austrian troops massed at the Belgian border, perhaps she will be proved right.

"What should a lawyer and a lady's companion— good citizens both—have to fear on a day such as this?"

I smile at Moustier again. The last time I left the Tuileries, it was to be displayed alongside the queen and the children at the theater. I do not like to be used as a prop. This outing, being of my own invention, however, makes me feel liberated. "We even have our tricolor cockades." As we stop to let a cart go by I touch his, pinned to the lapel of his coat.

"Tell me," Moustier asks, "why do you wish to see a man executed? I have seen men die, by swords, musket, and, er . . . other ways. But surely you have not."

"No. But I have seen animals die on my farm." I have killed chickens myself—being someone who wished to understand every aspect of the raising of my animals. I do not say this because it might shock Moustier, and he is looking rather shocked already. "Besides, I once met someone concerned with the cruelty of France's methods of execution, and it has been a matter of interest to me ever since."

When word of this new device reached me, my first thought was of Madame Condorcet, and of the pamphlet she gave me. As I promised her, I'd read the whole of it, and a few others on the same subject besides. The wheel, hanging, and many of the other things described seemed brutal to me, even if I could not accept the premise that death as punishment ought to be banned. I was very glad when my brother, after a man was saved from death on the wheel by an angry crowd, abolished that manner of execution. And I would like to think that my reflections on that topic, which I shared candidly with him, had some influence on his decision. I almost wrote to Sophie telling her what I had done. I wish now that I had.

"If I would not kill an animal in a manner that prolonged suffering, I surely wish those people found guilty of crimes and sentenced to die might do so swiftly, after seeking God's grace," I say to Moustier.

This is a rare point of agreement between myself and the Legislative Assembly—for it is they who decreed decapitation the only acceptable manner of executing the guilty. Dr. Joseph-Ignace Guillotin proposed this change of law and promoted the machine we will see today. I wonder how he feels about it being named for him.

Will Sophie Condorcet be in the crowd to witness this enlightened improvement—a manner of execution that is swift, sure, and without suffering? Might she recognize me, even after the passage of years? I never considered that. And if she does, will Sophie reveal me despite our former sympathetic discussion? No, it is foolishness to think she might espy me where none will reasonably expect me to be. And besides, I have already promised the vigilant Moustier we will stay at the fringes of the crowd.

"The condemned is a hardened highwayman," Moustier says. "I doubt he is a man for prayer."

"Ah, but the Bible teaches that no one is beyond redemption. Perhaps, faced with his end, he has confessed. And after a suitable stay in purgatory, he can attain heaven."

"I would be sorry to run into him there," my companion replies, looking extremely dubious. "But I suspect even in that setting we would move in different circles."

We enter the place de Grève. The crowd is so thick that, being short, I feel as if I am in a forest. But I can see the Hôtel de Ville rising over the heads of the others and before it, on a raised platform, is the guillotine. I give an involuntary shudder and my hand tightens on Moustier's arm.

I did not expect it to be red! But it is: tall and blood red. At its apex a pulley suspends a great blade, shining silver in the afternoon sun, its edge a dramatic angle. Below a small table extends behind the contraption. This must be where the highwayman will lie to put his neck through what looks like a wooden yoke. On the other side of that yoke a simple wicker basket sits.

Dear God, that must be for his head!

A massive roar announces the arrival of the condemned. A man mounts the steps between guards, followed by a drummer. I cannot see his face from this distance, but his shirt is red.

"So the blood will not be obvious," Moustier murmurs, suggesting that he likewise is caught off guard by this detail.

The man's arms are bound, and he is quickly lowered to the board, facedown. As the upper part of the "yoke" is secured so that only his neck and head protrude, the crowd falls eerily silent. It is as if the thousands of souls present hold one collective breath. Someone on the platform speaks but I hear only sound, not words. While the inaudible official pronouncements are made, a man with a shovel pushes a small wheelbarrow across the platform, coming to a stop near the condemned man's head.

There is a drumroll. At its last beat, a silver flash— and the man's head is gone! Gone so quickly that I do not see it go! There is nothing but a red stump where it used to be. The man with the shovel throws sawdust on the platform.

The crowd groans. I do not know what I was expecting but not a groan, and not grumbling, but that, too, starts immediately. "Too quick," someone shouts. A woman just beside me cups her hands around her mouth and yells, "Bring back the gallows!" Others take up the cry.

"The head! Show us the head." This demand grows to a roar.

The executioner stoops over the basket. Straightening, he holds up the dead man's head by its hair. The crowd is delighted. A cheer goes up. Apparently most people do not want swift and painless—they want blood, as if killing a man were sport.

I feel nauseated; not by the sight of the strange, lifeless trophy, but by my sobering realization about the nature of those I stand shoulder to shoulder with.

"Monsieur, I have seen enough. Please take me home."

"They want me to withdraw my veto of the twenty thousand troops."

"Louis?" I ask, startled. They are the first words my brother has spoken to me, other than those necessary to play backgammon, in days. When he has not been meeting with deputies or ministers, Louis has maintained a nearly absolute, dejected silence. Antoinette has been sick over it, and the children both have been in tears over their dear papa.

My brother meets my eyes. "At the meeting of my council today, my minister of the interior, Monsieur Roland, read aloud an extraordinary letter. It demanded I withdraw the royal veto preventing the establishment of twenty thousand provincial soldiers on the outskirts of Paris."

"Minister Roland, the man with the receding hairline and no proper buckles on his shoes?"

"Yes. His letter was a *reprimand*. There is no other word for it." Louis's eyes mirror the confusion I feel. Roland is a moderate Brissotin, and not a particularly notable one. I would not have expected such bold, and inappropriate, action from him. "Roland claims that my opposition shows a lack of enthusiasm for France's defense. A retreat from my avowed support of the constitution."

I snort. No matter how many times the king appears before the Assembly voicing his support for this or that action, the deputies are never satisfied. They want a level of fervor Louis will never manage, not only because dramatic statements are contrary to his nature, but because much of what he is asked to support is neither good for his crown nor good for France.

"One line in particular—" Louis shakes his head. "'The revolution has been made already in the people's minds; it will be accomplished and cemented at the cost of bloodshed unless wisdom forestalls evils which it is still possible to avoid.'"

"That sounds like a threat," I say. It also sounds very unlike the minister I've met in passing—a rather indecisive man without a particular flare for conversation. It seems to me the rumors that his wife writes his speeches and letters may be true. *What kind of woman must she be to think she has the privilege of advising a king when she is no minister—let alone has the right to reprimand one!* This thought is quickly followed by another: *I advise Louis. But that is different because he is my brother, my family, my blood.* Still, I think that those criticizing Manon Roland are too harsh. Although she oversteps in counseling a king, she surely does not do so in counseling her husband.

"It sounded like a threat to me as well." Louis's eyes are filled with dejection. "Just as twenty thousand provincial soldiers do. I fear such men will be called to Paris not to train—whatever the deputies insist—but in preparation for some attack upon us. Which is why I exercised my veto."

"Rightly," I say firmly, seeking to reinforce one of my brother's rare decisions that put himself and his family first. "You must not trust the deputies, or your ministers. Not even moderates like Roland, who enter the Tuileries with half bows and platitudes."

"They certainly do not trust me. Roland claims Parisians see my veto as a sign I am planning to use foreign forces against them and would have them defenseless so that I may more easily triumph. But I would not do such a thing!" Louis's face colors, and he picks up the game pieces, although we are not finished and he was winning. "In charitable moments, I tell myself the Assembly is only afraid. My people are afraid. Fear makes men foolish. It makes them entertain thoughts beneath them and causes them to act rashly. And my subjects are terrified of Austrian armies on French soil."

The king gives a deep sigh. "I am not a man for this epoch, Élisabeth. But, as I am not merely a man but a king, I must try."

"What does that mean, Louis? Surely you will not rescind the veto? The survival of the House of Bourbon may depend on your fortitude in upholding it," I push.

"No, I will let the veto stand. I believe I exercised it wisely. I have not used my veto a dozen times, but each time I do some faction finds the action offensive."

Relieved, I dare push him in a new direction. "While we speak of the veto, Louis, I would beg a favor. Please protect our beleaguered clergy from the Assembly's latest attack. Their decree providing that denounced priests will be sent to Guiana . . . it is a death sentence. Few deported there survive even a year. It is a place for criminals, not God's faithful servants."

"Yes, that is a wicked law." Louis puts his hand over mine on the game table. "I will veto it. I cannot imagine any but those who deny the very existence of God will blame me."

"The opinions of those who deny God, brother, are worthless. One should wear their bad regard as a crown."

Palace of the Tuileries, Paris, June 20, 1792

I knew the date as soon as my eyes opened this morning. A year ago, I sprang from my bed with a sense of purpose and full of hope. Today cries of "Tremble tyrant" and worse assail us on the feeble breeze. Below His Majesty's bedchamber windows, every gate is open and the gardens fill with "citizens" pushing past the National Guard, while these soldiers stand gape mouthed as if under a horrible enchantment. There are so many marchers, surely all Paris must lie deserted.

I am furious at the marchers, who believe the lies saying Louis works to surrender the capital to France's foreign enemies, but even more so at the newspapers and the ranting radicals who drive such sheep to the streets. And I have a particular resentment against now former minister Roland. His letter castigating Louis for vetoing the encampment of soldiers has been carried in too many papers to count. Or rather his *wife's* letter, for this past week there were nearly as many flyers showing him with the cuckold's horns as there were of Louis, and Manon Roland is widely being shamed and mocked for writing her husband's now famous tract, even as the letter itself is praised.

If I were to shame her, it would be on the content of her prose not because she was a woman writing it.

Staring at the crowd, my racing pulse quickens further as I notice banners decrying the king's veto protecting priests—the veto I urged upon him. Satan must be well pleased with the godless citizens of Paris.

The marchers carry more than lettered strips of bedsheet—they bear all manner of crude weapons: pikes; hatchets; tools of their various trades; anything, it would seem, that is sharp or heavy. As they pass directly below, a malodorous mix of sweat, grime, and I know not what else, rises up through the dreadful heat. I am tempted to take my handkerchief from my sleeve and cover my nose. But I would not have the grimacing, gloating men and women see the bit of cloth and think they have reduced me to tears.

"It seems the twentieth of June is not a day of good fortune for me," my brother remarks in a failed attempt at sangfroid.

The Princess de Lamballe comes running in. "They throw themselves at the gates to the grand courtyard!"

We race to take up places at windows in the king's antechamber overlooking the *cour*. Crowds surge against the gates on some unseen shouter's count. Then the gates are gone—opened, broken, I cannot tell—and a shouting horde sweeps up the château's outer staircase.

Madame Royale bursts into tears. The queen puts an arm around her, and we retreat to the bedchamber. We are there but a few moments before a knock comes. It is too civilized a sound to be the invaders, so Louis calls, "Enter."

The *chef de bataillon* of a company of the National Guard enters, flanked by a handful of grenadiers. "Your Majesty, the crowds are inside the palace. If you show yourself, they might be calmed."

"Or they might fall upon him in a frenzy and murder him, which some in the Assembly would dearly love!" The queen steps forward, lifting her chin and placing a hand on Louis's arm. Even as a voice somewhere in the rooms beyond can be heard calling for her head to mount on his pike, Antoinette remains unbowed.

"Majesty, upon my honor, I swear to you that we will do our duty to guard His Majesty. But there are not so many of us that we are likely to be successful should those approaching lose all control."

The sound of splintering wood, sadly familiar to me, punctuates the commander's point.

"If Your Majesty will deign to meet them in his antechamber, to receive their deputation, things may better remain within our power to control." The sounds of the crowd and of their destruction draw closer. "In haste, Your Majesty, please."

Louis steps forward and the grenadiers close around him. My *belle-soeur* loses her grasp. Another guard draws her in the opposite direction, while Lamballe urges Antoinette to secure the children.

The queen cannot follow Louis, she has other duties. But I can. Advising is no longer enough—I must act.

I push between two of the grenadiers accompanying Louis. I can see the surprise in their eyes, and I am surprised by my own physical strength, but not by the strength of my will. The door shuts behind me. I am close enough to hear the bolts sliding into place. They cannot force me back now.

I am jostled into a man in the middle years of his life. As he turns to see who runs upon him, I recognize Lieutenant Colonel François Louis Bartelemy de Sainte-Amaranthe, father of the beautiful Émilie. Sainte-Amaranthe has long been in my brother's service and was once a member of the king's Garde du Corps. Now he stands with his hand on his sword and a look of fire in his steel gray eyes that speaks both of his courage and of his devotion to Louis. Springing to a spot between the king and the outer door he declares, "They come, Majesty." Louis glances about, then climbs atop a coffer standing in one of the windows.

Good, this is a crowd that must be shown their relative place.

The first of the marchers breach the door and pour in, rushing forward as grenadiers move to join Sainte-Amaranthe, forming a protective line before the king. I press myself against the nearest wall. A member of the guard hangs back at my side.

He ought to be with the king! I have barely thought it when a man at the front of the mob raises an ax shouting, "The fat pig must die like one!"

In a flash, Colonel de Sainte-Amaranthe blocks the villain's arm, grabbing the handle of the ax, and with a single, violent twist ripping it from the man's hand. "This is your king!" the faithful colonel shouts, his face as distorted with anger as the would-be attacker's. His passion seems to surprise the assailant and those around him. *Did they think no one would resist? Are they so drunk on convenient Jacobin lies?*

Pushing the disarmed man back, Sainte-Amaranthe raises his chin and cries, "*Vive le roi!*" All around him grenadiers take up the chant. Despite their good intentions, their shouts draw additional marchers into the chamber. In a matter of moments the press of bodies is such that I cannot breathe.

Perhaps it is this desperation for air, but when the guard beside me surges forward to join those intent on pressing back the crowd, I go with him, then beyond, until I am through the mass of them and attempting to clamber up, gown lifted without thought for my personal dignity, beside my brother. As I teeter precariously on the edge of the coffer—as likely to topple backward into the sea of our enemies as to find myself securely atop it—Sainte-Amaranthe offers me his hand in assistance.

"It is the Austrian whore!" a voice tinged with hatred cries.

Sainte-Amaranthe opens his mouth. Squeezing his hand, I lean close and whisper, "Do not disabuse them." Then, having found steady footing on the window seat, I turn to face the mob.

A woman in front of me presses against the colonel, holding up a little gibbet, with a roughly fashioned cloth doll hanging from it labeled "*Marie-Antoinette à la lanterne.*" She laughs as I recoil, and then spits, barely missing me.

"We have her now!" someone shouts. "We are poor citizens if we let her escape alive!"

Under other circumstances, I might laugh at being

mistaken for Antoinette. With her slender frame, the more girlish me was long jealous of the fashions she could wear that I could not manage with my farmer's-wife figure. At this moment, however, being mistaken for the queen is serious business. But I like it very well. If this mob thinks I am she, Antoinette will be safe elsewhere and have time to secret the dauphin.

The tip of a pike brushes across my arm coming to rest at my breast. I look into the eyes of the man holding it. His face is nearly as red as his ugly bonnet rouge, and his eyes bulge, putting me in mind of one of the frogs at Montreuil. That image breaks the back of my fear.

"Take care, monsieur," I say, raising a hand and pushing the pike aside. "You might wound me, and I am sure you would be sorry for that." I lift my chin, mimicking the queen's familiar gesture. "I am not your enemy."

Mentally I add that lie to the things I must confess to the abbé. And if I do not live long enough to confess, I have already resigned myself to significant time in purgatory. Adding to it, both by my lie and by my lack of true repentance for it, seems but a little matter.

"You fools!" That voice! My eyes shoot to the doorway and find the figure I expect—the fruit seller who led the delegation of rain-soaked market women to

Versailles. It does not matter that nearly three years have passed. I could never forget that face, or the brash manner in which she met my eyes and pronounced her name, Louise Reine Audu, self-proclaimed Queen of the Market Women, in response to my inquiry as if she were my equal. "That is not the Austrian bitch. That is Princess Élisabeth."

My heart falls, and the crowd appears even more disappointed than I. There are curses and murmurs. Someone near the door slips out, and the hair on my neck stands up. Oh, how I hope Antoinette and the children are safely under guard.

"My sister Élisabeth is not your enemy, nor am I." The king raises his voice to be heard.

"Then, Monsieur-le-Royal-Veto, sign the Assembly's decrees!" someone shouts.

"Give Paris the soldiers needed to protect us from the Austrian devils," cries another.

"How can monsieur do that when he is a *cocu* in more ways than one? Show him, Pauline!"

A young woman in a striped skirt with a mass of dirty, light-colored curls spilling from beneath her bonnet rouge holds forth a pike with bloodied bull testicles dangling from it. "I'd like to cut yours off, you parasite." She spits the words, her eyes full of hatred. *How can she hate so very deeply a man she does not know?*

Louis does not retreat, despite the threat. "I vetoed in accordance with my conscience." He sounds remarkably patient—like a tutor explaining a simple mathematical problem to a young child. "The constitution gives me this right. It is my responsibility under law."

There is a burst of noise from the crowd—none of it flattering. Before us, the colonel and the other grenadiers tighten their ranks preparing to fend off an attack.

"If monsieur is such a good citizen, where is his bonnet rouge?"

This question is followed by cries of "Find him one!" Until, again on the end of a pike, one of the despicable hats is held out.

Plucking the bonnet from the pike, Louis puts it upon his head. It is too small and, to my eyes, makes the king ludicrous. But for the first time some of the sounds from the crowd are appreciative rather than derogatory.

"We shall toast France, mother of us all," the king declares with gusto.

Wine and glasses are quickly found and handed about. The toast is made. The glasses, like the wine, disappear—likely to be pawned by whichever rioters have pocketed them.

Surely, I think, the crowd will now disperse, appeased. And the crowd does begin to move, rotating as the hand of a clock, but as some marchers pass out of the antechamber, more enter, and we remain trapped as if reviewing troops. Only these troops are endless, and they do not fight on the same side of things. As this mass—*sans-culottes*; market women; tradesmen; even a handful of those I might, under other circumstances, consider respectable—parades past, each new assemblage repeats the demands of those who went before. Each must be treated to the same explanations by Louis, although he must be weary of making them, and although the idea that a king should explain himself to his subjects is, in itself, demeaning.

I give up listening and, fixing what I hope is a look of convincing composure on my features, watch the hands on Louis's tortoiseshell and gold ormolu clock. As the second hour of our horrible vigil draws to a close, a change in the atmosphere of the room commands my attention.

The mayor of Paris arrives. He is known to me, for he was another of those men deputized by the Assembly to bring us back from our failed escape that began one year ago today. He casts me a lewd glance, and I remember how he opened his knees when he sat next to me in the berline, pressing his thigh into mine until I felt dirty and humiliated. Recalling this unwanted contact, and how he bragged to the other deputy present that I fancied him, my cheeks grow hot where I stand.

The man was loathsome then, and has not changed. After tilting his head and smiling at me to let me know he sees my discomfort, he heaps accolades upon the creatures who torment us, commending the "dignity" with which they came. Then he finishes by inviting those who were not asked to enter the Tuileries in the first place to leave, and by calling the whole of the day a "civic fete."

The nerve!

But he is a man—being overly confident of his own worth and utterly without honor—precisely perfect for this crowd and this moment. And when he finishes, people begin to file out without being replaced, their shouted threats giving way to loud shows of good humor and bold assertions of "victory."

When the dreadful rioters are at last gone, I collapse on the coffer while my brother's face whitens. "The queen," he whispers, and a flurry of activity whirls us to Louis's bedchamber to wait as Colonel de Sainte-Amaranthe leads a search for Antoinette and the children. Neither Louis nor I are inclined to go to the windows and watch the retreat of the crowd; hearing their shouts is enough . . . or rather too much.

I do not know what to say to my brother. I have no

advice left. So instead of exhorting, I ask, "What will Your Majesty do?"

"Take this off, before Antoinette sees it," Louis replies, sweeping the bonnet rouge from his head.

The flash of red transports me—I see not the crimson bonnet, but the red of the tall, stretched beams of a guillotine, of a condemned man's shirt, chosen to match the blood that would be spilt. I sway slightly and reach out to steady myself, eyes falling to the floor where they come to rest on the toes of my shoes: bright scarlet.

And I know a true moment of resignation, fearful in both its content and its power.

There will be no restoration for our royal house. God will not save us. Our foreign allies will not save us. Our Royalist subjects, bless their loyalty, will not save us either.

And we cannot save ourselves. The taste for blood is too strong in the people of France.

This revolution will end for Louis as the English one did for Charles I—whose history my brother reads obsessively these days—in dethronement and death. I wish it were not so, but wishing changes nothing. All I can do from this moment is look toward the life of the next world and step forward boldly in this one as I did today: standing beside my brother—my king—until the bitter end.

PART IV

❖

The Politician

It is easier to avoid giving a man power
than to prevent him from abusing it.
—MANON ROLAND

Caen, August 1792

The Revolution has become a great whore, and I fear so have I.

We began the same. We began with vows: the Revolution with oaths recited to France on a tennis court, and I with oaths recited to Jean-Marie Roland in a church. We both began with such shining aspirations: to mold a nation, to mold a marriage. How did we both go wrong?

I walked slowly along the river, a dirt path soft beneath my shoes, which were better suited for city cobbles. I had come from Paris to Caen on the pretext of needing a few days of sea air and calm after the city's heat and violence, but in truth I had run here to escape my conscience. The river's lapping seemed to whisper accusation. *Harlot*, it said. *You and your new nation both.*

I cannot say where the Revolution began to career off course—to splinter from a passionate, united call for change into bitter factions clawing at one another and baying for blood. I was not in Paris to see it all begin—I was not in Caen, either, but in Lyon, helping build my husband's career as a wife should, both of us poring eagerly over newspapers full of Paris politics. So I did not see the Bastille fall; I did not see the women of Paris march to bring the king from Versailles—I only read about such things and wrote about them, too, as my husband began with my urging to enter politics, to correspond with leading assemblymen. It was only a year and a half ago that we arrived in Paris to set foot on the revolutionary stage.

There was nothing wrong then in my marriage, but I could see what was wrong with the Revolution. "It is absolute folly to put any faith in the king." Walking along the alien river here in Caen, I could hear the words I'd spoken in private to my husband, back in the days when there was still hope Louis would work with us all in good faith. "He has no belief in our constitution or our Legislative Assembly. Does no one realize that?" Perhaps the Revolution's spiral toward chaos wasn't entirely Louis's fault, but his stubbornness blocking every sensible move the Assembly made just gave the radicals more to froth about, as if anyone needed *that*. "The sooner he is put aside, the better."

My husband had laughed. "Hasty words, my dear. If the king is not sincere, he must be the biggest liar in the kingdom. No one can pretend to that extent!" Roland had been made minister of the interior by then, an appointment that had surprised many but certainly not me. I knew the worth of the man I married—naturally others would see the value of this man come from Lyon with his plain black suit and his heron-stooped posture from years of patient work over a desk and his shining faith in the new world we were creating. But in those days my husband and so many of his colleagues still believed we could have both a king and a constitution, and it nearly drove me to distraction waiting for them to wake up.

"Every time I see you go off to the council with that confident look on your face, I feel sure you are going to commit some folly," I said, dryly. I'd been going over my husband's papers in preparation for one of those useless meetings, highlighting the points for Roland to make to His Majesty. "You and the other ministers come home in a state of euphoria simply because the king has been polite to you. I fear you are all being fooled."

"But things are going quite well . . ."

Roland stopped saying that soon enough. August's heat had brought crisis and confusion to Paris in its wake: the National Guard storming the palace, the massacre of the Swiss Guard, the hero Lafayette forced into exile—there simply didn't seem to be an end to the things that could go wrong this summer. The day the royal family was at last placed under arrest, I prayed we'd finally seen the last of the bloodshed.

"I wish the king no ill will," I'd said softly, gripping my husband's hands tight. "He is not a bad man." Truly, I had taken no pleasure in the sight of Louis Capet's bewildered face as he and his draggled little family entered the ancient Temple's tower. But how could any man born and bred to be a despot believe in a cause other than his own power? How could anyone so steeped in luxury understand the desperation that drives the hungry? Royalty were all like that, even the most well-meaning—the king's sister, Madame Élisabeth, with her saintly reputation for generosity and good works had, according to her household accounts, bought *sixty-three pairs of shoes* in the span of less than three months! How can such people have any real notion what world their subjects live in?

No, it was far better to put them aside and let us rule ourselves. When the royal family went to the Temple, I pitied them but breathed a vast sigh of relief. Let the sun set on the Capets; the people of France no longer needed well-fed, diamond-decked kings and queens to determine their fate. France was moving forward now into a new government under an Executive Committee, a National Convention, and a Revolutionary Tribunal.

More committees, I couldn't help thinking. More

committees to disagree with one another, when you already couldn't round a street corner in Paris without tripping over a cluster of moderates chanting slogans at a cluster of radicals shaking fists. But I had done my best not to be cynical. At least now we had a nation made new, and the bloodshed would be stopped.

And for myself, I had a marriage to a great man, a man who would help lead France forward, and the wicked feelings inside me would be stopped.

So why wasn't any of it stopping? When did the slide become impossible to halt? A thousand steps from vows on a tennis court and vows in a church to the betrayal of all those vows—where did the fatal step happen?

I did not know.

But the Revolution was no longer cleaving to her new government like a faithful wife, but selling herself to every divisive new faction rising from within—to men who craved violence, power, and vengeance against the former ruling class more than they ever craved stability, peace, and prosperity.

And I had become unfaithful too. There was a letter hidden in my writing table in Paris that proved it—a letter from a man I could no longer pretend I did not desire—and I had run to Caen to get away from it, but there was no escape.

"Are you well, citizeness? You have gone quite pale."

I blinked, realizing that my footsteps had halted as I stared blind out at Caen's river. A woman had paused beside me—no, a girl; she did not look much more than twenty with her gray eyes, her dimpled chin, and her blue muslin gown. "I am quite well, thank you." From the book tucked under her arm, she had come to the river to read and stumbled instead on Manon Roland and her useless brooding. "I'm sorry to have intruded upon your reading."

"I've read it before." She showed me the book: Plutarch's *Parallel Lives*. I'd read it too. "Are you from Paris, citizeness? I could not help but notice your newspaper—"

She indicated the papers tucked under my arm. More from habit than anything else, I had carried on my aimless walk the latest newspapers from Paris. Seeing the eagerness in the girl's forthright gray eyes, I passed them over.

"*Le Pere Duchesne*, only two days old! It takes so long to get news out here . . . *ugh*, why bother with *L'Ami du Peuple*? It's such a rag, nothing but Citizen Marat ranting."

"Listen to an enemy rant and you can learn much about him," I said, liking her energy, her decisive contempt. I, too, had been a girl who devoured political journals rather than society gossip.

"If you detest the ranters as I do, then perhaps we should be friends." She smiled. "I am Charlotte Corday."

And I am a harlot, I thought. Even standing by this pretty river, talking politics to a gray-eyed child with a volume of Plutarch under her arm, there was no getting away from either the Revolution or my own sin.

"Are you staying in Caen long? I have so few people to discuss politics with—my cousin says a girl my age should be circumspect about such an enthusiasm." Anger glinted briefly in young Charlotte's eyes. "I say she is wrong."

"So she is. To take open interest in the shaping of a nation is the most appropriate enthusiasm imaginable." I put my hand up as she made to pass the newspapers back. "Keep them. I must return to Paris."

The flash of anger turned to wistfulness. "I wish I could go to Paris, Citizeness—?"

"Roland. Manon Roland."

She knew of me; I could tell from the blink. I made myself smile as I bid her farewell. Much as I wished I could stay here, I could not hide forever—not from the letter on my desk in Paris, not from the roiling of the Revolution, which threatened to spin out of control.

It was time to go home.

❈

Paris

It had only just turned September, and the noise of yet another angry crowd drifted up from the street below the ministry. *What makes them riot this time?* I thought, pushing aside the speech I was drafting and running to the window. Perhaps two hundred men had flooded into the courtyard below, all tricolor badges and reddened faces, waving crude cudgels and shouting. Surely all Paris was weary of mobs and bloodshed by now—what had brought them screaming and maddened to my doorstep?

"Maman—" My daughter tumbled white-faced through the door of my private study, blond curls flying. "They're shouting for Papa. Is he—"

"He is in session with the council, *mignonne*." As she ran to bury her face in my side, I shriveled in shame. An artist might have seen the picture I made before the window—a small, auburn-haired woman of thirty-eight clutching her ten-year-old daughter, muslins trembling as her eyes raked the crowd below for the face that mattered most—and titled the picture *Wife Prays in Virtuous Terror for Her Husband*. But a truer title would be *Harlot Swoons in Base Longing for Her Lover.* Because even as I cradled my daughter, I could not pretend my thoughts had flown first to her father with his receding hair and earnest expression. No, I searched in terror for a head of dark curls above broad shoulders, for bold dark eyes above a mouth that quirked in rueful humor. I knew he was not there, but my heart clutched in fear for him, anyway—the man who had penned the short letter that had sent me fleeing to Caen.

> *Manon, I love you. I cannot pretend I do not. I love your straight brows and your eager way of jumping from a carriage and your fine mind like a diamond. Tell me you love me too. Say the word and I will come to you.*

God help me, I thought, though it had been a long time since I called upon the God in whom I did not truly believe. I had come back to Paris and to my duty, but passion was still unraveling us both—Paris with her passion for blood, and Manon Roland with her passion for—

No, I thought, bringing myself up sharp. *Do not think his name. Nothing has unraveled that cannot be knit back up.* So I put my daughter from me with firm hands, saying, "Hide upstairs, *ma petite.*" I had no illusions as to what a crowd of Enragés might do to my sweet girl with her virginal looks and lovely fair hair. I'd been the same age when—but that was another thought to be cut off sharply.

Sweeping past the gilded cornices and Venetian mirrors to the antechamber below, I found my maids clutching each other and whimpering. They fell on me with a torrent of words.

"—riots in the prisons—the National Guard is killing prisoners in their cells—"

"—they're saying our men will march to defend Paris against foreign armies, and they cannot leave prisons full of aristos and counterrevolutionaries behind to seize the city—"

"Really, now," I scolded, trying to inject sense into the panic. "No pack of royalist sympathizers who has spent the last months sitting in prison straw is going to storm out of the prisons and seize the city."

But no one was listening. This was more fear whipped up in the streets by radical Jacobins, fear they could use for their own ends. Men like Citizen Danton, Citizen Robespierre—I'd invited those men to dine at my table in better days, and now their names made me want to spit.

"—the men outside are demanding to see the minister," a valet whispered.

"Send word to the crowd that the minister is not here," I said crisply.

"They are not listening, madame—I mean, citizeness."

The noise outside had grown uglier, but my blood pulsed coolly. Alarms, guns, and street agitation never sent me into hysterics as they did many women. My blood rose at such sounds in a kind of enthralled fascination, and now I was grateful for the distraction. I could put the letter upstairs out of mind as my heart beat to the familiar pulse of *Listen—this is the sound of great events happening, and you are privileged to find yourself at the center.* If danger came with that privilege, so be it.

I clasped my hands before me, noting that they were steady as granite. It was never danger that made me tremble, it was sin. But I hadn't sinned yet, not past all reckoning, and neither had the Revolution. "Go to the crowd below, and invite ten men upstairs to see me. Ten only."

"Madame—"

"Ten men," I repeated, sweeping up to my husband's study. I had never liked this ostentatious palace, which came with my husband's appointment, but I let the sumptuous gold-corniced ceiling and inlaid desk give me the weight of Roland's authority as I arrayed myself: white-clad, calm, and implacable.

They prowled into my presence, grinning: ten men in trousers, vests, and bonnets rouges, shirts open to the navel, restless with unslaked appetites. Frightening, yet I also had the urge to laugh—because I had never seen anything so second rate in my life. It was so difficult to make a revolution without becoming emotional; radicals like Danton and that frothing lunatic Marat were always whipping themselves into a frenzy, stirring panic and chaos in their followers—in men like these—to overcome any obstacle. Who needed to pass a vote in committee when you could get it done faster by whipping up a mob?

Whereas men like my husband appealed to reason and law, trusting in gravitas and intelligence to light the way. That division between emotion and logic, more than any other, was the one beginning to divide this new government. In the beginning it was the royalists and the revolutionaries, but now there were factions among the revolutionaries, and more than Jacobin or Girondin or any other party name they might call themselves, they were divided into the men of extremism and violence, and the men of moderation and reason.

Well, I would follow reason as long as I lived, and never abandon my faith that my fellow men would do the same. They needed only to be shown the calmer path.

"Welcome," I greeted the envoys. "How may I assist you?"

Their leader stepped forward with jutted chin. "Jean-Théophile Leclerc," he said, staring at me as if expecting a reaction. I didn't give him one, even though I knew exactly who he was—one of the founders of Les Enragés, a man who had joined the uprising in Martinique against slavery. I could laud him happily for such action, but not his swaggering and frothing now that he was back in Paris. Who can trust a man who refuses to deliver a speech full of ideals, but insists on shrieking it? "We're honest citizens, ready to set off to defend the city."

The news of Verdun falling to the attacking Prussians had swept over Paris yesterday like a great wave; rumormongers said the enemy would swarm the capital in three days. I wanted to roll my eyes and demand how any army laden with baggage trains and artillery could get here so quickly, but these men were clearly already seeing Paris burned and sacked by morning at the latest. "We have no arms, citizeness," the man continued rudely. "We've come to see the minister and demand weapons."

"The minister of the interior has never had arms at his disposal. You should address yourselves to the War Ministry."

"We've been there. No arms to be had there either." Leclerc spat, narrowly missing my hem. "All the ministers are traitors. We want to see Roland."

"He's not above arrest," came a mutter from the back. "No one's above arrest."

I wanted to swallow, but I would not let them see my throat move. "Is there a warrant?" Who would move against us? Had the split between the men of reason and the men of violence really deepened so quickly? "If there is, show me."

A thickened silence. "Maybe we will," the leader said, eyeing me. "Maybe we won't."

Another mutter from even farther back: "Maybe we don't need one."

They were all in motion, some pacing with jerky steps, some rocking on their feet and flexing their hands. I could feel that they wanted to come around behind me, make me look back and forth like a cornered mouse, but I had purposely set myself before the vast bulwark of Roland's desk and they could not encircle me. Since the age of ten, I had not gone into a room with any man without gauging where to set my back, for I swore I'd never let myself be flanked by someone with bright predatory eyes again.

They wanted me to beg to see their warrant, to beg for mercy. I deflected instead. "Well, whether it is a warrant you are to present or arms you wish to seize, the minister is not home. Come search the building with me; you will see." I spoke like a busy housewife with supper to get on the table; the best way to get restless men into line. After all, they had all once had mothers who clouted their ears and told them to behave themselves. "If you want Roland to speak to you, go to the Marine building where the council is in session . . ." *And just try to arrest my husband in front of the council,* I thought as I led them on a brisk tramp through our private apartments, waving them through empty rooms to show I hid nothing. By the time they realized I was speaking truth, they looked more like foolish small boys than burly swaggering men. As they withdrew, Leclerc even doffed his red cap and begged pardon for intruding.

"You are forgiven, citizen," I said graciously, even as some frozen part of my mind thought, *Had Roland been here, I think you might have killed him.*

My maids wept in relief as the doors closed and locked behind the men, but my pulse still beat fast and cold. Going to the window, I could see among the restless seething crowd a man in shirtsleeves waving a sword and yelling out that all ministers were traitors. "Fetch me a coach. I must warn Roland."

I was a child of the Seine, a daughter of Paris. My marriage took me to Lyon, but I grew up looking out over the smoky horizons beyond the Pont au Change. I had loved this city all my life, yet that night I learned to hate it.

"The murders at the prisons go on." My husband had a deep, fine voice that made up for his clipped way of speaking—his voice had been the first thing to draw me to him—but in the grainy gray light of this terrible dawn, he sounded as frail as a man one hundred years old. "In the Abbaye, at La Force, at the Bicêtre . . . yesterday evening in the Faubourg Saint-Germain, there was an attempt to move an overflow of prisoners to the Abbaye. People were lying in wait with pikes and swords. They murdered every man and woman, there in the open street, and all Paris watched." He shook his head, astonished and grieving. "After so many died at the Tuileries, I thought we were beyond such madness."

I sat on the floor with my head in my husband's lap, as exhausted as he. After delivering my warning to be

on his guard, all I could do was wait as the night deepened. Roland returned near midnight, and neither of
us had been able to sleep in the ostentatious bed with
its canopy of ostrich feathers.

Why? I could not stop thinking. *Why?*

The massacre at the Tuileries on August 10 had
been horrendous enough—perhaps six hundred of
the royal family's Swiss Guard torn to pieces; another
three hundred Parisians killed—but this was worse,
far worse. The Tuileries riot at least could be laid at the
door of panic and miscommunicated orders, but these
prisoners pulled from their cells had been slaughtered
in cold blood.

"It is not right," I whispered. "Jailed noblemen—
some may have been useless aristocratic parasites, but
it doesn't mean they were plotters. And there were so
many others who could not have been guilty—priests,
petty offenders . . ."

"Women." My husband's hand moved over my hair.
"The poor Princess de Lamballe—they say she was
raped, pulled to pieces, her limbs displayed on pikes . . ."

I'd heard of her, a silly blond creature who was one
of the queen's lovers if you believed the gutter press,
which I certainly did not. The poor woman hadn't
earned such a terrible fate. Nor had the other women
who died this night, down to the ragged prostitutes and

beggars of the Salpêtrière. This revolution could now say it had executed women . . . children, too, for we'd heard of small bodies lying among the dead.

A shiver racked me to my marrow. I had always thought that my sex and my daughter's youth would protect us from violence in this great endeavor but now I knew better.

No one is safe.

I shuddered again. "You say this was no vast mob of killers, just small bands of armed men. Did no one try to stop them?"

My husband sounded lifeless. "No one lifted a finger."

"I hate this city," I heard myself say, voice shaking.

"The citizens had no orders to defend the prisoners—"

"Orders!" I looked up, dashing away tears of rage. "Does a man need to receive orders from his officer when it is a question of rescuing people who are having their throats cut? How can liberty find a home among cowards who stand by watching violence that fifty men with a little backbone could have prevented?" I would not stand by to watch any man, woman, or child be dragged from a cell and butchered without trial. I would charge with my bare hands.

Roland only looked at me, helpless. "What do we do?"

It was the question that defined our marriage. *What do we do, Manon? How do we proceed, Manon? Tell* me, *Manon*. I looked at my husband—twenty years older than I, his complexion yellowed by strain, his hands hanging limp—and wished for a moment that I did not have to find the answer. That I did not *always* have to find the answer.

But Paris was drowning in blood, and if it could be saved from its worst impulses, the answer had to come from someone. It might as well be me.

"Acts of terror can be suppressed only by firmness," I said at last, rising to my knees and taking his hands between mine. "The men who encourage such acts hate you anyway, since you have tried to check them. Make them fear you. Impose your will."

He looked anxious. "How?"

I went upstairs to my writing desk, looking for a long moment at the letter still lying there. His handwriting. *Manon, I love you . . .*

I burned the letter in the hearth and sat down to a blank sheet of parchment. "Paris will not be allowed to surrender to her worst instincts," I muttered, sharpening my quill. "Nor will you, Manon Roland." And I began to write.

I never had the slightest temptation to become an author.

Any woman who acquires that title loses much more

than she gains—men dislike her, and women criticize her. If her work is bad, they make fun of her. If it is good, everybody says she cannot have written it herself. If forced to admit she was responsible for most of it, they turn to picking holes in her character. No, a woman gained nothing by picking up a pen and writing under her own name; she would only pay with her reputation, and I had spent my life avoiding *that* trap.

Yet that day, my pen flew swift and sure.

By evening I sat slumped and drained, as Roland paced before the dying fire reading my words. "'—it is the duty of the constituted authorities to put an end to this chaos, or see themselves reduced to nothing—' That is excellent, my dear."

I smiled faintly, looking at my husband: minister of the interior for the second time, reinstated this August after his fiery letter of reprimand to the king had gotten him dismissed in June. Never had I been prouder. Not of that letter, which had since become famous, but of the stand he had not been afraid to take, even if it cost him his office. Small wonder he had been reinstated after Louis Capet fell, as our revolution realized it needed men of principle. Roland read on now, light shining through his thinning hair—he had always scorned to wear a wig. "'—if this declaration exposes me to the fury of certain agitators, well, let them take my life . . .' Is that not too strong?"

"The times call for strong words."

"But to issue a direct challenge like that, that I am happy to die rather than abandon my stance or my post . . . there are many things to live for besides one's post, after all."

There is nothing to live for above duty, I thought. *A minister ought to stay at his post in the face of anything.* But I chose not to say that. Instead, I smiled, murmuring, "Amend it as you see best."

He sat down with my sheets and his quill.

I knew people whispered that I meddled in politics through my husband, that he never spoke a word in the Assembly not written by me. Of all the mud inevitably flung at people in public life, it was that charge that nettled me the most, not that I ever let that show. Why should I not share in my husband's work?

I would never put myself forward in any unseemly way; that was not a wife's place and I would never overstep my role. Not for me any notion of equality, all those silly notions put forward by women like Olympe de Gouges, penning her Declaration of the Rights of Woman and accomplishing nothing at all but to make every man in Paris either chuckle or froth. No, a woman's role was properly filled behind the scenes, behind her husband, and I was steeped in my husband's ideas. If I took up a pen to draft his speeches, well, it was because as a woman I had far more leisure for writing. Maybe I had a certain knack for imbuing his style with more boldness and strength than he might have achieved unaided—it had been my pen that drafted the famous letter he read aloud to the king in June—but once Roland discovered how well I could interpret his thoughts, he relied on me entirely. What would make a woman happier than to see her husband gain acclaim with her own words?

Watching him edit the address, I suddenly remembered my darling maman, gone these many years, looking over her embroidery at my young self and asking with some exasperation why I had turned down the latest suitor. "He has a high regard for you and will be happy to be guided by you. You could dominate him."

"Oh, Maman," I had said with a sigh. "I have no use for a man I could dominate. I cannot marry a great baby."

"*Mignonne*, you are very hard to please—for you do not seem to want a strong man either."

"I certainly do not want a man who would give me orders," I replied with all the assurance of a girl who knows nothing. "But neither do I want to have to control my husband. These little men who are five feet tall with great beards, who never cease making it clear that they are the masters . . . if a man like that started trying to make me accept his superiority, I should quickly resent it, while if another man gave way to me entirely I should be embarrassed by my own dominance."

Then came my mother's smile, wise and amused. "I see. You want to control a man in such a way that he thinks himself the master while doing exactly what you want."

"That is not it at all, Maman," I had sniffed at the time. I still think my mother was entirely wrong, wise as she was in other matters, but I couldn't help remembering her words.

"Come look at this, Manon," my husband called. "This phrase?"

He'd scratched out a bit of my wording, reworked it, then scratched that out and written my own back again. "I think you say it very well, my dear."

He kissed my cheek. "You should go to bed. You look tired."

He was the one who looked tired—his features drawn, his eyes sunken. How exhausting it was to stand alone in such a sea of chaos. *We will need allies in the days to come*, I thought, *because we cannot accomplish this work alone.* The schism in the new government must be healed—and it was the moderate men, our men, who must win.

Allies. I thought of the burned note in the handwriting that seared my eyes—*I love your straight brows and your eager way of jumping from a carriage and your fine mind like a diamond. Say the word and I will come.*

I did not want to write back. I was terrified to write back. But savage men who were the puppets of calculating men had come to our doorstep with blood on their minds, and it was just chance things had not turned violent—chance, and perhaps my will to face them down. But I could not count on that working again. The next crowd might not scruple to rend me to pieces like those poor women at the Salpêtrière.

We needed allies, and the man who loved me had a powerful voice.

Retreating to my bed, I sat under the absurd canopy of ostrich feathers and scribbled swiftly: *My friend, I cannot give you what you seek. But come to Paris for friendship alone, for the wolves are gathering.*

The address I drafted was well received—of course it was. Little men of little courage applauded my husband, showing all the boldness weak people show when they witness a courageous denunciation they would not be capable of themselves. Afterward, it was printed, distributed, posted to the masses, but nothing raised my spirits. The dead were still dead, and the blood of more than one thousand victims still stained the paving stones of Paris no matter how much vinegar was poured to scrub it away.

Yet the game of politics played on, and now we had a new stage.

"Who can keep it all straight?" I heard that cry often, as pamphleteers struggled to keep the public informed of the latest political factions.

For myself, I observed that the names changed but the debates didn't. The king's Estates General might have become the National Assembly, and the National Assembly might have become the Legislative Assembly, and now it was late September and we had the National Convention that had newly convened at the Tuileries. "Don't bother trying to tell the different assemblies and conventions apart," I advised a perplexed woman watching from the galleries at my side. "It might be different men, but they all sound the same, talking of their own merits the way a loose woman talks of her chastity."

Royalty abolished; the French Republic declared one and indivisible—those were advances of the Convention I could cheer, up in the spectator galleries where

I went daily to witness the debates, a tricolor sash at my waist and tricolor rosettes on my slippers. But oh, how much more debate there was than action! Men like my husband pressed to bring the killers of the prison massacres to justice, then some blocky coarse-featured fellow would rise from the high bleacher seats the radicals had made their own, and cry, "During revolutions, vigorous measures are necessary!" Then a colleague of my husband's would rise, thundering in full counter-cry, and nothing would be *done*.

I could have boxed their ears, every one of them. I could have stamped down to that floor and told them what was needed to restore order: dissolve the radical Paris faction that was determined to run everything to suit themselves (the rest of the nation be damned); re-organize the forces of public order; provide them with a commander chosen by the country's geographical sections. Was that not obvious? I wanted to bang my hands on the rail and shout down that not all France was Paris and we must have a federal system as the Americans did so that the whole of the country was represented and we might deprive these city mobs of the power to levy life and death. And I would have told Citizen Robespierre, now a deputy of the National Convention, and his increasing band of fanatics to go to the devil if they contradicted me.

So many men to evaluate from my place in the gallery, but the longer I watched, the more the true leaders of the Paris faction became clear. Seated in those high bleacher seats at the Convention—the Mountain seats, which made them the Montagnards—they formed a radical triumvirate, one to bring a republic low rather than raise it high as in the days of Rome. *You three*, I thought, eyes narrowing.

Robespierre—the small, cool, bewigged leader of the Jacobins who were becoming the voice of the fanatical Paris faction. I'd once liked him, or at least admired him, but now I had the powerful urge to wring his neck every time he enunciated *counterrevolutionary treason* in his high, precise voice.

Danton—our minister of justice, bulky, coarse, violent; all blunt-force charisma and brutal energy when he spoke. Him I had never liked; I'd taken one look at Danton when we met, fended off his fleshy hand—for he was one of those men who couldn't meet a woman without giving her rump a squeeze—and decided I could watch him glug to the bottom of the Seine without lifting a finger.

And finally, Marat of the newspaper *L'Ami du Peuple*—a rag and bone scarecrow, the worst of the gutter press lunatics, all wild eyes and half-mad followers, who was said to go into hiding in the city's sewers when his attacks in the paper went too far. I'd never met him, but had ample time to evaluate him now.

Robespierre, Danton, Marat: one could hardly see three men less alike, yet I saw them pulling unmistakably together. *You three,* I thought. *You brought bloodshed to the prisons and out into the streets. You seek my husband's end. And not just my husband's, but any man who called himself a Girondin.* A word that just meant a man was sensible and moderate in his politics, not frothing at the mouth like a wild dog, but there were those in this room who spat out *Girondin* with the same vitriol as *traitor.*

All is not lost, I reminded myself. We had fine leaders in the moderate camp. My husband, of course. Condorcet, the beak-nosed former marquis and current philosopher, whom I sometimes caught sleeping under the table in the chamber between discussions of bills so he could get more work done. François Buzot, who had burst upon the scene with such decisive leadership they were calling him General Buzot—whom Marat hated because he had proposed checks against mob violence, and whom Danton hated because he had rejected the creation of the Revolutionary Tribunal . . .

Danton was haranguing my husband now. The motion had been introduced that Roland continue as minister of the interior rather than serve as deputy in the Convention, as no man could do both, and Danton shoved back his chair and rose in bullish fury, roaring, "If you invite him to remain as minister, you should also extend the invitation to her." Sweeping his arm up to the galleries and pointing at me.

I jerked, startled, as hundreds of eyes turned in my direction. Danton grinned, clearly enjoying the color I could feel spreading across my face. I held myself spear straight, refusing to shrink. *You might make me blush but you can't make me flinch.*

Danton shook his head, turning his gaze to my husband standing embarrassed and awkward. "The nation needs ministers who can act without being led by their wives."

Laughter rippled, and I could see Roland shrivel. *Stand tall,* I wanted to shout down, *don't let them see you shrink—*

One voice rose above the cacophony of laughter and hoots. "I am, for one, proud to call Citizen Roland my friend." Dark eyes looked up from the Convention floor, but as soon as they found mine I looked away, refusing to gaze upon the man who wanted to be my lover. He had come straight from Normandy as soon as he received my letter, to throw his support to Roland

and the rest of our moderate-minded allies in the Convention. He came for that alone, I told myself. He knew I could give him only friendship.

Roland looked drawn and wasted in the privacy of our chamber that night. "Put the gibes from your mind," I said, massaging his aching shoulders. "It is classic Danton, you know. He tries to attack you by prowling around your family. Well, they can slander me to their hearts' content—they won't make me budge, or complain, or even care."

"They think me a fool," Roland muttered.

"You know you are no fool." I spoke gently. "Do not let them see how much their words shake you, and they will cease needling with such glee."

My husband pinched the bridge of his nose. "I sometimes wonder why I was so eager for political life, Manon. I do not like it. I cannot see how anyone likes it."

He spoke like a child, exhausted and petulant. I knelt and laid my head in his lap, yet even as I murmured something reassuring, I wondered why I so *loved* political life. Not the petty intrigues, but the true art of politics—for it is an art! The art of ruling men and organizing their happiness in society. Like any art it was frustrating, all-consuming, demanding everything one had and more, but was great art not worth the sacrifice? If I were a man I would lay my whole self down on that altar, but I was not a man, and no amount of ink spilled by women like Olympe de Gouges arguing for female votes and female equality would give me a man's power. My role was to inspire, to aid, to act as a sort of Providence in the background. I accepted that—but why were men, with the whole glory of the role open to them, so lacking in the courage to grasp it?

France was *drained* of men, I sometimes thought. Some I was not sorry to see the back of—the useless Feuillant faction, and outdated heroes like the great Marquis de Lafayette who was so loved by Paris and the Assembly for his heroic feats in America, until the fickle wind of public favor turned and he found himself burned in effigy, denounced by Robespierre, forced to flee, and currently sitting in a Prussian prison cell. Such men could not lead a new republic forward to glory, but who was left who could?

I looked about the Convention in the weeks that followed, as the conversation shifted from the recent violence in Paris to the army's success in pushing back the Prussians. Where was that greatness of soul Rousseau defined as the first attribute of the hero? Hardly anywhere, however far I looked.

Was that why Marat and Danton and the rabids of

the street and the Jacobin Club attacked me—not just my husband, but me? Were they afraid of the merest notion that heroes might be supplanted by heroines?

Was that why they called me to the bar of the Convention not long afterward, and accused me of treason?

"There she is, the harlot . . ."

"*La femme* Roland . . ."

"Traitorous slut . . ."

The whispers followed me as I made my way across the floor, looking neither right nor left. It was the first time a woman had been called to address the Convention, and I'd dressed for the occasion as though it were an honor: a blue gown that foamed about my feet as I stalked to the bar, a white fichu pinned with my tricolor cockade, red ribbons twined through my hair. A revolutionary patriot, top to toe. When I turned to face the questions, I let my eyes travel, bold and confident, to the high bleacher seats where the Montagnards held court.

Before the proceedings could even begin, some heckler from their ranks called, "How do you answer the charge, citizeness?"

I replied with calm contempt. "The charge is ludicrous, and all here know it."

It was a smear job of the crudest kind: an unsavory

informer reporting he had discovered a London conspiracy to restore the king, and that the Rolands were
complicit. My husband had already been summoned to
account for himself and had perhaps not done as well
as he might: he couldn't hide his indignation, and he
became flustered when the tone turned sneering. I
would not give my questioners a chance to sneer.

"The informer states clearly, Citizeness Roland, that
you—"

"I did not summon him." I spoke briskly, taking the
reins before my questioner could bring down the whip
and speed this interrogation to the pace my enemies
wanted. This was going to go at my pace, not theirs.
"From my files of letters I can see the man wrote to
me, asking for an interview with Minister Roland. I receive dozens of such requests every week."

"You do not deny you received the man?"

"He paid a brief call, and from his probing I concluded he was sent to sound us out about some scheme
or other." I smiled. "Or perhaps I was wrong. I am a
woman and not skilled in these matters."

The questioner took turns with his colleagues, trying
to turn my words on me, trying to talk me in circles.
As long as I had listened to politicians drone over my
dinner table, I could talk *anyone* in circles. I shredded
their accusations and stamped the shreds underfoot,

feeling the color rise in my cheeks—not embarrassment, but the fierce heat of pride. Was this what Roland felt when he addressed the Convention? This rush of power that tingled the fingertips, the confidence that my words were deploying like obedient soldiers and the crowd sat in the palm of my hand? Why would anyone who had command of this floor ever leave it?

Finally, I was excused to the sound of ringing applause, the charge dismissed in full, the honors of the session formally accorded to me. I looked from Robespierre to Danton to Marat with a wide bland smile as I glided out, and the smile became a beam as Roland drew me into the nearest empty hall.

"Thank goodness it's over." His face was creased with relief. "Let me take you home, calm your nerves."

"My nerves are calm, and I can take myself home. You stay, speak with those who need reassuring."

He kissed my forehead. "I hated seeing you up there," he muttered, before rushing back inside.

He'd hardly gone before a low voice spoke behind me, prickling my skin. "I loved seeing you up there. You were born to it."

I turned, smile draining away. The man who loved me stood feet planted wide, arms folded, dark hair rumpled—he must have been waiting to catch me alone.

"Citizen," I managed to say, not daring to put his name through my lips.

"You were brilliant," he said quietly. "Brave as a lioness." A voice of calm power for a man not yet thirty-three. Six years younger than I, what did that say about me? "They should have known better than to try to trap you in so crude a snare."

"That shabby excuse for a conspiracy might have been crude, but it was real, even if we had no involvement." I kept my voice brisk, turning the conversation to safer waters. "As long as the king lives, there will be plots to restore him. The matter will have to be dealt with."

"The king is just a man, and a small one."

"With a long shadow."

We both smiled involuntarily. It had always been like that with us, the eager cut-and-thrust of our minds. "If you wish to speak to my husband . . ."

But the man who loved me took my hand.

"Manon, I honor Roland and support him always. But I am here for you."

He brought my hand to his face as I turned. His jaw was rough under my fingertips, evidence that he'd stayed up all night again writing. I pulled away as his lips touched my palm, sending my heart thudding. "Please—anyone might see—" Being caught by one of these men so eager to hiss *traitorous slut* as I passed would be the end of me.

But he was already stepping back, leaving a scrap of paper in my hand. "Good day, citizeness," he said formally and was gone into the cold street outside. With shaking hands I unfolded his note.

I watched you today, and loved you more with every word you spoke. Just once, even if it leads to nothing else, I wish to hear you say you love me. Le Maison du Chocolat Léon, near the Palais—I will be there at noon tomorrow, and the day after, and the day after.

I burned the note. I was no slave to my heart, regardless of what it wanted, and I would not go.

Autumn, wet and cold, had turned to winter as the Convention blustered and brooded over the pressing issue of what to do with the king.

When I was not writing Roland's speeches or soothing his frayed feelings over the attacks that continued unabated in Marat's newspaper, I devoted myself to my daughter. At eleven she was pretty and phlegmatic, resisting all my attempts to make her imagination flower. Books bored her, which dismayed me since I could remember how at her age I had devoured them like sweets. *But she may be happier with a mind like a tight bud*, I thought, threading pink ribbon through her curls and smiling at her delight. *Bookish women are not the happiest females, for the world does not like to see a woman's head bent over anything but a cradle, a cooking pot, or a rosary.*

I surrendered to my daughter's begging one night and agreed to take her to the theater. I suspected she was more interested in *Le Marriage de Figaro*'s most dashing actor—"They say François Elleviou is singing, and he is *so* handsome, Maman!"—than in the politics, but perhaps I could steer her to a conversation on the underlying issues.

Roland was attending a salon so I was escorted to the theater by one of his deputies, full of news from the Society of the Friends of the Blacks. "Condorcet argued most passionately at our recent meeting for a complete ban from politics on any man who has engaged in the slave trade or owned slaves." Holding the carriage door for me, the deputy continued, "He has often said 'Anyone who votes against the rights of another, whatever his religion, color, or sex, automatically forfeits his own.'"

"Fine sentiments." We squeezed through the throng on the steps into the theater, my companion making way for my daughter and me in the crowd of Greek-styled gowns and bonnets rouges. It wasn't just the handsome François Elleviou on the stage tonight, but the notorious Claire Lacombe, mediocre actress and expert rabble-rouser, no doubt trying to drum up support for her absurd notion that revolutionary women deserved a political society of their own—the Enragés were out in force, and the smell of garlic and wine was overwhelming. "But fine sentiments mean nothing without action. When will there be a motion before the Convention to free the slaves in our colonies?" It was a matter long overdue: for many months we had seen passionate public debate as pro-enslavement and anti-enslavement factions went head-to-head, and rebellions against slavery raged in Martinique and Saint-Domingue. I doubt the oblivious royals would have ever noticed such uprisings until their spending was affected—heaven forbid the budget for satin shoes be curtailed!—but a Revolution that had only this April instated citizenship and equal political rights to free blacks could not remain so blind. Especially when former slaves from the colonies stood right there on the debate floor, arguing for those still enslaved across the sea. The Americans had neglected to amend the matter of slavery in their own revolution; surely we French could do better.

"We still face considerable resistance from those saying mass abolition would empty the nation's coffers at the worst time imaginable—"

"No republic is perfect if it allows slavery. We cannot simply turn away from the matter, or congratulate ourselves for offering sympathy but never help. If we want practical advances in the cause of abolition—"

We were pressing through the throng toward the box reserved for the minister of the interior, but as we neared it the embarrassed box attendant beside the door flapped his hands. "I am sorry, citizeness, but the box is occupied."

"Impossible." Entry to the box needed a ticket signed by my husband.

"The minister insisted on entering. You mustn't go in—"

Pushing the door open, I smelled a waft of strong wine and met the insolent eyes of three or four *sans-culottes* lounging, their shirts unlaced, two tawdry-looking women with rouged cheeks and gowns slipping off their shoulders—and a broad man with a brutal, pockmarked face.

Before I could retreat, Danton looked over his shoulder and saw me. "What ho, Citizeness Roland! Showing your virtuous face at the theater?"

I backed out, looking to my puzzled escort. "We must return home. Please fetch a cab." But as he disappeared back down the stairs, Danton emerged, blocking my path before I could follow.

"Join us, Madame Squeamish. I hear there's a pantomime in the wedding act that's quite an eye-opener. Claire Lacombe has the best tits in Paris, and when she gets them out—" He made an obscene gesture, and I hastily moved my daughter behind me out of sight. "Might learn a few things, eh? Better than sitting at home pen in hand."

"I prefer a pen, citizen."

"That's a boring life for a woman."

"Boredom is a malady of empty souls and resourceless minds. I hate wasting my time in gossip, and what I am bored by is fools."

"Come on, Manon. We never got along, but it's not for lack of my trying." He spoke true enough. When Roland was first instated as minister of the interior, Danton had been a frequent visitor, dropping in with bottles of wine and heavy-handed charm, not that he had ever charmed me. Men like that were far too easy to see through. "Have a drink," he cajoled now, raising a bottle. "We don't have to be enemies, you and I. Friendship could be profitable."

I turned to my daughter, wide-eyed behind me, and gave her a gentle push a few steps toward the stairs. "You'll see the fine gowns better from there, *ma petite*." When she was out of earshot, I turned back to Danton. "It is my husband you should speak to if you wish to—"

"Bollocks. I talk to the man in the marriage, and the man in your marriage is you. Roland does what you tell him, and you told him to show me the door."

I flushed. Roland *had* been more disposed to build bridges, once. "Danton has been useful in the Revolution," my husband had pointed out. "He has many friends, and there is no point in making an enemy unnecessarily."

I was aware I could be too severe in my assessments, too quick to form a dislike, but Danton's coolly assessing gaze and backslapping bonhomie had always made my flesh creep. "It is easier to avoid giving a man power than to prevent him from abusing it," I'd replied to my husband. After that it hadn't taken Danton long to realize he would get nowhere with either my husband or me, and he'd stopped dropping in.

"Most women like me," Danton said, eyes traveling to my bosom. "You don't. Why is that, Manon?"

I almost laughed. How puzzled men were when they met a woman who didn't blush and look pleased as she was greeted with a squeeze of the hip! "Why wouldn't I enjoy your company, citizen?" I said, looking him in the eye with an amused smile even as I kept watch on my child. "Doesn't everyone enjoy listening to men who imagine that every word they say is a revelation? Men who speak to women and think all they are capable of is stitching shirts and adding up figures?"

"You're a clever bitch, I'll give you that," Danton said frankly. "Watching you defend yourself on the Convention floor, I thought, 'That's a woman who needs a good fuck more than anyone I've ever seen—except maybe Robespierre—but she's got brains.' They won't do you any good, though. Or your husband."

"Do not speak of my husband." My smile evaporated. "He is an honorable man, and you sit in his theater box after months of spreading vile rumors about him. And you ask why we can't be *friends.*"

I headed for the stairs and my daughter, but Danton's big hand shot out and gripped my elbow. "You tell that gelding you married to fall in line. His day is done. It's my time now."

"Let go," I snapped like a nursemaid putting an ill-behaved child in their place.

People were watching now. Even Danton couldn't manhandle me in public before my husband's own theater box, and he knew it. But he took his time letting go, crowding me with his massive height, his smell of male sweat and newspaper ink. "You walk around like you're made of ice, but I know you, Manon. Under those skirts you're wet for it." He spoke softly, giving me another long up-and-down look. "Anytime you want a man in your bed instead of a cadaver, you know where to find me."

He saluted me with a grin and disappeared back into the box just as my escort fought his way back up the stairs to my side. "There was such a delay getting a cab—" I barely heard him over my own inner trembling. *Pull yourself together*, I told myself fiercely, calling my daughter to me and gripping her hand, but I could not stop shaking. I was ten years old again, smelling male sweat and feeling a male hand on my wrist, feeling naked and ashamed and *seen*. Danton of all people had looked at me and seen the whore I was. My husband with his great discernment did not see it; the man who sent me love letters did not see it.

Perhaps he should, I thought. *Perhaps then he would leave me be.* Right now, that was all I wanted—to be left alone to serve my husband and tend my child and play my small part in the service of the struggling new republic, and not be called a slut. Why was that too much to ask?

"Maman?" my daughter whispered.

I pulled her against my side. "We're going home, *mignonne*." But I could not stop trembling, and the next day I steeled myself in dread and shame and went at noon to the chocolate shop near the Palais.

He was there as I came down from the hired cab, leaning against the door in a blue coat, the winter wind ruffling his hair. He dropped his hat at the sight of me, picked it up again with a grin at his own foolishness, a grin that froze my insides hard with terrified longing.

I did not know how to begin, but he began for me. "It's one of the things I love."

I blinked, already off guard. "What?"

He gestured at the cab, now rumbling away down the street. "You never step from a carriage, you always jump. Like you can't wait to run to where you're going." Another grin. "For weeks I've been watching every cab, hoping I'd see you jump and run toward me."

"A foolish waste of time," I couldn't help saying, "when there is so much to do."

"I can dream of you and the republic at the same time, Manon. I planned most of my first Convention speech with my eyes closed, imagining your face."

"It was a good speech," I managed to say, breath puffing white in the cold. He had argued so passionately for reconciliation between the Paris faction and the rest of the country; for a law condemning the instigators of murder and not just the murderers; for a domestic force to rival the bands of armed *sans-culottes* roaming the streets. The kind of sensible, moderate action this country needed if we were to move forward with the business of governing ourselves. "A very good speech."

His eyes rested on me tender as a kiss. Curiously, that look steadied me. He would not look at me like that again when he heard what I had to say.

The little chocolate shop was nearly bare inside, no fragrant rolls or sweet buns on sale. Bread was dearer than gold in Paris at the moment.

He bought a single cup of chocolate. "All I can afford, I'm afraid. We'd better drink it outside if we don't want to be glared at." He looked back with a smile at Pauline Léon who had sold him the chocolate. The shop's owner was tall, raw-boned, her face young and her eyes old, light hair straggling under a proud red cap with a tattered tricolor cockade. She met my eyes with a glare, and so did the friend at her side, a woman with belligerent eyes and a pretty face ravaged by hunger. I recognized her, too—Louise Audu, the so-called Queen of the Market Women who had gained notoriety at Versailles years ago during the women's march.

Sans-culottes females like that were easily led, yapping at Marat's heels and sighing over Robespierre from the galleries. Yet some argued for giving women like these the vote!

"You give our sex and our revolution a bad name," I muttered, retreating from Louise's and Pauline's hostile glowers back to the cold street. We went around the side of the shop to a little alley between buildings, a space where we might stand squeezed close in some privacy.

He offered me the chocolate. "Do you love me, Manon?" he asked simply.

My stomach clenched. "I am a virtuous woman."

"You are." His mouth quirked. "You're also ducking the question."

I took a gulp of chocolate. It tasted bitter rather than sweet. "You respect and support my husband." Poor Roland, who suspected nothing of me or the man he called friend. "How can you make advances upon his wife?"

"I respect the man, but not the husband he makes

you. He takes your writing and calls it his own. I see him grow sulky if you take so much as a step from his side, even for your daughter. He demands every instant of your time, every bit of your care—"

"It is his right to demand that."

He took the cup, turning it so he could drink from the same place my lips had touched. "Passion is also a right—your right."

"You say so because of how I look," I replied bluntly. "Because physiognomists would say I am a woman made for passion." That was what men thought, when they saw a small voluptuous woman with a curving mouth and skin that blushed with every emotion—but no one so obviously made for voluptuous pleasure had ever enjoyed so little of it. "Liberty, equality, fraternity, those are my rights. Not passion."

"The Americans say the pursuit of happiness is a right." His hand upturned toward mine. "I believe I could make you happy."

"Happiness is rarer than one thinks." I pulled away before our hands could meet. "The consolations of virtue never fail."

"Cold consolations, Manon. Do you expect so little from life?"

"It is very wise to be able to lower one's expectations. We are not Americans; the pursuit of happiness is not a right I expect." I took a breath, dizzied by temptation, pulling from it angrily. "I cannot be your whore!"

His eyes were dark and steady. "You are the woman I love. Not a whore, not ever."

"Oh, but I am." I made myself look up at him, so much taller with so much yearning in his gaze. Time to wipe it away. "I was—at a very young age, I was—" I could not say it directly. I could not. I took refuge in vagueness. "You would do better not to yearn for fruit that has already been tainted while still green."

My hands were freezing. I thrust them into my muff, avoiding his gaze.

His breath caught for a long moment. I didn't raise my eyes. "What happened?" he said at last, quietly.

I shook my head. "It doesn't matter." And I'd promised my mother I would never tell. Her panicked eyes, her hands digging into my shoulders, her voice shooting a thousand questions. She took me to confession so I might be cleansed, but afterward made me swear on a crucifix that I would tell no one, not ever.

"Oh, Manon . . ." His voice was low. "Who harmed you?"

"I wasn't—it was not—" How could I tell, and not tell? A fifteen-year-old apprentice in my father's engraving shop, luring me close one afternoon, drawing my uncomprehending hand beneath the table to touch something I could not see. *What are you afraid of? Don't be stupid, I won't do you any harm.* I'd been so puzzled, so alarmed. *I won't say anything*, I kept saying. *Just let me go.*

"Did he try to force a husband's rights?" Quietly.

I managed a minute shake of my head. No, the boy had not—not fully, anyway. The second time it happened, the boy had pressed me between the window bench and his lap, his chest squashing against my back. *Are you still afraid? I'm not doing you any harm.*

But I want to go. My dress—

Never mind your dress, I'll see to that. Pulling it up, reaching underneath while at the same time reaching for himself. Doing something to himself I could not see. The way his eyes rolled up in his head afterward, his groan—

I should have run to my mother. I didn't. That was what made me a whore. I knew it was wrong, so why didn't I run to my mother? Some part of me must have been curious, must have wanted it. The apprentice boy had seen that.

My mother had seen it, too, once she saw the look on my face and pried the story out of me. Oh, God, her eyes as she babbled of religion, virtue, honor, reputation—she invoked them all, hugging me to her bosom and making me promise I would never transgress again, never take a man's advances so lightly. I'd soon been shaking with sobs, feeling myself the greatest slut on earth.

"Oh, *ma petite*," my mother said, comforting me through her own tears. "You are fortunate, never forget. He did not spoil you fully. No one will ever know."

But I *was* spoiled. I could live my life a virtuous woman, never prostitute myself as an author of words or a soiler of other men's beds, but I was what I was. Coarse-fibered Danton knew it when he saw me. Now the man who had loved me would too.

Good, I thought, *see what I am and leave me alone before I give in.* Because I did not have the strength to be a scarlet woman on the outside as well as in my soul.

I looked up with blurred eyes, hoping to see him recoil.

Instead, he drew my hand from my muff with a touch so light I could have broken it with a breath. He didn't bring my hand up to his lips—the same hand I'd scrubbed with harsh soap because it was the one the apprentice had taken and pulled under the table. Instead, he lowered his head and kissed each of my fingers in turn.

"You are supposed to revile me," I said, bewildered.

"Who in the name of God would revile you,

Manon?" For the first time he sounded angry. "Has Roland?"

"He does not know." I looked away. It had been a great struggle with my conscience, whether to tell him before we married. It would have been the honorable choice, but what if he had broken our betrothal? He had been reluctant to marry me; my birth was not equal to his, nor did my modest dowry make up for it. It had taken more than three years of courtship before he decided my youth and my serious mind would be recompense enough to merit an offer. I think I still might have told him—I did not fear spinsterhood so much as that—but my mother had made me promise silence. It had been a vow. The last vow I made to God, and I might not believe in God but I believed in my mother. She was gone and I couldn't betray the only promise she had ever forced from me.

"You did not break your promise in telling me." The big hand around mine squeezed, so gently. "You did not really tell—I asked questions, and your eyes gave answers rather than your voice. That broke no vow."

How had he read my mind? "You are supposed to go away," I said, near tears. "Why do you think I told you? So you would leave me."

"I will go if you want it. Do you want it?"

I knew what whores wanted. I could already feel myself melting into him, shaking as though I had a fever. Had he kissed me I would have flown away, but he only held me quietly against him, one arm holding me up so I wouldn't fall, the other stroking the length of my back as though he were stroking a terrified horse. Only I could feel the panic mounting even as my bones loosened. Since I was ten I had looked on every man who seemed friendly with a kind of terror. And since my marriage, no man but Roland had touched me past the press of a hand or a quick fraternal embrace. Now I was letting myself be touched, and I could feel the danger mounting.

I could take abuse. I could take slander. I had spoken truth to Roland when I said such things would not make me budge.

I could not take gentleness.

My breath came in uneven puffs on the cold air as I pulled away from my lover. It would be fair to call him my lover, I thought, even if he had not set his lips to more than my fingertips. In the ways that mattered, I'd surrendered. "Please let me go."

"As you wish, Manon." His face was drawn. "Anything that passes between us will always be as you wish."

I rushed out of the alley with blurring eyes, crashing straight into a red-capped figure blocking my way with arms akimbo. Pauline Léon made no effort to steady me as I staggered, and at her side, Louise Audu smirked. "Setting up a rendezvous with your fancy boy instead of working for the republic?"

"You Girondins can't keep your eyes on the prize," Pauline said, disapproving. "It won't be you who makes a new world."

"And it will be you?" I heard myself snarl, too brittle and close to tears to stop myself from snapping back rather than withdrawing with proper dignity. "You think pikes and slogans make a nation?"

"I didn't see you laboring on the streets alongside us, citizeness," Louise retorted pertly. "Or marching on the king to demand change."

"You didn't see me sawing a guardsman's head off with a filleting knife, either, like some of your friends," I lashed back. "A field of carnage does not make a nation."

"Nor do scruples." Pauline stepped out of my way with a sniff. "Women like you don't have the guts to do what needs to be done."

Yes, I do, I thought. And before my nerve could fail me, I went home, laid my repentant head in my husband's lap, and told him everything.

"**Is it** Danton?" Roland's voice was low and tight. The study was dim, the dying fire throwing shadows over his taut face as he looked down at me. "I see him looking after you—"

"Never." I flinched, unable to look my husband in the eyes from where I sat beside his chair on the floor. He had pushed my head from his lap after I finished my confession. "I would never look at Danton—"

"Robespierre? Did the Incorruptible corrupt you—"

"No—"

"Condorcet, then, with his half-baked philosophy and egg always showing on his cuffs from shoveling down omelets? Or Saint-Just, he's a handsome sprig—" Roland began throwing names at me, voice rising. All I could do was sit on the floor beside his chair, cringing. *You have earned this*, I repeated to myself. *You have earned all of this.*

"It is not any of them," I managed to say before Roland could reach the right name. I was robbing my husband of faith in his wife today; I would not rob him of trust in an ally. Because I knew my lover would remain faithful to Roland's support even if I would not come to him—he was not so petty as to throw over the only honest man in service of the republic simply because of a disappointed heart. And the bald truth was that Roland needed every friend in the Convention he could get, so I kept my lover's name to myself. "It does not matter who it is, because nothing has come of it or ever will. I tell you of his existence only to maintain honor between us." And to stop myself from falling further—that I freely admitted.

"I wish to know—" Roland began.

"I have not surrendered my virtue, and I never will." I looked up at my husband through swimming eyes. "Do you believe me?"

A long, dreadful moment. The fire crackled in the marble hearth. Such a cozy, connubial scene—I would have felt less out of place in the bloody September Massacres where the Princess de Lamballe had been torn to pieces. I felt I *was* being torn to pieces.

"I believe you didn't surrender your body," Roland said at last, stiffly. "If only because you take little pleasure in such pastimes."

I flinched. "You know I have done my best to please you."

Your best is not much. It hung in the air between us. Our first night of marriage had given me some disagreeable surprises—I had come to see my betrothed very comfortingly as a person without sex, a thinker in a folded neck-cloth devoted entirely to reason. To meet the flesh in the dark under the bedclothes, all gripping

hands and moist gasps, had been a great shock. Entirely my fault—since the incident with the apprentice
I had shut myself away from anything I might have
learned about congress of the flesh and come to my
marriage bed knowing worse than nothing. I had not
been able to stop myself from crying out in pain, and
my new husband had been very upset. He had married
a woman twenty years younger; he must have felt himself entitled to something softer and more welcoming
than the terrified board I could not stop myself from
becoming. He had not had the patience to loosen me,
and the promise to my mother had locked my mouth
helplessly when it came to telling him why I was such a
disappointment.

"We have been happy enough," I managed to say,
"despite my deficiency in that way." I had never denied
him my bed, no matter how stiff and panicked I felt,
and after our daughter's birth he'd seemed to feel his
advancing years and sought it less. Things eased then;
I threw myself into working intimately with him in
every other way to make up for my failings. "You know
I honor and cherish you. I would follow you to the ends
of the earth—"

"Yet you make it clear you are making a sacrifice to
do so," he snapped.

I have sacrificed everything I am in your service,

I thought before I could stop myself. *Can I not sacrifice one small portion of feeling to something else?* But I shoved that thought aside. I had no right to it. My husband was entitled to everything I had, everything I was. "What do you wish from me?" I asked instead. "I will do it."

He looked at the fire, his profile gaunt and tired. For a long moment neither of us said anything. "Go to bed."

I rose, smoothing my crumpled skirts with shaking hands. "Will you sit up tonight?"

"Yes, I have a report to study." I could see him grappling for the return of routine, taking refuge in business, and I could have wept. "From the inspector-general of national buildings."

"What about?" I asked, because I always asked, always encouraged.

"It seems a locksmith has come with a confession that he installed an iron safe for the king at the Tuileries. It bears investigation. Who knows what might be found."

"You should take witnesses with you to open it," I could not help saying. "Marat, Danton, they might accuse you of tampering—"

But my husband strode from the room. He was done listening to me, and I could not blame him.

❊

It was December before Louis Capet, our former king, was called to trial. These were long weeks when Danton let his mad dog Marat off his leash and pointed him at my family. The latest charges against my husband would have been laughable had not so many been willing to listen—that he had embezzled funds from the Republic, that he was a secret royalist. But I could not tell Roland to keep steady and hold his head high, because he would barely speak to me.

"Tell your husband to take care," our friends muttered. "Neither of you is safe in that marble shell of a palace—"

But I could only shake my head. A minister must stay at his post; so must a minister's wife. Even if the minister hated her.

It was with spittle clinging to the hem of my cloak that I passed before the hostile smirks from the Mountain and came to the gallery to watch the former king brought to trial. The appearance of Louis Capet was a shock to me after so many months spent listening to the Convention obsess over him—his specter had loomed like a Colossus over this room, yet he was just a pale, sickly looking man, blinking in his green coat as he heard the list of charges read. I could not help but pity him. Had he been born two hundred years earlier and married a sensible wife, he would have been no better remembered than many other French rulers who had come and gone without doing any good or any harm . . . But he had come to his throne in a time of change, and it was his ill fortune to suffer for it.

I wished he did not have to. I remembered the days of my husband's first term as minister of the interior, when he had returned from council meetings with so much hope that all might be solved.

There need never have been a trial, I thought as the ugly spectacle ground on. *The idea of attacking the monarchy would not have occurred to anyone had you sincerely backed the constitution, Louis Capet. If you find yourself here, it is your own doing as much as ours.*

The year turned to an iron-cold January of 1793 before the trial was done and the voting could begin. Tedium had worn away the novelty until everyone seemed used to the idea that a king might be judged and executed like any other man. Now the crowd bubbled with hot anticipation, not unlike the crowds who flocked to watch a condemned man broken on the wheel before the king, in one of his rare sensible judgments, banned such torture. I imagined the spectators of ancient Rome had looked very similar, waiting for

Christians to be pushed onto the sands of the Colosseum. What beasts men are . . .

It was past eight in the evening, the hall freezing and stuffy at once, when the voting began for the king's sentence. Up in the gallery, I clenched my hands when the word, at last, was spoken.

"Death."

The roll call went on as deputy after deputy rose. The watchers grew restless again as it became clear we would be here all night. I remained hour after hour, limbs growing numb, determined to see it to the end.

"May I join you, Citizeness Roland?"

I glanced up at the tall figure in white who had come through the throng at the rail. It was the former noblewoman Sophie Condorcet, her long dark hair loose over her shoulders in the republican way of the ancients, dimples set in a youthful round face. But she did not make those dimples deeper with a smile; her pink mouth was drawn tight and grave.

"Of course, citizeness," I said. I had never met Condorcet's wife publicly; she was one of those women who made herself a salonnière and mingled with men giving her opinion on all subjects—I couldn't help but think that such women sounded like yesterday's newspaper. But I liked her gravitas on this solemn occasion, so I made room for her at the rail.

She stared directly at her husband, awaiting his turn to vote, and nibbled at her lip. "How will Citizen Condorcet vote?" I asked.

"Justly," she said, whether because she didn't know, or because she didn't wish to say, I couldn't tell. That might have annoyed me, but my husband as minister of the interior had no vote, and I was not entitled to comment upon the vote my lover would cast. I could see him below, keeping his eyes from me, his shoulders tense when he stood and uttered "Death" with sorrow in his voice.

I hastily turned my thoughts and eyes back to my companion.

"Are you and Citizen Condorcet among those who believe Louis Capet should have been given no trial at all?" Such persons encompassed the opposing ends of French politics: one set were royalists bleating that the king could not be tried because of his God-given status, and the other set were those like Robespierre and Marat who stated that the king could not be tried because no red tape could make his death palatable, therefore he ought to be disposed of without a stage. Looking at both sets, I thought it would be hard to find stupider people.

Perhaps Sophie agreed with me, because she shook her head. "The trial was necessary. Everyone is entitled to the due process of law—wasn't that the reason for our revolution in the first place?"

"Law, and bread." I cast my eyes around the galleries, still packed and avid as the votes came. *Death. Death. Death.* "Though at times I wonder if our revolution has become bread and circuses."

She did not smile, but I saw a flicker of agreement in her eyes. "When people are forced to labor so hard to survive, they have no time to reflect or educate themselves about the qualities they share with other human beings . . ."

She trailed off, because her husband had risen to his feet to cast his vote. Condorcet was a shambling man with a truly Roman nose, less fastidious in his clothing than a man with an attentive wife would be. Bookish and quiet in the clamor of assemblies, the renowned philosopher had never been a powerful orator, but he chose this moment to make his voice carry. "I will vote death for no man, in no instance."

I looked at his wife, startled. Overwhelmingly through the long night hours, the votes had been for death. I had always found Condorcet timid—of all the times for the man to find a spine.

"Why would he give a dissenting vote to no purpose? The majority will still fall on the side of condemnation, and he risks being branded a counterrevolutionary."

The word made Sophie wince and she turned upon me, cheeks reddening. "He risks it for principle, citizeness."

"He should save his principle for a practical stance that will do some good. The streets run riot with *sansculottes*; we can hardly afford to lose our philosophers." Trying to convince philosophers of practicality—now there was a lost cause. "Is it from compassion, because Louis was a figure of sympathy at his trial? He was dignified enough, but there is no reason to give him credit for it. Kings are reared from childhood to act a part."

"Whatever part he has played, he is still a human being. We owe compassion on that basis alone. Why do you think Robespierre did not wish to try the king? He knows there is no moral way to deprive a man of his life."

"I disagree, when it is one life balanced against thousands. I see you despise such arguments," I said, seeing the disgust that flickered across her face, "but I make them out of common sense, not a desire for revenge. A dethroned king will attract conspiracies of all kinds, until the end of his life, and we cannot afford any attempt to place him back on the throne. I pity Louis Capet, but our republic will never be safe while he lives." I had clearly not convinced her, and I supposed I never would, but the hour was late, and with my nerves strained and jangling, I could not give up the argument. "We have the proof already that he was conspiring with Austria to regain his position. The letters from the iron safe in the Tuileries discovered by my husband—was that not clear enough evidence?"

Sophie's jaw tightened as she watched Condorcet, who was now being jeered from the galleries, and hostile eyes turned her way too. Perhaps it rattled her, because her tone became sharper. "This evidence—how much weight can anyone put on it, when it is vulnerable to the charge of having been tampered with? Could your husband have brought no reliable witnesses with him to retrieve the king's letters from that safe?"

It was my turn to redden, but I could hardly defend Roland in this because he *had* acted foolishly. He should have brought impartial colleagues to open the safe, but he had ignored my advice on that, too eager to see what winning cards he might pluck from it.

And whose fault is that?

I stared down at the men below, mute and furious, and saw Condorcet in a sea of accusing eyes and turned backs raise his gaze to us.

Sophie smiled at him—a tender, bittersweet smile of reassurance in this awful moment. *She knew how he would vote all along*, I thought. And despite his hostile surroundings, Condorcet smiled back at his wife as if she was the only person whose opinion mattered.

A pang of envy pierced my anger. Sophie Condorcet was younger than I, but Fate had dealt us not-dissimilar hands: staid husbands twenty years our senior, a passion for politics, and a place at this railing. But she had been lucky enough to find love in her lot, not the barren place of honorable resentment I occupied, unable to meet my own husband's eyes at all. Were he even to look, which he never did these days—except to ensure I was not looking elsewhere.

"Be careful." The warning came out of me unbidden. "You have a young daughter to think of, I believe—as I do. Your husband's vote won your family no friends today."

"When tempers cool, they will remember that we were amongst the first to declare for a republic in our newspaper. How can we be thought anything but patriots?"

"There are many newspapers now besides your husband's. What will they say of him, and you?"

"What they always say." She shrugged. "That he is cuckolded by me. That he is led by me. That he is not man enough. Though today has surely put all that to the lie." Another loving, prideful gaze downward before she asked, "What slanders do they pass about you?"

"The latest?" I gave a bitter-edged smile. "Marat barks at me; he never leaves me alone. I am a toothless hag who writes my husband's every speech, and a Circe reclining among the drained bodies of my lovers." Though there was no especial rumor singling out the one name I feared. "And really," I couldn't help exclaiming, "when does any busy woman during this revolution have time to recline *anywhere*?"

For the first time, amusement touched Sophie's mouth. Then it faded. "They would say all this about you whether you were busy or not. My husband says the faults of women are the work of men, just as the vices of nations are the crime of their tyrants. They will say anything to punish us for stepping outside of the role in which they confine us."

"But I have not stepped outside," I said, startled. "I do not write in my own name, I do not voice public opinions on political matters. The one time I spoke in public was when I was called to the floor to defend myself. Otherwise I keep behind my husband in all things."

"And it hasn't spared you, has it?"

I stared at her. My lips parted, but I could think of no response.

"Nothing spares women," Sophie said gently. "Whether we ask for the vote or only for bread, whether we march on the streets or keep to our salons, there are those who will find us at fault—and make us suffer for the crime of asking for more."

"I do not ask for more," I managed to say. "I have everything to which my sex entitles me."

"Decline to use your vote, then, once you have it. That is your right. I will continue to argue that you are entitled to that vote, as are all the women of France. That is *my* right."

I sealed my lips tight on hot words and turned back to the Convention floor. Sophie Condorcet and I traded no more conversation that night as the voting ground remorselessly on. Dawn broke to a pitiless morning as the final vote was cast, and an intake of breath was heard around the hall—around all France.

King Louis XVI would die.

Paris, January 21, 1793

"You are so eager to see royal blood flow?" Roland flung the question from his desk as I appeared at the study door in my cloak and muff, the revolutionary cockade at my bosom. "You will go to the place de la Révolution?"

"An era passes today," I said. Yesterday placards had

been distributed all over Paris, signed in my husband's name, giving the time and place where a former king would meet his end. "We should bear witness. Come with me?"

"No." He sat fiddling with his papers. "I have a speech to prepare."

"Then I will stay and work on it with you—"

"No!" he said sharply, turning away.

I bit down my flare of anger and went alone.

I heard the king's procession before I saw it: the sound of drums like heartbeats through the fog, wheels rattling like bones along the cobbles, and the hollow clopping of hooves. A silent crowd had pressed around the guard-enclosed carriage as it made its slow, agonizing way through the city toward the place de la Révolution, and I fell in among the tight-packed throng. Normally I might have been afraid; everywhere I'd gone for the last few months I had been glared at, spat on, called a counterrevolutionary slut, thanks to Marat and his gutter rag. But today there were bigger matters, and I walked unnoticed in the great crush as the people of Paris followed their king for the very last time.

A sudden commotion of shouts erupted around the carriage. I strained to make out the cause just as a man's voice called out above the clamor, "Follow me, my friends! Let us save the king! *Vive le roi!*"

Here and there, scattered voices shouted support. But a swelling wave of jeers rose even as a handful of Louis's foolhardy supporters tried to rally support for the condemned man. Another commotion as more National Guardsmen arrived, and the metallic clank of swords meeting swords made my heart hammer. Someone in the throng must have panicked and tried to flee, because guards were giving chase, running down the ringleaders.

And just as quickly, all was quiet again as the carriage rolled on toward the place de la Révolution.

It was nearly ten. I found myself wondering if Louis had taken a last communion this morning, if he had said farewell to his Austrian queen with anguish or with dignity. He was a husband and a father as well as a king, and I prayed his final parting with his family had brought him comfort—that his children had been spared the knowledge of what was coming, that frivolous Antoinette had been brave and sent him off consoled and at peace. That was what any wife should do, if her husband was called to die before her. As I would if Roland were taken . . . and I realized in dull horror that I would not be surprised if he was. This revolution was beginning to devour its children, and the honorable like my husband might make the first meal.

I shuddered, pushing that thought away as the carriage at last entered the strange, charged silence of the square. The entire waiting crowd drew breath as the hired cab rolled to a halt, surrounded by guards with drawn blades.

I felt a mass exhalation as the king appeared, gray-faced and drawn, looking around him in what seemed like bewilderment. *He means well*, I remembered Roland telling me from those early days when the Revolution had been young. *He sees himself as the father of his people. We can work with a man like this. He means so well!*

I wondered if that was what Louis was thinking as he mounted the scaffold. *But I meant so well . . .*

The executioner worked briskly, wasting no time. There was only one moment where the king reared back in protest, shaking his head. He would not have the rope bound around his hands, he was objecting fiercely, and I felt a moment's keen sympathy. I would not want my hands bound either; I would want freedom to the end, even if just the freedom to flex my wrists. For the first time I allowed myself to look squarely at the machine of execution; Dr. Guillotin's marvelous creation, its blade black-silhouetted in the strange light. Atavistic dread crawled up my spine. It was humane, I knew that—the quick descent of a blade took a head far more cleanly than a sword swung by human hands, to say nothing of the slower, crueler methods like the stake or the wheel. But I had never in my life seen a machine that looked more threatening, looming like a tall narrow doorway to some ghastly unknown realm.

It is justice, I thought. *It is necessary.* I still believed that, with all my soul. But justice could be a hard thing to witness. Perhaps it should be.

The former king at last allowed his hands to be bound. He faced the crowd, tried to say something—but it must have been agreed upon that he must say nothing, because I heard no more than a few muffled words before a drumroll drowned him out. His chin dropped, and then the executioner was moving with brutal efficiency, laying the plump, unresisting figure on the broad plank, closing the boards about his neck to hold it in place. Louis looked down into the basket of straw that would hold his head, and I pushed back a surge of nausea.

I had not prayed in earnest for a long time, but I prayed for Louis. I prayed for us all.

With a rattling sound, the blade released. You would hear it coming down as you lay there, I thought. The last sound you ever heard. Until the next sound ended it all—the wet, indescribable crunch.

A roar rose from the crowd as the executioner's assistant lifted the head. Bonnets rouges flew in the air, caps waved, a woman beside me tore off her tricolor sash and waved it ecstatically over her head. Then there was a different cry as a thin runnel of scarlet leaked from the edge of the scaffold, and I was buffeted on all sides as men, women, and children rushed forward to dip their fingers, their kerchiefs, their cuffs in the once-royal blood. I turned away, shoving down a surge of disgust, biting down hard on my own gloved knuckle to keep from vomiting.

The king is dead. The thought echoed inside my skull. *The king is dead.* Once, the responding cry would have been *Long live the king!* as a son took his father's place. Now the son was an orphan and a prisoner, never to be more than another Louis Capet, and the cry was *Long live the republic!*

The nausea would not fade. I took myself slowly home, light-headed and swaying, looking at the streets around me and wondering why no one else seemed affected by it all. Because within the hour the citizens of Paris seemed to have resumed their course: men jostling in groups, women arm in arm, children dashing over the cobbles, everyone talking and arguing and going about their business as usual. *Let this be the end,* I prayed, clutching my cloak against the cold. The arrest of the royal family had not been the end of the Revolution's violence; the September Massacres had not been the end—let this be the last of the bloodshed. Let one royal death see the end of strife.

Let us now begin the real business of building, of creating, of putting things to right.

I stared at my husband. "Resign as minister of the interior?"

My husband toyed with his pen. "At once."

"No—" I came to the desk, looking at the reports still to work on. "There is so much to do. Now that the problem of the king is solved, we can work in earnest."

"How?" Roland looked at me wearily. "I have only to rise in the Convention to be hooted and derided until I sit down. As soon as I raise my voice I am drowned out. The Jacobins and Montagnards, you have no idea how they tighten their grip every hour."

"Of course I know—"

But my husband wouldn't listen to me. "Robespierre and Marat and Danton are the ones listened to now. They're edging more of their men into new appointments and militia posts every day, and they won't hesitate to point that same militia at me—"

"Then we will find a way to be heard." I took his bony hand between my own. "We will not leave France in the hands of these rabid demagogues. We will speak for a national system, gain support from the provinces, reintroduce our notion of moving the center of government to Blois to break up this Paris cabal." I thought of my time in Caen, the chance meeting with a gray-eyed girl named Charlotte Corday who had devoured my newspapers so eagerly—why should her life in Normandy be ruled by those who legislated as though Paris was all that mattered? "There are practical measures we can suggest."

"The deputies in the provinces are too afraid of Robespierre's spies and Marat's tongue to speak for change. Anyone who does would find a mob on his doorstep by morning, and everyone knows it."

"I don't care. I am not afraid of Marat. I am not afraid of Robespierre or Danton or their mad dogs." I squeezed his hand as fiercely as I could. "I do not care if our table is heaped with threats of assassination. They do me honor to hate me. If our deputies must go about armed to the teeth, so will we—I will put a pistol in my muff and carry on. This is what it means to build a republic. No matter how hard the fight, we press onward—or else leave France to the madmen. Is that what you wish?"

"Yes," he whispered. "Let them have it. I am tired."

For the first and last time in my life, I shouted at my husband. "I do not care if you are tired!" I roared. "You are *minister*, Roland! That is what being a minister means. Working when you are tired, speaking when you are tired, fighting when you are tired. Looking down the barrel of a pistol and *dying* tired if that is what is needed! You are minister! You serve the republic, you serve those who love you, and you serve those who vilify you. *It does not matter if you are tired.*"

It was how I would see it were I minister. I would chain myself to my desk, fill my lungs on the floor of the Convention as I did when I was called to defend myself against treason, and roar as loud as a lion over any who would drown me out. I would never, ever, give up.

Roland's eyes swam with tears as he looked at me. "If only you'd been loyal—"

"Oh, for—" I nearly flung his hands away in my frustration, but he couldn't take another rebuff from me, even the slightest gesture. "Roland, surely there is more at stake here than the state of our marriage."

"You are my wife. There is nothing that should matter more to you."

There is, I thought. France was more than this marriage; the republic was more than this marriage. But my husband could not hear that. "I am loyal and I am here and I will never leave you." I dropped to my knees, gripping his hands so tight our knuckles whitened. "Together we can win this fight. Believe it."

I believed myself. Danton and Robespierre were not putting us aside with slander and rumor. For the first time in my life I did not care if I was called a whore— they could call me anything they liked, all they would make me was angrier. All the rage of this revolution was bottled in its women: in me, in the women with pikes like Pauline Léon and Louise Audu who had marched to Versailles to bring the king to Paris, in the hopeless idealists like young Charlotte Corday who devoured revolutionary newspapers like holy writ and snorted her contempt for the men who ranted in those pages rather than reasoned, in the dimpled salonnières like Sophie Condorcet who would fling mercy into the teeth of an entire hissing Convention. We were all so angry.

Perhaps that was why so many hated us. Why they called us names. The men of this revolution could raise their fists and ask for more, but not its women. We would have what we were given, when anyone got around to giving it to us, and we would say thank you.

I was done saying thank you. I wanted to rend and claw and scream and fight for my small corner, my small place on this stage.

"Fight alongside me," I begged my husband. "Please fight."

"No." He took his hands from mine, picked up his

pen again, began to sharpen it. "Leave me. I have my final speech to prepare."

In the end, I wrote it.

Roland delivered my words two days after the king's execution, hardly audible through all the derisive hissing. I would never have thought, if I had not seen it with my own eyes, that good judgment and fine character would be such rare commodities in this room, that so few men were fit to govern. As for expecting those qualities to be combined with honesty, it was asking for the moon.

The Jacobins looked pleased as they disposed of the last honest minister in Paris, while the Girondins on our own side shifted and fussed as they looked ahead to their own advantage. If our party of moderates ate itself and left the field to the madmen, it would be our own fault. We squabbled and jostled and fretted ourselves to pieces searching for the impossible, while Robespierre and his *sans-culottes* looked only for granite unity.

My lover caught us on the steps outside, bareheaded in the cold wind. "I am sorry," he told my husband, but his eyes looked to me. "I fought for you as hard as I could. I wish I could have done more."

If Roland had been willing to fight too . . . I pushed that thought away, for it was useless. "It is up to you now to lead the fight against the Jacobins," I said when my husband only sighed. "Brissot is too much the journalist—it must be you." My lover was the one they were calling the General, for all his marshaling to break the hold of the fanatical Paris faction. I wondered in a clutch of terror if he'd be the next to be eaten alive by Marat's gutter press.

A final kiss from the eyes of my lover, and he strode away after a bow to my husband. For one wild moment I wanted to pull my arm away from Roland's and run in pursuit. I wondered what it might have been like to soldier alongside a different kind of man, a man with my appetite for the fight. For an instant's shameful imagining I saw myself in my lover's apartments, him in his shirtsleeves, me wearing his blue coat over my nightdress to keep out the chill as we wrote at desks pushed side by side, passing the ink bottle back and forth. Trading drafts of our articles and reading, me scolding my lover for being too florid, him scolding me for being too dry, both of us laughing, sharing a cup of wine as we underlined and crossed out each other's words.

As quick as my mind painted that picture, I washed it away, and leaned my cheek against my husband's shoulder as we turned back toward the ministry. *The servants must begin moving our things out at once,* I thought. We were moving to the rue de la Harpe, a simple set of rooms. No more sleeping beneath a canopy of ostrich feathers. I'd never liked it anyway.

"It's him, isn't it?" Roland asked. "It's François Buzot."

I flinched, but I made myself speak. It didn't matter now; we were no longer public figures with alliances to maintain. "Yes." Just once I let myself speak his name. "It is François Buzot."

General Buzot, to whom our party must now look for leadership.

Roland sighed. I expected him to recoil and offer angry words, but he did not. "Has the world gone mad?" my husband asked instead, almost idly.

I considered the question. "Perhaps society calls any man mad who is not suffering from the general madness."

Through a mad new world, we walked in silence.

With madness came civil war and terror.

As winter advanced to spring, Marat incited his rabble to tear two Girondin newspaper offices to scraps as our currency dropped in value and grain prices soared.

Within months of the king's execution, a permanent guillotine loomed over the city.

In April there was a Committee of Public Safety, with not a Girondin to be seen on its roll. Our faction retaliated by having the Paris Commune investigated, which merely gained us a new enemy, and Marat arrested, which only built his status to mythic proportion once he was tried and released.

By May there was turmoil over the price of bread and calls from Robespierre for the people to rise up against the corrupt Girondin deputies of the Convention.

And then on the eve of June, there was a knock upon our door.

Six men loomed on the step. I remembered the ten men who came into the ministry the last time an arrest warrant had been threatened. I had stared them down, and no warrant had been produced. *Not this time*, I thought as the leader read the condemnation aloud in a toneless voice. *This is the end.*

Silence fell. For a moment, my husband appeared frozen. I touched his shoulder, and he cleared his throat. "I know of no law setting up the authority to which you refer, and I shall not comply. If you employ force, I can only offer you an old man's resistance, but I shall protest until the last."

For a moment the threat of violence hung in the balance. Would they seize him and drag him away? I met the eyes of the leader, summoning all the stone in my soul. His men behind him shuffled. He looked at me, back to Roland, and, at last, touched his cap. "I have no orders to employ force. Your reply will be reported to the Council of the Commune, but I must leave my colleagues here."

The thud of the door seemed very loud. My husband and I were left gazing at each other. His face was drained and gray, his hands worked. A dead calm swept over me. For so many months we had imagined this moment, had started at every knock on the door. Now that the moment was upon us, I was almost relieved. Vigorous characters like mine hate uncertainty more than anything else.

"Just a few more days," Roland muttered, glancing up the stairs to the chamber where our daughter worked at her sewing. We had been trying to get permission to leave Paris, but we were stymied at every turn, and Roland had become distracted by his crusade to get the Assembly to ratify the accounts he'd kept as minister. He didn't want to leave Paris under a cloud, he wanted his name at least cleared of any financial wrongdoing in office. I wondered where we might be if we had let the accounts go. But it had meant so much to him, to be counted an honest man . . .

An honest man, and now likely a dead one. Because the leader of the five men left outside would return with proper orders to make the arrest.

I reached for my veil and shawl. I would not stop fighting, not while I had breath. "We made plans for this," I said, keeping my voice brisk. "I will go to the Convention to denounce the situation publicly. With enough public outcry we can avoid your arrest or see you promptly released if they dare seize you."

He nodded. "I—I should stay here?"

"If you can get away unseen, leave word with the servants and go."

Armed men were everywhere at the Tuileries, which was surrounded by a growing crowd. I jumped down from the hired cab (*You never step from a carriage, you always jump down . . . no, Manon, do not think of that!*) and flew like a bird. Inside, the rooms were all shut up; guards kept anyone from entering. I managed to talk myself into a hall of petitioners and pass on a letter, but got no farther: I strode up and down for an hour, hearing the roar of men shouting.

"Paris is oppressed by tyrants who thirst for blood and dominion!" came one voice.

"Down! He defames Paris! He insults the people! Will we have a counterrevolution now?" came another.

"Citizeness, there is nothing to be done!" A colleague of Roland's came out at last, but he snapped at me before I could finish my plea. "The Assembly is in indescribable tumult. The petitioners now at the bar call for the arrest of the twenty-two." *Twenty-two who?* Roland would have asked, but I knew. The twenty-two that those in the high seats of the Mountain called their chief enemies. The Girondins. My husband would be on that list. My lover would too. And so many others, friends all . . . I swallowed, heart hammering as the man went on. "The Convention is surrounded by an armed force and no longer capable of doing good."

"It is perfectly capable!" I cried. "The majority of the people in Paris are simply asking to be told what to do. If I am admitted, I shall have the courage to say what must be said." If they would just allow me to defend my friends as I had defended my own good name. "I am afraid of nothing. Even if I cannot save Roland, I shall proclaim what the republic must hear." The man stared at me uncomprehending. I could feel the hair almost lifting off my head in my rage, blood boiling in my veins. All I loved in the world stood in mortal peril, and I could see my country's ruin before my eyes. "Let me *in!*"

"But there is a draft bill in six parts to be discussed—"

I nearly screamed my fury at the ceiling, but screaming would only mark me a hysterical woman fit for nothing. "Then I will go to warn our friends," I said and forced my rage into strength to carry me forward as long as I needed this terrible night. There is no bitter endurance like a woman's. Men call us fickle, yet we are the ones to bear witness, to bear warning, and to bear up when the world denounces us. And to bear it all silently, because we are not allowed to speak. Just once, my enemies had let me speak on the floor of this Convention, and I left with honors like victory laurels. The men in power at the moment would not make that mistake twice.

Because who knows what a woman will say when she is angry enough?

I flew to the various lodgings of our Girondin friends, leaving letters where I could not find servants to pass warnings. It was pitch dark by the time I returned to the Tuileries. Approaching the Carrousel by light of the streetlamps, I saw there were no more armed men, only a cabal of *sans-culottes* clustered about a cannon. For a moment I hesitated—these were the kind of people who had spit on me on the street—but it was dark and I was veiled; just another woman of Paris eager to know what had happened. "Citizens, did everything pass off well?"

"Marvelous well," a woman hiccuped. She smelled of gin and blood. "The Paris delegates were all embracing each other and singing 'La Marseillaise' under the tree of liberty."

"And the twenty-two?" My heart thudded. *Let me hear that order has been restored, that some measure of sanity has prevailed.*

"Kicked to the ditch," the woman snickered. "The municipality will arrest them. Robespierre says so."

My stomach sank. "He does not have the power to do that—"

"'Course he does. He does what needs to be done, to sort out those bastards—"

I took a moment to wonder just why there were so many women who worshipped Robespierre. Sophie Condorcet or perhaps her philosopher husband had commented that it was because the people of Paris had taken the Revolution as their religion, and Robespierre for their priest. The comparison was apt enough—like any good priest, Robespierre preached and censured; he could be furious or serious, melancholy or exalted. He thundered against the rich and the great, lived on little, and had only one mission: to talk. "And he talks all the time," I muttered, already running toward the street. I had to return to my husband; he would be wondering what to do without me.

Ahead I saw the dark shape of a coach for hire and lengthened my step—only to see the shadowy figures of a man and woman beside the wheel, their discussion a low, heated hiss. "Pardon my intrusion, but may I beg use of the cab—" I began, only to fall back a step as the man turned toward me as if summoned here by my thoughts. ". . . Citizen Robespierre."

"Citizeness Roland." He tipped his silk hat, immaculate even at the end of this terrible day where he must have been hours in the Convention whipping up his mob against my husband, my lover, and all my friends. His striped coat hung from his small frame in perfectly tailored folds, his hair was frizzed and powdered, his voice high and precise. "You should be home, surely."

"As should you," I parried. "A man who accosts women on the street in the night does not long keep a nickname like the Incorruptible."

"We will both depart," the woman at his side said quietly. "By your leave, Citizen Robespierre—" She touched his arm, the arc of her pale neck pure and beseeching in the lamplight, and I saw his face flicker. A curt nod, and he handed her up into the cab, me behind her. Another instant and we were rattling away. I could see Robespierre watching us go, spectacles reflecting two blank circles of light into the night.

I shivered, turning my gaze back to the girl quietly settling her skirts opposite. "Thank you," I said. "I feared I would be forced to walk home."

"You are the famous Madame Roland. I am happy to do you a service." A very young woman, surely not yet twenty—and beautiful, that I could see even in the shadowed coach. A slender, graceful figure, soft tumbles of hair, a passionate mouth.

"I do not know you, citizeness," I confessed, although she looked familiar.

"I am Madame de Sartine, but I was born Émilie de Sainte-Amaranthe." She smiled faintly at my start of recognition. "You might know my mother—the famous courtesan who ran the Cinquante gambling club. Having failed to earn an invitation to *le monde elegant* of Maman's salons and club, Robespierre seems to have set his sights on earning me." She sniffed and shrugged one shoulder as if having one of Paris's most influential Jacobins pursuing her was nothing more than a mere annoyance.

"The Incorruptible?" I said in surprise.

"Not so incorruptible." Her voice sounded far older

than her years. "I'm only the latest, for he has already despoiled one of his landlord's daughters."

"Do you return his interest?" It was not courteous to ask, but in this strange dark night I didn't know what constituted offense anymore. The world was upside down, and I could no longer hope for any good or be surprised by any evil.

"I loathe him," Émilie said conversationally. "He ordered me to the palace so I might see his triumph today. I did not dare refuse the invitation, though thanks to your arrival I was able to slip from his grasp before I had to refuse him something else."

"His triumph over my husband and my friends." I shook my head as my earlier rage stirred inside me again. "Does Robespierre need a woman to applaud him to make his victory complete? I did not think he had such passions in him."

"All men do," Émilie said. "My mother told me so, and I have seen nothing to make me disbelieve her."

"Then it will be his end." My mouth stretched into a smile, then the smile to a laugh. It was a laugh that skirted hysteria, but I could not stop myself. I had thought myself unfit for politics because passion had made me weak. But men were no less immune to fits of passion. Whether spasms of love or of rage, emotion sways us all like the tides. I wondered if Robespierre would follow his passion for the girl opposite, or if his passion for the guillotine would win.

"Passion thwarted turns to rage," I said, laughter fading as I thought of Robespierre's tight, ferocious gaze fixed on Émilie's beautiful throat. "Leave Paris while you still can."

She pleated a fold of her silk dress between her slim fingers. "Wherever I go, I doubt it will be far enough to escape him."

"I do not think I will escape him either," I heard myself saying. "Though it's hatred he has for me, rather than love." I had feared Danton with his crude flirtations and Marat with his obscene rantings more than Robespierre, but it was the small man with the quiet enmity flashing behind his spectacles who was the most dangerous. Too late, too late.

Émilie smiled faintly. "Hatred and love are not as different as you might think."

Our cab was stopped at the checkpoint of the Samaritaine. "Who's there?" the sentinel barked. "Two women all alone?"

I could see Émilie casting her eyes up in exasperation even as I bristled. "Alone, sir? Do you not observe Innocence and Truth, our traveling companions? What more is necessary?" He looked chastened, and Émilie burst into laughter as we rolled on into the night.

"I don't think I have been traveling companions with Innocence for quite some time." Amusement played around her lips as she met my gaze.

"Nor I," I said. In many ways Émilie was my opposite—young, no doubt royalist in her sympathies like her mother, seemingly unashamed to admit to her lack of purity. But here we were, in the same carriage upon the same dangerous avenue and afraid of the same man. Revolution had made France unsafe for everyone, regardless of loyalties or ideals. "You need not go out of your way to put me down on my doorstep; I can walk from here."

"Surely you, too, should flee while you still can, Citizeness Roland."

"I'm set in my ways," I returned lightly. "If anyone wishes to murder me, they can do it in my own home."

She squeezed my hand and grinned, suddenly and enchantingly. I smiled back. Just a moment's meeting between two women in the night, a touch of a woman's hand and the support of her smile, but it gave me strength for what was to come.

A murmured word from the porter let me know that my husband had fled, sneaking out via our landlord's lodging to avoid the guards at the door. After determining my daughter was still safe upstairs with the servants, I was soon on my own way and slipping inside a certain house nearby. I found Roland writing by the light of a shaded candle—his face shattered in relief as he saw me, and we flung our arms about each other. Soon we were sitting, hands clasped across the table.

"There is not much time," I began. "What arrangements have been made?"

"Our friends here will help me leave Paris. They have a passport for you, too, and clothes to disguise you as a peasant woman. And for our daughter—"

"We will slow you down." And if our friends had to hide three instead of one, it would put them in considerable danger. "Go ahead without us, Roland. It is you they want, not your wife and child. We will be safe."

"Not you. They hate you as much as me—"

"You must get away." I squeezed his hands fiercely. "You can still render great service in other parts of France where moderation still rules—if you can just escape this city and this crisis."

Someone had to stand against these Paris dictators and their mad little commune; I would help as many of my friends as possible escape into the provinces to set up an opposition. "The fight is not over."

"I cannot—"

"You must."

He continued to argue, but I would not. I kept repeating "You must" until he gave way with another weary sigh.

"Leave here as soon as you can, Roland. This hiding place won't be safe for long." I rose, pulling my shawl about my shoulders as he sat studying his folded hands.

"Remember the farm near Villefranche?" he said suddenly. "When we were first married. The hills of Beaujolais rising behind, the slopes covered in vines . . ."

"We will see it again." He clung to me as I embraced him. I would have to be the brave one for this farewell; his eyes were brimming so I kissed both his eyelids before they could overflow. "I love you," I whispered.

"I wish you loved me more," he answered.

"I will prove it every day as we grow old looking at the slopes of Beaujolais." I kissed him softly on the mouth. "Promise me you will continue the fight, Roland. No matter what happens."

When he finally nodded, I nodded back and slipped away, hoping with all my heart that he would keep the promise. I would keep mine—if we both survived, rode out this crisis together, and lived to see our hair grow white under the republic I loved so much, I would devote my life to loving him. *Just fight*, I prayed. *Find the strength to fight without me.* Because for the first time in years, I would not be by his side.

So why did I return home? I knew the dangers, but I still went. Why?

I could give a hundred answers. Because my daughter was there and I could not abandon her, or the servants who had served us so loyally. Because as much as I was loathed, Marat and Robespierre would find themselves called villains if they seized me. Because if they did seize me, that might be enough to slake their hatred so they would abandon their pursuit of my husband. And because even if the worst happened and I were to face the guillotine, I would rather die than witness this ruin of my country and the death of my revolution—I would consider it an honor to be counted amongst the heroic victims.

Most of all, I went home to wait because it was not in me to run. I had run from the memory of what happened to me as a girl, and it had brought me nothing but shame. I would not run from these men today.

I soothed my daughter's tears and sang her to sleep on my return; I calmed my servants and sent them to bed. Then I took a shaky breath and went up the dark stairs to my chamber, where a man's shadow detached from the wall as I slipped inside, and he drew me into his arms.

For the first time on this long, terrible day I let

myself sag, releasing a stifled sob. My husband was in flight, my friends were scattered, France had become a bloody arena where her children tore one another to pieces—but just a moment I let my shoulders sink under the weight of it all, as the strong arms I loved so much quietly held me up.

Then I straightened, wiped my eyes, and stepped back. "There," I told my lover. "You have seen me with your own eyes. Will you do the sensible thing and flee now, my general?"

"I am not general of anything," he answered, still holding me about the waist. "At least until I can get to the provinces and raise allies against that bastard Robespierre."

I knew he would fight. He did not know how to give up. We were alike in that—when I had dispatched a note to his lodgings this afternoon warning that arrests were coming, he had answered that he would not leave Paris without seeing me and would wait in my chamber until the end of time if necessary. "Did you come in through the window?" I asked, feeling a most unlikely smile crease my lips.

"Yes." He kissed my temple, the corner of my brow. "Manon—"

I laid a finger over his mouth. "I won't flee with you, any more than I would go with Roland. I will only slow you down, and I will not let either of you be caught because of me."

I suppose I should have felt like the greatest harlot in France, bidding my husband good-bye with my love, only to go home and bid my lover good-bye, also with my love. I did not know how to maintain honor here— only that the course of greatest honor seemed to be to let neither man die. They both loved me, and I loved both of them—did that make me a whore? I was no longer so sure. In the eye of the storm, in the shadow of the guillotine, we all walked in the glint of lightning. In such days, I could no longer think love a tarnished thing, even if it grew where it should not.

Honor, duty, love: these things would bind my beautiful Paris together again when the jackals were done rending it apart. I had to believe that.

I lifted my head off my lover's breast, saying simply, "Go now."

François Buzot bent his head and kissed me fiercely. The first kiss we had ever shared; the first kiss I had taken from any man but my husband. I had accustomed myself to remaining still for Roland's dry mouth, cursing the stiffness that always paralyzed me, but as my lover's wide hand tangled in my hair and his lips parted mine, I felt myself melting for the very first time in my life. I didn't know if it was his skill or something in me—exhaustion, fear, my furious resolve to defy my enemies—but something loosened the great block in my chest that had been there since I was ten years old and that greedy-handed apprentice fumbled beneath my skirts. For the first time in my life, I returned a man's kiss and wanted more.

My lover stopped with his forehead against mine and his breath coming harsh, fingers resting against the fastenings of my muslin gown. His stillness asked a question of me, and I wanted to answer *yes*. But, smiling, I shook my head. I could not pull him down on the narrow bed and forget the world, much as I wished to. I didn't know what the end of this revolution would be, but I would never betray my husband. I would share his fate and die as I'd lived, doing my duty, no matter how much it might cost me.

It was enough to know I *could* have lain on that bed, and for once not felt like a sadly incomplete woman. Passion could have been mine, had the world been different. That was enough.

My lover saw the good-bye in my smile and kissed me on the brow. "Fight," he whispered. "Fight, Manon."

"Fight," I whispered back and led him down the dark stair to the rear of the house where he might slip away unnoticed. I watched his shadow meld with the night as he slipped away, unnoticed, and then I locked the door and leaned against it, weeping for the men I loved. For myself. And for France.

Not twenty minutes later, they came for me.

The hesitant leader of yesterday had been replaced by another man, young and handsome and all insolent smiles under his red cap. "Remember me, Citizeness Roland?" I did. Théo Leclerc of Les Enragés, who never delivered a speech when he could shriek it, who had been one of the ten men forcing his way into my house nine months ago with threats and demands. Whom I had sent away empty-handed. Today he stood implacable, reading out a warrant for the arrest of Citizen and Citizeness Roland. I folded my hands through the recitation and considered my response. I might cite the law that forbid nocturnal arrests. I might cite the lack of legal grounds for any arrest at all . . .

Do not waste your time, Manon. At this moment, the law is now little more than a word used to deprive people of their rights. Force is the master here.

So I merely smiled. "How do we proceed, gentlemen?"

Dawn was breaking pink and new over Paris by the time my apartment had been picked over. I had said my farewells, clinging to every drop of my strength as I hugged my daughter, as I kept my voice calm and told her that I loved her, that she would be safe and must have no fear. I clung to the scent of her hair as I was, at last, marched out into the street. On my doorstep I found two rows of armed men leading all the way to the carriage. Behind these men gathered a jeering cluster of the avid and the curious. My heart beat steadily as I advanced between the gleaming rows of pikes.

A woman's voice rose, vicious and shrill: "To the guillotine!"

I found her face in the crowd and stared until she looked away.

"We can close the carriage windows." Théo Leclerc smirked as I stepped up into the coach.

"No, thank you." I sat, still feeling that curious calm. "I am not afraid of staring eyes and ask for no protection."

He settled into the seat opposite, rapping at the roof for the horses to drive on. "You have more character than many men, citizeness, to await justice so calmly. I'll give you that."

"Justice?" I allowed my smile to curl. "If justice were done, I should not be here in your power at all. But if this procedure leads me to the scaffold, I shall mount it calmly. I weep for my country. I blush for my mistake in thinking France was ready for liberty."

He looked affronted. "The citizens of Paris are the arbiters of liberty—"

"You citizens of Paris are the destroyers of your city. When you find yourself standing in its ruins, you will regret your cowardice."

He grunted. No doubt he thought me mad. But I'd never been more certain of anything in my life.

"On the throne today, tomorrow in irons. That is the common lot of the virtuous in time of revolution." I recorded those words the first night I spent in prison, the very first lines of my memoir. The pile of pages has grown since then, so fast—how long have I been here, nearly a month? My cell at the Abbaye is small, but my horizon limitless, and my soul ranges free outside these walls.

It follows my husband, who I have heard is safely in hiding in Rouen, and urges him to have courage. It follows my lover in his blue coat where he works to gather allies in Normandy against the Jacobins, and presses phantom kisses to his mouth. It follows my daughter, safe with friends who cherish her as though she were their own. My body is caged but I have pen and ink and free will—how can any man born call me imprisoned with such gifts?

My end is near, this I know. Any day I may be slaughtered or hauled before some tribunal where Robespierre, Danton, and Marat feed their enemies to the guillotine. I listen to the noise of the street out-side, interpreting the sounds of this city as a daughter of the Seine always can, and I know terror triumphs now. Marianne, as we named our national goddess of liberty, stalks above France like a scarlet specter, the blood of the innocent trailing from her red gown, no longer a lady of liberty but a lady of terror. In her wake, insolence and crime rage furiously together and the people bow down in mindless homage and abject fear. My vast and beautiful city has become gorged with blood and rotten with lies, wildly applauding the foul murders that are supposed to be necessary for its safety.

Yet I am at peace, because my part is done except for the very last act. Because a woman who is finished with life may simply *be*.

How long I have fretted and feared over the role life gave me! I never wrote a word in my own name; I kept behind my husband in all things; I turned away from love for the sake of virtue . . . and as Sophie Condorcet said, all my good behavior did not save me. She and I talk now and then—she is allowed to visit the prisoners here, where she sketches portraits of the condemned for their grieving families. She gives me news, prom-ises to look in on my daughter, and draws me as I write. We trade wry smiles: two women who have been called whores, simply because that is the word for any woman with an opinion and a voice to express it.

Well, no matter what the world calls me, I know I am no whore. I shake back my hair and smile as I realize that in the shadow of death, I am free.

Free to wish my husband well, knowing I stayed by him until the end.

Free to love the man who unlocked me with a kiss, now that I have no opportunity to give in to sin. My love for him hurts no one now. I would have given my life to my husband—now I will give my lover my last sigh.

Most of all, I am free to *write*.

Write for the first time under my own name, my own words, and to hell with what the world thinks. Write the memoirs of Manon Roland, who will fight to the end showing the world that a woman can face her death bravely as a lion. All the rage of this revolution was bottled in its women, I thought once—now I leave the rage to the women still taking up arms in the fight. I wish them well, and give them my strength for the battle ahead, in the hope they can give my daughter a republic that will not need her rage.

For myself, I will savor every moment within these drab walls. My jailers shall not prevent me from living to the full, right up until the last moment.

My memoir is being smuggled out of this cell, chapter by chapter, to friends who swear they will see it published. Each roll of pages is tied up with a red ribbon—the same ribbons twined through my hair the day I defended myself, with honors, on the floor of the National Convention. Now they bind up the story of my life. Not everything will go into this document that will be my legacy—someday my daughter will read it, and she does not need to know her mother loved a man besides her father. But I will put in the rest. My beginning, as a bookish girl yearning for the world . . . my womanhood, where I was privileged to serve the birth pangs of a republic in this incandescent time of change and chaos, terror and glory . . . and my end.

I have devoted a good deal of thought to that. What will be my last words when I mount the scaffold?

I speak aloud in the cold cell, breath puffing white in the air. "Liberty," I say slowly, "what crimes are committed in your name."

How does that sound?

PART V

The Assassin

Not a sensitive or generous heart beats
that does not shed tears of blood.
—CHARLOTTE CORDAY

PAULINE

Paris, July 7, 1793

The nightmare was always the same.

Being dragged into the alley outside my family's *chocolat* café. I had been walking home just after dark from a night of dinner with friends when they jumped me. Neighborhood ruffians. Beaten until bloodied and limp by too many meaty male fists. Robbed of the last coin in my purse—not even enough to buy a loaf of bread, if there were any to be found—and threatened with worse.

And I awakened from it as I always did—sweating, gasping, heart galloping out of my chest. Involuntary reactions to the terror some part of me could not let go, and which quickly gave way to a gut-deep conviction—I would never be defenseless again.

That beating two years ago had proved the final push I'd needed to risk my life and reputation for the people's Revolution. And yet, shortly after, when we'd stormed the Tuileries on 10 August in 1792, I'd been forced to give up my pike to a man.

Disarmed once more. At the mercy of those around me. It had been hard not to retreat into a corner or to run away.

This was the reason I was determined to give women a voice, and fight for our rights to bear arms, so that women could become equal in our new republic. This was the reason I woke every morning and started the day anew.

I whipped off the covers and stood in the heat of my room wishing there was a hint of a breeze coming through the open window, but all we had for the past few weeks in Paris was sweltering heat that was driving the whole city mad.

I touched the scar on my left forearm, puckered and pink. It always throbbed after I dreamed of the attack. They'd tried to stab me in the belly, but I blocked it with my arm. I flexed my fingers, the smallest one still tingly, never having fully regained feeling. A reminder that I was alive, and what my purpose was.

"Bastards," I murmured.

The door to my bedroom burst open and two tiny faces peered into the room.

"Pauline, why are you still sleeping? We are starving!"

I couldn't help smiling at my younger siblings. They looked like Maman and smiled just as sweetly as our departed papa. I hugged them, feeling the warmth of sleep still on their skin.

"Where is Maman?" I asked.

"Baking."

With Papa gone, the running of the café and the raising of my siblings was left to Maman and me. "Ah. Go and wash up and I will see if I can find you some eggs."

They hurried out of the room, scrambling over each other like puppies going after a ball. Two little girls who remembered nothing before the Revolution. Two little girls who thought the madness of our city was normal. When I first witnessed the execution of peasants who had rioted for bread, who were starving and demanding their king do something about their rumbling bellies and dying children, I knew this world was wrong. I would riot for my *petit* brothers and sisters. Would I be killed for trying to feed them? If so, it was a worthy cause.

This was why our government must change, why we'd run those swindling Girondins out of town. Why they must be executed along with every other traitor. You were either with us or against us. Before the king's execution in January, the Girondins had voted for Louis to be spared. But living, he left open a door, even if just a crack, for the return of the monarchy. And we'd come too far and bled too much for that. If our country was going to make its true transformation, it had to be all the way. No king living, and no heirs to take up his mantle. Which meant that his wife and his children needed to follow him to the guillotine, and soon. Their lives were a necessary sacrifice. The death of one family to spare the lives and secure the just futures of the rest.

I dressed quickly, tugging my chemise down from the drying cord where I'd hung it the night before. I tried to tame my mass of blond curls into a bun at the nape of my neck, but little rebellious wisps sprang free. They did not want to be contained any more than I did.

I picked up the tiny kitchen knife and tucked it securely into my boot, my need to carry it a stark reminder of what could happen to any woman on the street. Women might not yet have the right to bear arms, but no one could tell me not to protect myself. I'd knife a man without hesitation if he tried to harm me. Gut him right where he stood. What I did, I did for my sisters across France as much as for myself. I aim to leave behind a legacy. So I can depart the world knowing I've done something for every woman in the republic. Given her a voice, equal rights, and the kind of meaningful citizenship we all strived for.

Citizen Condorcet, the representative in my neighborhood of Faubourg Saint-Germain, is fond of saying, "Be careful not to mistake heat of head for heat of soul; because what you want is not heat, but force, not violence but steadfastness."

I disagree. I am force, I am heat, I am steadfastness, but I am also not opposed to violence. Let them just try and stand in my way.

Paris, July 9, 1793

"*Ma petite fille*, you are an inspiration," Maman said as she fussed at pinning my tricolor cockade to my bonnet rouge. The cap had become synonymous with not only the revolutionaries, but the women of the Société des Républicaines-Révolutionnaires, a highly respected society of women activists, and a branch of the Jacobin Club.

A society that was now mine to lead.

"It's fine, Maman," I said as she tried to tame my curls where they escaped from my bonnet. "It's almost time." Below, the men waiting for the start of the club's meeting in our *café au chocolat* grew rowdier by the second.

Admittedly, I was overeager to flee her grasp, but that was because today's meeting was special. Today, I was leading the first march as president of the women's Société des Républicaines-Révolutionnaires. My dear friend Claire Lacombe, a former actress and great beauty, secretary of our women's club, would join me. I've strived for respect amongst my peers since that moment when I'd been disarmed at the Tuileries. Claire and Louise—the Queen of the Market Women—were like sisters to me, had been given awards for their service in that same battle. Louise had gone head to head with a Swiss Guard and won. If I'd not been disarmed, maybe I would have been recognized too.

Where was my glory? It was coming, I could feel it.

My stomach made a loud rumbling noise. Maman ran her hands over my shoulders. "I fear you will get nothing to eat with all those downstairs. They will want to hear you speak."

"They do not come to see me, Maman, they come because they know you have made progress with your potato flour, and everyone is hungry for something better than dust."

My mother blushed. At one time, we'd been famous for our *chocolat chaud*. A favorite drink of one of King Louis's mistresses, Madame du Barry. Le Maison du Chocolat Léon had been popular, and our coffers overflowed. Everything changed when the old king died and the new king married his Austrian *chienne*. Widow Capet brought her own chocolatier to court and would have none of our peasant concoction.

I took great satisfaction in knowing she has no *chocolat* now. Well, at least not any that wasn't tainted with the spit of her enemies.

"We shall take their sous either way." Maman clucked her tongue and pinned her cockade to her apron. "The coin will help keep you in bonnets rouges and feed your brothers and sisters."

They cheered us and called out flatteries as we entered the café.

Louise shoved aside a few men, giving one a few choice words when he dared jostle her back. "Madame President." She gave a mocking bow. In recent months, there had been a gradual change with Louise. We used to be like sisters, and now there seemed to be an ever-widening divide between us, the reason for which remained hidden to me.

"La Reine Audu," I teased back.

"I managed to convince Jeanne that we should move our cart to the Champs de Mars for the rally. So I will be there."

"Thank you, my friend." I squeezed her hand, feeling a sudden course of raw emotion.

Louise was still painfully thin with sunken half-moons beneath her eyes, which were more often wide with intensity now than before. A fervor for our Revolution, or something deeper and more complicated?

"I saved a few rotten apples to throw at anyone who tries to ruin your day." She jerked her hand away, staring down at it for a minute before giving a raspy laugh.

I laughed too, though there was no humor in it. "I have no doubt you'll find a use for them." I wanted to ask her what was wrong, why she was pulling away from me, but a shout from behind interrupted us.

"Pauline, there you are!" Claire leapt onto a table, her dark curls bouncing around her shoulders, and her bright coffee-colored eyes vibrant. Claire played a bonne Goddess of Liberty and had a talent for inspiring a crowd. With no preamble she pressed her hand to her heart and began to recite the speech I gave at the National Assembly last year. The one in support of the right of women to bear arms for which I'd gathered hundreds of signatures. I could still feel all those eyes on me. The sweat that prickled beneath my arms. A thrumming of heat through my limbs. The anger of most of the men as they rejected not only me, but all of my gender. How dare we rise up? How dare we try to take from men their due? Run back to the kitchen, to the birthing room, that was what they shouted. Only a few were quiet, or even nodded slightly in agreement. The few who knew and saw. The few who understood that women, half the population, had a place in this world. A place in change.

In fairness, I must admit our representative Condorcet had been among those few. But even though he wished to help women in our fight for equality and was reputed to give his wife, Sophie, an unusual degree of freedom and autonomy, he was not a man who got things done. I could never respect him for opposing the king's execution. But Sophie, she was beautiful, intelligent, and perhaps the only aristo I might spare, for she'd befriended Louise, taught her, and had helped to educate many women with her school. She'd visited our little *chocolat* shop a few times now and was always kind.

As Claire recited my words, this group of men looked at me appraisingly—some with approval in their eyes and others with resentment darkening their expressions. Let them resent me all they would. Because every day, a growing number of us women vowed: we will not go back, we will not sit down, we will not be quiet. I was certainly one of them.

We didn't always agree on every point—instead, we ran the gamut from progressives like myself to those conservative Girondins, such as Madame Roland, who called themselves revolutionaries but only accepted half measures. Oh, how the Girondins cause my blood to boil. That was how ingrained antiquated ideas about a woman's place were, that even some revolutionaries could only accept single women in the ranks of the marchers and agitators, but not the married ones. And some likewise insisted a mother's place was at home. I glanced across the café at my mother. She spent her days taking care of her children and the café, and she still found time to promote the rights of women. I saw no reason why we couldn't be both mother and activist. Wasn't the duty of a mother to show her daughter that she, too, had a voice?

Then there were the royalist-friendly women who catered to the men, like Citizeness de Sainte-Amaranthe, a courtesan, of all things, who ran the gambling club Cinquante. Of course she was a royalist. Flaunting luxuries like high-paying whores and tossing coin into the gutter just like that bitch Widow Capet.

"Attention seeker." Louise snorted in Claire's direction.

I grinned. There was nothing more refreshing than Louise's brutal honesty. But for the most part, Claire and I were on the same side of things. And we'd risen together through the ranks of our society and the clubs. We were both held in respect by other republicans: especially the men who sat above the Convention floor in the seats known as the Mountain, and by Danton and Robespierre themselves. I knew this because such men mostly kept their filthy hands off us—though I wasn't sure Claire had been entirely able to escape their roving touches.

Even enlightened men sometimes felt beautiful women were things they might possess.

Which was one more reason why, together, the women of the Société des Républicaines-Révolutionnaires meant to make good on the promises of the Revolution. To no longer pay a king's ransom for a loaf of bread. To no longer fear that any child born might soon starve. To end the hypocrisy and the blatant disregard for the lives of those who kept this country alive—peasants, soldiers, women.

Claire came to my favorite part of my speech, and I interrupted her, taking over, reliving the words, and letting my voice carry over the crowd. "You cannot refuse us and society cannot remove from us this right which nature gives us, unless it is alleged that the Declaration of Rights is not applicable to women and that they must allow their throats to be slit, like sheep, without having the right to defend themselves!"

I jumped up on the table beside my friend and continued. "Well, what choice do we have but to protect ourselves? My fellow lovers of a free nation, what say you join us today on our march to the Champs to Mars where we will celebrate our rise to victory? We will leave on the hour!"

Cheers, applause, and thumping hands upon the wooden tables nearly shook the shop. Grinning, Claire tossed her arm about my shoulder and kissed my cheeks. "Today is a good day, *mon amie.*"

"*Oui*, a great day." I leapt off the table to make ready for our march that would take place when the hour struck. As soon as the rest of our members arrived, we'd take the streets by storm, gathering anyone we could as we went.

As Claire launched into another speech, her alleged lover and fellow activist Jean-Théophile Leclerc sidled closer to my side. I battled away the attraction I felt for him, for it was out of place and impossible. And yet, Théo was the only man to give me a weapon when others disarmed me. How could I not admire him for that?

"Citizeness," he crooned, running a hand through his short-cropped *noir* hair. "Look at all these people who have come here for you."

He'd been casting me dark looks full of lust and not a little rage for months now. This constant simmering of anger and outrage was the very reason he'd been kicked out of the Jacobin Club and formed his own political group which he named Les Enragés.

He and others like him had made a name defending the lower class, the less fortunate—people like me and the rest of the *sans-culottes*, working-class poor who wore pantaloons instead of bourgeois knee breeches.

I respected Théo for fighting for the rights of *every* man, woman, and child. The man had a courage that surpassed all others. Every day he woke, ready to fight, despite the dangers. This was who he was, an enraged one. Even years earlier, after he'd been arrested in Martinique for aiding in the slave revolt, he'd returned to the islands to defend other revolutionists who'd taken a stand. And we could all count on that same commitment today, for we'd seen progress already.

I looked away, because I hated the way the desire in Théo's eyes made me question my own choice to remain without a man. Because I liked that he looked at me that way. And because I hated the way liking it made me a betrayer to my friend. I did not have time for the weakness that so often came when a woman spread her legs. For centuries, women had been considered fit only for breeding. Now we had a chance to make a difference. I would not let this moment be taken from me by base desires that might push me into the role of mother. If the only way to remain politically active was to maintain a stoic abstinence, then so be it.

I respected Théo for aiding in the expulsion of the Girondins from power in order to see his beliefs—*my* beliefs—realized. Respect for him—that was all I would allow myself. Thanks to that expulsion, the Montagnards, who we jokingly called our voices on the Mountain, wielded control of the Convention. Minister Roland—and don't mistake me, I do not mean the man, but his *wife*—had finally been arrested, even though her husband escaped. And I couldn't wait to see her head roll. I wanted her to look out into the crowd and see me, and know that indeed our pikes and slogans—which she'd once dismissed—had made a nation.

I was bitterly disappointed that the rest of "the twenty-two" who ought to have been arrested and awaiting death along with Madame Roland had been able to escape. Olympe, too, but not for long. The list of gathered evidence against her was longer than the line of men at our café. A defender of women, of slaves, I wish I could have admired her, but having aligned herself to my enemies, I could look at her no other way. We'd find them all. Just like we'd found the king and his family.

There was no escaping justice.

The only way to show true power was to feed these

enemies of the republic to Madame Guillotine. I had made a vow that I'd find the rotten bastards and make them pay for their views in blood. For the Girondins made promises in vain and profited from the Revolution at the expense of the working class and destitute. Their greed had ruined the finances of France to a point we might never recover. Yet, where was the promised bread? The distribution of wealth? Why must widows whose husbands and sons were sent to the battlefield for the cause of freedom pay a year's wages for the cotton to wipe their tears? This was why we fought still, women like myself, and Théo and his fellow Enragés, because even though the king was dead, we still suffered.

"Any news on the Girondins who escaped Paris?" I asked Théo softly, not wanting to drag anyone's attention from Claire, who was still speaking, toward us.

"There have been rumors from the north." Théo lifted a cup of coffee to his lips, sipping as he met my eyes over the rim. "Your maman makes good coffee." He smirked. "Do you make coffee so well as she?"

I gritted my teeth at his subtle hint to women's work. "Not as many are drinking *chocolat* as we wish. If the men of this revolution wish to sit all day sipping and shouting, I want our share of their coin. How else to come out of this revolution with clothes on my siblings' backs and food enough in their bellies?"

"How are your brothers and sisters?"

I glanced up at him with narrowed eyes. There was only one reason for such small talk. Well, perhaps not among friends, but Théo was not my friend. He was a reveler, a man willing to be unfaithful to my friend, and a potential seducer. Claire leaped down from the table.

"They are well." I flicked my gaze back at him for a moment, thoughtful. Théo was handsome, there could be no doubt. Did Claire find him desirable because he believed women should have the right to fight, to be politically active? Because if I were to make a partner of the opposite sex, that belief would be essential.

A slight smile twitched at the side of his mouth, and he winked, his masculine charms unexpectedly taking my breath. Did he know what I was thinking? I wanted to pound my head into the wall for it. Then Claire was beside us, grabbing his hand and doing a twirl, drawing him into a dance without music. A spike of jealousy lanced through me, and I had to turn away in disgust with them and with myself.

The door opened and another Enragés leader sauntered in. Claire tugged Théo away with a delighted shout about a speech the other man was preparing. Théo glanced back over his shoulder, a question in his eyes I couldn't and wouldn't decipher.

"Pauline, come help with this." My mother waved me over, and I carried a stack of crates out back. "Are you ready?" Pride shone in my mother's eyes.

"*Oui*, Maman. We will leave shortly." I hefted two more crates.

"Allow me, citizeness." Théo took another pile from my mother's grasp and indicated for me to lead the way out the back.

Cautiously, I allowed him to follow me. "Right here is fine," I said, setting down my stack. I turned my back to go inside when he stopped me. Why wasn't he with Claire? Why had he followed me out here?

"I wish to speak with you about something."

I glanced toward the back door of our café. I didn't want to be alone with Théo. Didn't want to feel that quickening in my chest that seemed to happen every time he was near me. But I didn't want him to know he made me uncomfortable, either—to give him that power—so I narrowed my eyes. "I need to get back inside. We are to march."

"One moment, that is all."

The summer heat was stifling, and the fabric of my clothes quickly started to stick.

"I have an appointment with Marat this afternoon," he said, pausing for dramatic effect.

And it worked, damn him. Because Marat and his

newspaper, *L'ami de Peuple*, were critical to the revolutionary cause—helping rouse the people, spread
important speeches from the Convention, and unify
our movement. "Go on."

"I am going to ask him to publish this." Théo pulled
a small bundle of papers from his pocket and handed it
to me.

I opened them, hoping to see something about Claire
and me and our society of women, how we were forg-
ing our way ahead and advocating for women's rights.
If after presenting herself to the Convention, being received at the Jacobin Club, Jeanne Odo, a former slave
of Saint-Domingue, was able to affect change for men of
color, certainly change was imminent for women, too.
Instead, Théo's neatly scrawled writing proclaimed the
Girondins must be found and held accountable for their
many sins. That they must meet Madame Guillotine,
and after them, in their footsteps, all the hoarders, and
everyone with a drop of royal blood must die as well.

Despite my disappointment, a shiver of excitement
coursed through me. If there was one person in all
Paris who felt as I did about the Girondins, I thought it
must be Théo.

"This is good," I said, though it was nothing more
than what was in the papers constantly. But for some
reason, which I couldn't explain, I sought to placate him.

"I was hoping you would think so."

I handed him back the papers, avoiding eye contact. "Marat will be impressed."

Théo smiled. "I was hoping to impress you, citizeness."

"Why?" I eyed him defiantly.

Without warning, Théo gripped my elbow. Panic knocked the breath from me. The forceful touch an instant reminder of what happened to me before. I tried to shove him away, and he lightened his touch but didn't let go. Our eyes locked, and the panic ebbed. This wasn't an attack, but a clumsy attempt at wooing.

"You fascinate me," he said.

I didn't know if I should be more disturbed by the fact that the closeness between us sent a hot shiver coursing through me, or the disgust I felt at such weakness.

"What are you doing, citizen?" I asked, trying for formal when all I felt was a base need to grind my body against his. Instead, I halfheartedly shoved at his chest.

His blue eyes were intent on mine as he skimmed a hand over my cheek and down my neck. How many other women had he touched like this? Taking what he wanted without permission. Why was I letting him? "What I've wanted to do for a long time."

What *he* wanted.

I narrowed my eyes, frowning and working hard to seem the tough termagant he knew me to be. "Molest a woman behind her place of work?"

Théo smiled, his hand gripping my hip and squeezing. "Is my touch unwanted?"

I wanted to shout *oui*, but my throat was closed tight, because while half of me wanted him to leave me alone, the other half wanted to feel the power of his longing for me as he crushed my body beneath him.

"Get off me," I hissed.

"We both need this."

"I do not need any man."

Théo's grin widened. "Ah, but there you are wrong, *ma petite fille*, because you do need me. You need me to tell the Mountain that you are worthy of their vote." He leaned closer, so that his breath fanned on my face and I wanted to pummel him. I did need the support of the Mountain in moving women's rights forward, and for Théo to dangle it before my nose like a carrot was manipulation at its worst. Was he suggesting I sleep with him to advance my cause? Was that not paradoxical? "You need me to stockpile your weapons. To march beside you."

"You flatter yourself." I'd marched beside women without him and seen our cause through. "We brought the king from Versailles, toppled the Bastille, and raised hell at the Tuileries without you."

"But you want me. I don't flatter myself in that. Your body tells me the truth."

I shoved against his chest again, this time harder, and Théo laughed as he backed away. The evidence of his arousal pressed to his pants, and heat flushed my cheeks for having looked.

"If you want to impress me, citizen, then write about me, write about women, for Marat's paper."

He pursed his lips, studying me. "Perhaps I will."

I straightened my bonnet. "Claire would not be happy to find us together like this."

"What does Claire have to do with anything? We have done nothing wrong."

I gritted my teeth. "Keep your mind on the cause, citizen. It is desires of the flesh that have sunk this country into its current state."

"Even warriors need to feel something." He touched my cheek.

Again, a wash of yearning clashed with disgust. Why could I not brush him aside? The answer was simple. Because he was the leader of a powerful group and had influence in the Assembly. But to continue to play these games was to betray my friend.

"I do not," I lied.

"I don't believe you."

"It doesn't matter if you do." The truth was, I did want him.

"Doesn't it?"

"No. We must go." I turned my back on him, on what he offered, and walked inside.

It was time to march.

"Citizens!" I called, my blood thrumming, my hands still trembling from my encounter with Théo. "We march for *liberté*! *Égalité!*"

My mother's admiring eyes looked on from behind the counter as I led everyone out to the street. Excitement and a sense of power thrummed in my veins. "*Vive la révolution!*" I cried as we marched, the crowd behind me crying out in answer. People joined our ranks until we were hundreds marching on the Champs de Mars.

We arrived in the center of the Champs, and I climbed onto the back of a wagon with Théo and Claire, who called out to anyone who wanted to witness history being made.

Then Théo lifted my hand into the air, exposing my long, jagged scar, either intentionally or not. "Behold, the president of the Women's Revolution!"

Shouts of approval rippled over the crowd, and I turned to smile at Claire in triumph over what we'd accomplished. The first women-run political group, and I its leader. Then I gazed out over the crowd of women, men, and children who cheered for our progress, my mother among them, eyes bright with unshed tears of happiness.

I pulled my hand from Théo's. This was a woman's moment, not his. I took a step forward, partially blocking him from view of the crowd. "Women, mothers, wives, widows!" I locked eyes with my mother who was all those things and felt her joy radiating. "Sisters-in-arms!"

The courtyard resounded in a cheer. I could see Louise, unsmiling, in the background with her fruit cart, and purchasing an apple was Sophie Condorcet. The woman watched me attentively, though blank-faced. Would she ever wield a pike, or would she choose an umbrella like her husband?

Sliding my gaze away from her, I found my mother once more. "We have marched together. We have bled together. We have shared cries of triumph and wiped at each other's tears of sorrow. Freedom has given us wings! We fly like eagles! No longer will we keep our mouths shut, no longer will we hide in corners like wounded animals. This is our fight. No longer will we allow our children to starve. No longer will we feel the pangs of hunger in our own bellies when hoarders take our bread. Never again will we be victims of the partisans of tyranny. We are the face of this new republic—one, indivisible and indestructible! Fly, my sisters, to the defense of our golden republic!"

My ears rang with the deafening cries of my sisters, and my throat felt dry and scratchy for having shouted every meaningful word. This was another step on a ladder I built with my own hands.

No matter what happened in the end, I was going to make a difference for women everywhere.

CHARLOTTE

I am no stranger to death. No stranger to taking life. I have gutted fish. Chopped the head off a writhing chicken. Suffered the blade of a knife cutting through the bone and sinew of a game animal. Shrunk at the sensation of warm blood spilling over my fingers. But that is not the same as thrusting a knife into a man's heart. To feel his last breath wash over your skin.

I am not a murderer. I am a patriot. Like Joan of Arc, I am a savior of France.

I am stalwart. And it is too late for me now. France needed a hero, and I gave them one.

Paris, July 11, 1793

I had hoped upon finally reaching Paris from Caen that I might feel a moment of triumph, but instead, trepidation ran cold in my veins.

The previous two days spent in and out of a stagecoach had made my bones throb. Worse still was watching France's beautiful landscape be replaced by the stench of the city. Paris seemed encased in tall buildings of marble hardness, the perfect reflection of the men who ran it. Unfeeling stacks of stone.

Through the windows of the stagecoach, the noise from the city was overwhelming, and I found myself longing for the quiet gardens of my cousin in Caen who so graciously took me in when I had nowhere else to go. At least I'd brought with me the words of the scholars and poets I'd explored in those gardens. I reminded myself of Plutarch's words: "Courage consists not in hazarding without fear, but being resolutely minded in a just cause."

No one knew I was here. Not my cousin, nor my friends—friends I'd come to love in my twenty-five years of life. My purpose in coming here meant I would lose them all.

There would be no welcoming face to greet me here in Paris. In fact, I fully expected that once my mission was complete, the rage it was destined to cause would swallow me whole.

I worried the cuff of my sleeve under which my rosary lay hidden, and I fretted over whether or not my cousin had seen my note of farewell, and whether she'd forgive me for abandoning her when all she'd ever shown me was kindness.

It'd been nearly two years since the National Convention closed down the abbey that had sheltered my sister and me when Papa cast us out. We were a burden to him in his grief, a grief now over a decade old at the loss of my mother. A constant burden to the little coin he'd ever had. Even before Maman's death, we'd always been poor and at the mercy of others' charity.

Still, all I'd ever wanted was to make my papa proud. Would he notice me now that I'd taken his republican teachings with me to Paris? Would he praise me at the hour of my death?

I touched the beads beneath my sleeve, rolling their solidness between my fingers. Even now, I could still feel the itch of homespun on my skin, though the gown I wore was made of a finer cotton. The bodies in the stagecoach pressed close, making my lungs hurt from breathing in the stale air.

I missed the abbey, the companions I'd spent time with there. It was an institution established by William the Conqueror's wife, Matilda, to educate aristocratic ladies, and the few poor nobles like myself taken in for charity. I'd stayed on when my education was complete in hopes of taking vows. Hopes that were dashed by the radicals in Paris.

I had a new calling now. France needed me and that bolstered me, especially in dark moments when I reflected on the pain I knew my family and friends would feel when they found out what I'd done. But it was my ancestor Corneille who said, "Treachery is noble when aimed at tyranny." And I hoped they would understand.

For I was going to kill a man.

The man responsible for urging the closings of the abbeys that left my sister, myself, and countless others homeless. The same man who sent nearly a dozen Girondin men to hide in Caen to escape death. Those who had unjustly arrested Madame Roland, whom I knew personally to be gracious, intelligent, and stalwart. I'll never forget seeing her on the banks of the river in Caen, staring out into the void like I sometimes did. Her support of my political interests bolstered me in seeking out meetings with the Girondins hiding over the past months in our town. How I wish that I could see her now, visit with her, and tell her that soon I would help set her free by taking the life of a monster.

The madman who encouraged the blood lust that led to the September Massacres, when innocents were yanked from the prisons and hacked to death in the streets. The poor Princess Lamballe, viciously murdered . . . the horror of the images I'd seen in a pamphlet still tormented me when I closed my eyes at night. She might have been royal born, but she did not deserve a death like that. No one did.

And all this fanaticism could be laid at the doorstep of one man: Jean-Paul Marat, Jacobin leader and owner of a heinous tabloid impersonating a credible paper. A man who cared little for France or human life.

Marat needed to die, and his newspaper with him. There needed to be an end to his call for terror and his determination to see heads roll while he splashed in his victims' blood.

When they heard what I'd done, my family and friends would not understand why I was determined to become Marat's executioner. But I hoped to show them that my actions were the same as any soldier. The same as any man protecting his country. I prayed that they would trust in me and in God that Marat's death was the only option to save the country from utter destruction. For just as in a game of dominoes, when one radical leader fell, so too the rest would follow. Continuing, I could only hope, with the so-called *l'Incorruptible* and his henchman in the Convention, Danton. And I wouldn't think it unjust for other rabid Jacobin newspapermen like Jacques Hébert to fall either.

On the ride to Paris, there had been a moment when I wished I could turn around. That I didn't have to go into this place of nightmares. This place where riots were daily, and massacres normalized. Staring out the coach window there was a chance I might witness such an atrocity. That a head on a pike might wave past my window. Instead of Princess Lamballe's, would it be Princess Élisabeth's or the queen's? I must make it clear that I was not a royalist, lest my wish for them to retain their lives bring about confusion.

I corresponded with the princess for some years while I was still at the convent, and she was always kind, trying to uplift my spirits, as well as encouraging me in my pursuit of taking vows. I knew she was not the depraved and villainous soul Marat and his hounds would have us think.

I crossed myself, remembering the insurrection in Caen when I'd barely avoided watching a man be torn to pieces. Paris, as ugly and violent as it was, was not the only city to suffer horror. No, the contagion of terror spread. Yet, those living outside the city had almost no representation and no voice, because the cry of the Paris Commune's extremism was so loud.

And that was why I'd come. To put an end to all of it. The key was Marat, champion of terrorists, voice of the bloodthirsty, and enemy to God.

Upon every side, factions were breaking. The Mountain alone triumphed by the strength of its wickedness and despotism. Despicable plots that have been hatched by monsters feed on the people of France's blood, dragging us all into destruction. And Marat, supposedly a man of the people, a representative in the National Convention, watched gleefully as the people tore one another apart at his command. The vilest of scoundrels, Marat, whose name alone conjured images of every kind of brutal crime, had the power to make Danton and Robespierre pale.

A body pressed closer to me. "Marry me, citizeness."

I turned to the lecherous man who'd been pestering me during the whole of our journey. Why would he not take my deflections as a firm answer?

I narrowed my eyes at him, having grown tired of his songs and watchful eyes. "This is quite a comedy of cross-purposes we are playing at, monsieur. It is a pity that so much of your talent should remain without an audience. Shall I invite the rest of our companions to share in the jest?"

The man frowned. "You are spiteful, citizeness."

I pursed my lips and turned away. How should I be called spiteful merely for thrusting his unwelcomed attentions back in his face? How very backward it all seemed.

The old lady beside me took a piece of fruit from her bag and began to eat it, the sounds of her chewing, the crunch and slurp, making me queasy. I'd not eaten that morning, and I probably wouldn't eat again, not if I was about my purpose right away. The hunger kept me focused, though, and reminded me of those who starved for bread. Just as our Lord starved for us.

At last, the stagecoach jerked to a stop.

"Tuileries Palace." Our driver hopped down from his seat and opened our door.

I found myself pausing on the coach step as the sights, sounds, and scents of Paris assailed me.

The older woman jostled me from behind. "Go on then, we all want to get out."

I lurched forward, my shoes hitting the muck-covered cobblestones hard, jarring my bones. With everyone disembarked, the coach moved off, and those I'd spent the last few days with melted into the crowd— except for my ardent, annoying admirer.

"You must give me your address in Paris," he demanded. "Or at least the name of your father so I might request your hand in marriage."

"What if I told you it was the Conciergerie?"

His eyes widened at my mention of the infamous prison, and he held up his hands backing away. "I am sorry, I mistook you for someone else."

I watched him hurry away, biting my lip to keep from laughing. How little he understood that I spoke the truth.

I silently gawked at the carved marble of the palace of horror before me, ignoring everything around me. The Tuileries. Its massive bulk represented so very much what I both loved and hated. Political change and oppression.

I stared at the cobbles, imagining I could still see the bloodstains of the innocent as they'd been hacked to death last September. Was I imagining it? With so much blood, would it not be stained for eternity? Again, I wanted to cross myself, but settled for pinching the beads beneath my sleeve. *Have courage. Be brave.*

My gaze shifted to those passing by. They were like something out of the newspapers we read in Caen— dirty, starved, hurried. It was harder to tell at first glance if they were made hard with righteousness as the papers reported. I knew from those papers that years of political unrest, revolution, and chance had trans- formed Paris into a city of ugliness and hate. That fact had been conveyed again and again, not only in words but in images. Fear and pandemonium. And always the September Massacres were in my mind. A shiver ran up my spine as I imagined what it would be like to be dragged, pleading for mercy, to my death.

In this great big hateful city, I would be inconspicuous—and that suited my purpose. Though my sister had always told me I was pretty, there was nothing particularly noteworthy about a girl with brown hair and pale skin, whose clothes were plain at best.

I was attempting to acclimate when the bite of a whip on my shoulder had me leaping out of the way with a cry. Dear God, is it the death I have imagined? Is a new slaughter about to begin?

"Get out of the street!" The driver of a wagon grumbled as he rolled past.

I clutched at the spot that still stung. And at the same time the mark of the whip seemed a perfect reminder . . .

This was the Paris that had been lashed open by the devil himself, Marat, who used his power as a journalist to spread false propaganda and instigate massacres. Perhaps with Jean-Paul Marat's death the city would be washed clean. Though the king would not come back to life, perhaps Marat's call for blood of anyone who wished to pardon the rest of the royal family would die unheeded and the blood would stop.

Another jostle had me fearing I'd once more stepped into the street, but instead, I faced a young woman in a bonnet rouge, blond curls falling from beneath. Bedraggled and haggard, there was a roughness about her eyes that spoke of scenes that could not be unseen.

"Where is your cockade, hussy?" she spat at me.

I touched my bare bonnet, my eyes falling on the tricolor rosette pinned to hers, realizing I'd not thought of this important detail and should have. "It must have fallen," I lied. "Where can I get a new one?"

She snarled at me and pointed toward a dressmaker's shop. "Better get one soon, else we'll see you stripped and whipped." She laughed as she walked away.

She must be a *femmes sans-culottes*. The femmes were Marat's hounds, often illustrated in fanatical pamphlets standing on the corpses of aristocrats, or eating their entrails. I stared after the woman as she wove her way through the crowd and disappeared down an alley.

"A sou, citizeness? Just one is all I need for the paper." A tiny hand tugged at my sleeve and I glanced down to see a child who looked as though he'd not eaten in weeks.

"What paper is it?" I asked, though I could see it was the very one I hated most of all.

"Oh, it is the best, citizeness. By the brave Citizen

Marat." The boy shook the paper. "He writes it all just over there." He pointed to the Tuileries.

The home of the National Convention was there but it was certainly not where Marat wrote. But perhaps that was what he wanted the people to believe, that he lived on his Mountain and preached vitriol from there by both tongue and pen. A tremor shook my spine.

How misled the people of Paris were, even down to this young child. Had he been born to different parents, he would have had his throat slit by now. If anyone were to find out that aristocratic blood ran through my veins, I might meet the same fate. That idea enraged me. I might have been born of noble blood, but I believed in a free republic. When born, we could not help whose blood we shared. Why should we be made to suffer on that fact alone? Oughtn't a person be judged on her actions and beliefs?

I held out a coin. The lad took it and handed me the paper, then ran away. I studied the Tuileries, hoping Marat was indeed inside at that very moment.

If I could just get in there now, I could see the deed done before even an hour passed. But too many people milled all around, each of them with tricolor cockades. And my bonnet, missing what they believed to be an incredibly important symbol, made me stand out when

I needed to blend in. Without a cockade, I wouldn't get past the mob.

Inside the dressmaker's shop, dust-covered lush fabrics filled shelves from floor to ceiling on one side, and the dull colors of the working-class fabrics were on the other. Standing before the lusher fabrics was a swan of a girl who looked to be around my age. Blond ringlets settled around delicate shoulders, and she fingered the vibrant bolts with desire in her bright blue eyes.

"Émilie, *non, ma cherie*," an older woman tsked beside her. "You're a married woman now, a wife must dress the part, less flamboyant."

Émilie flashed her gaze on me as the door clicked closed behind me, disappointment turning her bow-shaped mouth downward.

"Citizeness de Sainte-Amaranthe," the dressmaker called from behind the counter.

The older woman interrupted her, "My daughter is Citizeness Sartine now."

"Ah, congratulations, Citizeness Sartine. I have the perfect fabric for you in the back." Then she eyed me wearily, as if just noticing me standing there. "Can I help you?"

"A cockade, *s'il vous plait.*"

I bought a cockade and fastened it to my bonnet, ignoring the twinge of guilt. I would have to think of it as a costume for the role I was to play, and not a betrayal of my own beliefs and those of the great Lafayette, who'd first decided on the colors of blue, white, and red. And to think the Jacobins had helped spur the imprisonment of the creator of the very rosette they so revered! At least Lafayette was not held in Paris where he might have been dragged from prison and murdered in the streets. Oh, how the tricolor had been corrupted over time. The symbols of the republic that I loved were tarnished by the condoning of carnage.

I sneezed my way out of the dusty shop and back onto the putrid-smelling streets. I once more considered making my way into the Tuileries, but without a means with which to dispatch the Monster on his Mountain, it made no sense to try and enter just yet.

I was drawn, instead, to the Palais-Royal, where in the courtyard people gathered to listen to speakers, merchants hawked their wares, and little boys and girls picked the pockets of anyone who looked as though they had a few livres to spare. I tucked my purse closer, not wanting to be one of their victims.

"Buy an apple."

I turned to a woman with mousy brown hair tucked beneath a dingy cap, holding a piece of fruit outstretched toward me, smirking, as though she challenged me to say no. Beside her was another woman—the same who'd accosted me earlier about my lack of a cockade—a piece of fruit in her outstretched hand. Sneering, she stared at me with an intensity bordering on fanaticism, her gaze raking me over before alighting on the cockade. The two femmes stood before a vendor cart—a rickety thing with apples, pears, and peaches, and half filled with vegetables.

"Louise . . ." The blonde elbowed the fruit seller. "Maybe she only buys fruit from Girondins, not patriots."

"Hush, Pauline." Louise eyed the marketplace warily before her gaze fell back on me. "Come, citizeness," she urged, "buy an apple and show your patriotism. Your dress is clean, and so is your skin. You've not had to work a day in your life I'd guess. So buy my apple before I call attention to you. Or before I let Pauline show you what we do to counterrevolutionaries."

Pauline smirked.

"How much?" I tried to keep my voice strong, to hide the fear that they might just decide to do as they threatened.

"How much do you have?" Pauline asked.

I didn't want to play games, but neither did I want attention drawn to myself. I pulled out two sous and handed them over.

"I would have only charged one. Your loss." Louise pocketed the coins and tossed me the apple.

I'd barely time to catch it, but I did, and then I hurried away from the marketers, not wanting to go through a similar scenario with anyone else. It was time to find lodgings. I spied a likely place under a sign for *l'hôtel de Providence*, and I ducked inside. "A *chambre, s'il vous plait.*"

The proprietor, a woman with brown hair streaked with gray, gave me a dull look. "Are you alone, citizeness?"

"*Oui.*"

"And you have money to pay? The room is not free." She named her price and I handed it over without haggling. "I have a small room on this floor with a single bed." She called to the porter. "Show her to number seven."

"*Merci,* citizeness."

I followed the porter through the winding corridors to my dusty room with a small, lumpy-looking bed, a crumpled and dingy white coverlet upon it.

"Could I have new sheets?"

"*Oui.*" He grumbled, returning a moment later with a fresh set. "You come from Caen? My sister lives there. I have not heard from her in some weeks. What is the state of the town?"

"Not as riotous as Paris. But there has been some recent violence." I spied a copy of *L'Ami du Peuple* on a side table, folded and wrinkled as though it had been well read. I set mine beside it. "Do you know of Citizen Marat? Friend of the people?"

"Ah, *oui*, everyone in Paris, indeed all France, knows of Citizen Marat. The patriots are besotted with him, but the aristocrats, as you can guess, are not." He drew his finger across his throat in a way that sent a shiver of dread up my spine. The porter smoothed the sheet over the sagging mattress. "There is much talk of his health lately throughout the city. He has been very ill and missing from the Convention. They say he is working on the paper from his home—from his very bed! However ill he is, it does not keep him from writing and inciting the passion of the nation."

"Passion?" I retorted sharply. I had to bite the tip of my tongue to keep from saying more—to avoid lashing out at the man for comparing the riots and massacres fomented by Marat's writings to passion.

"Apologies, citizeness, I did not mean to offend."

I smiled, because I didn't want him to think me a royalist and run to tell anyone who would listen. "I am not offended, citizen, merely tired from my journey."

My mind was whirling. I'd have to change my plan. If Marat no longer made appearances at the National

Convention, I would have to get to him at his residence. But how?

"Citizen, can you get me writing materials?" I held out a coin.

"Of course." When he was gone, I walked across the creaking, sagging wood floor to look out the window. A group of women in bonnets rouges walked by with arms raised, hands fisted. No doubt they were headed to the Palais-Royal. They shouted about the injustices pressed upon the people, the fault of the dead king's wretched wife. How the only way to truly liberate the poor and the good citizens of France was to cut off the heads of everyone of noble blood.

How long, unhappy French men and women, will you delight in strife and division? I turned away from their angry faces, their vile shouts.

When the porter returned with the writing implements, I penned a quick note to be delivered to Marat begging him to receive me, telling him that I bore news from Caen concerning counterrevolutionists. I closed by saying that I would come to his residence on rue des Cordeliers in two days' time at one o'clock.

In the quiet stillness of my room, I glanced at the remaining paper. All the words that had been rushing around in my head needed an outlet. If Marat could address the people with such vicious propaganda, perhaps I should address them as well, and my gift could be one of peace.

I let the words rush out, my own treatise to the people of France.

Oh, France, your happiness depends on the execution of the law, but I break none in killing Marat. He is condemned by the world from where he stands on the opposite side of the law. Who would condemn me? If I'm guilty, so too was Hercules when he destroyed the monsters. You will not miss an odious beast who has grown fat on your blood. And you sad aristocrats left abused by the Revolution will not begrudge me.

My French people, you know your enemies. Arise! March! Strike!

Paris, July 13, 1793

"Arm yourselves, citizenesses," came the shouts of women in the courtyard of the Palais-Royal. "Women must be able to protect themselves."

Was it sad that I had to agree? Perhaps even just so I could protect myself from these women. But I had to concede, much as I might find them frightening or loathsome, these *femme sans-culottes* needed protection also.

Too long already party leaders in France, and other scoundrels like Marat, preferred the interests of their ambition in the place of the general well-being of the people, and especially that of women.

I'd stayed up all night writing, and the plight of these women made me feel more deeply my conviction in what I was to do. I did it for them too.

These women wanted pikes and daggers. But I was the weapon women needed.

Soon, I thought, looking at their angry, dirty, hate-filled faces, they could heal. A rush of pride and sense of urgency burst through me. There was no time to waste in saving the women, the people, of France.

A bell over the door jingled as I entered a cutler's shop. The proprietor waved though he didn't look up. A few other patrons milled about, but I kept my head down and began looking. Many of the knives appeared used. How would that be, to stab the devil with an old knife that someone had once used to carve up the carcass of a hog?

Fitting I should think. Marat, himself, was a butcher.

I picked up a knife and turned it over, holding the blade against the flat of my palm. Perhaps five or six inches long, the handle was smooth and dark. It was not too long to be inconspicuously concealed. There was nothing particularly special about this knife—no pearl handle, no chaste silver. But then again, there had never been anything particularly special about me. Which was why I knew that it would be my weapon of choice.

Glancing to make certain no one was paying attention, I held it to my breast to see if it would fit unnoticed into my bodice. A bubble of excitement burst in my throat. Justice would soon be delivered.

I carried the knife to the counter. I expected the clerk to ask what a young lady might need with a knife, but instead, he tucked it into a cloth sheath, told me how much it cost, and held out his hand for payment.

How easy that was! I wasn't certain why, but I kept imagining I would be caught, or stopped. I glanced furtively out the windows of the shop, my hands trembling as I paid and shoved the knife in my purse. I was one step closer to my goal and the idea both thrilled and terrified me.

I am a soldier, I kept telling myself. Soldiers didn't doubt their duty, and I couldn't either. *Have courage.*

On the street once more, I began walking to Marat's establishment, on the rue des Cordeliers, where he rented an apartment. It was nearly one o'clock. The woman I kept running into—Pauline—stood in front of a building perhaps a block, no more, down the street, with a group of other femmes. Dressed in dingy striped skirts with crimson bonnets covering their hair, the women made me nervous. There was a hunger in their eyes that was almost feral, as though just the slightest provocation might set them off.

They heckled people passing, creating a ruckus. Squaring my shoulders, I picked up my pace, feeling myself tremble. I kept my eyes downcast. Perhaps if I did not look at them . . .

As I approached the group I debated whether to leave or continue with my quest to enter the residence with its high windows and somber, sagging roof. The idea of being done with my task, efficiently, bravely, even, while his flock gathered on the street made me smile. So I wove my way through them, head high now, and they jostled me like the wind jostles a blade of grass in a field. That was what I have been most of my life—blowing with the vagaries of fate, but that would change today. Today I was not the blade of grass. Today I was the wind. And I refused to let their sharp words stop me.

Inside the residence and up the stairs I went, as though I belonged. How odd it was that when you believed you belonged, others did too. People were coming and going from a door on the first floor, and I determined that to be my destination. But a woman stopped me at the threshold. Sweat caused the hair at her temples to stick to her skin. She was plump, and her gown threadbare.

"What can I do for you?" she asked.

"I need to speak with Marat."

"He is unavailable."

I could tell by the way she looked at me that she thought Marat had better things to do. Perhaps if I'd come wearing a bonnet rouge and spouting hatred she might have thought otherwise. Perhaps if I'd come dressed like a man. Perhaps if I'd come shouting at the injustices of the world and laying them at the feet of a child, the dauphin, whom they wanted to murder next.

"It is quite an important matter," I insisted, not taking my eyes off hers. I could tell by the way she fidgeted that she didn't like how direct I was. Most people didn't. "I sent him a note mentioning that I would come today at one o'clock. My name is Citizeness Corday."

The woman's eyes narrowed and she shook her head. "He gave no instruction to admit you."

"I come to report on a Girondin uprising in Caen, which I referenced in my letter."

That grabbed her attention. "He is in his bath, citizeness, quite ill, but I will tell him," she said.

Unfortunately, because it was a name she didn't know, she looked dubious about the possibility that I might have information worth sharing. She dismissed me then, but I wasn't giving up, I would keep going back as many times as it took.

"I will return in a few hours when he is no longer indisposed."

Two hours later, after pacing the surrounding streets of rue de Cordeliers, I returned, and she once more barred my entry.

Two days had passed since I'd arrived in Paris and I had nothing to show for it other than a knife in my purse. Was it bad luck? Bad planning? The woman was an unexpected obstacle, and I was now convinced by her presence and the protective possessiveness she showed for Marat that she must be his mistress.

No matter. Tonight, I would make his mistress let me in. Or she might find herself another sacrifice on the altar of peace.

After eating a small meal to alleviate my gnawing hunger, I pinned my letter to the people of France along with my baptismal papers into the folds of my fichu, in case I did not make it out of Marat's residence alive. My letter would show what a delicate hand could accomplish when driven by self-sacrifice. If I should fail, I would have at least shown the people the way.

"Dear God, may none of my family or friends suffer for my act, for none knew of my plans," I murmured, crossing myself.

Again I traveled through the streets, this time in a hired cab, for my feet were sore from all the walking earlier in the day. The way was familiar now. I watched the starving children, pushing in and out of the crowds, begging, stealing. I noticed how every man and woman I passed looked haggard, starved, tired. And this suffering bolstered me and steadied my resolve.

When I arrived, there was a man delivering a package and no gatekeeper. I snuck through the door only to be stopped at the last minute by the buxom figure I'd come to know so well these last days.

She openly rolled her eyes at me. "You again? I told you before he is ill. Why do you continue to pester him?"

I swallowed away my nerves, hoping to come across as confident. This time, I wasn't leaving without an audience. "Because I must speak to him. We cannot let the Girondins regain their power."

She hesitated. She clearly hated the Girondins, and why wouldn't she—it was the fashion at the moment. But she did not stand aside. Doubtless she still thought I might just be one of Marat's admirers, like the *femmes sans-culottes* I'd passed again outside.

"Please, citizeness, allow me to speak to him. Our glorious victory over the Girondins may depend on it."

Before she could reply, from somewhere in the apartment, a man's voice called out, "Let her in, *mon amie*, that she might leave us in peace."

My heart skipped a beat. My mouth was suddenly dry and a thrill rushed through my veins. The woman visibly gritted her teeth and glowered. "Make it quick. We are to dine soon, and he is still in his bath."

"I will be quick," I assured her.

And you will dine alone.

Marat's mistress led me through their apartment. With every step, I felt my toes going numb, my neck hot.

She opened a door to reveal a bathing room. A man sat in a copper, boot-shaped tub. "*Merci, mon amie*," he said, smiling at her, the gesture grotesque on him. "Leave us."

"Quickly," she hissed at me as she backed out of the room.

I stood staring at him. The overwhelming scent of the room was of sulfur and rotting flesh. Through the linen of his shirt, I could see the outlines of scaly sores, some of them oozing blood and pus that bled through. His hair was thinning and greasy, and his face was lined with deep unforgiving grooves.

This man, this invalid, was the powerful devil who

had so outrageously been able to turn an entire country on its head?

It was almost impossible to believe. Had he been left out in nature, he would not have survived. He would've been mauled and left for dead, his pain ended long ago. The tender part of me—yes, there was such a part—felt sorry for him. And perhaps what I would do was a mercy not just to France, but to its monster too.

"Come inside," he murmured, one long, thin arm gesturing toward a chair in the corner. He seemed quite comfortable receiving guests in his bathroom, as if he made a habit of it. His gaze raked my form, causing my skin to crawl.

He held a copy of his own newspaper, and he was making comments in the margins, grasping the pen in shriveled, spindly fingers, tipped with long, sharpened nails and covered in black ink stains. His inkwell sat atop an overturned wooden box set on the tub like a desk. As I watched, a wet knuckle brushed the paper, leaving a damp line. The same paper that had been stirring up the crowds in Paris and now Caen. The paper that incited the violence and death of not only the September Massacres but so many others.

I thought when I first saw him I'd be scared. But I wasn't. An intense feeling of calm filled me. All the days, no, weeks, of planning had finally come to a head.

The cool steel of the knife against my breast was reassuring. I wasn't even trembling; instead, I was incredibly still and knew exactly what I had to do.

Marat studied me as though I were some foreign creature. "So you are Charlotte Corday, of Caen. The little bird from the north. I got your earlier missive."

I nodded, trying not to bristle at his description of me as a little creature he could crush in his hand.

"I didn't think this day would come," I said a little breathlessly.

He grinned, showing crooked yellow teeth, taking my words for flattery and having no idea of my true purpose. "I am glad you saw fit to do your patriotic duty, and I'm impressed you would travel all this way rather than merely writing."

I swallowed to loosen my tongue where it was stuck to the roof of my mouth. "I thought what needed to be relayed was too important to leave to the care of paper and quill."

"Well then, let's hear it. What of this Girondin plot?"

I glanced down at the damp floor, knowing that I'd have to step closer to thrust the knife deep. My pulse thundered in my ears, making every word spoken from both him and myself sound far away. "I know where the escaped Girondins are."

He narrowed his eyes at me. "Why would you give them up?"

Undoubtedly, Marat had spoken to many liars. Could he see through me? I willed my hands to still. "They are traitors and deserve to die a traitor's death." I stepped forward, steady.

"Indeed they do. So, tell me then."

I could barely breathe, not because I was nervous, but because the air was so thick and hot in the stifling room. Nevertheless, I found the air to speak the names of the patriots he had helped to condemn: the members of Madame Roland's faction, her husband included. Perhaps with Marat's death, they'd be released. With each name I took another small step forward. All the while my gaze was trained on the softly thumping center of his chest.

I stopped very close to the tub. "They are in Caen. I saw them with my own eyes."

"We've been searching all through France for them. And to think they were so close all along." His gleeful laugh scraped unpleasantly down my spine. "We'll bring them back to Paris and they'll be guillotined within a week. We'll paint the streets of Paris with their blood." As he spoke, he licked his lips with what I took for demonic hunger.

I couldn't comment, for fear my voice would crack

with the emotion his gleeful declaration of death evoked in me. Instead, I reached into my bodice and pulled out the knife, letting the sheath that protected the blade fall to the floor. He looked up at me strangely, his eyes on the knife.

"What are you—"

Before he could say more, I raised the weapon up over my head. Time seemed to stand still as my body arced over his. Marat's voice faded to a silent scream and he dropped his quill into the water. The paper fell to the side, halfway over the tub. I cut my knife through the air thick with steam and stench, plunging the blade into his chest exactly in the place I felt my own heart beat. There was a sickening thunk as it pierced him. My forearm jarred painfully as I sank the knife through bone and sinew, all the way to the hilt.

His mouth grew wide, pain etched his features, and a guttural sound issued from his throat. "Help, *mon amie!*" he managed to cry.

A weak hand moved to the hilt, as though he might pull it out, but then quickly fell away, as the life bled out of him in ribbons of scarlet.

I took a shuddering step back, my hands jerking to my sides, fists clenched and slick with his blood. A moment of relief filled me. As though I were no longer in the room, but floating overhead. It was done. I stared at the slowly growing splotch of bright red on the wet fabric of his shirt. A wash of heat pulsed through my arms, my chest, up my neck to face. I watched in exultant fascination.

Footsteps pounded. But it was too late. Too late for Marat. And too late for me, too, for soon they would be upon me. I could try to escape. But, looking at the small window above his bath and hearing the shouts of the *sans-culottes* on the street below, I realized that I would rather die at the guillotine's mercy than let myself fall into such hands as Princess Lamballe had. I'd used up all the bravery I had in that one act and was afraid I might not find it again.

But I must. I drew upon the wisdom of my favorite philosopher Plutarch once more. "Those who aim at great deeds must also suffer greatly."

I touched the papers pinned in my fichu. Would I ever get to say those words aloud? No matter. The sacrifice of my life would be my most eloquent oratory. I stepped into the corner of the bathroom and waited for the doors to open, determined not to be afraid.

Only a breath more, and they were there. Marat's mistress and another woman, a maid perhaps, rushed in. "Jean-Paul," his mistress cried, dropping to her knees, grabbing his hand, clutching it. "*Mon Dieu!* What has she done to you?" I found it ironic that a godless woman would take the Lord's name in vain. No one could save him now. Not even the devil.

Marat's eyes focused briefly and he reached out for her but his touch fell short. And then he was nothing.

"You killed him!" she turned her wide eyes on me.

I nodded. I wasn't afraid or ashamed. Only relieved. I'd been brave enough to see it through.

A man burst through the door. "What happened?" He let out a curse when he saw Marat's lifeless body.

More men came. They pulled Marat's lifeless body from his tub and carried him away. Then and only then did one of the men lunge for me and toss me to the ground as if to keep me from fleeing. Overtaken with rage and vengeance he lifted the wooden chair from the corner, bringing it down on my side. Pain crushed through my body as the chair cracked against my ribs again and again. He didn't stop even when the chair was broken. Instead, while I moaned in agony, he raised the pieces in his hand to beat me again, standing over me like a dog of hell, foaming at the mouth.

"*Arrêtez!*" Two guards pulled the rabid man from me, and I sat up, pain ricocheting deep inside my body. I fought down the urge to return the man's blows. My fingers flexed against the soft carpet covering the hard floor, as I glared up at them, refusing to be sorry for what I'd done.

"Commissioner, she has murdered Marat," the hound-man cried, swiping at sweat upon his brow to a third man who entered.

Blood rushed in my ears as I was lifted, moaning, from the ground. They dragged me into Marat's salon and tossed me onto a chair. My mind was blank, the sounds of men and women rushing to and fro muted by a whirring noise in my ears and the screaming of my ribs. Several officers came into the room, their white knee breeches blinding, and the candle's reflections shone in the gleam of their boots and gold buttons on their blue coats. I focused on their shiny buttons and not on the next beating that was sure to come.

"Do not move," the commissioner barked.

"Where would I go?" A little part of me threatened to shatter inside. Murder was a cardinal sin. *I'm a soldier, executing an enemy of my country.* If God had not wanted me to do this, I would have been turned away again. But Marat himself had invited me in. I gathered up the pieces of my insides, trying to put them back together as the men stared at me as if I were an indecipherable puzzle.

While one of the officers loomed behind me, standing guard should I bolt, the commissioner tasked one of the other men to take notes. So I was to be questioned.

"What is your name?"

They would only listen if I remained calm. Oh, but how hard it was to do that. Taking a ragged breath, I straightened in my chair as best I could. The rungs of the back pressing against me heightened the ache from the beating, but I would not slump before such men. "Marie-Anne Charlotte de Corday d'Armont is my full name, but I am called Charlotte."

They asked me other mundane questions. But their last question was the one I'd been waiting for them to ask.

"What possessed you to kill Citizen Marat?"

I glanced up with confidence and righteous. "For love of my country! Marat has threatened our republic from where he has stood again and again on the opposite side of the law. And you would condemn me? Civil war is breaking out all over France with him at the helm of every wretched tragedy. Someone had to stop him. I waited for a man to do it, and I watched as many people died at Marat's instigation. So I determined I must sacrifice my own life to save France."

My interrogator frowned, then blinked, then shook his head as if to dismiss my confession. "Who commissioned you to do this? A father? A brother? A lover?"

How dare they think that I, a woman, could not be capable of such heroism without a man to put the idea in my head. "I assure you, it was my enterprise alone."

"Search her." The commissioner ordered one of the officers. He dumped my purse, revealing a silver thimble that was once my mother's, white thread, my passport, and some money.

Still hidden within my bodice, pinned to the inner folds of my fichu, was the letter I'd written. I'd planned for them to find it when they disposed of my body. Now I wanted to hold it close, unsure of whom to entrust it to.

Unsatisfied with what his officer found, the commissioner came close, bending to eye level with me. "Tell us who sent you." His voice was threatening, but for the first time in my life, I refused to hide behind a façade of calm humility.

Curling my lip with distaste, I said, "No one sent me. I made up my own mind. I came for the people of France."

I was numb, both in mind and aching body. Hours had passed and I was still at Marat's, trapped.

"This woman came to my house this morning!" an older man exclaimed, his body wiggling with unrestrained excitement as he pointed at me. I'd never seen him before. "She would've killed me had I not seen the viciousness in her eyes and barred the door against her."

I raised a single, ironic brow and muttered, "You are mistaken, citizen."

"I am not," he sneered, and I could see by the set of his thin-lined mouth that he wanted blood. *My* blood.

I sat up taller. "A man such as yourself is not capable of being a leader, and therefore of being a tyrant dangerous to this country, monsieur," I said, licking my dry lips, for I was parched. "Do not flatter yourself. You would not have been worth my life. I only had intentions of striking Marat."

My accuser's double chin jiggled, his gray hair seeming to rise up at the roots. I could clearly see the desire to strike me in his rheumy eyes.

But I would not be cowed. I was still not afraid.

"How did you know to strike so accurately at his heart?" one of the men asked.

"The indignation that swelled in my own breast showed me the place." I could have offered a better answer, but why give him the satisfaction?

At that moment, Chabot, a defrocked Capuchin monk and another of Marat's sycophants, reached forward, gripping the gold watch dangling on a chatelaine around my waist. He tugged hard enough to jar my already abused body. The watch came free and he pocketed it.

"Have you forgotten that you are supposed to be

under a vow of poverty?" I asked, accusing him of thievery. Such a reminder would strike at his heart and humiliate him in present company. If I'd been a woman with something to lose, I might not have goaded him, but he'd just stolen my watch, my one last possession, which had belonged to my mother.

"You are bold, citizeness," he said, eyes roaming over my figure.

"As are you," I retorted.

Chabot came close once more, tugging on a lock of my dark hair. "Where is your lover hiding?"

Indignation filled my heart and I jerked away. "I am no harlot."

"That is what all harlots say." Chabot nodded to one of the guards. "Give me rope to bind her."

"There is no need to bind me. I am in possession of no weapon and I have no intention of striking anyone."

But he gripped my arms, squeezing hard, enjoying it. Chabot tugged me to stand and slid his vile hands down my arms to my wrists.

"You're a murderess," he whispered in my ear. "Do you know what we do to women who kill?"

I didn't answer, paralyzed for a moment with fear, for I had a very good idea. His breath was hot on my neck, making my stomach turn. I could smell the onions and eggs he had for dinner.

"You will suffer endlessly before Madame Guillotine grants you compassion unless you do what I say," he said. "You are at my mercy." He tugged my hands back, brushing them against a part of his body no decent man would expect an honest woman to touch without the bonds of marriage. I jerked forward in disgust.

He yanked me back with a grunt. There was no escaping him. And no one came to my defense. When he was done tying the ropes, I thought at last I might be taken from this wretched place and away from him. I'd never been manhandled so vilely in my life. I wished I could have edited my address to the people to add his name along with the other monsters.

"What have you hidden in your fichu?" His voice was soft and menacing, his face so close to mine I could make out the broken red vessels in the whites of his eyes.

I kept my stare locked with his. It took every ounce of willpower I had not to spit in his face. "Untie me, citizen." My voice remained calm.

He laughed and grabbed at my breasts, running a finger along the inside of my fichu. I jerked back at his touch, and his eyes widened as he encountered the paper. My address to the people. He pulled out my scarf and threw it to the ground and a moment later the sharp ping of my bodice fastenings coming undone echoed in the room. I stumbled away, heat burning my cheeks. My breasts were fully exposed and I whirled to face the wall, trying to hold back tears.

Not one of the guards, not even the commissioner, sought to cover or aid me. And I wasn't surprised, even if I was furious. How many illustrations had I seen in the radical propaganda that depicted bare-breasted women in the streets? Well, if none would fight for me, I would fight for myself.

"I must be allowed to fix my bodice. This is indecent, citizens! Is this how I am to be presented in the street? Would you wish this on your wives? Your daughters? Help me," I appealed directly to the commissioner, "unless you are so cruel that you mean to let him rape me."

"Allow her to adjust her clothing," the commissioner said wearily. "We are not so cruel, citizeness."

But I knew they could be.

A guard untied me so I could fix my gown, and I nearly sobbed with relief at this small bit of mercy. I might have been willing to sacrifice my life for France's cause, but not my modesty or dignity. I'd expected to die instantly once I plunged the knife. By now, at long last, I was trembling. I had thought I'd either be killed or taken to prison, not abused and violated. Would they have done this to a soldier? I doubted so. But a woman was another matter. They wanted me humiliated.

Have courage. Be brave. Stand up for yourself.

Though I was dizzy with humiliation and exhaustion, I stifled the sob that hung at the back of my throat, straightened my shoulders, and worked to bring my trembling to a stop. I could not let them see my fear. I had to remain strong, or it would all be for naught.

"Sign this confession." The commissioner shoved the notes they'd taken toward me, his meaty hand covering the words.

"Let me read it."

The men grumbled as though surprised I could read, and reluctantly the commissioner removed his hand. It was nothing more than what I'd said, and so I signed without hesitation.

Then he took me by the elbow and led me into the adjoining room where Marat's corpse was lain out on a bed. I looked at his ashen face, mouth slack, eyes unseeing. He no longer wore his shirt, revealing the grotesque and puffy sores on his skin. The knife had been removed to reveal the yawning wound in his chest. I swallowed the bile in my throat and looked away. I didn't regret at all what I'd done, but to view the horror of it . . . I'd not prepared myself for that.

Marat's mistress knelt beside the bed, sobbing, her

face a ghostly white. She pointed at me, lips moving as though she wanted to say something.

A part of me wished to give her comfort, but the part of me that hated that monster couldn't understand how this woman might have loved him. Corneille had written "Love is a tyrant sparing none," and it had not spared this poor woman.

I suppose I had hoped that with Marat's death, his mistress would be free of whatever spell he cast on her. That France would be free of his spell. But if she was not, then would others be? I silently beseeched my God that it would be so.

I did not like to think I might have given my life for nothing.

PAULINE

"Marat is dead." I stared at Théo where he sat hunched over a writing desk at the Cordeliers Club.

The screams from Marat's mistress still echoed in my ears. How could the world go on the same way it had in the face of such catastrophe? My eyes burned from the tears I'd shed, and my stomach hurt. I couldn't stop shaking. I'd not been able to find Claire, and so naturally, I came looking for Théo, thinking she must be with him.

Théo startled and his gaze jerked to me. "What?" The light from the candle on the desk brought out the redness from lack of sleep in his wide, disbelieving eyes. He was tireless, as was I.

My throat was tight with grief. "Murdered in his bathtub by some whore."

Shaking his head, Théo looked dazed, as if I had made up some dark jest. "Impossible. Marat has never been one for whores." Outside, a series of shouts had him glancing behind me. "His mistress would never allow it."

"His death seems impossible, and yet it is true." I shook my head in disbelief. "I talked to him only today about our rally on the Palais-Royal. I was there, outside, when his blood was spilled. I could have stopped her. Could have saved him." My voice cracked with pent-up emotion.

"*Non, cherie, non.*" Théo stood and rounded the desk, approaching as though he might embrace me, but I backed up a step, not wanting to feel a spark of yearning for him, when our dear friend, our staunchest ally, had just been murdered.

Guilt riddled me. Was I partially to blame for Marat's

death? Could I have somehow stopped the she-devil who'd come from nowhere to snuff out the voice of our revolution? Who was she? Who sent her? I had to know!

The same thought seemed to occur to Théo. "Where is the assassin now?" Théo touched my elbow and I realized suddenly that he'd closed the distance between us.

"Still at Marat's apartments."

"We'll go there."

"What of Claire?"

"She'll be along when she hears the news," he said dismissively.

I looked down at where he held me, wanting to ask what they meant to each other. I wanted to say *touch me*, because in this moment of sorrow, I wanted to be somewhere else. I wanted to be with him. Some part of myself was willing to abandon my ideals and give in to that desire.

"I want to kill her," I said.

"Claire?" Théo's eyes widened.

"No." I shook my head and pressed a hand to where he held my elbow. "The assassin." What if this was just part of the royalists' plans to regain control of France? The precursor to an invasion? Who was the assassin? Where had she come from? Was she Austrian? Who would be next? It was a stark reminder that none of us were safe.

"Do not worry, Pauline. Justice will be done," Théo said, his voice was tight. "She will meet Madame Guillotine. We have to make sure of it."

"We must show Paris that she has killed a great man." My hands fisted at my sides, and I looked around for a weapon, something I could take with us and use to maim the witch.

"I'll get Hébert on it right away," he said, referring to Jacques Hébert, the editor of the *Le Père Duchesne* newspaper, another radical favorite among all *sans-culottes*. "He believes as well as we do that Marat is a saint of the revolution."

"That's perfect," I murmured. Between his voting position on the Paris Commune and his newspaper, Hébert was perhaps only second to Marat in his ability to influence our great revolution in the most radical directions. "Let all the nation mourn our tremendous loss. Let them know that they can send as many assassins as they want, we will stomp them down."

Suddenly, Théo swallowed thickly and ran his hand through his mussed hair. "I can't believe he's dead."

"Me neither." I picked up a candlestick and set it back down again. "But his legend will live on. We won't let it die."

Don't let us die.

Théo stared hard at me; tears of rage and grief moist-ened his eyes. And then his hands were on me pulling me to him, as his lips sought mine.

I shoved him away, my words stuck on the tip of my tongue, wanting to tell him that if he wanted a new mistress, he could take his interest somewhere else. But a different sort of thought struck me instead. A traitorous one that only made me angrier. What if I returned his affection?

No! This was only grief talking. To give in would be to betray myself and everything I believed in. I might as well have ripped off my tricolor cockade and stomped on it.

"Do not be like every other rutting dog, citizen," I rebuked. "We mourn."

But even as fear coursed through me, I was shoving myself forward into his body and pressing him to the opposite wall. Because fear and lust and the need for protection filled me. I clutched onto his shirt, my mouth crushing against his.

Théo gripped my behind and whirled me around, taking me to the couch and laying me down. I lifted my leg up around his hip, feeling the heat of his arousal press against me. Lust drove me, anger emboldened me. We fumbled hurriedly, our mouths hot and frenzied.

"Oh, Pauline," Théo murmured against my mouth as he took me.

Out in the open room of the club, where anyone could walk in. I'd become the very thing I accused my enemy of being. A weak, lust-crazed harlot, rutting for anyone to see.

But I didn't stop.

I reeled into it, gasping for breath, and abhorring the pleasure at the same time I took it.

Outside of Marat's house, crowds had gathered to see the murderess. To demand her head. To tie her four limbs to horses and watch her body be torn apart. We wanted to leap on her like we had during the massacres, to each feel the thrust of a blade piercing her flesh. Would they let us? Could we demand it?

Théo shoved through the throng, holding my hand so I would not be swallowed and lost among them. Like the rest of the pulsing, violently angry crowd, my blood surged with a thirst for vengeance.

"*Vive la république!*" I cried. "Give us her traitorous head!"

We shoved our way to the door where a line of guards stood sentry.

"We are friends of Marat and we demand justice for the assassin," I said. "Let us in."

The guards looked me over with a mixture of surprise and disgust. They did not like me, or what I represented—a woman making demands.

"Step aside," Théo ordered the guards.

"We cannot, citizen."

Théo's voice took on a dangerous edge. "Do you know who I am?"

"Yes, Citizen Leclerc," one of them said. "We know you lead Les Enragés, that you are a friend to Marat. But we have been ordered by the commissioner not to let anyone in."

"You know Marat would want me in there if he had a voice. Now let us pass."

The guards shifted. "If it were up to us, citizen, we would. We could send a message to the commissioner if that is your request?"

Théo glanced at me, anger shining red in his eyes.

A commotion from inside the building claimed the guards' attention and ours.

There she was . . .

The murderess wore a white gown I expected to be covered in blood, but it was decidedly clean. Then I saw her white bonnet tied with green ribbons, and a tricolor cockade pinned to its side as if she were a patriot.

"Rip that off her!" I shouted, nearly unhinged with rage. "She desecrates our cockade with the blood of Marat on her hands!"

The assassin looked right at me with piercing eyes the color of smoke, and there was triumph there, pride, and it took my breath away. Because I realized that I had seen her before. I was the one who instructed her to get the cockade! And I'd seen her again, in the marketplace. She was the one at Louise's fruit stand whom we'd taunted with the apple. The one who'd appeared here at the residence several times earlier today. *Putain!* I should have known. Should have sensed her danger, her false patriotism. Should have stopped her!

I'd failed. Maybe I'd never failed more in my whole life.

"Your misfortunes tear my heart!" the assassin cried, her cheeks crimson with fever. "I can only offer you my life and give thanks to heaven for the liberty that I have to dispose of it. My last dying breath will be to have helped my fellow citizens. Let my death be a rallying cry for all the friends of the law! Let the wavering Mountain see its fall with my blood! Let me be the last victim of those blood-fattened monsters. For any of you who might view my conduct in a different light, know this—I care not. You know your enemies. Arise! March! Strike!"

What crazed speech was this? I recognized in her a frenzied passion for what she believed was right. But what she thought was right was a terrible evil. Looking at her, clean and well fed, clearly a woman who had never known a day of suffering in her life, my hatred nearly blinded me.

"Kill her! Give us her head! Kill her! Give us her head!" the crowd chanted.

I made ready to shout at the murderess witch myself, when suddenly she sagged, held upright only by the guard's hands on her elbows.

One of the guards pinched the sagging woman's cheeks, but her eyes rolled back in her head, and from the limpness of her body it was evident she had fainted. *Weak*, I told myself; she could not stand to hear our cries, to face those who would judge her.

"Death to the traitorous bitch!" I thundered, and my demand was echoed in the crowd.

CHARLOTTE

Paris, July 14, 1793

I am a prisoner.

I awoke with a start in the dark, my hands out-stretched, fingers brushing on the cool, wet stone of the wall at the Prison de l'Abbeye. I lay on a narrow bed with a thick, itchy woolen blanket beneath me. A small iron-barred window admitted vile smells from the street, but no light on this moonless night.

As my eyes adjusted, I realized there were two hulking shadows standing just inside the cell's wooden door, obstructing the small barred window and blocking most of the torchlight from the corridor beyond.

My pulse leapt. "Who are you?" My voice sounded so far away, my tongue dry, throat scratchy.

"Chabot has ordered us to stand guard here," one man said.

Not Chabot, thank God.

"It is indecent for you to watch me sleep," I said. When they ignored me, I sat up and hugged myself. "Perhaps you could fetch me pen and ink so I might write letters to my family?"

"I will ask, citizeness. I believe they allowed Madame Roland the use of such tools during her time here."

Madame Roland stayed in this cell? Slept on this bed? Touched these walls? How lucky was I to follow in such footsteps. Where was she now? I wanted to ask but was afraid of the answer. The ghost of her presence comforted me somewhat. This was a sign from God, was it not?

"Thank you." I lay back down, but did not close my

eyes, fearful of what they might do to me while I slept. Was this a tactic the Mountaineers have used with every woman? Or only those they feared might kill them?

"Citizeness." A sharp voice woke me from my fitful sleep. The sun had risen, and so had the stench. The guards were still in their place but now the prison keeper stood on my threshold as well, addressing me. "You have been given permission to take a walk with the other prisoners."

"Why?" I rubbed sleep from my eyes.

"The Tribunal is not yet ready for you."

The Tribunal. So I would get a hearing. What was the point? I confessed to the murder, and they'd already told me I would die. All that was left was the killing— and my legacy: *Charlotte Corday, martyr to the people of France.* "Who prepares the case against me?"

"Fouquier-Tinville."

"I have not been asked if I want a defender, *messieurs.*"

"We can pass on that request."

A small smile curled inside me, but I tried to hide it. "Do you think I should request Robespierre, or even Chabot who would love another chance to abuse me?"

"If that is your desire, citizeness." The keeper's voice sounded uncertain.

What did anyone care of my desires? "I will ask a friend in Caen to come to my defense. What of my writing implements?"

"We are still waiting, citizeness," one of the guards replied.

I nodded. I would be wholly surprised if Fouquier-Tinville allowed me even this small kindness.

"Are you prepared to go outside?"

"Will you allow me a moment's privacy?"

They eyed each other, perhaps afraid of what would happen if they allowed me a moment alone with the chamber pot. But eventually they relented.

Outside, the sun beamed down. I closed my eyes and tilted my face toward the sky, grateful for the tiny gift of the warmth on my face, as though God Himself were giving me His grace one last time.

And then came another gift.

"You are Charlotte Corday, aren't you? Praise to you for what you have done," a woman said approaching me outside in the prison courtyard. "I rot in this prison thanks to Marat. You have taken down the Mountain."

That same rush of warmth I'd experienced in Marat's bathroom rippled over my limbs. "I wanted only to establish peace."

She nodded and another woman grasped my hands. These prisoners, these wretched victims of a Jacobin government, knew what I had done for them. It was a sweet vindication after the vicious jeering for my blood by the mob the night before.

"Pray with me," I said. They looked at one another as though I'd asked them to eat spiders. It was a great risk to kneel before God within the sight of our oppressors.

But one by one, they took that risk, sinking to their knees until we made a little circle. We held hands as our words of worship stroked the rays of sun.

For two days, I was allowed outside. On the second day I returned to find paper, pen, and ink in my cell.

My first letter was a request to the Committee of Public Safety to have my portrait commissioned. I wanted the people of France to know and remember what a woman of faith had done for her country. I wanted those who were grateful for my sacrifice to see me for the good citizen I knew myself to be. And for those who were curious or thought me a criminal, I wished to make sure they would never forget that I'd died for them too.

Then I wrote a much more difficult letter.

Forgive me, my dear papa, for having disposed of my existence without your permission . . .

I was not sorry for having acted upon my design, nor did I feel that I needed permission from a man who'd abandoned me at every turn to do with my life what I wanted. But I did so wish for my father's forgiveness, as every dying person wishes to be absolved of any perceived sin.

"Papa, can you see me now?" I whispered to a memory of his thin frame.

I have avenged many innocent victims and prevented many new disasters. Someday, when the people are disabused of their errors, they will rejoice that I delivered them from a tyrant.

Would he understand? Or would he abandon me to eternity as he'd done in life?

Paris, July 16, 1793

"Time to go," a guard from the Convention said.

I stood up from where I'd been kneeling in prayer and stared up through the tiny window.

"The Tribunal is ready for your trial. You will be moved to the Conciergerie afterward."

I looked around. This cell had never been comfortable and I would not miss it. Only the pen, paper, and ink were to be regretted. But the Conciergerie could be expected to be worse. It was infamous. As I followed the men from my cell, I thought of my lecherous traveling companion whom I'd told when I arrived in Paris that my address would be that notorious prison, and now it would be so.

My journey to the Revolutionary Tribunal was a blur. I feared facing Antoine Fouquier-Tinville, for he was another monster. At home among the legion of devils dancing as men in Paris at the moment. I wasn't afraid of the truth, but of how I knew he would try to twist it.

They ushered me into a room filled with people, their faces hazy because my eyes refused to focus. Despite how shaken I felt on the inside, I would not let these men know. In the crowd I recognized the proprietor of my hotel, Marat's mistress, the *sans-culotte* woman named Pauline, and the fruit seller, Louise, who'd accosted me in the Palais-Royal. Sitting higher was a man I recognized from pamphlets as Robespierre himself, surrounded by men and women in red caps.

I listened to men speak of my crimes and tried to remain calm, as I stood for hours at the bar, my hands bound. Fouquier-Tinville and the president of the Tribunal laced the truth with lies to fit their version of what had happened and my motivations. They made me out to be a villainess whore. The lover of every Girondin who'd fled Paris to Caen and put up to the crime of killing by these men. A crazed madwoman who burst through the doors of Marat's residence flailing my knife in an attempt to kill anyone in sight. That if I wasn't shackled at the bar, I might, even now, attempt to maim those in the courtroom.

They called witnesses I had never met or seen, who claimed to know me so very well. Those false witnesses declared they'd heard me lament of wanting to kill every Jacobin in France. All the men of the Convention. How dangerous they must've deemed the truth if they felt the need to so embellish it with all these lies. I stood stoically through it, utterly alone in a room full of my enemies. I was allowed no comment, no response.

At last, they moved to my interrogation. This I welcomed. For surely now I would have the chance, again, to speak my own truth, to right the lies that had been spoken all morning.

He placed a paper flat in front of me. My letter to the people. "Did you pen this?"

I nodded, for there was no denying it, the letter had been found on me.

"Behold, the writings of a madwoman, in which she

admits to being a counterrevolutionist and her desire to see France fall." Fouquier-Tinville held aloft my address, not reading even one line of it to the people.

Anger made my heart pound and I leaned forward. "No, citizen, I desire only to see France rise."

But he ignored me. "What was the purpose of your journey to Paris?"

"I came to kill Marat. Despite what others say, I had no other purpose." I kept my voice steady, strong, and clear but calm, and I stood straight. I'd faced down a monster in his lair; I could face these men too.

"What was your motive?"

I jutted my chin forward. "To punish him for his many crimes."

My interrogator rolled his eyes, pursed his lips, and then snorted derisively—showing the crowd that he thought me a bad liar and a silly woman. Many in the courtroom chuckled.

I could not react, for if I did, if I lost my composure, I might be seen as the silly woman he wanted me to be. So I merely sniffed down at him when he turned back to face me.

"And what crimes can you attribute to Marat, who was such a friend of the people?"

Friend of the people. It was a crime to call such a monster a friend. I stared out toward Pauline, a woman who claimed to be close with Marat. Why? What could she gain by aligning herself to such men, unless her own lust for blood was just as potent.

"Treason, monsieur. The betrayal of France."

Angry, disbelieving mumbles swelled from those in attendance. I bit the inside of my cheek to keep from screaming. I would be worthy in this moment. Men like Marat said every base thing that came to their minds. But people could control themselves. I certainly could.

"You accuse him of treason, upon what foundation?"

"He instigated the massacres of last September. He wanted to be chosen dictator amongst the people." My voice grew louder, stronger, as I continued. "He attempted to infringe upon the sovereignty of the citizens of France by causing the arrest and imprisonment of the Girondin deputies of the Convention in May."

"The Girondins are the traitors. And even if they were not, what proof have you that Marat was the orchestrator of their arrest?"

I bristled. "The opinions of those in Paris are not the same as the opinions of those elsewhere across France. Arresting citizens, men who speak for the people, is a vile offense against the rights of the citizens of France. Marat called for their arrest, and he said to me himself he would see the Girondins sent to the guillotine. Marat hid his designs behind a mask of patriotism, but do not be mistaken, he wished to rule as a tyrant over you all."

"Silence!" he shouted, spittle flying from his mouth. "I will not allow you to poison our ears with your lies."

The room fell silent, and the air became heavy and expectant. Fouquier-Tinville frowned at me for a long moment, then he slapped the surface of the wooden bar in front of me. "Your action, murder, is so atrocious it could never have been conceived or committed by a woman of your age unless you were incited by someone. Tell us who sent you."

Why did they refuse to believe that a woman could be capable of heroism? Of soldiering on and taking out an enemy? Again, my eyes found Pauline. She glowered at me, but I could see something inside her breaking when I spoke next. "Do all women act only on the commands of a man? Are women mere puppets? Can we not form our own opinions and act upon them? I tell you again, I did not confide my plans to anyone, nor conceive of them with another person. In killing Marat I did not kill a human, but a wild beast who was devouring the people of my beloved country."

A light blinked in the prosecutor's eyes. "You assume he was a wild beast?"

"In the ways in which men possessed by evil are, *oui*."

"I do not believe you did this on your own, Citizeness Corday. No one does. Now, tell us, who instructed you? Who are you so unwilling to name?"

The prosecutor began to guess at names. And I straightened, refusing to expose friends who had nothing to do with me killing Marat, even as I became unsettled by the names I heard. A neighbor and friend of my dearly departed mother. How far into my past had they gone? Was my sister, my cousin in danger?

"You, and those who agree with you, show poor knowledge of the human heart," I managed, even as nerves made my voice waver. It was important for me to insulate my kin as much as I could by convincing these men that I acted alone. "It is easier to carry out such a design upon the strength of one's own hatred than upon that of others."

The prosecutor blustered, his cheeks growing red, clearly frustrated that I was not breaking under his interrogation. "Did the Girondins in Caen not ask you to give them an account of your journey? Did they not know your motive?"

I swallowed around my outrage. I'd made friends with the Girondins. "No."

"Then what is this? Taken from your own cell?"

He placed my letter to Barbaroux, a Girondin I'd met in Caen on the table. How had they found it? After writing it, I'd slipped it inside my mattress, in a small slit I'd found, certain they would find it if I'd left it out in the open.

"That is a letter I wrote home to a friend." I licked my lips, feeling more nervous than before.

"A Girondin."

"No," I lied.

"Citizen Barbaroux is a known Girondin. Is he not the person to whom you addressed this letter?"

I swallowed, seeing his name plainly written in ink. "He is a friend in Caen. I wrote to him of my journey." Good God . . . Barbaroux and the other Girondins had wanted to know the state Paris was in from someone they could trust. And now they may die, because of me.

"You wrote of more of your journey, Citizeness Corday. You wrote of your crime. If he was not involved, not the instigator of your crimes, you would not have written him such correspondence. You would not have so openly given him every detail."

There was nothing I could say in my defense, because I could see why he would think so, even if it wasn't true. "You will twist whatever I say to fit your version of the truth, just as you have twisted the words I've written."

The man bristled. "Did your Girondin friends not warn you that if you killed Marat you would immediately be executed?"

"No one warned me, as no one knew what I was going to do. But I was convinced that it would be so, yes. It was for that reason I explained my motive in my address to the French, which was found upon my person. I assumed I would have no chance to speak for myself and wanted the truth to be known after my death."

His lip curled in derision. "We shall resume again tomorrow."

The sun had already set by the time we arrived at the Conciergerie. Outside, a mob had gathered to scream at me. As I was escorted to a new gloomy chamber I received the honor I believed I was due: condemned women and men cheered me. My name was on my fellow prisoners' lips and the sound of them crying out to me was the sweetest music, for I felt loved, perhaps for the first time. Inside this dark place, I had found light.

PAULINE

Paris, July 16, 1793

The sun shone off the shirt stained with Marat's sacred blood, which I held aloft. Beside me, Claire and other women from our Société des Républicaines-

Révolutionnaires carried the copper tub Marat had been murdered in. Louise had declined to attend, feigning illness—another of her lies to keep away from the women she'd once fought beside. Behind us, Marat's lover followed, sobbing for the great man.

A martyr to our cause.

And though I myself wished to sob, both for the loss of my friend and for the nation's loss, this was not the time for tears. The fate of a nation depended on no one man—or woman. The promise of liberty was that when one hero fell, another worthy one might pick up the mantle.

And so, I have picked it up. And I will try to carry it forward for all France.

I was drawn back to that moment at the Tribunal when the Corday bitch's eyes met mine, and she asked if women were puppets. She all but accused me of being one. I hated her for that, for what she saw in me—that I was powerless without men. And she was not wrong. I realized that as our eyes met and bitterness filled me along with that awful truth.

Overhead, the skies darkened as clouds rolled in, and a rumble of thunder threatened us. How many times had rain poured down on us when we marched? The day of the Women's March, in 1789, I'd tramped through the muddy streets toward Versailles with

Louise by my side, but hour after hour of rain did not stop us, did not send us running home. I missed her desperately, but if she no longer wanted to fight for our cause, how could I still call her a friend? No amount of rain was going to stop women now. The more I thought of it, maybe rain was a sign of rebirth, of feeding the earth. Rain meant we should carry on.

I was surrounded by people who'd loved Marat and who believed in the cause. My sisters-at-arms, Théo and his fellow Enragés, and Hébert, who the people were already embracing as Marat's natural and perhaps even more radical successor. I even caught sight of Danton, though he tried to remain inconspicuous. He'd been a good friend to Marat. They'd sat beside each other in the Convention. Commiserated together. Plotted. And now his friend was gone, and he, too, was trying to fade into the background, perhaps before he suffered a similar fate. *Coward.*

Waving Marat's bloodied shirt, I cried, "We Revolutionary Republican Women will populate this country, our nation, the land of liberty, with as many men like Marat as there are children born! We will raise those children in adoration of the Revolution and swear to put in their hands no gospel other than *L'Ami du Peuple.* And we will teach them to curse the Angel of Assassination, that murderous harlot from Caen!"

Angel of Assassination was the name they'd given the Corday bitch in the papers. She'd made her mark. She had a moniker that would stick. And worse, even I had to admit she'd been brave. Close to my age, she stood stoic in the courtroom, meeting everyone's gaze with a pride that was as shameless and terrifying as it was . . . inspiring.

If ever someone could have rivaled me in dedication to a cause, it was she.

I hated her all the more for it, because she'd made a name for herself. Even if it was as an infamous traitor. And who was I? Who would remember me?

On the street, to my friends, to strangers, I called the Corday bitch every vulgar word I'd ever heard. Marat had been one of our cause's staunchest supporters. His death was a major blow to the Jacobin party. Already I'd heard there were rumblings in the National Convention, from the Jacobins and the Mountain, that women should not have the right to assemble, let alone any other rights we wanted. And without Marat, Robespierre now had more power than before. And he hated me. Hated my society. And could undo all our efforts if he put his influence to it. Turning the people against us—against women.

What a joke these men were. Wanting to frame a republican nation without half the population's input.

In fairness, I had to admit more than a little agreement with Corday on one point—women *could* and *did* form and act upon their own opinions. And even the most progressive men seemed to have difficulty accepting that. At least we had the backing of Théo and the rest of Les Enragés.

I hoped that was enough. No, I had to do more than hope. I had to make it so.

CHARLOTTE

Paris, July 17, 1793

Dressed in the same white gown I'd worn to execute Marat, I was escorted back to the Tribunal shortly after eight o'clock in the morning. More people were present than on the first day of my trial. I searched the faces, looking for anyone familiar, but found solely those who hated me.

"Monster! Murderess!"

I kept my head high and, when I reached the bar, the crowd quieted, and I steeled myself for another day of false accusations.

The president of the Tribunal, Jacques Montané, paced before me. "Who have you chosen as counsel for your defense?"

They knew who. I'd already told them, but my counsel had not come, and I was not surprised. Gustave was a Girondin, one whom I'd known since my days at the abbey in Caen. There was no question that he would abandon me to save himself. A coward, as I might have been if I'd had anything to lose.

"Gustave Doulcet, deputy to the Convention from Caen."

"A Girondin." He stared at me intently, then turned to face those in attendance. "An enemy of the people."

My hands curled into fists until my nails bit into the delicate skin of my palms. "He is no more an enemy of the people than I. You, citizen, are an enemy of our great country."

The president's face flamed, and I immediately regretted letting anger get the better of me. He leaned close, both of his fattened hands pressed to the wooden bar in front of me. "You will meet death soon, citizeness, and we will rejoice in killing you."

I rose, my spine straight, face serene. "So it will be."

I'd spoken my truth. The rest would unfold as I knew it must. Now all that remained was to have my moment before the people in the square where I would die.

From the way Montané paced in front of me, I was certain he would like nothing more than to toss me out to the wolves now. "Chauveau de la Garde and his assistant will make an attempt at a defense."

I nodded, glancing at them uneasily. I wanted to tell my defender it was not necessary, that he should go home.

Witnesses were then called by the prosecutor, the first of whom was Marat's mistress. I listened to her explain the details of that night once more, anger rising in my chest as the woman spoke falsely of my murderous face, my threats and shouts, how I'd come into their home resembling a raving lunatic. For the first time in the trial, I was affected, and not because of the insults she flung. But because she had loved Marat. She was in pain. And it was through her pain that she lied. Perhaps it was through the pain inflicted on all France that we lied, and that is how we got to this place. This betrayal of our revolution. I needed the pain and the lying to end. For love of country.

"*Oui*, it was I who killed him!" I shouted, interrupting them all. "I wished to sacrifice him for the greater good of the country."

I'd bested them at the first Tribunal. But they were wiser now and breaking down my defenses. The next assault was made by showing me the knife with which my deed was done, still stained with Marat's blood. "Do you recognize this?"

Bile rose in my throat, and emotion swiftly carried me over the edge of my serenity. I'd managed to remain mostly calm until now. Still believed wholeheartedly in my cause, but at the base root of my soul, I was not a murderer. And I was still a Christian. So the sight of the crusted blood on the blade . . . "*Oui*, of course I recognize it." I shuddered.

"Oh, what practice you must have taken to hit such a vital spot to have killed the man so proficiently. Who did you practice on?" Montané taunted.

I leaned over the bar looking the man right in the face, fury coursing through my veins. "Oh, you're a monster! You accuse me of being some common killer, stabbing anyone without discrimination. But that is not who I am. I am a woman of God and a soldier for the people."

The president sneered and pulled from his coat folded slips of paper. My letters. The ones I'd written in prison. The ones they'd never sent. I had expected that they would read my letters, but I hadn't considered the possibility that they would not send them.

He read them aloud to the great delight of the crowd, and when he came to the words I'd written my father, bitter tears clouded my eyes. I raised my head, fighting down the sobs, and stared at every face before me, willing him to be there, to acknowledge his daughter. Once again, I was left disappointed.

But then Montané reached the last line, reading it louder than the rest, "The shame lies in the crime, not in the scaffold. What does that mean, citizeness?"

Hearing those words of my ancestor Corneille, my spirits were strengthened. All my tears dried up, replaced by a surge of pride. "I was a republican before the Revolution started, and I have always been willing to sacrifice myself for my country. Does a soldier commit a crime when he executes an enemy? I have committed no crime. I have no shame. And I die with honor."

I thought for a moment that Montané might leap up over the bar and attack me. When he spoke, spittle flew from his lips, "Is there anything you wish to add to these letters, citizeness?"

My gaze swept the room as I sought to meet each pair of eyes one more time. They wanted to break my spirit, this mob, but I would not let them. Then I stared at each of the officials presiding over my trial in turn. They could take their powdered hair and go to the devil.

"*Oui*, there is one last thing I would like to add, and it is this: the leader of anarchy is no more. France shall now have peace."

"We shall have your head." His viciousness, the sneer that peeled his lips back could've sent me over the edge, had I not seen my counsel regarding me with what could only be called respect. Perhaps I was not wholly surrounded by enemies after all.

At last, one of my prosecutors announced to the Tribunal that this folly had come to an end.

I watched de la Garde stand, his eyes on me. I wondered what he was going to say. I did not want a defense, but after all he had been assigned to give me one.

Those of the Tribunal had tried to portray me as if I were mad. Did they want my defender to agree? Was that the condition under which he had been appointed? I looked at their faces and thought, yes, they want him to tell everyone that. They wanted him to state that a woman killing for political reasons was proof of insanity.

They wanted my defender to agree in an effort to save my life—a useless effort since my prosecutor had all but guaranteed my death.

I held my breath. Would this man aid in the mockery of me, assist men in degrading and diminishing me?

He cleared his throat, stepped away from his chair. "The prisoner confesses with great calmness the horrible crime she has committed. She confesses calmly having premeditated the deed. She confesses its most dreadful details. In a word, she confesses everything and does not even seek to justify herself other than to say she wanted to save the people of our great nation from tyranny." He glanced back at me, and I worked hard to keep my face impassive. "That, citizens, is her whole defense. This imperturbable calm, this entire rejection of remorse, even in the very presence of death itself, this sublime calm under such circumstances are contrary to nature. They can only be explained by the excitement of political devotion that armed her hand."

De la Garde had not betrayed me! He'd let me retain my purpose, my dignity. And the outrage on Montané's and Fouquier-Tinville's faces was telling. But I blessed him and silently prayed that his brave actions would not result in his ruin.

I was not surprised when they ordered my death. I dearly hoped that all France would be told of my defense, of my last gift to them all.

They sent a priest—a constitutional clergyman, a man sworn to the republic not to Rome. To my mind such a nonjuring clergyman was no priest at all.

"Sir, I do not require your ministrations."

He seemed quite astounded. "Citizeness, allow me, *s'il vous plait*, to hear your confession and administer a blessing."

"No."

Shortly after he left, the portraitist from the Tribunal arrived. He'd painted me while I stood at the bar, and I'd requested to see the likeness. The miniature was fascinating, and accurate: even down to the soft chestnut curls around my ears.

"You are very good, monsieur." I'd given up on the pretexts of revolutionary addresses now that I'd been consigned to death. I met his gaze, hoping he'd show mercy on a woman about to die. "Will you paint me again now? Something for my father?" A portrait of me, so he might see what I'd become, and know that despite his having forsaken me, I was still proud.

"*Oui*, citizeness."

I stood by the window so the light would touch my face, and he sat at my writing desk, setting out his paints. He sketched my face and then painted what he'd drawn. When he was finished, he gestured me closer.

"Looks like me," I mused, delighted in the way he'd been able to manipulate the colors to show the sun upon me.

The door to my cell opened to reveal the formidable figure of the executioner dressed all in black with a sash across his middle in red, white, and blue. My face paled, and I whispered, "What, already?" feeling a small pang of anguish for those I'd not been able to say good-bye to.

Charles-Henri Sanson was legendary throughout France. He'd inherited his position from his father before him and was fourth in a long line of executioners by the same name. The tall, broad-shouldered man before me performed his duty with infamous talent— even helping to design the instrument of my death. I'd heard he could execute upwards of a dozen people in nearly the same number of minutes. How many souls had he collected so far?

"We bid you *au revoir*, citizeness." His voice was deep, gravelly, as though his throat were constantly tight. And why wouldn't it be? He was the principal soul-taker in all Paris. Sanson was Death.

The executioner held out a red linen overgown, which they made all the condemned wear to disguise the blood. "I'm sorry to make you wear this, mademoiselle, but it is the law. And we must cut your hair."

"Red flatters me," I replied, moving my chair to the center of the room for the man to begin his work. Seated, I tugged off my white linen cap. My long hair fell around my shoulders. He hacked away with terrifying sheers. When it was done, I could have sobbed at the lightness, the coldness of the loss, but kept a brave face.

"A lock of my hair for you, monsieur," I picked up a curl from my lap and held it out to the painter. "For you have troubled yourself much on my behalf. Please accept it as a keepsake." The portraitist stared at my outstretched hand, uncertainly. "Do not fret, monsieur, I am at peace."

The men left me alone for a moment. I stood, praying my knees would hold me, and with slightly trembling hands, I pulled the crimson gown—the gown of my death—over the top of my white dress, my breath catching as I realized this would be the last time I dressed myself. A great shudder racked my body, and I wrapped my arms around myself, trying to breathe steadily and finding my body did not cooperate.

The executioner returned. "It is time."

Time for me to die. Time for me to offer up the greatest sacrifice anyone can give—their life. And I wanted to do it like a patriot, which meant, freely. "Please, monsieur, do not bind me."

But of course, even the king had been bound at the last moment with his own handkerchief. And no exception could be made for me. So I held out my hands to show the bruises that still marred my flesh from my capture. "May I at least be allowed to wear gloves to prevent pain?"

"You may wear gloves, but I promise I will not hurt

you as they have." His eyes widened, and he stared at me for a moment with a look of shame for what he'd said.

Not hurt me? He was only the man who would take my life . . .

I smiled, though my lips trembled with fear. "I would guess you have more experience than they do."

"Perhaps, mademoiselle."

There was kindness in Sanson. And a deep respect I would not have expected from a man who had taken so many lives. Knowing that he had to live with the guilt of what he did, I wondered, did he worry that on the day of his death God would send him to the bowels of hell for taking so many innocent lives?

He was gentle just as he'd promised, and when he finished binding my wrists, I looked into his eyes, smiled, and said, "I am ready. Lead me now to immortality."

PAULINE

Paris, July 17, 1793

The Corday bitch stood stoically in the back of the tumbrel, her hands tied. It had rained steadily through the night, and there seemed to be no end to it. The

Angel of Assassination kept her back straight, and even though she wore condemned red, she somehow made *us* feel like sinners. The rain soaked through her garments, flattened her cap, dripped from the tip of her nose, and still she smiled.

I took hurried steps to keep up with the wagon, water sloshing in my clogs. I wanted to see her to the very end.

Her hair was shorn, and I couldn't help but wonder what had been done with the discarded locks. I hated that every last strand would soon be a prize. That all her worldly possessions would be coveted.

Because she was infamous.

Her name filled the papers. Théo had taken up Marat's position publishing *L'Ami du Peuple*, adding *According to Leclerc* as a subtitle, and he had become obsessed with her. He talked of her endlessly. He wrote that she was heinous to behold, that she was a wicked fornicator, that she had been the lover of every Girondin, royalist, and traitor. But even when he was writing these things, or saying these things, I saw in his eyes a great lust; he wanted to possess her.

Claire did not seem to see it. But I had long begun to suspect that I knew her lover better than she did. And when I drew her attention to it, she said that of course every man lusted for her, that was what men did. Crowds filled the street, making it difficult for the executioner's cart to roll over the cobbles. They shouted at her and threw rotten fruits and vegetables. We marched for over an hour, and all the while I held Marat's bloody shirt on a pike in the air for all to see.

"Harlot!" I screamed at her. "Murderess! Sinner! Shame!"

My words did not seem to bother her any more than the words of the others. Not once did she flinch at our insults or even when hit by some foul object. It was as if she already floated in a heaven we all knew didn't exist.

At the place of execution, she climbed out of the cart without assistance and up to the scaffold as though she were climbing the stairs to a dais. The executioner took her elbow, gently guiding her. He smiled kindly, and I was even more disgusted. It seemed the vile traitoress had won the heart of the man who must end her.

I shoved my way to the front of the crowd with Théo at my side.

As Sanson turned to prepare, the assistant grasped the fichu covering Corday's breasts, and tore it away with such violence he ripped part of her gown. The action incited the crowd to surge forward. The whore's face reddened, her mouth gaping open, and she jerked as though to cover herself, but it was useless as her hands were tied behind her back. Her humiliation was acute.

And I enjoyed it.

The crowd cheered. And all that creamy white flesh exposed had my own breath catching. The woman was perfection. And as if the sky above mocked us, the rain ceased, the clouds parted, and the sun beamed down on her.

Corday opened her mouth to say something. Why wouldn't she just die and let her words die with her? She was cut off by the steady beat of the drums and the demands of the crowd for her head. And when it was clear that they wouldn't be silenced, I shouted, "*Vive la république!*" But soon my throat was too tight to do more than mouth the words.

The assistant shoved Corday forward, and as she reached the bench, the sun glinted off the metal of the angled guillotine blade, casting her in a light that only served to call more attention to her serene countenance. Did it make the others present question whether we were right to shun God? The question certainly came to my mind.

Théo breathed heavily beside me, lusting for blood, or perhaps, even in this moment, for carnal possession of the woman on the scaffold. I could have shoved him to the ground and stomped on his heart.

The crowd quieted, taken in by her beauty, by her smile. How could she smile like that, as though she'd won, when she was about to die? Angry tears threatened to spill from my eyes, but I forced them back and pinched my forearm to refocus myself.

Corday knelt on the bench before the block, then jerked back when the executioner went to pull her feet, lengthening her legs so she lay flat on her belly. I could almost feel the scrape of the wooden bench on my own knees, the rope at my wrists, and when she laid her pretty head down for the last time, I, too, felt the sun-warmed wood on my cheek. Saw the waiting, bloodied basket, hungry for my head.

I held my breath in anticipation, all while Théo panted.

Then the guillotine screamed as it dropped, as if in protest for what it must do. A jolt of satisfaction went through me as the blade made its clean cut.

As soon as the assassin's delicate head was in the basket, a man hired to assist with the guillotine lifted it up by the shorn hair showing it to the crowd, and then slapped the peacefully smiling face hard on each cheek. Beside me, Théo gaped with shock, and I did too. Because at this insult, the disembodied head of Charlotte Corday reacted. Her cheeks reddened, her mouth thinned in outrage, and her eyebrows dipped with consternation, as though she were still very much alive and offended.

As I said before, she would not die.

I stormed through the doors of Hébert's Cordeliers Club and went in the direction of Saint-Germain, having had enough of Théo and his impassioned hypocritical speeches. The long walk would do me good. I ached to be home surrounded by the scents of *chocolat*, the warmth of my siblings, and quiet.

"Pauline!" Théo's voice came from behind me.

I quickened my pace, ignoring him, and rushed past the few men and women still out at this hour. Long fingers gripped my elbow and he tugged me into an alleyway, pressing me against the wall, caging me in with his hands pressed to the brick on either side of my face. The possessiveness of his move, the way he effortlessly positioned me made me furious.

"What are you doing?" Even in the dim light cast off by the streetlamps I could read the accusation of desertion in his eyes.

"Going home, what did you think I'm doing?"

"Running away."

"What have I to run from?"

"Me."

I crossed my arms over my chest, hoping to mask

my uneven breaths. "Why would I run from you? You are no threat to me." But that was a lie. Fear gripped me, deep in my gut. No woman was safe in all this. No matter what we'd tried to accomplish, one false word from a man could tear us down. He was a threat, all men were.

"Did you not like my speech? I wrote it for you."

I rolled my eyes and glanced toward the street. "I thought it well done for a hypocrite."

Théo jerked back as though I'd slapped him. "What do you mean?"

"You speak of patriotism and inciting the fairer sex to rise up, and yet no one believes that Charlotte Corday could have acted on her own. None of you truly believe that we women, myself and those of my society, can either. Knowing you do not believe makes your speech, your support, nothing but patronizing."

"That is a lie, Pauline."

But I didn't stop. "They believe us all to be whores at our core, so much so they subjected her body to an examination. Did you know that? Her headless body! She had no lover whispering in her ear to kill Marat. She was no whore."

"That bitch was *virgo intacta*?"

I pursed my lips to keep from railing even more. The news of Charlotte Corday's innocent, lustless body had crushed me. We were exact opposites in nearly every way. Though she was dead, she still had the power to torment me. To show me all my own failures.

I hated the danger that Charlotte Corday's execution meant for other women. The way they humiliated her. The way they lusted for her. Les Enragés, the Jacobins, they might all say they were on our side, but were they really? Or were we all just pawns in the games they played? Fear made me shudder.

Théo narrowed his eyes, the muscle in his jaw clenching. He wanted to say something, but kept silent. Good. Because I had nothing more to say to this man whom I'd once thought held me in such high regard.

I turned my back on him and walked away.

Paris, September 5, 1793

Terror was the order given by Robespierre on behalf of the Convention. And we took that order gleefully in hand.

Marat's death hadn't been in vain, for more politicians and citizens alike began to embrace the radical beliefs and approaches that the Enragés and Hébertists championed. Between Corday's murderous actions and local revolts and the threat of looming foreign invasions, it was clear that Terror was the only way to protect the Revolution's achievements—including our new constitution, which promised a breathtaking array of rights and the redistribution of wealth. And though only men had been permitted to vote on the new constitution, it was in all citizens' interest to protect such sweeping changes, so I firmly believed that the republic's enemies had to be repressed at any cost.

Just before noon, as we readied for a protest at the Tuileries, an eclipse covered most of the sun, putting Paris into near darkness. An omen, not to us, but to those who were against us, that soon we would unleash darkness on them.

Hundreds of *sans-culottes* crowded in front of the Tuileries, fists raised, bodies pressed closely together, smelling of determination and sweat, shouting for bread. "*Du pain! Du pain!*"

We demanded the arrest of anyone noble, anyone hoarding wheat. We demanded their heads.

All the while the men inside decided our fates.

Pawns. All of us, waiting hungrily with our hands outstretched, and there was nothing we could do. The power I'd felt when I led the march on the Champs de

Mars, when women and men, too, counted on me, had slowly been chipped away, until it felt like I stood here with nothing left.

Paris, October 26, 1793

"Down with bonnets rouges! Down with Jacobin women! Down with cockades! You are all scoundrels and whores who have brought misfortune upon France!"

I jerked my gaze up when the market woman barged into our Société des Républicaines-Révolutionnaires meeting, pointing her finger at us. Her hair was disheveled, and the first thing I noticed on her dingy gray cap, besides its color, was the missing cockade. The second thing I noticed was that it was Louise, my once dear friend, leading the disturbance. Behind her were what looked like dozens more women. For weeks now, we'd been divided with the working-class women of Paris who thought we were too extreme. Run-ins on the streets had even gotten us noticed in the Convention, and they were not happy with what they saw as riotous behavior not conducive to their own plans.

The men were scared we women were going mad.

The divide between Louise and I had been growing for months, but never once did I think she would turn against me, against our cause. Why? What had happened? She was barely the woman I'd known before, and the way she stared at me now . . . I might not have recognized her had I passed her in the marketplace.

"Pull off their bonnets!" Louise shouted, then stared right at me. "You cannot tell us what to wear. You cannot tell us what to do. You are the reason we're being attacked by men in the streets. Did you know that? Just last week a man tore the red bonnet off my head and shoved me to the ground, kicking me in the ribs. We'll not conform to your militant ways any longer. We'll not risk our own livelihoods in the process."

The tragedy of women turning against women, because men had forced them to, was not lost on me.

"The men are the ones making you choose, Louise. All of you. Do not bow to them."

Louise shook her head, her scowl deepening. "It is too late."

"What happened to us?" I pleaded, searching the vacant eyes for the friend I'd once known.

"You went too far."

"Whores!" came a chant from the market women behind Louise, the venom in their voices enough to stun us all.

And with that one word, Louise was lost to me.

Did they not realize what we did, we did for them? Did they not realize they'd once stood beside us?

"There she is, the *new* Corday!" They pointed at Claire, their accusations of her being a counterrevolutionary loud and clear. "Get the terrible woman and tear her to pieces!"

Claire startled beside me. Our run-ins with the market women had become ever more violent as they defied the wearing of cockades and bonnets rouges, claiming violence against them for wearing the symbol of freedom, never mind men were calling it militant. They despised us for our desire to see women's rights grow. Through it all, Louise had avoided me. She must have felt the tightening noose because she stood beside such women daily to earn enough coin to feed herself—was that why she'd turned? But I knew it had to be more than that. Louise was lost inside herself.

And now, these ungrateful wretches had come into our meeting attempting to start a riot. Well, if it was a fight they wanted, we would give them one.

"To arms, citizenesses! Do not let these bitches tear us down," I shouted.

The battle was bloody; women leapt over chairs and overturned tables in an effort to rip one another apart. Our opponents ripped off our cockades, and we raked our nails over their flesh. Heads were bashed, and clothing torn, lips bloodied and eyes blackened. The vicious invaders tried to destroy our society's symbols, and when Théo's fellow Enragés leader ran in to intercede, shouting for them to stop, they turned on the man as well like a pack of wild animals.

I was no less wild. My fists were bloodied and my head pounded from where someone had hit me with a broken chair leg. The cockade from my bonnet had been stripped, the ribbons unthreaded in wrinkled red, white, and blue waves at my feet. Indiscriminately unraveled the way our revolution seemed to be coming undone around me.

When the police arrived, breaking up the bloody scene, I stood panting, my sleeve torn off, my lip bleeding, and all I could think was, is this what we've become?

I leapt into this revolution to protect women, not fight them.

Breathing hard, I regarded Claire. She looked more furious than I'd ever seen before, even when she was arrested the previous month, accused of being a counterrevolutionary. Citizen Maillard, once our friend, was behind her arrest. He now had spies all over the city. It would seem that friends turned on one another these days. Maillard had certainly learned that in his turn, for even as I stood pressing the cut on my temple that pulsed with pain, Maillard sat in prison. Claire joined me, one eye already swollen shut. This wasn't the first brawl we'd been in, and I hazarded a guess that it wouldn't be our last.

She smirked. "Market bitches."

Where could we go from here, when it would seem we could so easily turn on one another? We'd marched with these market women, to Versailles, to the Bastille, to the Tuileries. Fought side by side. When had we become enemies?

Paris, November 8, 1793

They would silence us all.

One woman at a time.

First the Angel of Assassination. Then Widow Capet, who had once been queen. Olympe de Gouges five days ago. Now proud Manon Roland.

A professed Girondin, Manon was still against tyranny and had been an advocate for the republic since the dawn of the Terror. Once, I wouldn't have been able to admit that, but I could admit it now. Now that it's too late.

I heard later that Madame Roland's pathetic husband shot himself as soon as he heard she was dead, and even her lover didn't make it much longer. Though it was never confirmed Buzot was her lover—the bitch kept her lips tight around that secret—they say that a miniature of her was found on Buzot's body. If that wasn't proof enough of their liaison, then I don't know what is. Who could blame her for taking a lover considering the stick she was married to? But even Buzot was a coward. He'd taken his own life rather than be captured and face the Tribunal after an attempt to raise troops against the Convention failed.

As I watched her mount the scaffold at the place de la Révolution, this woman who, to her very last, was confident in her political views, her activism, and her political achievements, I could not help seeing myself. For I, too, was once confident in all those things. I lived for them.

Manon glanced toward the clay statue of Marianne, Goddess of Liberty, who stood tall on her pedestal, looking down on the proceedings, judging our hypocrisy. Manon's last words clawed at my heart. "Oh Liberty, what crimes are committed in your name!"

And then she was lain out, her head put in position, and rather than thirsting for the spurt of blood I knew was coming as I had in the past, inside I rebelled. I wished for someone to come and break that guillotine, like years ago a crowd had broken a wheel and stopped an execution.

But the blade dropped, and as it cut short Manon's life, a sob escaped my throat and I bit hard on the inside of my cheek to keep from letting out another sound. If anyone noticed, they did not let on, and thank goodness, else they drag me away in chains demanding my head too.

Would I be next? Already I was embroiled, my name high on the flapping tongues of men who wished to crush any rights of women's liberty.

"Pauline?" Théo's voice cut into my thoughts, and he looked at me as though I might have suddenly sprouted the former queen's ridiculous hairpieces.

"I am pregnant." The words were out before I could stop them. Just over a week had passed since I'd talked with Claire, and I'd not had the courage yet to tell him, and she'd surprisingly not betrayed my trust, nor hated me for it.

"Is it . . . mine?" His brows raised, and whether real or imagined, I saw dread.

"*Oui.*"

Théo let out a curse under his breath. "I should have been more careful."

For the first time at an execution, Théo was silent,

even as the crowd around us screamed with delight at the executioner holding up Manon's once brilliant head.

"I didn't want . . ." I couldn't finish the sentence; there were so many things I didn't want.

"We must marry. You've no other choice," he continued when I didn't respond. "What will your mother think? You cannot abandon her, or your brothers and sisters."

"And you would have me abandon my cause?"

Théo shook his head. "Together, we will see this revolution through to the end."

Théo kissed my knuckles in an absurd gesture of chivalry, so much in opposition for the way in which I'd found myself in this situation—captured by lust and weakness.

We had wanted liberty in France. But what freedom was there now? I had none. Théo would possess me utterly. I knew it, because the look he gave me had me wanting to crumble to the ground. All the choices I'd fought years for had been stripped away.

And now, I was nothing.

PART VI

The Beauty

It was a sensual delight for
l'homme rouge to see fall
in the basket these charming heads
and their ruby blood streaming
under the hideous cleaver.
—ARCHIVES NATIONALE

Sucy-en-Brie, France, March 1794

When love came to me, it was in the dead of night, under cover of darkness, and always in disguise. For those were the indignities that marriage and revolution had imposed upon me, and both had done violence to the gaiety of society at the exact moment when, by the dictums of youth, fashion, and inclination, I should have been at the center of Paris's *le monde élégant*.

But, alas, nothing was as it should have been.

Which was why I found myself moving stealthily about our country château in Sucy-en-Brie, where my family had for months been in self-imposed exile from the paranoia of the Jacobin government, the great mobs of *sans-culottes*, and the willingness of neighbor to turn against neighbor to win favor with both. Trusting not even my lady's maid to assist me, I went from room to room and window to window to set up the signal of lights that would tell my love it was safe to come to me, then I snuck outside into the gardens to wait.

Finally, he was there, slipping through the secret little door into the park beside our home. "Oh, my Georgette," he whispered, pulling me into his arms.

"Oh, Philippe," I said, allowing myself to be swept up into his kisses for only a moment. "Come, we must hurry."

Hand in hand, we raced among the early spring blooms cloaked in twilight dew until we reached the château. Inside, I removed my slippers and he his boots, and we made ghosts of ourselves until we were finally shut up in my suite of rooms, laughing and kissing.

"Did you have any trouble, my love?" I asked, feeling almost as if I could exhale in his warm, familiar presence.

He shed his short carmagnole coat and cap upon the bed, revealing to me his handsome face and rakish brown curls. Along with the *pantalon* he wore, every part of his outfit was borrowed costuming from the Théâtre Favart where he frequently performed. For everything was theater in France now, and Philippe and Georgette were but code names we used to hide all that we'd become to each other since I first saw Jean-Baptiste-François Elleviou sing his famed one-act opera, *Philippe et Georgette*, from Maman's box at the Comédie nearly five years before. Our love had been fast and intense and exciting, full of late-night parties at the theater and stolen, heated moments wherever we could find them—our secrecy the result of my mother's disapproval and my need to maintain an image of availability for my work at Cinquante, Paris's most famous gambling house.

"The patrols were heavier tonight," he said. "Executing the latest faction seems to have done little to assuage the Committee of Public Safety's belief that a foreign conspiracy plots to invade France, assassinate Robespierre, and overthrow the Revolution." François took me into his arms again. "But I missed you too much to stay away, *mon trésor.*"

"The whole of France has gone mad," I said, concern for him—for all of us—making it hard for me to relax into his embrace. And I'd come by that concern honestly after what'd happened to my papa . . .

"It has," he said, soothingly stroking his fingers through the long, loose golden curls of my hair, almost chasing away the troubling thoughts. "From day to day, it's impossible to know what will happen. But we have this day, when you possess all those beaming charms that inspire the most ardent passions. Which is why I must have you now."

François's words wove a spell that bade me to forget the world as his mouth dipped to mine. Clever fingers went to the pink silk sash tied about the waist of my gauzy *chemise à la reine.* I sighed in surrender as he walked us toward the bed, toward oblivion, toward—

An insistent pounding upon the front door echoed through the château. Then again. "Open in the name of the republic!" came a loud command.

On a gasp, I broke free of the embrace and dashed for the window. A group of men gathered upon our portico while a patrol waited in formation just outside our gate, sending a shiver of cold dread down my spine. No good ever came from the arrival of self-styled patriots at one's door. It wasn't the first time and probably wouldn't be the last, though we'd hoped our flight from the city would not only remove us from their sights, but also from their minds.

Someone permitted them entrance, and then the crier's voice boomed from inside our parlor. "Search the premises!"

"Come," I said, pulse racing as I grabbed the discarded pieces of my lover's costume and pulled him to the closet.

François stumbled into the hanging fabric of my outdated *robes à la française* and the wide-hooped panniers that went beneath them. "Émilie, wait—"

"Say no more," I whispered, hearing footsteps upon the grand staircase. "And stay hidden behind the gowns until I return for you."

If I returned.

For the Jacobins had long been resentful of my

mother for being the daughter of a marquis and for running Cinquante—the favorite gambling establishment among the city's aristocracy and, therefore, of its royalists and moderates. That resentment extended to me, too, not only for helping her run the club, but also for not returning the interest of the men who frequented it—or wished to. Men who had now gained power, like Robespierre, recent president of the National Convention and primary defender of *la Terreur*, a man so powerful he'd created his own religion by proclamation a few months before; and Louis Saint-Just, the revolution's so-called Angel of Death and the National Convention's youngest delegate, who'd done more than anyone to convince that body to execute Louis XVI. Many times I'd dreamt of Robespierre pinning me against the wheel of a carriage the night the Convention had turned on the Girondins and ordered their detainment, except in the nightmare, Madame Roland never interrupted and I had no safe way to deny his desires . . .

I shuddered and forced the memory away, because closing Cinquante and leaving Paris hadn't lessened that resentment. Though it'd been months since our family had retreated to Sucy, Maman still possessed enough friends in elevated places for us to learn that we were even now denounced to the Committee of General Security. After all, in a moment when everyone coveted *more* than what they had—not just freedom and rights, but more influence, more power, and more status, too—spiteful jealousy ran wild.

So I knew not which of us might be the patrol's intended prey. Maman? Myself? I might not have run our club, but I'd committed the additional sin of being known for my supposed dazzling beauty.

The latter had always been for me a double-edged sword. Attracting the unwanted attention of admirers in one moment, but providing a blessed distraction in another. I only hoped it might somehow save us now.

Wrenching open the carved doors to the *armoire de mariage* my dear papa had given me years before, I tore through the piles of antique linens, ruffles of delicate lace, and other parts of my trousseau to find the basket of tricolored ribbons I'd worked into rosettes. Mine was the last suite on the long hallway, so I took just another moment to pin one of the cockades to the gauzy muslin at my breast. My hands trembled so much that I pricked the skin over my heart, but I couldn't give that a thought as I spilled into the hallway with my basket. The door closed behind me just as three municipal officers emerged from my younger brother Louis's neighboring suite.

Upon seeing me, the men nearly knocked into one

another before falling into bows. It would've been comical were the situation not so precarious.

"*Mon dieu!*" I said, pressing my hand to my heart as if their presence had given me a fright, an impression beneath which there was some truth. "Is something the matter?"

"We didn't mean to startle you, Citizeness de Sainte-Amaranthe," the senior officer said, stepping forward. I didn't bother to correct him, though I hadn't gone by that family name for nearly two years. In this moment, I preferred for him to think of me as innocent, virginal, uncorrupted . . . "We received a report of a suspect upon the property."

"Oh, dear." I held the basket in front of me so that the fine satin tendrils of blue, white, and red spilled over the edge in plain sight. Had someone seen François? Certainly, he'd make the Jacobins a notable prize as he'd become one of the most celebrated singers in France—and though that brought him fame and stature, it also brought jealousy and a desire to be the one to take a notable down a few pegs. But if he was their prey, that would mean we were being watched even here in the country. I swallowed hard. "A suspect? Have you found anything? Are we in danger?"

"Do not worry. All appears as it should," the man said in an officious tone as his fellows nodded.

"Well, you deserve our gratitude." I swallowed back bile and smiled at each of them in turn. I moved closer so they could smell my rose water perfume, and I fingered the ribbon upon my breast, inviting their gazes to linger there. "I was just on my way to present these cockades I made to my family. But I would be honored if such fine citizens as yourselves would wear one."

"The honor would be ours," the first officer said. With sheepish nods, the commissioners agreed, and I made a little project of pinning the ribbons upon each man's lapel, making sure to give them the same private smile I used to give Maman's players at Cinquante. The one that made the men believe they might receive even more special attention later—and in the meanwhile, order another round of drinks or play another set at the tables. Sometimes it felt as though my whole life had been about learning to trade one mask for another. At the club, in polite society, with men . . . When I was done with the cockades, the senior commissioner gave me another bow and gestured to the grand staircase. "*Merci*, mademoiselle. Now, may we escort you down to your family while we complete our business?"

Still playing the innocent coquette, I readily assented and descended ahead of the men, who followed seemingly without realizing they'd never searched my rooms. Just as I'd hoped, the beautiful, innocent façade

I presented hid all my secrets—not just François's presence in my chamber, but the misgivings I shared with Maman about the Jacobins' extremism in our revolution. Then again, how could we not question it when the Jacobins had cut down faithful servants like my papa, an officer in King Louis's guard who'd been butchered nearly two years ago in the insurrection of 10 August?

I blinked away the sudden rushing threat of hot, angry tears.

The commissioners led me to our parlor, where they'd gathered the rest of my family—Maman, my brother, and my husband of almost two years, Charles de Sartine, at whom a sentry glared and pointed his bayonet. Despite working for the revolutionary government as a senior judicial officer in the Council of State, Charles lived forever under the shadow cast by his father. Antoine de Sartine had served as lieutenant general of the police and had the detestable habit of imprisoning people without trial. After the fall of the Bastille, the mob meant to seek their revenge against him, and so Antoine had fled to Spain, leaving Charles to prove his loyalty to the republic, which he'd done quite admirably.

But still, the people remembered.

"Are you all right, *mon amour*?" Charles asked as I rushed to his side.

"Quite." I dropped my basket onto an armchair and heaved a calming breath. "The commissioners explained everything and I'm grateful to them for being so diligent."

"As are we all." Charles slanted me a glance that suspected too much.

Our praise made the commissioner puff up, putting his cockade on display. "It is nothing more than our duty to protect our citizens from enemies of the republic." Just then, a clang rang out from the hallway, and the officer turned on his heel. "You there, be careful!"

On hands and knees, a boy, perhaps my brother's same age of sixteen, gathered our kitchen utensils from where they'd scattered upon the marble floor, confiscated, no doubt, to be melted and made into weapons as was the custom whenever the authorities conducted a search. I smiled serenely until the commissioners and their patrolmen finally took their leave.

"Why would they suspect us of harboring enemies?" my brother fumed. "This revolution promised liberty, equality, and fraternity, but all it seems capable of is tyranny and death!" Louis stormed out of the room. Ever since Papa's murder, he'd harbored a simmering anger that took little to ignite into outright rage. Not that I could blame him.

With a sad, resigned smile, Maman squeezed my

shoulder. "I'll talk to him." Nodding, I watched her go. With her golden curls and still-pleasing figure, my mother was as beautiful as she'd ever been, with grace and polish and a pointed wit that could hold a whole salon in thrall. But as she turned away, I couldn't help noticing how she seemed to have aged—silver now streaked through the gold here and there, and she braced her hand against the back of the settee as she passed it, as if she required the support. Once, at the zenith of French society, men had attempted to flatter Maman by telling her she and I must be sisters. But whatever youthfulness had occasioned those fawning compliments had given way under the weight of widowhood and the loss of our lives and livelihood in Paris, not to mention all her friends who had disappeared over the last year . . .

When her footsteps retreated upon the stairs, my husband pulled me aside. "He's here again, isn't he?"

Guilt stirred in my belly. "Charles—"

He shook me by the shoulders, dark eyes flashing and his handsome mouth set in a hard frown. "Damn it, Émilie. Now is not the time for recklessness. If this regime is willing to execute radicals like Jacques Hébert and his faction, then God help us all."

I shuddered upon hearing the man's name, though I regretted his death not at all. Like Marat, Hébert had begun as an angry newspaperman, aiming his poison pen first at the royal family, then at moderates like the Marquis de Lafayette, and then against the reasonable Girondins. In the process, he'd been catapulted into the political leadership of the Montagnard extremists who favored martial law, a system of Terror to root out so-called counterrevolutionaries, and a program of dechristianization for all France. And now that all the reasonable men and women had mostly been silenced, the radicals were turning on one another. "Hébert died for charging that Robespierre was not radical enough."

"That is exactly my point," Charles said. "France's leaders have spent the year since Marat's death convincing themselves that assassins and counterrevolutionary plotters lurk around every corner. And Robespierre himself has become a tyrant used to getting his way at any cost. In such an atmosphere, no one is safe."

Weariness weighed upon my shoulders, and I sighed. Must even love wither and die because of this damnable revolution? "I know, but—"

"I told you what Marie said. As long as the Committee of Public Safety believes that some foreign faction plots Robespierre's assassination, suspicion and calumny are having their day. The longer they cannot catch the leaders of this supposed conspiracy, the more their frustration leads them to seize anyone who could, rightly or wrongly, be suspected of intrigue, corruption, or even merely lukewarm support. You must be smart."

At that, I flashed him a look. "I kept them from finding him, didn't I?"

After a moment, the anger bled out of my husband's expression. "The cockades?"

A slow grin crept over my face. "'I'd be so honored if such fine citizens as yourselves would wear one,'" I said mockingly. But my smile fell away again. "It's not fair that you can go to Paris to see your actress whenever you wish while François and I can only see each other at great risk."

"It's not," Charles agreed as he pulled me into a comforting embrace, for we'd been friends long before circumstance had forced us to marry. Friends who'd first come to know each other through the community of Théâtre Favart, where I'd met François, and Charles had courted Mademoiselle Marie Grandmaison, an Italian actress who'd risen in popularity here in France.

When the Jacobins murdered Papa, Maman determined that the security of our family necessitated that I give up my lover and marry, preferably someone serving the new government. She'd gone so far as to invite her recommended choices to join us on a sojourn to the country, where I'd allowed her to introduce me to Monsieur Charles-Louis-Antoine de Sartine as if Charles and I hadn't been drinking wine together with our lovers and other theater friends several nights a week. And so I married him in hopes that I could secure my family's future—without either Charles or myself having to give up the love we'd found in others, making my marriage just one more role I played.

Now I wondered how much more of ourselves we'd have to sacrifice in an effort to make ourselves free.

"When is it all going to end, Charles?" I asked, because I couldn't see a way out of the madness. Despair threatened to dig its claws into my heart.

He sighed and shook his head, and his voice was gentle when he spoke. "I don't know. Marie hears that, privately, some officials are questioning *la Terreur*, so maybe sooner rather than later." Charles's work in the city allowed him opportunities to see his mistress, who was now a source of vital information. For the theater had become a hotbed of Jacobinism, and Marie passed to us secrets of policy and intrigue from inside the Convention that were recounted by several actors who'd become fiery patriots and befriended Robespierre himself.

Pulling away, I nodded. "I'll tell François not to come for a few weeks until we know better how the winds are blowing."

Charles tilted his head and gave me a little smirk. "And tell him I'll give him a good knockabout if I need to."

I rolled my eyes but appreciated Charles's playfulness and camaraderie in that moment. For our long friendship and unconventional understanding made him the only person in whom I could confide about François. "I don't think that will be necessary," I said, retreating to the doorway.

"Wait." I turned to find Charles bringing my basket of cockades. "Wouldn't want to forget these."

"Indeed." I took it from him, making the blue, white, and red strands flutter. "*Liberté, égalité, fraternité*," I said with false enthusiasm. And then I turned and raced back to the arms of my lover.

Where I could finally take off all my masks and be myself—and try to forget just how close we had come to losing it all.

This is *too great a risk*, I thought as the carriage came to a hard stop before the grand town house. I wasn't sure whether it was the night air or my own dread that caused me to shiver. I tugged my blue jacket tighter around me.

We hadn't been in the city in weeks, yet Maman had readily accepted a coded invitation to a private gathering of those wishing to be initiated into Robespierre's new religion, which he called the Cult of the Supreme Being. Ever since Robespierre had first announced it last December—when he'd issued a surprising proclamation prohibiting all measures contrary to the freedom of worship—Maman had begun looking at him with a sense of hope that he might be the one to restore some order after all. I feared it was her flirtation with the Jacobin's brother, Augustin, that had helped cast the demagogue in a new light.

In my experience with the man, he did nothing that didn't benefit himself. So I remained skeptical.

After all, how could we ever trust Robespierre when he'd built France's current government upon a foundation coated in my father's blood? To say nothing of how many times the so-called *l'Incorruptible* had tried to press his advantage upon me in the back hallways of parties or in dark shadows upon a nighttime street, transgressions I'd kept from Maman fearing she'd be so unwise as to try to defend my honor. Already, I worried that my resistance might have earned his ire, for it had never been riskier for a woman to reject a man's advances or reveal the limitations of his self-control. Especially when anyone who crossed Robespierre ended up losing their head.

"Are you sure this is a good idea, Maman?" I whispered, finally giving voice to my misgivings.

The footman helped my mother and me alight from the conveyance, and we held up our white silk chemise dresses to keep the hems from dragging through puddles leftover from a springtime rain. Charles followed closely behind, also in a blue coat over a white outfit—all of us in the attire specified in the invitation.

Only when the carriage pulled away did Maman finally respond. "The Cult of the Supreme Being stands for ending religious persecutions, abolishing the scaffold, and restoring peace, whereupon we'll finally be able to return to Paris and reopen our house. If anyone can bring these things about, it is Robespierre. Why, with a single proclamation, he made it safe to believe in God again. And even now, he has the Convention debating recognition of the cult as our new official religion. So we must play the odds, darling."

She walked ahead, her stiff posture and the regal tilt of her chin forbidding further discussion. For Maman was not used to being questioned. Indeed, it wasn't so many months ago that her influence had been such that men sometimes joked about which of their younger children they might sell off to receive an invitation to join Cinquante.

But my teeth ached from how tightly I clenched them, and I saw my own uncertainty reflected in Charles's dark gaze. I took his arm and found a small measure of comfort in his steadfastness as he guided us up the tall staircase to the grand front doors. "I fear they're bad odds," I finally muttered under my breath.

"Perhaps, but we must nonetheless be entirely convincing in our enthusiasm," Charles whispered, though we could say no more before we were being greeted and ushered inside, where all was oddly dark and quiet.

Occasional candles cast just enough light to allow us to make our way to a large parlor where perhaps a dozen others were congregated. Notable among them was Monsieur de Quesvremont, who came immediately to Maman's side and kissed her cheeks. Formerly an intimate of the House of Orleans and a friend of Papa's, the man had been whispering in Maman's ear about being initiated since the Proclamation of the Supreme Being. Monsieur de Q was convinced that the end of religious persecutions, as well as Robespierre's much-rumored design to reign over France, raised legitimate hopes of clemency for royalists.

Monsieur de Q was not alone in these hopes. Indeed, some darkly jested that Robespierre was at this moment more popular among the party of the victims than that of the executioners!

We'd barely exchanged hushed greetings before our hostess stepped to the front of the assembly. Only a few years older than me, Victorine, the Marquise de Chastenay, was as devout a believer as she was beautiful. She extended her lithe arms and seemed to hold the whole room rapt. "Come, mortals, share the immortality of the Mother of God."

Our shoes barely made a sound upon the carpets as we moved en masse into another parlor. Three knocks rang out upon the far wall, and then a curtain billowed despite the stillness in the room. It hid yet another door through which our silent assemblage passed. I clutched tighter to Charles's arm.

The only illumination in this new chamber was a single tall candelabra, which cast just enough light to reveal the silhouettes of several who waited for us within. We formed a line, whereupon Victorine presented each of us with a necklace. "Truth and strength," she said, giving me a warm, vivacious smile as she helped me fasten mine on, as if we were meeting amidst the gaiety of one of Baron de Grand Cour's magnificent suppers. Slowly, my eyes adjusted to the dimness sufficiently to make out the pendants that now hung around my neck—a mirror and a dagger. The truth of reflection and the strength of the blade.

Three figures stepped into the ring of light cast by

the candelabra—two young girls, who immediately knelt, and an elderly woman dressed in a nun's black habit. I gasped.

It was the Mother of God.

Catherine Théot was her name. But she was better known among the people for declaring herself the second coming of the Virgin Mary, the new Eve, and the Mother of God. For her claims, she'd been imprisoned for years, but her persecution only strengthened some people's belief in her. After her release, believers flocked to her, along with those who wished to hear her prophecies for a price—and we counted more than a few of our aristocratic friends among her clients. And then, after Robespierre's proclamation, she'd proclaimed the arrival of the Messiah, the one who would comfort the poor, redeem mankind, and create a government inspired by the divine.

Most believed they knew *exactly* whom the *Mère de Dieu* meant, which was, of course, why we were here.

My pulse raced, and perspiration broke out across my brow. Whether that was from the heat quickly overtaking the dark, shrouded room or from being in the presence of the famed prophetess with whom Robespierre had joined forces in this new religion, I didn't know.

The flickering candlelight revealed a pinched, severe

face beneath her veil. She held out her hands as if in invitation. Victorine guided the first supplicant through the appropriate gestures. I watched as Monsieur de Q kissed the prophetess's cheek and hands, then got down on his knees and bent to kiss her feet. One by one, the others did the same, until finally it was my turn to stand before her petite form. A shiver ran through me and I was intensely aware of being watched.

But the elderly woman radiated a confidence that almost promised to wipe away all my misgivings, and there was a certainty in her pale blue eyes that made me feel exposed, as if she knew the fears harbored deep inside my heart. "You are most welcome, child."

Her words spurred me to do my duty before her. I hesitated only for the space of a breath, for I heard Charles's voice again: *We must be entirely convincing in our enthusiasm . . .* So I kissed her weathered cheeks, bent to kiss her gnarled hands, and knelt upon the thick, woven rug to kiss her feet. When I rose, the infirm Sybil placed a kiss of peace upon my forehead, and though the mystic seemed kindly, I couldn't help but count my dignity as another casualty of the times.

When everyone had presented themselves, Victorine stood before us once more. "Friends of God, prepare to meet the Supreme Being. Do you swear obedience to the Mother of God and submission to her prophets?"

"I do," came the others' reply a half beat before I, too, gave my answer. Charles slanted me a deep frown that told me to do better.

"Do you swear to pour the last drop of your blood for the sake of the Supreme Being, either weapons in hand or by all possible kinds of death?" Victorine asked in a tone that almost mesmerized.

"I do," I said, hastening to answer in time with the rest despite the feeling that we were not being asked to make this vow to God at all. Years before, the Revolution's Cult of Reason had declared God dead, and heralded liberty, equality, fraternity, freedom, and justice as supreme. Now we were allowed to believe in the deity again, but was that who these people now believe reigned above all? Or was it instead someone of this mortal plane?

After we gave our pledges, the Mother of God was escorted away and more candles were lit, revealing that none other than Maximilien Robespierre sat off to the side in a gilded beechwood armchair upholstered in blood red silk, as if he'd been orchestrating the whole of this strange ceremony. And perhaps he had. Other men sat around him, but I could only look into the assured brown eyes of the man who'd once delighted in making sport of me. But now he seemed to gaze at me with what I could only describe as reverence.

He made a show of rising slowly, gracefully. He, too, wore white and blue, though his silks were finer, his lace necktie was more delicate, and the indigo dye of his coat was bolder. Then he spoke to the newly initiated one by one. When it was our turn to receive his attention, I knew not what to expect.

He kissed Maman's cheeks. "Grace is poured on all those who embrace the Supreme Being."

"As I now do," she said, bowing her head.

"And it is a credit to your whole family," he said, making me wonder if the words contained a promise of safety. "Please also allow me to convey greetings from my brother to you, madame." Everything in his round-faced expression read as sincere.

"*Merci.*" Maman gave him one of her secret, knowing smiles.

He turned next to Charles, and they shook hands. "Sartine, welcome. The whole of nature awaits its salvation, and it is only we who can deliver it."

"Yes, sir," Charles said stiffly. "It will be our privilege."

We? So Robespierre saw us as all on one side? Kissing the prophetess's feet was well worth it if that was the case.

"Indeed." Next, he moved to me, placing kisses on each of my cheeks. "Paris's most celebrated beauty."

My stomach clenched, for standing out as superior in any way was these days an unpardonable transgression. "Is it not the Supreme Being whose immortal hand engraves on the heart of man all things? The code of justice and equality? The decrees of liberty, faith, and justice?"

"Yes," I whispered, wondering whether such a being truly existed, and, if so, what he might have engraved on this man's heart.

"Yes," he repeated fervently, brown eyes blazing as he stared at me for a moment that stretched on uncomfortably long. Finally, he continued, "He created men to help each other, to love each other mutually, and to attain to happiness by the way of virtue. That is what we do here, madame. And I am delighted to count you among us."

This reserved and devout Robespierre was so different from the man I remembered and expected that I hardly knew how to reply. "Thank you."

Afterward, Robespierre invited a few of us to stay for a supper of cured ham, foie gras terrine with a conserve of figs, rillettes of suckling pig, and warm, poached asparagus. I was already surprised that we'd been among those singled out for this honor, but I was further astounded when he bade Victorine, Maman, and me to sit closest to him. But perhaps what was most astonishing was the offer he made as we savored the fine meal, of which he ate very little.

"Ladies," he said, addressing my mother and me with a glance. "I invite you to interview me, that I might make my views clear to you."

I nearly dropped my fork upon Victorine's fine porcelain. Maman gave a little cough as she worked to swallow a bite of the savory ham. For one did not simply question Robespierre. Not if they wished their head to remain attached to their shoulders. Was this some kind of trick?

"Citizen Robespierre," my mother began. "Surely we could not—"

"Come now, madame." He sat forward with his elbows upon the table. "You were until not very long ago a renowned salonnière. Your gift for sparkling conversation on the great ideas of the day is well known."

My mother actually blushed, and her knuckles went white where she gripped the armrest of her chair.

As much as one couldn't question *l'Incorruptible*, Maman also couldn't safely refuse him. So I rushed to cover her rare speechlessness. "Is . . . is it true that the Cult of the Supreme Being stands for extinguishing religious persecutions and abolishing the scaffold?" I asked, my voice soft and meek.

A slow grin crept up his face. "Ah, leave it to you,

Madame Sartine, to go right to the heart of it, *oui*?" He nodded to himself, clearly enjoying the way all our gazes were riveted upon his every expression, gesture, and word. "The answer to the first is unequivocally yes. A republic requires public virtue, something that can only be obtained by perfecting private virtue. Thus, religious faith and the grace of the Supreme Being are indispensable to orderly, civilized society."

I sipped my wine and hoped he wouldn't notice how my hand shook around the goblet. But his words made clear exactly why Hébert and his faction had been killed, for the most radical revolutionaries' program of dechristianization ran directly counter to what Robespierre was saying now.

"As to your second . . ." He hummed and tilted his head as if in thought. "What is the goal for which we strive?" His gaze swept the table, holding the whole room in his thrall. "The peaceful enjoyment of liberty and equality, the rule of justice and law, and a nation that safeguards the welfare of each individual. A France where all can enjoy the prosperity and glory of the republic."

Nods and murmurs of approval circled the table, urging Robespierre on. And though I, too, nodded, something about the coolness with which he spoke unleashed a shiver down my spine.

"What kind of government can realize these marvels?" He stabbed at the table with his finger. "A democratic government. But to build this requires the public virtue of which I spoke before." His gaze returned to me. "Democracy requires a virtuous people. Anyone who does not support democracy lacks the requisite virtue and is an enemy of the people—and is therefore deserving of the tyranny of the Terror."

He sipped at his wine, then stared at its movement in his glass for a long moment, as if working the problem and looking for the solution.

Finally, he said, "Our peaceful republican citizens deserve all the protection we can afford them, but those who ally with foreign conspirators and seek to restore the monarchy are not true citizens but strangers and enemies among us. For them, the scaffold is swift, severe, indomitable justice. Any delay in rendering judgment against them is equal to impunity, and any uncertainty of punishment encourages the guilty. Virtue without Terror is defenseless, and so we see that the Terror flows, then, from virtue."

For a moment, the whole table hung in a suspended silence. And then one of the men in Robespierre's entourage rose to his feet and raised his glass. "*Vive la république!*" It was all I could do to keep from clutching my throat.

Still, I joined the others in rushing to rise and offer the salute. "*Vive la république!*" I cried with the truest enthusiasm I'd mustered all night. For nothing short of complete sincerity—or at least the convincing feigning of it—would suffice. Despite the naive dreams of my mother and my father's friend, I perceived no hope of clemency for royalists or even moderates in the thinking of a man who believed that his political opponents deserved death. To say nothing of the warm, thoughtful charm with which he'd talked about the Terror as if he wasn't discussing cutting off the heads of mothers and fathers, husbands and wives, in front of one another and a bloodthirsty crowd!

Which was when I knew for sure what surviving this revolution would require of me. Not just that I accept my papa's death and the precariousness of life without him. Not just the sacrifice of my love, or the gaiety that should've been the right of a young belle of nineteen. And not just my belief in God, the practice of my religion, and my dignity. Nay, the price of my and my family's survival was the complete submission of my selfhood to the role of rabid patriot.

The truth of that had been staring me in the face for months. Perhaps even years. But having heard Robespierre spell out his intellectual intolerance in such brutal plainness after praising our initiation into a society that demanded the sacrifice of our very blood, I finally understood. And it was as if my whole life of learning to play my part and exchange one mask for another had been preparing me for *this* role.

In the space of one moment, I felt as if I'd aged a lifetime.

And in the next, I donned the costume of my warmest and most adoring smile and turned it upon the man at the head of the table basking in our praise and adulation.

If keeping my family and myself alive meant that I had to act the part of Robespierre's faithful admirer every second of every day until someone finally cut *his* head off, I would gladly do just that.

"I had a terrible nightmare last night," Maman said two mornings later after having remained abed until noon. "You will laugh at me, but I dreamt I was the mother of three bats." She blinked back tears and gave off such a doleful and dejected air that I was immediately alarmed.

"It was just a dream, Maman," I said, going to her and feeling her forehead. "Are you unwell?" I despised seeing her brought so low.

Just yesterday we'd received word that the Revolution had devoured yet another old friend and great mind—the Marquis de Condorcet, who used to hold everyone in his thrall at the gambling tables with his predictions for the future. Some months ago, a warrant had been issued for the arrest of the marquis for the unpardonable crime of debating the language in France's new constitution, despite being a member of the committee that'd been tasked with drafting the document. He'd been forced into hiding but had been found out—or betrayed. And died in a jail cell.

Already people whispered that his jailers had murdered the old philosopher because he was too well loved and respected to be publicly executed.

His poor wife! I remembered with great fondness the marquise's kindness and wit, and the friendship we'd struck up after she'd bade me to call her Grouchette and I'd covered for her speechlessness with the Marquis de Lafayette, with whom she'd seemed to be desperately infatuated. But that was before she'd married Condorcet. From all accounts, it had become a true love match.

My heart ached for my friend's loss, especially when Maman said, "She had to divorce him, you know. He pleaded with her do it. Otherwise, they'd have seized everything and put their poor little orphaned daughter on the street. She had no choice, even if it broke her heart. Mothers have no choices—not even mothers of bats." Shaking her head, Maman stepped to the windows of the solarium and stared out at the ornate gardens beyond. "Bats are creatures of the night. Symbols of death and rebirth . . ."

I exchanged a glance with my husband, where he sat playing backgammon with my brother, whose attention was also on our mother. Maman had rarely been one to give in to melancholy, even after Papa died, and it was plain that her unusual sadness distressed Louis as much as it did me. I put my arm around her. "The weather is glorious. Let's take a turn about the gardens."

"Not now, darling." She managed the faintest of smiles before drifting away like a wounded bird. And I could only let her go, for there was no role I could play that would change the reality of our friends disappearing one by one by one . . .

Despite the beautiful sunshine, the lively conversation occasioned by the arrival of one of Charles's friends, and a lovely al fresco dinner amid the new blooms of our garden, a feeling of darkness hung over the whole château, as if the house knew something we didn't and was trying to warn us.

But the true warning came from another quarter altogether. A most surprising quarter.

We were lounging in robes and slippers in the sitting room when there was a sudden knocking upon the back door. At ten o'clock at night . . .

Charles jumped immediately to his feet. "Stay here," he commanded, rushing into his study from whence he quickly returned, flintlock pistol in hand. The candle-light flashed off the bright steel surfaces of the barrel and lockplate, causing my heart to thunder against my breast, and I thought to beg him not to leave us there. But before I could, my husband disappeared.

"It's all right," I said aloud, though I knew not whether I meant to comfort myself or my mother, whose face had gone pale.

After an impossibly long minute, Charles returned with an envelope. "It's addressed to you, Mother," he said, taking the missive to Maman. "Whoever delivered it made off through the deer park as soon as I opened the door. I heard the retreating mount."

My mother carefully unfolded the letter. Her eyes and mouth grew wide with shock. "We've been denounced."

"Again?" I asked, even as dread lanced through my veins. Because while we had been denounced repeatedly—for everything from running our gambling parlor, to hosting dinners for one hundred crown per head, to Maman's supposed impertinence and haughty

manners, and many other supposed offenses besides—
I'd never seen her react with such utter fright.

Charles took the page from her shaking hand and
read aloud:

*"Your family has been caught in the tempest of
denunciation. Charges of complicity in a foreign
conspiracy are being drawn up even now. Fly with
all haste."*

Charles blinked at me, his face ashen.

Heart in my throat, I flew to his side and peered at
the letter for myself, half hoping Charles had somehow
misunderstood. But of course he had not. Moreover, a
splatter of ink revealed the obvious haste with which
the missive had been written, lending its warning all
the more credence. "It's unsigned," I managed.

Charles peered at me with desolation in his dark
eyes. "It doesn't need to be signed. It's the handwriting
of Robespierre himself."

I gasped. The man whose libidinous advances I'd
many times fended off, and who spoke so calmly of the
justice of murdering royalists . . . was warning us? I
was immediately suspicious.

As if hearing the man's name roused Maman from

the melancholy that had gripped her all day, she rose to her feet. "Are you certain?"

He gave a single nod. "I've seen enough of his correspondence come through the Council of State office to recognize it."

"Then we must heed his advice."

The decisiveness of my mother's words sent my pulse into flight. "But why would *l'Incorruptible* warn us? What if this is a trick or a test?"

"I don't know," Charles said. "Perhaps because of our vow to the Cult of the Supreme Being? Or perhaps he warns us as an admirer of the women in this family. His fondness for Paris's two Sainte-Amaranthe beauties was on plain display the evening that we pledged." Charles took my hand and looked at me with a devastating mix of sadness and affection. "What if it's not a trick? Ever since the execution of Charlotte Corday, the National Convention has suspected foreign conspiracies and assassination plots coming from every quarter, even as the police have been unable to apprehend even one aristocratic conspirator. The failure of their investigation is an embarrassment for them, and it's made it permissible and even necessary for them to suspect everyone."

That was true enough. The general feeling of apprehension over conspiracies to restore the monarchy was so strong that no one in Paris would have been surprised to learn one morning that the entire Convention had been massacred and King Louis XVII had been installed on the throne! But Charles was right, we had far more to lose by assuming the warning was false if it was not.

"Do we go to Grandpapa's then?" I asked, for when we'd first retreated to the country, Maman had told me that if we had to flee farther, her ancestral home was where she wanted to go as it was so far distant from Paris.

With steel in her spine and in her voice, my mother had a ready answer. "Yes, we go to Besançon, and from there into Switzerland. Charles, have the groom prepare the carriage." She turned to me. "Émilie, wake Louis. Both of you pack just like we discussed. Take only what you must."

We flew into a panicked rush of preparations to leave our lives and all our worldly possessions behind. Not to mention our country, which in trying to cure one disease, had caused another. And its malignancy finally threatened to consume us.

It was the moment that we'd secretly feared but never allowed ourselves to fully believe would arrive.

"Louis, wake up," I said, lighting the candle on his bedside table. "Louis!"

He came awake on a gasp, eyes squinting at me as he lifted his head. "What are you doing?"

"Get up and dress, then pack a satchel with a few essentials." It was only searches like the one we'd endured weeks before that kept us from having bags packed and ready for flight.

His feet hit the floor. "There's trouble?" The shadows on his face made him appear older. A younger version of our beloved papa.

"Yes. Make haste, we leave for Grandpapa's as quickly as we can."

"Grandpapa's?" He rose. "But that's a three-day ride."

"All the more reason to hurry." I rushed into my own room and donned the gauzy dress I'd worn earlier. I threw an empty valise upon the bed and rushed to collect the few pieces of my wardrobe and trousseau I couldn't do without. Was this really all one packed for the rest of their lives?

But neither the answer nor my efforts mattered, because at that very moment, pounding at the front door nearly shook the whole château. "Open in the name of the republic!"

And this time I knew that neither my beauty, my acting, the truth, nor even our innocence could save us.

❧

Sainte-Pélagie Prison, Paris, France, April 1794

Just as we'd been warned, we were charged with conspiring with Jean, the Baron de Batz, in a vast foreign conspiracy against the republic with the aim of restoring the monarchy. Myself, Maman, Charles, and even my sixteen-year-old brother, Louis.

The baron had been an adviser to King Louis XVI before the insurrection of 10 August, so my papa had many occasions to see the man at the Tuileries. But Maman and I had only met him socially a handful of times before the king's imprisonment and Papa's murder. At the king's execution, the baron had reportedly attempted to stir the crowd of onlookers to save their king and been forced to flee France when he failed.

We were beside ourselves trying to understand how we were supposed to have known him well enough to have conspired with him, since we hadn't seen him in nearly two years!

Neither had the French authorities, despite a six-month-long hunt for the baron and his ringleaders.

Since the Committee could not discover the true offenders, they diverted the accusations toward the innocent, whom they made to bear the consequences of
their own incapacity.

Which was how we found ourselves imprisoned at
the infamous Sainte-Pélagie, with its thick stone walls,
oozing dirt floors, bone-rattling cold, and bottomless
despair.

"You have a visitor," one of the guards said, calling to me as he came to the bars of the cell my family
had been moved to just that morning. "Ten minutes."
He retreated to reveal a voluptuous black-eyed beauty
with cascading brown ringlets and a yellow gown that
looked out of place amid the dreariness and next to our
shabbiness, even after just two days.

Marie!

I traded glances with Charles as we all huddled at
the bars to see why my husband's lover had come.

"Mademoiselle Grandmaison, what news?" my husband asked, his voice strained. His barely concealed
emotion made me a little jealous that it wasn't my François who'd come. Then again, it was a risk for *anyone*
to associate with us now, which made me especially
grateful to Marie.

"I've learned the main evidence against you," she
said in a hushed voice, and then she turned her pained,

sympathetic gaze on me. "First, there have been reports of a disguised man coming and going from your
country house, and they are persuaded it was the
baron."

"That's preposterous," Maman bit out.

My stomach plummeted, and sudden dizziness forced
me to grip the bars. "I'm sorry," I said. Were we truly
all to lose our lives because of who I loved? "This is all
my fault. I'm so sorry."

Maman frowned, confusion plain on her face as she
looked from me to Marie to Charles. Then understanding dawned, and her suspicious gaze cut to me again.
"Who was it?"

Tears threatened, but I blinked them away as I
looked into the eyes of the woman who'd taught me
how and when and which masks to don throughout
my life—and with whom I'd worn the biggest mask of
all in having spent the last two years going against her
wishes. "Monsieur Elleviou."

My mother blanched and glanced at Charles as if astonished I'd admitted to my infidelity before him, but
he was shaking his head and peering at me with sad
understanding. "This isn't your fault, Émilie."

He was generous to say it, even though it wasn't true.
"You warned me, Charles." Sadness welled up inside
me, and it was the first time since the patrol had ar-

rived at our house the night before that despair threatened to overwhelm me.

"Am I to understand that you knew about this?" Maman asked my husband.

"Maman." I winced at the depth of her shock and censure. For though I knew she'd disapproved of François, as the mistress to more than one influential aristocrat, I never expected her to have such a care for the propriety of the situation. "This isn't his doing—"

"Ladies, please," Charles said in a rare show of temper. "The guard will be returning to escort Marie away. If we must discuss the private understanding that exists between myself and my wife, let us do it after we hear all there is to know." Without waiting for our response, he turned back to his lover. "What is the other evidence?"

Her gaze locked with his, some intimate communication passing between them. "That . . . that I facilitated meetings between you and the baron at Théâtre Favart."

Charles sighed, then looked to me again. "See? Not your fault after all. Years ago, the Baron de Batz frequently attended performances there and became a supporter of the stage. So they think they've connected me to him as well."

I took his hand, heartbroken for the both of us. That

love should be responsible for our predicament was as ludicrous as it was devastating.

"Anything else?" he asked.

"Only whispers." Marie looked both ways down the empty stone corridor, then leaned closer. Her voice dropped into a whisper. "That the bitterness of important men who Émilie rejected made her a target."

I gasped. "Robespierre?" If so, it made his assistance last night even more confusing—or it confirmed that there'd been even more skullduggery afoot than we realized. And, by God, after we'd prostrated ourselves before him by joining his cult! Had he been mocking us the whole time?

"I'll bet it was that ruthless disciplinarian, Saint-Just," Maman said. "That puppy always had an eye for you and was jealous that despite all his social climbing he never rose sufficiently to attend my salons."

Saint-Just? For a moment I was stunned. Could the so-called Angel of Death have really been so wounded by the nervous rejection of a naive fifteen-year-old girl that he'd employ such brutal revenge for it four years later?

If that was the character of France's new republican citizens, then there was no hope of justice for anyone except the demagogues, tyrants, and deplorable opportunists among us.

"I cannot believe it," I managed, my head spinning at the thought that I should be punished for how my appearance made men react. So the value of my life was truly to be determined by whether I'd spread my legs for the right man. It was one thing to know such ideas about my sex existed, but a whole other thing to bear the application of such a principle to the question of my very survival.

Maman breathed a sigh of resignation, and I hated the defeat in it. "If it's true, then I must accept the blame. For I was the one who displayed your beauty as an attraction at Cinquante."

"No, Maman. Our evenings there were nothing but a delight." I shook my head, anger steadily replacing the sadness and shame inside me. "If my supposed beauty is the cause of our arrest, what it truly reveals is that this revolution's ideals of liberty, equality, and fraternity are meant for men alone." It'd only been five months since the Jacobins had executed playwright and philosopher Olympe de Gouges for daring to argue that if a woman had the right to mount the scaffold, she must possess equally the right to mount the speaker's platform—a right that she exercised again and again until they silenced her altogether.

The realization sweeping over me now ought to have come upon me then. But even as the injustices had mounted against others over these past months, we'd allowed some part of our hearts and brains to rationalize them away until we'd all but accepted as normal the political persecution of one group after another. Perhaps it was naivete or disbelief or fear. Any means of coping with *la Terreur* all around.

Until it came for us too.

And de Gouges wasn't the only woman whose independent thinking forced her to kneel before the nation's razor. Madame Roland, the wife of the former minister of the interior, was rumored to have authored some of his official correspondence with such a sharp pen that it cost Monsieur Roland his ministry. Worse, after her husband's fall, the Jacobins blamed his wife's influence for every word and act they found objectionable. Olympe's blood had barely dried upon the blade before Madame Roland, who once rescued me from a difficult moment, met the same fate.

And to think that I perhaps stood in the same cells that had confined both these ladies. Perhaps their spirits roamed within this ancient prison, ill at rest for the injustices done to them and the ongoing misogyny of the Revolution's leaders. For a moment, I imagined they were still here with us, silent witnesses to the struggles of the living—and I wondered how they might judge *me*.

Or how they might influence me . . .

"Marie," I said, inspiration striking, "will you carry a message to François for me?"

"Of course."

The guard appeared behind her. "Time's up."

My heart took flight as the words rushed out of me. "Tell him all that has transpired and implore him to ask for an interview with the members of the Committee." It was a risk, I knew, but perhaps François's fame and popularity would offer all of us protection.

"Come now unless you wish to join them, mademoiselle," the jailer groused.

My plea spilled out faster as she took halting steps toward the door. "If he confesses that he was the mysterious individual, his testimony could clear our names."

"I will," she said as the guard all but dragged Marie through the doorway.

For days, we heard nothing. And then it was as if every prisoner's outside eyes and ears brought news.

Another faction of Robespierre's opponents, this one under the leadership of National Convention deputy Danton, had been executed. Their crime: vying with Robespierre for power and advocating that France attempt to make peace with its continental neighbors. Naturally, such an idea made the faction vulnerable to charges of complicity with the foreign conspiracy. But the Dantonists weren't the only ones to find their heads separated from their shoulders. Word reached us again and again that the pace of arrests and executions escalated, touching every sort of people until there was almost no family in all France that didn't feel the sharp edge of the blade.

Which seemed increasingly likely to be our fate too.

For when Marie finally returned, it was with tears in her eyes as she relayed her conversation with François. "He finds such a measure repugnant and believes it would be useless, and says his grief for you leaves him in no fit state to take action. I'm so sorry, Émilie."

He wouldn't even try? It was one thing to have risked all for love, but quite another to learn that only one of us was truly willing to take that risk. And after I'd protected him that day at our château. The coward! My chest ached with a gripping hollowness that turned white hot, and I found his grief not even a cold comfort, especially as I realized that having spread my legs for a man hadn't guaranteed my safety after all. I scoffed. "Was that all he had to say?"

His expression as dark as a gathering storm, Charles put his arm around my shoulders, his strong embrace keeping me from flying to pieces.

Marie forced a smile and a false cheer into her voice.

"He . . . he still hopes that a thorough inquiry will bring light to your innocence or that you'll be forgotten in prison like so many others until the revolutionary troubles are over."

Hopes? He *hopes*? "*Merde!*" I spat, for I put no stock in such wishful thinking, nor in the speculation running rampant that the killing of the factions was a sign that the Revolution was coming to an end. Because if that wasn't true, François's cowardice might've just signed our death warrants. And I wasn't willing to do nothing until it became clear whether I was right or wrong. That night, I whispered to Maman, "Perhaps if you appealed to the brother of *l'Incorruptible*."

She touched her forehead to mine. "You are my daughter, aren't you? I've already done it."

But no reply came from Maman's admirer.

Several days later, we were suddenly informed that all the members of our family were to be moved across the city to a house of detention called the Anglaises. The jailer's cart was cramped and jolting, and our countrymen skirted their gazes away from the slatted windows as if merely looking upon us might bring trouble their way. But we could hardly be bothered by such a thing when it was the first time in weeks that we'd breathed fresh air or felt the sun on our faces. So it was a crushing torment to return to confinement, this time within the small barren cells of a former Benedictine convent confiscated by the Jacobins for government use.

And then my mother fell ill with a rattling cough that drained her energy and her appetite until I feared she might never again rise from her sickbed. More than a month had passed since our arrest, and between my worry for Maman, my fear for all of us, gnawing hunger, and the unending monotony of this horrible place, I sometimes feared I might go mad. So I attempted to distract myself and rouse Maman by recounting to her the news as it reached us.

"Maman, Robespierre did it. He had the Cult of the Supreme Being established as the official religion of the Republic." There was no questioning the man's ability to see an idea through from germination to reality, and now I acknowledged that perhaps Maman had been right to think we should align ourselves with his mysticism. "I think that could be good news for us, don't you? Just as you suspected."

"We can only hope," she said in a flat, quiet voice before looking away.

But not all the news was of a hopeful nature. For we

learned a few days later that the king's sister, the devout Madame Élisabeth, had been executed. And supposedly against Robespierre's will!

Like Condorcet, much of the public respected and loved the princess, viewing her very differently than her *belle-soeur* the former queen. But unlike Condorcet, who had undeniably been active at the center of the Revolution's political whirl, Élisabeth's life had been devoted to charity not politics. So she was widely regarded as innocent and the accusations at her trial that she had molested her nephew the dauphin had horrified many. Moreover, stories already multiplied about how she'd kept her faith until the end, going so far as to comfort and reassure her fellow victims that they would soon lay down the trials, injustices, and pains of this life for a more glorious one in heaven.

"Maman," I said, hoping she, too, would find some solace in this part of the tragic story. "When they took her head, the crowd did not cheer. And people say that the scent of roses filled the square. Some say it was a miracle."

When my mother finally spoke, her voice was weak. "Are the people aroused against Robespierre for this?"

I nodded, and Maman turned over to face the wall beside the narrow pallet we shared. "Give Louis my rations" was her only response.

Other news that reached us filled me with a sense of righteousness. After years of debate, the National Convention had several months ago outlawed slavery in its colonies—an expedient step the growing revolution on the far-off island of Saint-Domingue had forced them to take. But it was apparently too little too late, because I'd heard the guards whisper that France had lost control of nearly the entire colony now as the British and the Spanish came to the aid of the black forces with the goal of expelling the French.

"An actual foreign conspiracy," Charles said, wryly. "One the Jacobins brought on themselves."

"Yet here we sit in this miserable place," I bit out, "imprisoned because of an imaginary one." I found myself hoping the black rebels broke free of France, if for no other reason than to hurt the corrupt Convention.

I couldn't arouse Maman at all to relate this news, as she was too weak with fever to remain awake. What could I do?

I found myself thinking about the dignity of the princess's last hours. Élisabeth might have railed against the injustice of the accusations against her, or complained about her ill-treatment, or broken down in a dozen other ways. Instead, she'd turned her care and concern outward toward her fellow victims.

I resolved to do that too.

I mopped Maman's sweaty forehead with a cool cloth I begged from one of the guards. I tried to cheer and distract my brother with stories from our childhood and by playing a made-up game using naught but little pebbles we found upon the hard floor. And I showered my husband with affection and appreciation, for he struck a deal with a guard to bring us extra rations of food and herbal medicines from the apothecary in exchange for payment from Marie at the theater.

"You're a good man, Charles. I am fortunate to have you for my husband," I said one night when I awoke to find him sitting in the corner instead of on the little pallet he shared with Louis.

He bumped my shoulder and gave me a rueful smile. "Have a care, Émilie. You'll make me think you've fallen in love with me at long last."

I stared at him in the darkness, only the moonlight through the small window offering any illumination, and was stunned to feel a welling pressure in my chest. "I do love you," I whispered. Sudden tears filled my eyes at the realization that I'd come to cherish him as much more than a friend. When had that happened? "You're the only one who has ever accepted me just as I am and valued me for more than the youthful beauty that nature must soon diminish."

"Oh, my darling girl. My heart is yours and always has been."

I gasped. "What do you mean?"

He kissed me and pulled me against him. "I have loved you from nearly the moment I first met you."

His words made me ache utterly. "But then . . . why . . ." I struggled to untangle the knot of memories and thoughts and emotions inside me. I'd already been with François when first I'd met Charles and Marie, who found each other soon thereafter. ". . . why didn't you—"

His fingers fell upon my lips. "I was happy as long as you were happy. It's all I've ever wanted."

And though he'd had me before, the way we came together in the darkness of that cell was altogether different. For the first time, I wasn't playing a role with Charles. Instead, I could be and could give him my true self—who was just a girl daring to hope that she'd found a happy future in the arms of the man she loved. Our hushed union was full of understanding and soul-deep connection. A moment of perfection amid the ruins of France.

Afterward, Charles cradled me against him, and I whispered, "Do you think, if we are released—"

"When," he said, stroking my hair. "*When* we are released."

I nodded, finding strength in his certainty. "Do you think, when we're released, that we might come to a new . . ." In a rare fit of embarrassment, I searched for the words that expressed my desire and worried that he'd think my request selfish. For his lover hadn't abandoned him as mine had.

Charles's fingers tipped up my chin so that he could look into my eyes. "Charlotte-Rose-Émilie Davasse de Sainte-Amaranthe, would you consent to be my wife? And mine alone?"

"Yes," I managed, utterly overwhelmed. Elation filled me with such a lightness of being, and it was as vital as it was out of place amid all this despair.

"And I pledge to be your husband, forsaking all others," he said before sealing our vows with a kiss.

But in the days that followed, circumstances threw more and more shadow over the lightness I'd found. We learned that there'd been assassination attempts on both Robespierre and Collot d'Herbois, the butcher who'd killed thousands in Lyon last autumn and was now a member of the Committee of Public Safety. Suspicion gripped all Paris and the arrests again accelerated, crowding our cells with so many new arrivals that our already meager rations of corn and a watery vegetable soup were halved. And then, in the wake of Robespierre's election to the presidency of the National Convention, that body passed a law that made me tremble. For the Revolutionary Tribunal that adjudicated the cases of all those accused in the Terror was transformed into a court of condemnation without need of witnesses.

More than two months had passed since our arrest. Occasionally, I allowed myself to believe that we had been forgotten after all. But if we were still to be tried, our chances for acquittal would be far worse than if we'd been tried under the old system. Maybe Maman's letter to Augustin Robespierre explained our long neglect. If so, perhaps we'd never stand before any tribunal at all. It was that slender hope to which I clung.

The middle of June brought an unusual heat wave that turned the old convent into an oven. Prisoners died in such numbers that the stench of rotting flesh combined with the reek of unwashed bodies and overfull chamber pots was enough to make us retch. Finally, the warden offered us the smallest of mercies—the opportunity for groups of prisoners to take the air in the square green courtyard that sat at the center of the Anglaises. Our respite lasted only fifteen minutes, but the reprieve from the horrors accumulating inside the jail lifted my spirits enough that I could imagine surviving for one more day. And then one more day after that.

Standing in the dappled sunlight, I tipped my face to the sky and inhaled a deep, cleansing breath. Once I'd prized the finest silks and collected pearl strands and every manner of paste jewelry . . . now I could've fallen to my knees in worship of the sun.

My spirits were further lightened when I recognized a face amidst the strolling prisoners one day. For a moment, I struggled to place the wraith of a young woman, her brown locks long and scraggly, and the hollows beneath her eyes a deep purple. And then, in my mind's eye, I saw her. The fearless fruit seller who'd risked our butler and my mother's ire by forcing her way into a party at our salon so that she could deliver a letter from François . . .

Louise something . . . Louise Audu!

"Mademoiselle Audu," I said, recalling how much I'd appreciated her pluck.

She whirled on me and charged, holding out a stick as if it were a saber. "You think you will sneak up on me as you did them?"

I stumbled away until my back came up against the wall of the convent. "I'm sorry," I cried, my pulse racing as confusion swamped me. "I didn't mean to sneak . . . Louise, please, I only meant to say hello."

Glaring, she held the tip of her stick a mere inch from my chest, eyes wild and distant. And that was when I noticed the rat's nest of her hair and the way her dirty shift hung on the too-apparent frame of her bones. "You aristocrats are all alike. Thinking you can use us and discard us. Just like you did to my maman and my friend." She spat on the ground. "Well, not me. You won't use and discard me." She jabbed the stick against the bare skin above my breast.

I choked back a cry, for the volume of Louise's ranting had caught the notice of a guard who appeared to be debating whether it was worth his time to intervene. I hoped he wouldn't. Something terrible had happened to the spirited girl I'd met, and my heart was just sick over it, sick of all the ways in which this revolution had used and discarded so many of us.

Perhaps that was why I managed to offer her kindness instead of anger at her treatment of me when I said, "Louise, I mean you no harm. I'm still grateful for the way you risked yourself to deliver a letter to me years ago. Do you recall? You shouted my name and brought the entire party to a halt, and then you stayed to eat."

Her gaze narrowed and roamed over my face, and her head twitched in what seemed an unconscious tic. "And I swiped a whole plate of macarons into my basket."

I laughed. "So that's what became of them."

Her mouth slid into a slow smile. "You were amiable."

"Of course," I said.

Just as soon, her glare returned. "But you're an aristocrat, which means you can't be trusted."

I shook my head. "Are we really so different, Louise? Look around, we've suffered the very same fate."

For just a moment, it seemed as though I might've gotten through to her, but then hatred twisted her harsh features once more. "We are nothing alike." She emphasized her point with another jab of the stick, and then she stepped back. "Stay away from me, royalist scum. Or I'll run you through like it's the tenth of August all over again."

I gasped at the reference to the attack on the Tuileries. "You were there?"

"I was no mere bystander," Louise sneered in offense, and her head jerked in another tic. "I was a decorated soldier. The Paris Commune recognized my bravery and patriotism with the 'Sword of Honour.'"

Trembling, I stared at her anew, caught between horror on the one hand and defeated resignation on the other. Thank God Maman hadn't been up to taking the air, because I wasn't sure she had strength enough to face the girl whose very sword might've put an end to my father's life. It was almost more than I could bear myself. My breath caught and my hands fisted, and it was all I could do to keep from launching myself at her and throttling her delicate neck.

But what would that get me? Perhaps a beating from the guards, or separation from my family. And Papa would still be dead . . . as would Louise's maman and sister.

It was that last thought that drained the fight from my body. I hated the Jacobins for what they'd done to my father. And if she hated royalists for what they'd done to her family, how could I blame her? Especially when, in the end, Louise had fared no better than I had. Finding this grace of understanding wasn't easy, and the grief I still carried wished to rise up in outrage against her. But it struck me with such clarity—there were angels and demons on both sides, and I wondered if anyone truly knew the full accounting of good and evil that'd occurred these past five years, or if anyone ever would . . .

I thought once more of Princess Élisabeth's dignity and compassion and decided that whatever wrongs Louise might've perpetrated had been revisited upon her enough already.

The guard rang the bell signaling the end of our respite.

"*Adieu*, Louise," I managed.

She blinked and her eyes narrowed. "How do you know my name?"

The question brought tears to my eyes, but I dashed them away. If I allowed tears to fall in this place, over a once-fierce girl losing her senses or anything else, I might not ever get them to stop.

We'd all lost so much. Too much. But still, the Revolution raged on, taking even more.

Conciergerie Prison, Paris, France, June 17, 1794

"Did you make an attempt upon the lives of Robespierre and Collot d'Herbois, representatives of the people?" the president of the Revolutionary Tribunal asked.

I sat trembling, my head still spinning over how fast our lives were unraveling. One moment, we were asleep in our cramped cell. And the next, we were being hauled out of the Anglaises and roughly shoved into a prison cart by an angry usher to the Tribunal who'd grumbled that he'd never before had to visit seven different jails to find prisoners gone missing from the Tribunal's register.

We arrived at the Conciergerie just before daybreak, and I shuddered as the cart rolled through the foreboding gate of the prison that was also the home of the Revolutionary Tribunal. Inside, the registrar was frustrated by the apparent disorder of our paperwork, and he fired a series of impatient questions at us about why there'd never been an inquiry into our case and how we'd been so long imprisoned without taking part in even preliminary proceedings. We knew no more about these violations of judicial procedure than he did . . . unless *la famille* Robespierre had, after all, been trying to protect us by erasing our confinement from the record so thoroughly that none of the authorities even knew where we were.

Yet, even if such a ruse had been going on during these long months, it now appeared that not even the Robespierres had the power and influence to shield us forever. When the clock tolled ten in the morning, we were lined up with dozens of others, more than fifty in all, as haggard and terrified as ourselves. A narrow wooden door opened at the front of the line, letting in the warm glow of sunlight and the loud roar of shouts and applause. One by one, we were pushed out of doors onto an immense tier of benches overlooking the public enclosure of the Revolutionary Tribunal.

The registrar shouted a roll call of all our names.

Each new victim received a new round of hooting, hissing, and jeering from the spectators crowded all around the platform.

Then it was my turn.

"Émilie de Sartine, née de Sainte-Amaranthe," a man called out.

For the space of one heartbeat, I was shamed by the dirty, limp cascade of my hair, and by the way the white gauze of my dress had turned a dingy brown. But such things no longer mattered, did they? Appearance— even beauty itself—meant nothing in a world in which innocence was no defense from accusation. So I lifted my chin, straightened my spine, and stepped into the light.

The sheer number of eyes upon me was in itself overwhelming, for there was not a free space in the entire courtyard. Red-capped spectators pushed one another and strained for a chance to see the most beautiful girl in all Paris brought low. Lewd taunts rang out from some quarters, but enough others fell silent that the roar dulled to a low rumble. And then the dizzying moment of presentation was over, and a gendarme accompanied me to a seat next to my mother.

When my family had been reunited upon the rough-hewn benches, I clutched Charles's hand on the one side, and Maman's on the other. Poor Louis lost his fight against tears and buried his face in Maman's shoulder. And, dear God, there were familiar faces among the other victims. The Vicomte de Pons, a warm and generous man and another of Maman's admirers, to whom Louis and I bore such a striking resemblance that tongues wagged about our true parentage, now sat just behind me and gave me the saddest smile of affection and greeting.

And, oh, poor Marie, who'd been such a friend and a help to us, along with her most trusted servant and her landlady, were presented in their turn. For less than a heartbeat, my gaze locked with Marie's, and I felt a pang of guilt that, in what could be our final hours, I'd won Charles's love at her expense. But then Charles squeezed my hand and looked at me with such longing that I cast away that guilt, because to find love amidst terror was too miraculous a thing to ever regret.

I couldn't decide if it was a solace or a further outrage that François was not among the crowd of the accused, but even his cowardice was no reason that he should die.

But there was one person whom I was grateful into my very soul was not there. For the first and only time, I found myself glad that Papa was dead. To be happy about my father's murder was so despicable a thought that a sharp pain momentarily seized my breast. But I was certain that his death would've been all the more painful if he'd fallen at the hands of this mockery of justice than having fallen in defense of king and country. Certain, too, that seeing his beloved family here awaiting their fate would have been worse to him than death.

When all the prisoners were seated, the Court entered. Jacobins all, of course.

An usher commanded silence, and then the president of the Tribunal, wearing a tricolored ribbon around his neck and a black-plumed hat, rose and read from a document: "This session of the Revolutionary Tribunal is now called to order. The cases before us today prove the existence of the Foreign Conspiracy dated from the end of July 1793 to the present, which had as its principal objects to carry off the widow Capet, to dissolve the National Convention, and to effect a counterrevolution. All the levers that were intended to overthrow the republic were moved by a single man, who prompted numerous allied tyrants—de Batz, baron and ex-deputy of the Constituent Assembly, is the atrocious brigand who directed the blackest crimes of kings against humanity." The crowd booed at the baron's name, forcing the official to wait until the clamor died down. "Batz had intermediary agents in every section of Paris, in the country, in the municipality, in the official departments, and in the very prisons, many of whom will stand before this Tribunal today." This time, the crowd cheered.

My stomach rolled and I trembled, for the scenario playing out around me was the very one that had kept me awake in our cell many nights. With all we'd heard from those newly imprisoned at the Anglaises since the assassination attempts on d'Herbois and Robespierre, we knew that the Committee of Public Safety was under great pressure to prove it could protect the republic by capturing the nearly mythological Baron de Batz. But if they couldn't catch the baron, they could distract the public with a spectacle of a trial against a large group of notables. No matter if denunciations against them bore the faintest of connections to the baron or not.

One by one, we were brought forward to sit and face the Tribunal's accusation.

First, a man they called Admiral, who boldly answered, "Yes!" to the accusation of the attempted assassination of Citizen d'Herbois. "I have but one regret, and that is that I missed that scoundrel," he said belligerently, earning the boos of the spectators. Undeterred, he continued, "I would've been admired by the whole of France if I'd achieved my purpose!"

Next upon the stool was a girl who appeared not quite my age. But that was where the similarities ended, for where I was terrified, she was entirely self-possessed. Moreover, she spoke with utter calmness and not a little disdain as she insisted upon her innocence, adding, "I never intended to kill Robespierre. I merely regarded him as one of the principal oppressors of my country." Her father, brother, and aunt each faced the Tribunal after her.

They were followed by a comte who imagined himself to be in a court of justice and attempted to present evidence and read a written defense. But the president cut him short, refusing to accept the documents. And why would they accept them, when the Convention's recent law had made it legal for the Tribunal to pass judgment without consideration of evidence? No evidence was wanted. So instead they merely asked the comte the question that would be put to each of us in our turn: "Did you engage in the attempted murder of Robespierre and Collot d'Herbois?"

"No!" the comte shouted. Outraged and desperate, he turned to the crowd. "I am suspected merely because I am an *émigré*. This so-called conspiracy is a falsehood and a calumny! How could we have conspired when we have been kept apart in prison, and when most of us are entirely unknown to one another before today?"

But the crowd wanted blood, and so did the Tribunal.

Which was why the Court went through the farce of asking the rest of us that same question, and nothing more.

All we could do was defend our innocence even as this court connived at an appalling massacre. Mama's voice was strong when she offered her refutation. And then it was my turn to sit before them. Heaving a calming breath, I met the gazes of the closest onlookers and let them see the truth of me.

"No," I replied to the Tribunal.

I rose from the stool, but did not immediately make way for the next prisoner. Resisting the gendarme, I stood there for a long moment, meeting the gazes of my curious countrymen. If beauty was truly to be the reason for my death, then I wanted them to look. To see and appreciate. And then to watch that beauty be desecrated, just as France was being desecrated by tyrants bent on covering the whole of our country in blood.

It was over in an instant, this singular moment to speak in defense of a whole life. But instead of feeling despair, I felt the oddest sense of peace. If I was judged innocent, I would live in happiness with my beloved Charles. And if I was found guilty, then I was naught but a ghost, already dead in every way but one.

It took the jury mere minutes to decide.

"The verdict of the jury is in the affirmative on all the questions concerning all the prisoners!"

A storm of anger and despair rose up from the prisoners all around me.

"We have not been tried!" one man shouted.

"You are murderers!" another cried, shaking his fist in the air.

Amid the sobbing and curses, I turned to Charles and said the only thing that mattered, "*Je t'aime.*" I love you.

For the first time of our whole ordeal, he had tears in his eyes. "Oh, my love. I'm sorry I couldn't protect you."

I shook my head. "Let's not waste a single moment on apologies." I kissed him, then pressed my forehead to his. "Our life together would've been so beautiful."

A tear escaped from the corner of his eyes. "Would there have been children?" he asked, his voice tight with emotion.

"Oh, yes. Two, I should think. A boy and a girl." I let the pain of the imagining tear through me.

"With my dark hair and your blue eyes," Charles said, seeing it with me. "Oh, Émilie," he rasped, hugging me tight until I lost the fight with my own tears.

In a confused rush, the whole group of us were herded into the registrar's office, where it was explained that we would prepare for the scaffold. There were so many prisoners that the authorities had to open a second room, the office of the head jailer, who was quite taken aback as more than twenty prisoners, wailing and shouting, spilled into his space.

Four hours passed in this horrible place between life and death. Many fell into such despair that they wouldn't speak and their eyes refused even to focus. Others attempted to negotiate for another outcome with the jailers and guards. All the while, the loud murmur of the crowd that thronged the court buildings was ever present. For a long time, I sat in a little circle with Charles, Maman, and Louis, all of us clutching tight to one another as we struggled to confront that the worst had come to pass. It seemed impossible, unbelievable, so utterly unjust that I labored to breathe. My heart thundered within my breast, as if even my blood raged against my fate.

"Maybe your friend will help us yet again, Maman," Louis said, tears straining his voice.

My mother appeared so fragile that I told the lie for her, "Perhaps he will, Louis. Why keep us alive this long only to allow us to perish now?" If my sixteen-year-old brother, whose age should've shielded him from the guillotine, required lies to get through his final hours, I would give them to him again and again.

After a while, assistants of the public prosecutor came around with a pair of sheers and a basket filled with hair—dark, fair, and gray together. When it was my turn for the sheers, I sat and held out my hand, then serenely gathered the long lengths of my once marvelous hair and cut it off as close to the neck as I could. When it was done, I held my tresses out to the jailer. "Take it, monsieur. I am robbing the executioner, but this is the only legacy I can leave to our friends. They will hear of it, and perhaps someday they will come to claim this souvenir of us. I rely on your honesty to keep it for them."

The man carefully clutched at the long rope of my hair as if he were holding strands of gold. "You have my word," he said solemnly.

I cut the hair of the rest of my family, too, and when I was done, one of the prosecutor's assistants called me over toward the far door and handed me a note. Bewildered, I opened it to find a message from Prosecutor Fouquier-Tinville—the purveyor to the guillotine—himself.

Madame de Sartine, you might be spared if you would declare yourself enceinte.

~Fouquier

My eyes flashed to those of the messenger, and my heart ached at the idea that a pregnancy might be the thing to save us after Charles and I had just imagined the very thing. "And my family?"

A single shake of his head. "The offer is for you alone, madame."

The momentary flare of hope now was like a dagger sinking slowly, but no less violently, into my chest. "And what would be the payment for this clemency?" I managed, knowing such a favor would never come for free. Not from a man like Fouquier, who seemed exactly the type who'd require a woman to buy her liberty without recognizing the hypocrisy. To say nothing of how the offer revealed what this brave new republic valued about women.

In that regard, it seemed to me there had been no revolution at all.

The assistant gave me a meaningful look, which decided it for me entirely. If the only way I could live was by lying with one of the most evil men in all France, I would rather face the guillotine.

Let them destroy me and every beautiful thing in this country until they stood among nothing but ash and ruin.

Without another word, I left the assistant at the

door and returned to find my Charles and Louis already bound, their hands tied behind their backs with cords still damp with blood from an earlier execution. Nausea rolled over me so harshly that I clutched my stomach. And then one of Fouquier's assistants tied Maman's hands. To see my proud, beautiful, witty mother treated in such a manner was a thing that couldn't be borne, and only a desire to shield her from the depths of my grief kept me quiet.

An official came to me next—the same man who'd passed me Fouquier's offer. "What a waste," he muttered as he trussed my wrists.

"Yes, killing fifty-four of your countrymen *is* a terrible waste, monsieur," I said.

He cinched the bindings unmercifully tight, but I refused to give him the satisfaction of voicing my discomfort. And then he came to stand in front of me, where he wrenched the fabric of my sleeves from my shoulders, exposing them.

"Don't touch her!" Charles shouted before nearly charging the man. Only the restraint of another of the prosecutor's assistants held him back.

Louis sobbed aloud, and then Maman let out an anguished shriek and swooned to the floor.

"Maman!" I sank to my knees beside her. But I

couldn't rouse her or stroke her face or help her up because of the damned restraints.

"Let me help her," the Vicomte de Pons said in a kindly voice. Still unrestrained, he stroked his hand over her forehead and stared down at her with an ancient longing. "Madame. Madame, please." He squeezed her hand. "Jeanne, it is I, your old friend, Pons."

Her eyelids fluttered. For just a second, a smile began to grow on her face at seeing the vicomte, but I saw the moment awareness returned to her, because she let out a sorrowful sob. "I'm sorry," she said. "I'm just so . . . sorry."

"Don't apologize, Maman," I said from beside her. "Never apologize for giving me a life I loved."

"It is time!" a deep voice rang out. "Line up, women first."

Mon Dieu, this was really the beginning of the end.

Rough hands pushed us this way and that, and the mob seemed to know the time was upon them, as it roared with renewed vigor. But from my position near the door to the courtyard, raised voices reached my ears. A debate or an argument of some sort, complete with curses.

Fouquier marched through the door, his gaze taking

me in even as he spoke to all. "We are postponed. Be seated."

Cautious elation rolled through the assembled prisoners. More than one person shouted, "Have we been pardoned?"

Meanwhile, I couldn't help but wonder if the delay was Robespierre's doing yet again. No matter how many times I attempted to smother that dangerous hope, it managed to take root. Meeting Maman's gaze, it was clear that she wondered the same. Long minutes of suspension between hope and despair stretched into more than an hour, and a few who hadn't lost their senses already were on the verge of doing so now.

Suddenly, the courtyard door opened again to reveal Fouquier's assistants carrying sacks that they placed upon a table.

Shirts and even shawls in every kind of material and varying shades of red, as if they'd grabbed whatever red clothing they could on such short notice.

Which was when I recalled that after reading the verdict, the Tribunal had decreed that we should be dressed in red for our executions, as assassins and murderers of the people's representatives.

There was to be no reprieve, then. They had merely been waiting for our absurd costumes.

A hollow pain racked through me, even as I donned

a fine handwoven shawl, which reminded me of another young woman who'd been forced to don this mark of shame. I hadn't known Charlotte Corday, who'd been executed last summer for murdering that terrible Marat, but I'd secretly held this young lady in high regard for risking all for something bigger than herself. "I knew that Marat was perverting France," she'd said at her trial. "I have killed one man to save a hundred thousand."

From the Terror, she'd meant. The very thing leading us to our deaths even now.

For perpetrating an act that many people believed transgressed societal norms for a woman—not so much murder, as making a political statement by murdering a representative of the government—some whispered that Corday's actions had made the Revolution more dangerous for women. Others went so far as to blame Corday for the executions of Olympe de Gouges, Madame Roland, and even the queen herself, all of which came in the months that followed Marat's assassination. But since Corday had been attempting to exorcise the very same radical Jacobinism now using the Terror to kill my countrymen in the tens of thousands—to kill *us* this very day—I couldn't help but think that she'd been right and her actions just.

Because as much as they killed my countrymen,

they seemed to take a sick, perverted glee in killing my *countrywomen*.

They killed us for being too political, too intelligent, too opinionated, too daring, too pretty.

At long last, as the church bells marked the four o'clock hour, we were loaded into carts for the procession to the scaffold. Under the hot June sun, spectators lined the rue de la Vieille-Draperie, with women in bright dresses carrying gaily-colored parasols. Everywhere there was laughter and merriment intermixed with jeers and shouts, giving the whole affair an almost festive air. And it was a fresh wound to see the people enjoying the imminent death of innocents as if it were mere entertainment.

Louis had been permitted to ride with us on account of his age, and between Maman and me, we tried to support and encourage him despite our bound hands. As we turned on rue de la Lanterne toward the Pont Notre-Dame, I sat as straight and proud upon the cart's hard bench as I had upon the accused's armchair. I met the gazes of those I could, wanting them to see me as a person, and not an object for their entertainment. And with my eyes, I willed them to see something else. It was me today, but it could very well be them tomorrow.

Something curious began to happen then—instead

of celebrating or jeering as our cart trundled by, the crowds began to hush.

"There she is, there's Émilie!" someone shouted.

"*Adieu*, beautiful madame!" someone else cried out, doffing his bonnet rouge. The gesture lit an ember of hope in my breast—not for myself, nor for my family. But for the future of France.

"So many victims to avenge Robespierre!" a third voice dared say.

"Some are too young to die!" came another bold cry. The bravery behind these subtle criticisms sparked that ember brighter inside me. Perhaps, one day, enough people of compassion and courage would come forward and say, *It is enough.*

Hours passed as we made our sad, slow procession across the city, over the bridge, passed the quays, and through neighborhoods, where people hung from the windows and parapets and lined the streets so densely that sometimes our carts could barely move. Finally, we approached the place du Trône-Renversé, which was when I noticed a woman at the edge of the crowd, her head bent over a drawing canvas. Just then, she looked up, as if the weight of my gaze had called to her.

She looked so broken. So grief-stricken. But I knew her.

Oh, Grouchette!

She held up her hand in a small sympathetic wave of recognition before pressing her trembling fingers to her mouth. And then she gathered up her belongings and rushed into the crowd.

I was at once overwhelmed and utterly heartened to know our old friend had come to witness our parting. I tried to watch her as she made her way toward the street, but I lost sight of her as the crowd pushed and the carts rolled. Finally, she reappeared, closer now, and I cried out, "Oh, please, let the citizeness pass."

The people closest to the cart relayed my wishes from one person to the next, until a gap opened through which Madame Condorcet passed until she was walking alongside us. "My dear girl," she whispered, her eyes filled with tears. "How has it come to this? It should be me, not you."

It might well be you next, I thought, leaning toward her. She'd aged in the years since we'd last met, and her hair was shot through with gray. Maybe that was just an impression created by the drab workaday dress she wore, or maybe it was the result of all she'd lost. "Promise me, Grouchette, that you will survive this madness."

"I will try," she said.

"And promise me you'll remember us," I pleaded.

She reached up and squeezed my shoulder. "I will never forget."

It was seven o'clock before the cart jolted to a halt, and what I saw before me was so terrifying that, for a moment, my legs wouldn't work.

Eight guillotines sat in a line. The wood of the machines was stained red with the blood of countless other victims, the blades gleaming darkly in the sun as they were loaded into the killing position. Beneath the platforms sat blood-soaked baskets that would soon hold the heads of everyone I loved.

It was a thing too despicable to contemplate.

Shouted commands directed us to alight from the carts and sit upon rows of wooden benches around the guillotines. I found myself seated between Maman, who trembled violently as Louis cried into her neck, and the Vicomte de Pons, who pressed his shoulder to mine and said, "You are a dear girl, Émilie."

I blinked against the sudden rush of tears, and then couldn't hold them back when Charles stopped before me, smiled, and recited a line from the opera:

"*La mort même est une faveur,*
Puisque la tombeau nous rassemble."

Even death is a favor, since the tomb brings us together. He kissed my forehead before being pushed toward a bench.

And then it began.

Upon the guillotine beside our own, the young woman who had been so brave before the tribunal matter-of-factly ascended the steps and dropped herself upon the plank. The blade fell, and I flinched away as the crowds gathered closest to the machines reacted, some with cheers and others with disapproval. But Maman did watch, and the sight of the girl's decapitation left her shrieking and crying. "Take me first, please. Please let me die before my children!"

I wanted to scream, to wail, to tell my mother that it would soon be all right, but I could do none of those because the executioner grabbed a now sobbing Louis. Breathless with fright, I cried out for him. "Louis! Louis, I love you!" Everything inside me raged against what would transpire within the very next seconds. And then it did. Maman slumped to the ground in a dead swoon. I knew not whether she was even alive.

The executioner came for me.

I didn't make him grab me, but rose on my own and held my head high. The breeze caught the edge of my red shawl, sending it fluttering off one shoulder as I climbed the steps. And then I stood upon the platform and looked out at the faces surrounding me. Beloved Charles, who managed a heartbreaking smile, as if he wished to offer strength until the very last. Dear Grouchette, who had made her way boldly close to the guillotine. And then there were the thousands of strangers besides.

How would I be remembered by them, or would I be remembered at all? For memories were soon all that was to be left of me. And the sole, final hope I had was that somehow the memory of me would matter—to my friends, to my lovers, to my country.

The wind kicked up, pulling the shawl free of my shoulders, and I met Sophie's tear-filled gaze as it sailed on the breeze toward her, a ribbon of scarlet upon the wind.

The executioner urged me toward the plank, and I lay upon the sun-warmed wood. The weight of a yoke held me in place. I hadn't the time to react to the gore beneath me nor to succumb to the grief inside me. Instead, I found Charles's face again and returned his smile.

The crowd around my guillotine hushed and cried, but around others the people cheered and celebrated.

Beautiful, terrible humanity. Capable of the most inspiring and creative genius and the greatest and most unimaginable abominations.

And as the blade fell, I knew France's revolution was both.

Epilogue

Ten years later . . .

"You never forget, do you?" my young lover asks from his side of my rumpled bed. He's a natural politician with unruly dark hair and a perfectly proportioned nose. He's nothing like Condorcet, which is, I suppose, why I chose him. "You let me make love to you, Sophie, but in your head . . . you're with a dead man!"

"And you are jealous of one," I accuse, snapping the bedsheet back to go in search of my robe.

This is not the first time we have had this argument; he is not entirely wrong. After all these years, now that the Revolution is over, there is very little of me still in this world. Mostly, I reside with my ghosts. With my husband, my love, the father of my child.

And the rest of them . . .

The royal family, all dead now, with many of our friends. Our enemies too. Even Robespierre was eventually dragged to the guillotine. They say it was Émilie's death that turned people against him and the Terror— the tragic act that finally sated the worst of the blood lust in France.

Maybe it was her beauty. Maybe it was something else. Certainly, of all the people I have seen murdered, my thoughts always return to that sweet girl who once saved me from the silly embarrassments of youth. That sweet girl who died for love. I keep her crimson scarf hidden in my dressing table and finger it each morning, like a talisman from a religion in which I never believed.

I wonder if my lover would understand if I told him.

I don't think so. He is too young. He does not live for the past or the future. He lives for today. He lives in this world we built upon enlightened ideals and the fading memory of blood-drenched scaffolds. A world in which there will soon be an election to make Napoleon Bonaparte the new emperor of the French.

Which doesn't sound nearly as *new* as so many of us had hoped.

But my lover isn't thinking about that farce now; instead, he angrily gestures to the stacks of Condorcet's papers that I'm assembling for publication. "You make me sound like an unreasonable child to be jealous, as if *the great philosopher* were not right here in the bedroom, mocking my love for you morning and night, and I cannot even call him out for a duel!"

I sputter in dark exasperation, nearly laughing at the idea. "Condorcet wasn't a man for mockery or for duels."

Red anger spreads splotchy down his bare, muscled chest. "Oh, yes. Condorcet was a perfect man. A paragon of virtue—"

"Don't," I warn. There are limits to how far I will let him go, even when I have pushed him there. "You *are* being unreasonable. It's important his papers are published. And it will keep a roof over our heads."

In the years since Nicolas died, during the height of the Terror, I've sold portraits and lingerie to keep my daughter clothed and fed and educated. I've also published my translation of Adam Smith's *Theory of Moral Sentiments*, with my notes. My work has allowed me to buy this house in Paris near the Champs-Elysées and provided my lover support so that he, too, can write about the injustices of special tribunals. But he doesn't like to be reminded of that. He reaches for my arm, a longing in his eyes. "I want to be rid of sad memories, to make a life for us together. I want to marry you, Sophie."

He's said this before. This time, I know he means it. More's the pity. I slip out of his grasp and go to my easel next to the fireplace and start smudging charcoal lines for my latest portrait. It is a woman. I don't know which one.

Maybe all of them.

About the mouth, there is a touch of Manon Roland's sardonic smile as she delivered her tart, well-chosen, final words on the scaffold. But the eyes are Madame Élisabeth—clear and royal and lifted heavenward like the nun she once wished to be. Of course, the assassin Charlotte Corday's eyes were like that, too, now that I think about it, just before the executioner's assistant slapped the cheek of her decapitated head.

But I don't think the woman I'm sketching is a politician, or a saint, or a self-proclaimed soldier. There is too much sadness, madness, and disappointment in the portrait. The kind of emotions that belong to the living. Perhaps I am drawing the so-called survivors of the Revolution, like Pauline Léon who once carried a pike at Versailles but now trails meekly after her husband, the army officer. Or my onetime student, Louise Audu, who is locked now in an asylum for lunatics if the gossip is true. Or the *sans-culotte* in a butcher's apron I saw screaming in the crowd when Marie-Antoinette mounted the scaffold. Or the woman in a lace fichu who sobbed when Lafayette's kinswomen were beheaded. So many women . . .

Yet, I begin to believe I am drawing myself. "Our friends told me Condorcet slipped away from his attic hideaway," I say. "*He's escaped to America. He will send for you.*" My lover's mouth thins. He's heard this story before. He doesn't want to hear it again. But I need to tell him. "Three months he was dead, and I didn't know."

"Sophie, I said I want to marry you."

"I heard you," I whisper, numbly, my fingers still trying to capture the essence of a person on the canvas. "It was an omelet that killed him. He went into a tavern, pretending to be a carpenter, and ordered one. I used to tell him that a hearty omelet gave me hope for a new day. Had he been hopeful that morning?"

Raking a hand through his glorious hair, my lover replies, "He was probably hungry."

I glare. "*How many eggs*, the cook asked. Nicolas said a dozen. That's how they knew he was a nobleman who had never cooked for himself . . . When they arrested him he gave the name of the boy we tried to save together. Pierre Simare. So that I would know him after he was dead even if no one else would. They beat him, and dragged him to jail, and there he poisoned himself so as not to give up anyone who helped him."

My lover nods, teeth clenched. "Condorcet was a brave man. I know. You loved him. I know. You had hope for the future and now you don't. I want to give you some. Why won't you take it?"

Perhaps he believes me to be like Elleviou, who abandoned his love to the scaffold without a backward glance. I refuse to go to the Opéra-Comique where that man has gone on to earn great fame and fortune. The mere sound of that callow coward's dulcet voice would make me retch with disgust. For him and for myself, both.

But I do not say this to my lover. Instead, my reply spills free in a rush, more instinct than logic. "Hopes are dangerous. Reach for them and you can lose everything, even your life."

"*Don't* reach for them and you are already dead," he replies. "I'm going to say it a third time. I want to marry you. And so help me, Sophie, if you don't answer—"

"What will you do if I don't answer?" I am defiant.

And he is a wounded animal who lashes out. "You are not the only woman who loves me."

As much as it hurts, this doesn't startle me. I have suspected a flirtation with one of my friends, but did not wish to hasten a painful parting with an accusation. "Then you should leave me. If there is someone else you want more, go to her. I will not stop you. You are not bound."

"Not like you?" he asks, stricken. "You are not married to Condorcet anymore, Sophie. You are not even his widow. Do you forget you divorced the man?"

In an instant, all the air in the room is gone. I can scarcely breathe. He's said the one unforgivable thing. He presses a fist to his mouth as if to call back the word, but it's too late. "*Mon Dieu*, I'm sorry. I—"

"Get out," I say, quietly.

I don't see him go or even hear the door close behind him because I am already lost, lost in memories . . .

A divorce will be nothing but farce and mummery, Nicolas promised. *Only a piece of paper. A meaningless ritual.*

He'd been in hiding for several months, living in the attic of a tenderhearted widow who risked her life to shelter him. I would cross the city in beggar's rags—taking a different path each time—watching over my shoulder to make certain I was not followed. I brought him food, if I could find it. Paper. Ink. What he needed was a warm coat, but I couldn't get one for him. So we nestled together for warmth on the little attic bed and spoke of an enlightened future, in which he still believed. Always, though, he would end our visits by pleading with me to divorce him lest I leave our daughter an orphan.

In the end, I did as he wished. I did as Émilie wished too. I survived. Part of me anyway.

Because divorcing Condorcet had already killed some other part of me as brutally as a blade. I, who had never wanted to marry, wanted even less to dissolve my marriage. I, who had believed in the sanctity of nothing, had found faith in love. To divorce was to betray and defile that faith. I have never forgiven myself for it. I never will.

"Maman?" My daughter knocks upon my door and peers inside, seemingly shocked to find me in robe and slippers, face in my hands. "Will we go to the salon tonight, or . . ."

My daughter is fourteen now, on the cusp of womanhood, with dark, arresting eyes like her father. I think she is more worried about missing her first salon than about my lover's absence. She has been trying on jewelry with her dress for weeks, pouting only a little when I told her that no daughter of republicans should wear a diadem upon her brow, even if it is now the imperial fashion.

I rouse myself from my stupor. "We will go together, sweet girl."

Relieved, she smiles and holds up two ribbons against her gown. "The blue or the red?"

"Red," I say, thinking of her father—and remembering how, in the wake of Émilie's death, red scarves, crimson shawls, and scarlet ribbons became a symbol of quiet defiance. "Definitely the red."

We go over the river to the old residence of Madame Helvetius whose heirs still allow me to host my salons in her spacious manor house where Ben Franklin and Thomas Jefferson once strolled. How the grand house survived the Revolution is a mystery, but it's a comforting monument to the past. And I try to remake my salon there, cultivating young intellects and gathering together what remains of the old ones.

Even those with whom I have had my quarrels.

Lafayette sometimes comes with *his* daughter, who has become fast friends with mine. How he survived the Revolution is also a mystery—but he is another comforting monument of the past, even bent and broken by his long imprisonment as he is.

I should still hold against him that day on the Champs de Mars when he ordered his men to fire on the crowd. I was there, with my child in my arms, asking for a republic, being forced to run for my life. I have blamed him a very long time for that—sure that if he had been less torn between his republican values and his loyalty to the royal family . . . it might have all turned out differently. But now, I don't know that any single moment or decision could have changed the course of things. And when I look at Lafayette, I wonder if he, too, lives with ghosts.

So, once I have introduced my daughter to the most brilliant minds in the room, and left her chatting with other young thinkers, I seek out Lafayette where he sits quietly at the far edge of the crowd. Using his cane, he tries to rise in respect, but I wave him back into his seat and ask, without preamble, "Will you vote for the Corsican to be our emperor?"

He rubs at the back of his neck. "What do you think?"

Sitting beside him, I sigh to see Manon Roland's daughter in the crowd. Though I cannot hear the word *Girondin* spoken without pain for the memories, the young lady is here at my invitation, as I made a promise to her mother to keep an eye on her. But she shows no interest in the political discussions that captivated her mother and me. And she is probably happier for it. "I think it doesn't matter. People are tired of revolution."

The parties will never be as dazzling as they were before, but there is wine to drink and bread to eat again; I suppose that is why they will make Napoleon

Bonaparte a tyrant over us. The people are happy to trade the freedom so many people bled for in exchange for security. And who am I to judge them given the way our revolution spoiled itself until there was more blood than liberty? In the end, it was all for nothing.

"I still think it matters," Lafayette says quietly, staring into his glass.

I wonder if Lafayette really *will* defy the hard and wily Bonaparte when he could scarcely find it within himself to defy the soft and guileless King Louis. I wonder, too, if there is any point in doing so.

"You would do it again, even knowing what we know now?"

"Not all revolutions turn out this way," he says, and I think he means his beloved America, where three men have already taken a turn presiding as president over a republic without blood running in the streets.

And yet, women are not equal citizens in either of those places.

As that thought occurs to me, my guests all rise to their feet. There is an uncomfortable murmur by the archway, and gasps can be heard as the crowd parts to reveal a newcomer. A man of only moderate physical stature, balding a bit, dressed in civilian garb that doesn't suit. A man who is instantly recognizable anywhere.

It is Napoleon Bonaparte, the very same man about whom all these fine thinkers have been gossiping for the past hour. Having been caught out at what might seem a seditious gathering, they do not seem to know whether to glare or bow in submission to the man who will soon be crowned above us.

As he approaches, a lupine smile upon his face, I don't know which I will do either. "What brings you to our gathering, General?" I ask, with a curtsy that fills me with indignation.

"Curiosity, madame," Bonaparte replies, "or do you prefer *citizeness*?"

He is baiting me and I should not rise to it, but I see that, in cleaning up to be presentable in society, I have missed a line of charcoal dust on my thumb. And I am reminded of my unfinished sketch of the mysterious woman. I give a sweet smile, a little falsely. "I would prefer *Citizeness* if women had any rights of citizenship in France, but as we don't . . ."

Bonaparte laughs, also a little falsely. "You have not changed it would seem." He looks at Lafayette, pointedly. "Neither has he. But the world has changed."

"Has it?" I ask. "It seems to me that we have only spun round again to the same place. And that our revolution is a great wheel of torture upon which women have been broken and silenced." *Marie-Antoinette. Princess*

Élisabeth. Olympe de Gouges. Manon Roland. Louise Audu. Charlotte Corday. Pauline Léon. Émilie de Sartine. The list went on and on.

"And yet, *you* are not silent," Bonaparte says. "You should know that I dislike women who meddle in politics, madame."

At this, the old fire kindles in my belly, the light of conviction that some things are worth risking for. I hadn't realized the fire was even still there. And so I do not cower before Bonaparte. "Ah, but *mon Général,* so long as you men take it upon yourselves to behead us, we will want to know why."

I glance over to where my daughter stands, nervously holding hands with the daughters of Lafayette and Manon Roland, and I am struck by a pang. A bittersweet revelation that for them—for all of them—and for their daughters, too, I would turn that wheel again for the chance that, next time, it might turn out some other way . . .

Acknowledgments

No novel is ever the product of the author alone, and that is particularly true in a cowritten work such as this. As a group, we extend our thanks to our agent on this project, Kevan Lyon, who championed this book from the moment its idea was born. Thanks also to our editor, Tessa Woodward, for believing in and wanting to be a part of the sororité of the novel right from the start. We also extend our gratitude to the whole team at William Morrow, and to Kathie Bennett and her publicity team at Magic Time Literary, and to Kelly Simmon of InkSlinger PR for helping us get word out about the book—we appreciate all you're doing! Our deep appreciation goes to Allison Pataki, whose schedule prevented her from participating as an author but who graciously agreed to write the foreword and did it with such style and panache.

Among the many people we'd like to thank is historical figure Olympe de Gouges, the French playwright and author of the Declaration of the Rights of Woman and the Female Citizen. She was always on our minds and at the heart of the story even though the structure of the novel didn't allow us to give her a point of view. Her contributions were many, her shadow very large, and the sacrifice of her life at the guillotine too courageous not to mention.

We are grateful to our friends, families, critique partners, beta readers, and individual agents for their unstinting support. Enormous thanks to Sheila Accongio, Brenna Ash, Lori Ann Bailey, Christi Barth, Desserts by Regine (of Carlisle, PA), Julianne Douglas, Adam Dray, Hazel Gaynor, Ashleigh Inglesby, D. and L. Inglesby, Hoff Inglesby, Brian Kamoie, Cara Kamoie, Julia Kamoie, Madeline Martin, Michelle Moran, Lea Nolan, Kelly Quinn, Margaret Rodenberg, Kerry Schafer, Andrea Snider, Jacques de Spoelberch, Jennifer Thomas, Kris Waldherr, Misty Waters, and Sonja Yoerg.

For resources, we acknowledge that discussions about legal reform and Dupaty's case in prerevolutionary France, including his quote about the criminal jurisprudence being barbaric, were used here, with permission, from *Private Lives and Public Affairs: The*

Causes Célèbres of Prerevolutionary France, by Sarah Maza, University of California Press. Biographical information about Condorcet came from *Condorcet and Modernity,* by David Williams, including the quote from Condorcet's pamphlet about the matter of the three peasants, which appears with permission from Cambridge University Press. English-translation quotes from *Letters on Sympathy (1798): A Critical Edition,* Volume 98, edited by Karin Brown and James Edward McClellan, appear with permission from the American Philosophical Society.

Finally, the Scarlet Sisters would all like to thank the Kraken. She knows who she is.